KU-527-671

DOUBLE-EDGED
DETECTIVE

BY

MALLORY KANE

ights Reserved ... ion in whole
... or any form. This edition is published by arrangement with Har...
... is II B.V./S.à.r.l. The text of this publication or any part thereof
... reproduced or transmitted in any form or by any means, electron
... including photocopying, recording, storage in an inform
... val system, or otherwise, without the written permission of the publ

... is sold subject to the condition that it shall not, by way of tra
... e, be lent, resold, hired out or otherwise circulated without the
... of the publisher in any form of binding or cover other than th
... is published and without a similar condition including this con
... imposed on the subsequent purchaser.

... are trademarks owned and used by the trademark owner and/
... Trademarks marked with ® are registered with the United Kin
... ... ffice and/or the Office for Harmonisation in the Internal Marke
... countries.

... lished in Great Britain 2011
... & Bose, an imprint of Harlequin (UK) Limited

DID YOU PURCHASE THIS BOOK WITHOUT A COVER?
If you did, you should be aware it is **stolen property** as it was reported
unsold and destroyed by a retailer. Neither the author nor the publisher
has received any payment for this book.

All the characters in this book have no existence outside the imagination of
the author, and have no relation whatsoever to anyone bearing the same name
or names. They are not even distantly inspired by any individual known or
unknown to the author, and all the incidents are pure invention.

All Rights ~~reserved including the right of reproduction in whole~~ or in
part in a ~~~~ ~~with~~ Harlequin
Enterpri~~~~ ~~any part there~~f may
not be re~~~~ ~~by any means, elect~~nic or
mechani~~~~ ~~storage in an info~~ation
retrieval ~~~~ ~~without the written permission of the p~~isher.

This boo~~~~ that it shall not, by way of ~~rade or
otherwis~~~~ ~~circulated without~~ prior
consent ~~~~ ~~any form of cover other than~~ that in
which it ~~~~ ~~a similar condition~~ ~~including this co~~dition
being im~~~~ ~~subsequent purchase~~.

® and ™~~~~ ~~and~~ ~~trade mark owner an~~ or its
licensee. ~~~~ ~~with ® are registered with the United K~~ingdom
Patent O~~ffice and/or the Office for Harmonisation in the Internal Mar~~ket and
in other c~~ountries~~.

LONDON BOROUGH OF WANDSWORTH		
9030 00001 9485 5		
Askews & Holts	27-Oct-2011	
AF KANE	£5.30	

First pub~~lished in Great Britain 201~~
by Mills & ~~Boon, an imprint of Harlequin (UK) Limited~~,
Eton House, 18-24 Paradise Road, Richmond, Surrey TW9 1SR

© Rickey R. Mallory 2010

ISBN: 978 0 263 88560 6

46-1111

Harlequin (UK) policy is to use papers that are natural, renewable and
recyclable products and made from wood grown in sustainable forests. The
logging and manufacturing processes conform to the legal environmental
regulations of the country of origin.

Printed and bound in Spain
by Blackprint CPI, Barcelona

Mallory Kane has two very good reasons for loving reading and writing. Her mother was a librarian, who taught her to love and respect books as a precious resource. Her father could hold listeners spellbound for hours with his stories. He was always her biggest fan.

Mallory loves romantic suspense with dangerous heroes and dauntless heroines, and enjoys tossing in a bit of her medical knowledge for an extra dose of intrigue. Mallory lives in Mississippi with her computer-genius husband and three exceptionally intelligent cats.

She enjoys hearing from readers. You can write her at mallory@mallorykane.com

To my mother,
who only ever wished the best for me.

Chapter One

Albert Moser sat in his worn easy chair with his daughters' photo album on his lap. It bulged with photos, snapshots and small remembrances of happy times and places.

Christmas Leigh and Autumn Lynn, each named for the time of year they were born. Moser slid his fingers along the edge of the pages. The first half of the album was about his daughters' lives. He'd devoted the last half of the book to something else entirely.

He looked up at the calendar he'd hung on the wall next to his TV so he could watch the months, the weeks, the days go by. And they had. Somehow, he'd made it through another year. Somehow, it was October again.

He flipped over to the back of the album, where he'd pasted newspaper clippings, notes and baby photos. Behind them, stuck between two pages, was a small stack of insurance forms. Four years ago, the stack had seemed huge. During his career, he'd sold a lot of life insurance policies to parents for their newborns. Then, when Rudolfo Gomez had retired, Albert had taken over his customers, too.

Once he'd culled out the males and the people who had moved away or died, the stack had dwindled to ten. He counted. Only six were left. Six policies taken out at birth on six baby girls. Now they were grown. Young women with their lives ahead of them, just like his Autumn.

And like his daughter, they had no idea that one of them had only a few days to live.

Albert Moser sighed. He didn't want to do it. The weight of the women's lives was heavy on his shoulders. He wasn't sure he could stand under the weight of another one. It had been four years.

For a brief moment, he considered turning himself in and begging them to find his daughter's killer. He'd tried begging. But the police had dismissed Autumn's murder as a mugging. He knew it wasn't. He just *knew* it.

The telephone rang. Albert started and almost dropped the album. He didn't have to wonder who was calling. It was Christy. His older daughter was the only one who ever called him. He picked up the handset.

"Dad? Hi. How are you?"

"I'm okay. How're you doing? Is it cold in Boston?"

"Always," she said with a laugh. Her low, slightly husky voice reminded him of her mother. "So how are you doing? Are you eating? Taking care of yourself?"

"I'm doing okay."

"Dad, you need to get out. Why don't you call some of your buddies and play some golf?"

Albert didn't answer. Christy had been pushing him ever since Autumn's death to get out, get some exercise, see some of his old friends.

"Well, I just wanted to call and see how you are, and—"

"Autumn's birthday's in six days," Albert interjected. "She'd be twenty-six now, you know."

"I know." Christy sighed. "Dad, I called tonight because I'm leaving for Germany tomorrow. I'll be gone for a week. I'm speaking at the Children's Health Issues Summit in Munich."

"Okay."

"Think about coming to Boston for Christmas, Dad. I can't get time off. Christmas is always a busy time for pediatricians. But we could sightsee, go to some good restaurants."

"I'll see," Albert said. He shuffled the insurance forms he held, looking at the birth dates on the policies. "You know, Christy, the police still aren't doing anything about Autumn's murder."

"Dad—"

"She was murdered. You know how scared she was of that man she was seeing. He killed her. I'm sure of it."

"Dad, please stop trying to figure out who it was. It's eating you up inside."

"You're right there. It is."

"Think about coming up here for Christmas."

"I'll think about it."

Christy said goodbye and hung up, leaving Albert feeling more lonely than he had before she called. Her voice echoed through the empty house.

It's eating you up inside.

Yes, it was. And there was only one thing that would stop the gnawing pain.

He had to continue his crusade. Eventually, the police would look back and know he'd been right all along. Autumn Moser was murdered. Then they'd realize that these young women wouldn't have had to die if they'd paid attention to him. They'd be sorry they'd dismissed him.

DETECTIVE RYKER DELANCEY polished off the last bite of Coquilles St. Jacques and took a final sip of wine. He sat back and glanced at his watch. Almost eleven o'clock. Closing time. Only a few late diners were still lingering over coffee or dessert at L'Orage.

It hadn't been easy to adapt to eating dinner so late,

but with the anniversary date about to roll around, Ryker wasn't taking any chances with his only living victim.

Speaking of—a familiar figure in a white coat emerged from the kitchen. Nicole Beckham. She smiled as she greeted a couple a few tables away. Ryker had no trouble hearing their conversation in the subdued, intimate atmosphere of the upscale continental restaurant. The two were regulars, and they always asked to speak to the chef. Nicole always responded the same way.

"I'm so happy you enjoyed it. It's always wonderful to see you." Nicole's green eyes sparkled with genuine pleasure. Her pixieish face lit up when she smiled. She acted as if the couple were the only people in the room.

Ryker glanced around at the lingering diners. A woman he'd seen a few times before was reading what looked like a legal brief as she ate. As he watched, she glanced up at Nicole, then pulled out her cell phone. She spoke briefly then set it down beside her plate and went back to her reading. Three tables beyond her a young couple were feeding each other white chocolate bread pudding and kisses. Ryker knew how their evening was going to end.

His gaze traveled to the last patron, a regular in his mid-fifties who was looking at his watch and wiping his mouth at the same time. The man glanced up and met Ryker's gaze. He nodded, then folded his napkin and reached into his back pocket for his wallet.

Ryker glanced back at Nicole, just as she turned toward the kitchen. Her gaze met his and just like every time she saw him, her eyes widened for an instant, and then her smile faded.

Ryker's mouth twisted wryly. No warm greeting or dazzling smile for him. She didn't want him in her restaurant. He couldn't blame her. She'd informed him in no uncertain terms the first time he'd showed up here that seeing him brought back the memory of her attack a year ago. He regretted that. But he wasn't about to leave her alone and unprotected. Especially now, only one week before the anniversary date of her home invasion.

Since that first confrontation, she'd been polite, but aloof. He'd never gone out of his way to speak to her. In fact he rarely saw her because she rarely emerged from the kitchen.

Still, he knew she was there, and that made him feel better. If she was there at the restaurant, cooking, then she was safe.

As he set his napkin beside his plate and glanced around for his waiter, he saw her turn on her heel and head his way with a determined glint in her eye. Leaning back casually, he waited to see what she was going to do. She wouldn't make a scene. She was executive chef. It would be in bad taste.

"Detective Delancey," she greeted him in her low voice.

"Call me Ryker," he offered, as he had on each of the few occasions she'd spoken to him.

"I hope you enjoyed your dinner." She crossed her arms and lifted her chin.

She no more hoped he enjoyed his dinner than she hoped he'd come back tomorrow night, and the next and the next.

"I did," he said politely. "My compliments to the chef."

Her lips tightened. "You've been coming in later the past two weeks or so." It sounded like an accusation.

"I'm flattered you noticed."

"Don't be."

He smiled. "I've been working later. We're short-handed."

A flicker of her eyelids told him she didn't like that answer. Or believe it.

He wondered how she would react if he told her the whole truth. Yes, they were shorthanded, but the real reason he'd been dining later was so he could wait outside the restaurant until it closed, and watch her until she was safely inside her apartment three blocks away.

She was his only living connection to a killer he was convinced had committed three murders of young women in the past four years. Each killing had occurred during the fourth week in October, and the only reason the killer wasn't four for four was because Nicole's roommate had come home early and interrupted him.

But with all the evidence he had, he still couldn't convince his chief that the murders were the work of one man. Deputy Chief Mike Davis needed more than just the coincidence of the dates.

"May I sit?" Nicole asked, gesturing to a chair.

He nodded. What was she up to? Judging by the tiny wrinkle between her brows, she was worried about something. He hoped it was her safety.

She sat on the edge of the chair and rested her clasped hands on the tabletop. "I don't mean to be rude, but why are you here every night?"

"I'm not here every night."

She glared at him. "Practically. You sometimes miss Thursdays, and we're closed on Mondays, but the rest of the week…" She shrugged. "I mean, the food here isn't exactly cheap. Or low-calorie."

"Are you calling me fat?"

"Of course not. I—"

"You're wondering how a St. Tammany Parish Sheriff's Office detective can afford to eat like this every day?"

Her cheeks turned red.

"I told you I'd keep an eye on you."

"And I told you that wasn't necessary."

He glanced down at her entwined fingers. The knuckles were white. She spread her fingers, then squeezed them again.

He waited.

Finally she spoke, her voice muted. "I heard what you said that night, about the other women."

Ryker cursed silently. He knew exactly what night she meant, and what conversation. She was referring to the night the killer had broken into her apartment. He hadn't meant for anyone there to overhear his telephone conversation, certainly not her, the victim. He'd been trying to talk his chief into letting him combine the cases, now that he had a live victim. "You weren't supposed to hear that. It had nothing to do with you."

That was a lie. It had everything to do with her.

Her gaze told him she knew it. "I'm not stupid, Detective. You talked about combining murder cases. You said I was *damned lucky* to be alive. And you said my attack was the fourth in four years, all during the fourth week of October." She paused and her eyes bored into his. "You think the man who broke into my apartment killed those other women."

Ryker clenched his jaw. How was he supposed to answer her? He'd been given specific orders by Deputy Chief Mike Davis to drop his crusade to connect the murders.

"Obviously, next week will be the fourth week in October. If you're right about him, that means he'll kill again." Her eyes narrowed. "You're here because you think he'll come after me, aren't you?"

Ryker opened his mouth, but immediately closed it and gritted his teeth. He couldn't deny her words, but he didn't want to confirm them, either. He wasn't sure why the killer hadn't tried again to kill Nicole. He'd like to think it was because the man didn't know where she was, but that was highly unlikely. Her name had been in the paper and on television the day after the break-in.

Across from him, Nicole swallowed audibly. "Why hasn't he come after me already?" she asked as if reading his mind.

Ryker's own mouth went dry at her question. He shook his head. "I don't know. He's obsessive. The fact that he only kills once a year attests to that. For whatever reason, the last full week in October has some extremely important meaning for him."

"This week," she muttered. "What do you suggest I do?"

"Get out of town, preferably permanently, but at least for the next week or two."

"I can't do that." Nicole bit her lower lip and looked down at her hands, then peered up at him, her green eyes hard as jade. "I bought double-locking dead bolts, even for the balcony doors. If you want to, you could check them. See if they're strong enough. I could make you a cup of coffee."

Ryker grimaced inwardly. There were very few things in the world he'd rather do than get to know Nicole Beckham better. He couldn't deny the sexual attraction he'd felt for her ever since he'd first seen her a year ago, when he'd responded to the 911 call about the break-in.

Nicole Beckham was stunning in an understated way. Her hair was the color of old gold, and cut weirdly—shorter in back than in front. It suited her small, sharp features and heart-shaped face. If things were different, he'd accept her invitation in a heartbeat.

But things weren't different. He was a detective with the major crimes division of the St. Tammany Parish Sheriff's

Office, and she was the victim of a crime. There was no way they would ever have any other relationship than that.

As much as he wished he could say yes, he shook his head. He couldn't go with her to her apartment for more than one reason. If the killer was watching her, he'd be tipped off that she had a bodyguard. Not to mention that the guy may have seen Ryker before, at other crime scenes. Serial killers were notorious for visiting crime scenes in the guise of an innocent onlooker. The killer might recognize him as a detective.

"Who installed your locks?"

"I called a locksmith from the phone book. He said they were the top-of-the-line residential locks."

"Then I'm sure they are. Look. I know you don't want me in your apartment. Just accept that I've decided this is the best restaurant in Mandeville, and you're the best chef."

Nicole pushed her chair back and stood. "Have you always eaten all your meals out?"

"Ninety percent anyway. I'm not much of a cook."

"So where did you eat before you started coming here?"

Ryker smiled up at her. "The Lakeview Diner," he said blandly, naming a fly-specked dive down near the lake.

Nicole bit her lip. It looked as if she was trying to keep from laughing. "Well then, thank you for choosing L'Orage, Detective Delancey."

"Call me Ryker," he said.

"Good night, Detective."

RYKER SAT IN HIS PARKED CAR on the side of the road about three-fourths of a block east of the restaurant. He watched the time. As always, by ten minutes after eleven,

Nicole appeared. Her golden-brown hair shone in the light from the streetlamps as she walked confidently along the sidewalk with a tote bag slung over her shoulder.

Ryker knew what was inside the bag. Her knives. Every decent chef had their own set. He also knew Nicole's knife case was missing one knife. Her attacker had fled out the back door with it when her roommate came home early and interrupted him.

The idea of the killer having that super-sharp knife that was engraved with Nicole's initials really bothered Ryker. The sheriff's department had managed to keep her name out of the papers after the first mention. But even if by some miracle the killer didn't already know her name, knowing she was a chef and having her initials on the knife gave him a clear advantage in finding her.

Ryker waited until she was half a block beyond his car before he started his engine. His BMW 3 Series sedan started quietly and purred almost inaudibly. He pulled forward at a snail's pace, keeping her in his sight.

The short three blocks from the restaurant to her apartment building were well lit and open, an ideal neighborhood to walk to and from work. But Ryker would be much happier if she drove.

After her near miss last October, Nicole had quit her position as executive chef at the finest restaurant in Chef Voleur. She'd moved to Mandeville, several miles away, and taken this job.

Both Mandeville and Chef Voleur were in St. Tammany Parish, so her new job and her new apartment were still in his jurisdiction.

As Ryker watched her walk, and lectured himself about eyeing her shapely backside accentuated by the snug-fitting black jeans she wore, he noticed a movement in the shadows behind her.

A figure in a dark hooded sweatshirt staggered out of the shadows of a side street, less than a hundred feet behind Nicole. His head was down, his hands were in his pockets and he weaved slightly as he walked.

Ryker tensed. Nicole's attacker had worn a dark hoodie and jeans. It was the only description Ryker had, because Nicole had seen nothing but a silhouette holding a knife. And her roommate, who'd surprised the attacker, had barely glimpsed his back as he'd fled through the kitchen door.

Pulling his Sig Sauer from his underarm holster, Ryker pressed the button to roll down the car window. The man had come from the direction of the restaurant. Had the woman who'd looked at Nicole and made a call been giving instructions to this punk?

Nicole's shoulders stiffened visibly, she pulled her tote bag tighter against her body and she lifted her chin. She'd noticed the man.

The guy in the hoodie stumbled, and staggered forward a few steps, as if trying to regain his balance. His awkward dance could have been a misstep, or it could have been designed to get him twenty feet closer to Nicole.

Whatever his intent, that was twenty feet too close.

Ryker killed his engine and got out of the car, not closing the driver's-side door. He moved silently and quickly across the street and crept up behind the hooded guy.

The guy lifted his head. Had he noticed Ryker? He didn't turn around. But he did take his hands out of his pockets, clench his fists and push himself to a quicker pace.

"Hey, lady," he rasped, reaching out with one hand. "Lady, stop."

Nicole's shoulders tensed under the short-sleeved green top she wore. Her head turned slightly, acknowledging the guy's voice.

"Lady, I just need to—"

Ryker didn't wait to find out what he needed to do. He grabbed the back of the hoodie and jerked the lightweight sideways and threw him up against a chain-link fence.

Nicole spun around with a small cry.

The guy whooped and hollered in a squeaky voice. Ryker stuck his gun barrel just behind the guy's ear. "Shut up and freeze!" he ordered him.

The guy's legs collapsed underneath him and suddenly Ryker's hand on the back of his shirt was the only thing holding him up.

"Stand up! Get your hands up." Ryker jerked the hood down and pushed the side of his face against the fence. In the lights from the streetlamps, Ryker saw that he was a kid—eighteen or nineteen at the most.

"I didn't do nothing," the kid whined. "You're hurting me."

"Not yet I'm not. Shut up or I will. Spread your feet."

The kid obeyed, nearly falling down in his haste to do what Ryker told him to. Without looking at her, Ryker spoke to Nicole. "You okay?"

"Yes."

He quickly patted the kid down and found a wadded-up dollar bill and a few coins, a pack of cigarettes with a book of matches stuck inside the cellophane and—no surprise— a pipe. Probably a crack pipe. He fished it out.

"Turn around."

The kid obliged, his gaze darting around, as if assessing the likelihood of an escape.

"Don't even think about it. Look at me," Ryker yelled. "And get your hands up."

The kid raised his arms, but he had trouble keeping them up. He was fidgety, his face was pale and clammy and his nose was running. He lowered one arm and wiped his nose on his sleeve.

Ryker assessed the likelihood that he and the woman in the restaurant were in cahoots. By the contrast in their looks and dress, he doubted it, but he couldn't afford to take a chance. The kid didn't have a phone, but he could have ditched it.

"Who are you? Who sent you to follow her?"

"Who—? Nobody, man. Nobody sent me nowhere and I ain't following nobody. I—" The kid giggled. "I don't even know what street I'm on. I lost my car. I'm just trying to get home."

The kid's words were slurred and slow. Ryker peered at his face. His eyes never stopped moving. They were red-rimmed and teary. Sure enough, he'd been doing crack. He probably wasn't lying when he said he had no idea where he was, much less where his car was. If he even had a car.

"Car? Where are your keys?"

"Oh, man." The kid giggled again. "I musta lost 'em."

Ryker's irritation ratcheted up a few notches. He got in the kid's face. "Listen to me. If you don't quit lying—" he doubled a fist "—I'll fix it so you can't talk at all. Got it?"

"Y-yes sir," the kid stammered.

"What's your name?"

"Duane."

"What were you going to do, Duane? Rob her?"

"No, no man. I just wanted a couple bucks. You know, to catch the bus home."

"Okay, Duane. Where's your ID?"

Duane lowered his arms and pulled up his pants. "I left it at home," he whined.

Ryker decided to believe him. For an instant he considered letting the scared kid go with a warning. But he decided he'd better do what he was supposed to do. He used his cell phone to call Central Dispatch and request a couple of Mandeville patrolmen to run the kid in and check for priors.

"Wait right here under this streetlight," he told Nicole, then grabbed the kid by an arm and marched him over to his car. He pushed him against the car's frame.

"Spread your feet," he commanded.

"Aw, man. I ain't never been arrested. Gimme a break."

"Spread 'em. You lost your chance at a break when you accosted the woman." He pushed the kid's head down against the back window. "Stay there."

Reaching through the open driver's-side door, he retrieved a flexible strap cuff and quickly secured the kid's hands behind him. By the time he finished, a car marked St. Tammany Parish Sheriff's Office pulled up and two uniformed deputies got out.

"Detective Ryker Delancey," he said. "Got one for you."

"Sweet," the younger deputy said, while the older one groaned.

"Another hour and we'd be off duty. Now we got paperwork."

"Sorry," Ryker said, grinning. "He's all yours."

They marched the kid to the cruiser, settled him in the backseat and then drove away.

Ryker holstered his gun, locked his car and returned to Nicole's side, ready to console and reassure her.

She glared at him. "You were *following* me?"

Ryker stared at her. "*That's* what you got out of all this? Did you even notice that little jerk behind you?"

"Of course I did. But I'm less than fifty feet from my building."

"Fifty feet?" Ryker laughed. "Might as well be fifty miles, if your throat is cut."

Nicole's head jerked slightly, probably at the image his words conjured.

"No." She recovered and cut a hand through the air. "You're just trying to distract me. You *were* following me. Have you done this for the whole past year?"

He shook his head.

"I don't believe you."

"I have been keeping an eye on you, but no. I haven't been following you home until recently."

Her eyes widened. "Because it's the last week in October." Her throat moved as she swallowed. "You do think that man is going to come back, don't you?"

"Let's say I'm afraid he will. I wasn't supposed to talk about the previous cases, because I can't convince my chief that they're all related."

"Your chief doesn't think they're related?" Nicole's voice rose in hope. "Why do you?"

He pushed his fingers through his short hair, leaving it spiked. "Because of the dates of the attacks. Because of a connection among the victims that hasn't been released to the public."

"A connection? What connection?"

Ryker studied her. Would it hurt for her to know the reason he was so sure the same man had committed all the murders and tried to kill her? Hopefully it would convince her of the danger she could be in. He believed that *forewarned is forearmed.*

"Birthdays," he said. "All of your birthdays are within about a week of each other. The dates range from the twenty-first of October to the first of November. Mike isn't convinced the birthdays are important. He's relying on the MOs, which are all different."

"MOs. That's—"

"Modus operandi. Or method of operation. Basically,

things that are unique to the killer. What weapon or weapons he uses, similarities in how he gains entrance, who he targets. That kind of thing." Ryker sighed. "He's got a point. Normally serial killers don't change their methods."

A dark car sped by close to them. Nicole jumped and stepped closer to Ryker. He put his hand on the small of her back. "Are you okay?"

She nodded. "Just a little jumpy." She looked up at him, and her demeanor changed. "I apologize. I know you're trying to protect me."

Ryker stared at her. Suddenly, the hostility that had honed every word she'd said was gone. In its place was a husky softness that slid through him straight to his groin. Surely she wasn't doing that on purpose.

As if to prove that she wasn't, she stepped back, putting space between them. "I could make you that cup of coffee," she said hesitantly.

Ryker swallowed. He'd be a fool to accept her invitation, the way he was feeling right now. His pulse had sped up, and in just a few seconds, if he didn't get himself under control, he might embarrass himself and her. The best thing to do would be to decline again, and head for his car and get the hell out of there.

"I'd better get going," he said. "I just wanted to be sure you got home safely."

"Oh, of course. I need to go, too." She gestured vaguely behind her, in the direction of her apartment.

"I'll walk you to your door."

Glancing back at him, she shook her head. "Please don't. I walk to and from work every day. I don't want to be one of those women who's afraid of going anywhere."

"Yeah? Well, for what it's worth, I'm pretty sure you'll never be one of those women. But do me a favor and take your car to work for the next couple of weeks."

"Good night," she called as she walked away.

Ryker stood and watched her until she got to her building and walked up the stairs to the second-floor landing. She looked down at him as she unlocked her door, then she stepped inside and closed it behind her. He waited until he saw lights go on behind her curtains.

"Damn it, Nicole," he whispered as he got into his car and cranked it. She was no more going to drive to the restaurant than there was a man in the moon. Another light came on in her apartment. Her bedroom, probably.

The thought of her getting undressed, bathing, slipping between the sheets, stirred him again. He gritted his teeth and pulled away from the curb. "Down, boy," he muttered. "No getting the hots for the pretty victim. That's stepping over the line."

Chapter Two

Albert Moser entered his house through the garage and headed straight for the photo album. He knew the man who'd come to Nicole Beckham's rescue tonight. He'd seen him somewhere, he was sure.

The encroaching date on the calendar had sent him out looking for Nicole Beckham. He was ninety-nine percent sure she hadn't seen his face a year ago. Still, she was unfinished business.

He knew where she worked, so he'd waited outside the restaurant until it closed and she emerged. He was delighted when he saw that she was walking home. He'd figured it would be easy to follow her and force his way into her apartment as she unlocked the door.

But then a small drama had unfolded, and Albert realized Nicole Beckham had a protector. And not just any protector—a cop. He'd grabbed the kid who'd been walking behind Nicole, cuffed him and called a couple of his buddies to take the kid in. Meanwhile, Albert was able to get a good look at his face.

He'd seen him before.

He sat down with the photo album and thumbed through all the newspaper clippings he'd saved from the murders. He'd seen that cop before. It could have been several years ago, during the brief time the police were investigating his daughter's murder. Or maybe his picture had been in the newspaper.

It didn't matter where he'd seen him. What mattered was, he was a cop and he was watching out for Nicole. Did that mean the police were finally taking the murder of young women seriously?

If so, then Albert had to be doubly vigilant, and doubly careful. He sorted through the six insurance forms, looking at the birth dates. He narrowed his choice down to two, both of whom had been born on the twenty-fifth day of October, three days after his daughter.

THE NEXT MORNING, Deputy Chief Mike Davis of the St. Tammany Parish Sheriff's Office satellite office in Chef Voleur leaned back in his desk chair and frowned at Ryker. "I just got off the phone with Lieutenant James Faraday in Mandeville."

"Yes, sir?"

"Don't give me 'yes, sir.' Tell me what you were doing arresting a kid in Mandeville at midnight last night. And don't tell me this has anything to do with your serial killer obsession."

"I'm afraid I can't do both, sir."

Mike scowled. "What the hell are you doing?"

"I was off duty. I observed a kid accosting—someone. He was acting drunk or high. I dispatched a couple of locals to run him in."

Mike Davis sighed and sat up straight. "And the some-one? That wouldn't be that young woman whom you've been *stalking,* would it?"

Ryker studied the toes of his shoes. "The victim of last year's foiled attack. Yes, sir."

"Didn't I refuse to provide protection for her?" Mike's voice rose in volume.

"As I said, I was off duty," Ryker said mildly. Mike couldn't tell him what to do on his own time, but Ryker didn't like bucking authority. He believed in going by the book. He also believed Nicole's life was in danger.

And that belief took priority over any other.

"You're going to give me apoplexy, Detective Delancey."

Ryker wasn't sure what apoplexy was, but he'd already noticed Mike's red ears, a sure sign of an impending explosion. Now the redness was creeping down his neck and up his cheeks.

"Sir, I know that the man who broke into Nicole Beckham's apartment last year is the same man who killed those other women. I know it."

Mike sighed and ran a hand over his face. "I've already told you, my hands are tied. If I combine the cases and make it official that we believe the deaths are the work of one man, I'll have to appoint a task force, and involve the district attorney's office. The media will be all over us."

"Women are dying."

"Not to mention that we're shorthanded already. I need more evidence—a lot more."

"Damn it, Mike. How much more evidence will it take? For four years he's struck during the same week in October. It's always a nighttime home invasion, always when the women are alone. *And* they were all born in October."

"I thought one of them was born on November 1."

Ryker gritted his teeth. "One day."

"I understand what you're saying, but there's not enough consistency. You can't connect the women. You've got different weapons, different dates." Mike stood. "And it doesn't help your case that you have a history with one of the victims."

"It was a few dates back in college. I hadn't seen her in—"

Mike held up a hand. "Spare me. I've heard it before. Now I've got a meeting. This discussion is over."

"Fine." Ryker blew out a frustrated breath. "Within the week, he'll strike again, and I'll get you your evidence. It's a shame that another woman has to die to convince you."

"Get out of here, before I fire your ass."

Ryker beat a hasty retreat. Mike couldn't fire him. Not without cause. But he understood his deputy chief's frustration.

Even so, there was no way he was going to leave Nicole unprotected. It was October 21. Within the next few days, he fully expected the killer to strike again. There was no way he could stop him. But he'd be damned if the victim was Nicole.

THAT NIGHT AS NICOLE EXITED the restaurant, Ryker fell into step beside her.

She jumped and pressed her hand to her chest.

"I see you paid no attention to me," he remarked. "I told you to drive."

"I see you're still following me."

"Somebody has to look out for you if you aren't going to take care of yourself."

She sped up. He was surprised her heels didn't strike sparks off the sidewalk. "I do not intend to act like a victim," she threw back over her shoulder.

Ryker easily caught up to her. "Taking reasonable precautions is not acting like a victim."

"I take reasonable precautions."

"Walking alone at midnight is not a reasonable precaution."

Nicole stopped at the stairwell that led up to the second-floor landing of her apartment building. "Look, Detective. After the break-in, I was so spooked that I gave up my job and my apartment. I will *never* feel that way again."

He saw the beginnings of tears in her eyes. "I understand. Is that offer for a cup of coffee still open? I'd like to tell you about this killer."

Her eyes widened and shimmered. "Why? To terrify me?"

He shook his head. "No. To prepare you, in case he comes back to finish what he started."

She shuddered. "In other words, to terrify me."

He knew his words were harsh, but at this point, with only a few days' window for the next attack, he'd do anything to get her attention. "If you insist on looking at it that way. But the more you know, the better prepared you'll be."

She swallowed and pressed her lips together as she studied his face. "Fine. Please," she said wryly. "By all means, come in and have a cup of coffee and tell me about the killer who's after me."

She turned and climbed the stairs. Ryker followed her, taking the opportunity to admire her backside in the jeans she wore. She was trim, but with curves in the right places. He liked that. He didn't like stick-thin women who looked as if they hadn't eaten in weeks.

He gave his head a shake. This wasn't about admiring her figure or considering how her firm curves would feel under his hands.

By the time she got to the top of the stairs she was digging in her purse. Ryker heard keys jangle. He grimaced. He'd have thought every woman everywhere knew to have keys out and ready. It could be dangerous to be fumbling for keys outside in the dark.

Nicole felt Ryker's disapproving gaze on her as she unlocked her apartment door.

"I usually have my keys out before I get up here." She winced at her tone. She sounded like a wimp. She had no need to make explanations to him. In any case, it was his fault she hadn't pulled out her keys earlier. When he'd stepped up beside her out of the shadows he'd given her a scare.

"Maybe you could look at my locks while you're here," she said as she walked through the door ahead of him.

He paused for a second and glanced around the landing, then stepped inside and gave the locks a brief inspection before closing the door. "They look good," he said. "Nice apartment."

"Not as nice as the one I gave up in Chef Voleur," she said, an accusatory note in her voice as she stepped behind the butcher-block island into the kitchen area.

She swallowed nervously. Ryker Delancey made her small apartment feel tiny. He wasn't a real big man. He was six feet tall, but lean. He probably only weighed about one-ninety, but he filled up her living room—and her senses.

He sat on one of the bar stools at the island. "You didn't grow up in Chef Voleur." He made it a statement, not a question.

"No. I moved there when I got the job at the restaurant."

"Where did you grow up?"

Nicole winced internally. *In an apartment half this size with a mother who wasn't there even when she was there.*

"Baton Rouge," she said noncommittally. "Do you really want coffee, or would you rather have something else?" She opened the refrigerator. "I have—water. There might be some bourbon—"

Ryker laughed. "Coffee's fine with me."

"Do you mind if I make it decaf?"

He shook his head.

She grabbed the decaffeinated beans from the cabinet and put them in the grinder. By the time they were ground, she realized he was standing beside her. "How do you do that?"

"Do what?"

His voice rumbled near her ear, disturbing and enticing. She took a fraction of a step away from his imposing presence.

"Just appear, like you did on the sidewalk. You don't make any noise."

"Nobody moves without making any noise. You're not paying attention. Being unaware of your surroundings could get you killed."

"Do you think you could lay off the scare tactics for a minute or two?"

"You have a real espresso machine. That's impressive."

Nicole laughed. "Okay. Nice segue. Yes. I do have a real espresso machine. I like coffee, probably a little too much."

"I know what you mean. I've always wanted one. Show me how to use it."

Together, they made two mugs of decaf cappuccino, and Nicole put sugar in hers. She leaned against the kitchen counter and sipped her coffee. Ryker leaned next to her.

Nicole felt the subtle brush of his sleeve against her bare arm, and realized that this was the first time a man had been in her apartment—other than the moving crew and the locksmith. Thinking of that, it occurred to her that she hadn't been out on a single date in the year since the break-in.

Why was she even thinking about dating? Her gaze lit on Ryker's hands holding her jazz festival mug. They were large and square, with long fingers. The sleeves of his shirt were rolled up and his tanned forearms were dusted with golden hair, lighter than the light brown hair on his head.

He was attractive. Very attractive.

And strong, in the way that basketball players and soccer players were. Lean and wiry. She liked lean and wiry. Maybe that was why she was suddenly thinking about dating.

Okay, stop. He was in her apartment because she'd been the victim of a home invasion, and he, the investigator on the case, thought her life was in danger. That was a far cry from dating.

She shivered.

He glanced at her sidelong. "You okay?" he asked.

"Not really. Do you think that boy last night was following me?"

Ryker put his mug down and turned toward her. "No. I think he was high as a kite and lost, like he said he was. But it ought to illustrate to you what could happen. Someone could easily follow you. In the few minutes it takes you to walk from the restaurant to here, you could be grabbed."

"There you go again with the scare tactics. You can't manipulate me by scaring me. I will not quit this job. I already had to give up one job because of this person. I will not lose this one, too."

"I hope you won't. He hasn't come after you, and it's been almost a year. Maybe he won't. Maybe I'm wrong, and your attack had nothing to do with the others."

"But you don't believe that, do you? Otherwise you wouldn't have eaten at L'Orage every night for almost a year."

Nicole looked up into his blue eyes, searching for a

denial of what she'd just said. But as surely as he was standing there in front of her, she knew he was right.

"You believe before this week is out, he's coming to get me, don't you?"

Nicole's green eyes filled with tears, then wavered and dropped to the cup she held.

Ryker took the cup and set it aside, then took her hands in his. "Listen to me, okay? Just listen to me. I'm going to make sure that nothing—*nothing*—happens to you."

Her fingers squeezed his. "Okay," she whispered, meeting his gaze. "I believe you." Then she blinked, and a fat tear spilled over onto her lower lashes and hung there, sparkling in the light.

That tear almost undid Ryker. He was a sucker for tears. So much so that he'd had to teach himself to remain detached when he questioned victims or interrogated suspects. He couldn't afford to get his emotions entangled in his job. He'd seen the devastating effects of emotion up close, and he wasn't about to become a slave to his feelings like his father had.

Before he'd even finished his internal lecture, he'd defied it by reaching out and catching the teardrop with his thumb. When he did, her eyes closed. He laid his palm against her cheek.

He'd kept an eye on her for a year, ever since the break-in. She was his only living connection to his serial killer. He'd seen her leave her job and move. Watched over her as she searched for a new job in Mandeville and finally took the executive chef position at L'Orage.

He was intimately familiar with her honey-colored hair and skin, her sharp, beautiful green eyes, her graceful yet determined walk and the sweet smile she shared with everyone around her. When had he become so fascinated with her?

As soon as the question arose in his mind, he dismissed it. *He wasn't*. Well, except as a victim of the killer he was trying to catch. She was his connection to his killer. That was all.

At that moment, Nicole's eyes opened. Tears had matted her lashes until they looked like dark starbursts around her green eyes. Before he could work up the willpower to stop himself, he bent his head, urged her chin up with his fingers and kissed her.

She kissed him back. She tasted like coffee and cream. Hot, sweet, intense. A fire erupted inside him. The fire of lust—raging, consuming. He was instantly hard and burning for release.

Then the fire enveloped her, and her response was as hungry and frenzied as his own.

He backed her against the counter and kissed her deeply and thoroughly. She gave as good as she got, doubling her fists in the lapels of his jacket to pull him closer, taking his openmouthed kisses and returning them fully. He pressed the full length of his body against her, revealing how turned on he was.

She uttered a small cry and pushed at his chest. Somewhere in his brain, he felt relief. At least one of them had some self-control.

"What is that?" she panted, squirming.

He stared, incredulous. "Are you kidding me?" he muttered.

She shook her head. "Not that." She touched the leather strap around his midsection. "This."

Oh. His gun. She was talking about his gun. He had on his shoulder holster and she'd felt hard metal pressing against her. He stepped backward. "Sorry."

"Just take it off." Her green eyes were stormy, yet amazingly, still filled with passion.

He took off his jacket and then unbuckled the holster and shrugged out of it. By the time he was done, his lust had waned slightly. He breathed deeply. "Maybe I should go."

Nicole didn't say anything. He looked up at her, his holster dangling from one hand.

Her tongue slid out to moisten her lips and she shook her head no.

His hand tightened on the leather strap. He could stop right now. He could put the holster back on, and the jacket, and walk right out the door.

But he didn't. Against his better judgment, he let the holster drop to the floor. Then he reached for her. Before he could take her in his arms, though, she grasped his hand and pulled him toward her bedroom. At the bedroom door, he stopped and turned her around to face him. "Are you sure?" he panted.

She pulled his head down and kissed him intimately. "If I want to, or if it's a good idea?" she asked.

"Good idea."

"No."

"Yeah, me neither." He pulled her close and kissed her again as she maneuvered them closer to the bed. When the backs of his calves hit the mattress, he tumbled, taking her with him. They ended up laughing in a tangle of clothes and sheets and throw pillows.

Nicole tugged a bright orange pillow out from under his shoulders, and a turquoise one that was tangled in her legs. Ryker chuckled as he tossed the rest of them onto the floor.

"What are those things for anyhow?" he asked, between kisses.

"Throw pillows?" she answered. "To throw, I guess."

She leaned over the side of the bed, reaching for one. "I'll show you."

Ryker caught her waist and pulled her back. He turned her around to face him and slid her green top up and over her head. She wore a pink bra—not sexy at all. Utilitarian. It did have a front clasp though, so he disposed of it quickly. He decided that her full, round breasts were the most beautiful he'd ever seen. They were lush, firm, creamy-smooth. His mouth watered to taste them, but he restrained himself.

Once he got started, he didn't want to be hindered by clothes, so he quickly undid the top button of his shirt and tugged it off over his head, then shed his khaki pants.

By the time he was out of his clothes, Nicole had stripped down to her pink panties. Now *they* were sexy.

He didn't remove them. Not yet. Instead, he slid his hands along her firm, soft skin. He caressed her breasts, trailing his fingers across their tips and watching them tighten in response. He traced the curve of her waist and the swell of that enticing backside. Just as he'd thought, it was as firm and silky smooth as the rest of her. Then he hooked his fingers around the bikini panties and pulled them off and tossed them aside. He dipped into her, sliding, touching, coaxing her body into response.

"There are condoms in that drawer," Nicole whispered raggedly.

The box of condoms was sealed, and he couldn't help wondering how long she'd had it as he tore the cardboard top and retrieved one. He fumbled like a teenager, but finally got it on. In the midst of it, as his cheeks warmed in embarrassment and he thought about stopping while he still had one rational brain cell in his head, Nicole wrapped her hand around him, and that one last coherent thought scattered like dandelion seeds in the wind.

He kissed her again, and retraced the path of his fingers with his tongue. He kissed the petal-smooth skin of her cheek, her neck, her collarbone. Then he traced the little tunnel between her breasts. He cupped them again, lavishing more attention on their tips. Once they stood erect, he tasted each one in turn, then grazed them with his teeth. To his delight, she arched her back and moaned with pleasure.

Her skin tasted fresh and sweet, like a crisp, cool melon. His mouth watered as he traced the indentation below her breastbone and slid his hand down to palm her flat belly.

She sat up and pulled him back to kiss his mouth again, while her hand cupped him and caressed him until his erection pulsed against her palm. Then she guided him. He groaned with the effort of controlling himself as he slid into her.

Nicole was riding a wave of hot delicious pleasure like nothing she'd ever felt before. Her few experiences had let her know she enjoyed sex, but this, with Ryker, was something far beyond mere enjoyment.

Her entire body vibrated with almost unbearable desire, building from her sexual core like a volcano about to erupt. And when he sank deeply into her, filling her, the shock of her instantaneous climax caused her to cry out.

He immediately stopped. "Are you okay?" he asked breathlessly, his forehead pressed against hers. His erection throbbed inside her, as her own body pulsed in tiny aftershocks.

"Yes," she breathed, and arched upward to take him in more fully. "Don't stop."

With a low growl, he began thrusting rhythmically, stirring her already satiated desire to new life. Each thrust took them higher and higher still, until he rose up on his arms and drove her to a new, dizzying pinnacle.

Both of them cried out as they came together. Then Ryker kissed her gently on the lips, floated a fleeting kiss to each eyelid, then pressed his face into the sweet spot between her shoulder and neck. His harsh breaths slowly returned to normal.

Nicole felt as if she had melted into the mattress. Her limbs might as well have been boneless, and her body still trembled in an occasional tiny contraction.

But the most amazing thing was that she felt as if she could drift off to sleep. Ryker lay beside her and pulled her into the crook of his arm. He kissed her temple and murmured, "Are you okay?"

She nodded. "Better than okay."

"Good." Then, within a few seconds, his breathing slowed and evened out.

"Are you?" she whispered, but he didn't answer. Did he feel as safe and comfortable as she did? Or was he one of those self-absorbed guys who fell asleep as soon as they were done?

No, he wasn't one of those guys. He'd been too attentive, too considerate. And he'd definitely thought of her pleasure. Her very, very nice pleasure.

Her…pleasurable…pleasure…

Drowsily, she realized her thoughts were drifting. She closed her eyes and took a deep breath, filling her head with his clean, soapy scent, and her mind with his promise.

I'm going to make sure that nothing—nothing—happens to you.

Chapter Three

Ryker emerged into consciousness, leaving behind a sexy dream involving Nicole Beckham. The subtle scent of melon and an afterthought of coffee tickled his nostrils. He shifted, and realized he was lying on his back, sprawled diagonally across a double bed. His eyes opened to a slit, and he saw that faint light was seeping in from behind a set of pale green curtains.

Was he still dreaming? He took another breath and his mouth watered at the scent of melon and coffee. Memories of the night before stirred his desire. Nope. This was definitely not a memory. It was reality.

He frowned and squinted. Surprisingly, he'd slept through the night, something he rarely did—never if there was a woman in bed with him. He tried to lift his arm to check his watch, and found that he couldn't. His arm was weighted down by Nicole's shoulder. Her honey-smooth, naked, rounded shoulder.

Then he noticed that more of her was draped across him. She was on her stomach and her face was buried in her pillow. He raised his head and admired the sexy curve of her buttocks half-hidden by a sheet. He looked further. Her legs were sprawled across his calf.

Without allowing himself too much time to think about why he was so reluctant to move, when usually he couldn't wait to get home after a date, he slid his leg out from under hers, turned over and pressed a kiss to the curve of her shoulder, then slipped his arm out from beneath her.

She lifted her head and gazed at him through heavy-lidded, sleepy eyes. Then her gaze went to the window behind him. "It's daylight," she said, sounding surprised.

"We slept all night," he responded, smiling at her. "How are you doing this morning?"

She sat up, pulling the rumpled sheet with her and pushed her tousled hair back from her face. "I'm fine," she said on a yawn, then smiled sheepishly. "I don't usually sleep all night, especially—"

"With someone else in the bed?" he finished. "Me neither."

She looked at him thoughtfully.

"What?" he asked, sitting up beside her and making sure the sheet covered him.

She blinked. "Nothing. Are you hungry?"

"Starving. What've you got?"

"Not much. I rarely eat at home."

Ryker grinned. "Come on. Surely you have eggs."

"I think so."

"And we know you have coffee. So you stay here, and I'll make breakfast. When I'm done, you can make the coffee in that fancy espresso machine of yours."

"I thought you said you didn't cook."

"I said I didn't cook much." He put a finger against her mouth. "Just say thank you. You've cooked for me practically every night for almost a year. Let me return the favor."

"Thank you," she said against his finger. He leaned over and gave her a quick kiss, then sat up and grabbed his briefs and jeans and headed for the bathroom.

Once Ryker had gone into the kitchen, Nicole put her hands over her mouth and squealed silently.

What had she done? In the year since the break-in, she hadn't had one date. Not one. She hadn't even thought about dating. Certainly hadn't missed it. She'd been too busy making a reputation for herself as a chef all over again at a new restaurant.

Now, suddenly, she'd fallen into bed with a man—a cop—whose only interest in her was that she'd managed to survive his faceless killer.

What was the matter with her? In the first place, she *never* did that. *Never.*

Certainly not with a stranger.

Leaning back against the headboard and pulling the sheet up over her, Nicole indulged in a bit of morning-after basking. Last night she'd slept better than she had in over a year. Maybe in forever. Her mother's job as a night cleaning woman in Baton Rouge hadn't contributed to sleeping well. Her hours had been from 10:00 p.m. to 8:00 a.m. while she left her young daughter alone on the couch that they made into a bed in their room in a run-down rooming house.

Was it bizarre that the man who was trying to convince her that her life was in danger was the same man who made her feel safer than she'd ever felt before in her life?

Most definitely.

Nicole heard pans rattling in the kitchen. She couldn't imagine what Ryker was cooking up out of her sparsely stocked refrigerator. She hoped the eggs weren't too old. She couldn't remember when she'd bought them.

Jumping up, she ran to the bathroom and washed and brushed her teeth, then pulled on a pair of jeans and a T-shirt that read Kiss the Chef. Just as she was running a comb through her hair, she heard Ryker.

"Come on and make the coffee," he called.

"Whatever you found to cook, it smells wonderful," she said as she came into the kitchen and headed for the espresso machine. By the time she had the mugs filled, the plates were on the table. "I assume the eggs were okay?"

"I floated them in water. They sank." He leaned forward and kissed her, grinning like the proverbial Cheshire Cat.

"What?" she asked as her heart gave a little leap. He was even more handsome this morning. His hair, damp from his shower, looked darker, which somehow made his eyes look bluer.

"Just following instructions," he said, planting a soft kiss on her nose, then looking down at the front of her T-shirt. He gently traced the letters.

"Oh, that." She shivered and her cheeks flamed as his fingertips slid across her breasts. She set a mug down near his plate, then sat. "I never really thought about what it says. What kind of eggs are these?"

"My special scrambled eggs. The only bread I found was green, and I didn't think green toast and eggs sounded good, so eggs is all you get."

"That's fine." She picked up a fork and tasted the dish. The eggs were fluffy and creamy, with a hint of something savory. "They're amazing," she remarked.

"You don't have to sound so surprised," he said with a laugh. "Although I have to admit, this is pretty much the extent of my cooking skills. Well, this and sausage gumbo."

"You can make gumbo? That's quite a talent."

"My mother taught me how to make a perfect roux, and as anyone in Louisiana knows—"

"You can't have a good gumbo without a good roux," Nicole finished, smiling. "What's in here that makes them so creamy? I know there's no cream in the refrigerator."

Ryker shook his head as he shoveled forkfuls of eggs down and chased them with coffee. "Mayonnaise."

"Mayonnaise." She'd never thought about mixing mayonnaise and eggs, although they obviously complemented each other perfectly. "And the savory flavor?"

"Onions. I had to use dried minced onions. You *really* don't keep much food around, for a chef."

Nicole's mouth was full, so she had to swallow and drink some coffee before she could answer. "I told you. It's a lot of trouble to cook for one person," she said, wiping her mouth on a sheet of paper towel Ryker had folded for a napkin.

"Tell me about it."

"But I am totally stealing your scrambled egg recipe," she teased.

"No, you're not. That's my copyrighted recipe. Not unless you call it Eggs Delancey."

"How about Ryker's Amazing Morning-After Breakfast?" she teased.

"That's a mouthful."

She picked up her plate and stood at the very instant he did the same thing. They nearly collided.

Ryker slid his plate under hers and took them both. "I've got the dishes." He leaned over and kissed her again. As before, it started as a tease, a little peck on the lips, but she leaned forward, too, and the simple little kiss turned into much more.

Ryker put his hand holding the mug around her and pulled her closer, until the plates in his other hand were pressing into her breastbone. Coffee and salt mingled with bits of egg as their kiss deepened.

Nicole felt the fire starting deep inside her. She made a little involuntary sound in her throat.

Ryker pulled back and looked into her eyes. "Think the dishes could wait?" he whispered.

"I definitely think they could—" A harsh jangle interrupted her.

"Damn," he said. "That's my phone." He retrieved his jacket from the floor beside the front door.

It was William Crenshaw, a friend and fellow detective. "What's up, Bill?"

"We got another one."

"Another what?" Ryker glanced at Nicole. She was rinsing dishes and putting them in the dishwasher. He turned his back to her.

Bill sucked in a deep breath. "Another girl. Dead in her apartment."

Ryker's whole body went on alert. Everybody on the force knew about his certainty that St. Tammany Parish had a serial killer. Three young women had been killed in three years, all inside their homes, and all with weapons of convenience.

"When?" he barked.

"The Courtyard Apartments on Main Street in Chef Voleur. Neighbors saw her lying on her patio this morning. Looks like she collapsed while trying to escape."

"Damn it. Today's the—" he held the phone away from his ear and glanced at the date "—twenty-second. Okay. I'll be right there." Ryker hung up and turned to find Nicole looking at him. The running water was off. How much had she heard? He didn't want her to know that another woman had been killed.

"You have to go?" she asked.

He nodded. "Got a situation." He ran a hand across his damp hair.

"Is it bad?"

"It might be."

She wrapped her arms around herself. "I don't know how you do what you do. Chasing the bad guys. Putting yourself in danger, day after day."

He shrugged, suddenly wanting to be out of there, and not just because he had a new murder to investigate.

Nicole was going to keep on asking questions, and eventually, she'd get around to questions he didn't want to answer. Questions she really didn't want to know the answers to.

He tucked in his shirt, donned his shoulder holster and fastened it, and shook out his jacket. "I'll see you later," he said, glancing around to make sure he hadn't left anything.

Nicole started toward him, but he grabbed the front doorknob.

"I'll call you," he tossed back over his shoulder as he headed out, closing the door behind him. As he vaulted down the stairs, he winced at his words. He'd meant them, but the offhand phrase had become a cliché for one-night stands. All he could do was hope that Nicole had sense enough to know that when he was called, he had to go.

He got in his car and took off, his mind already turning to the crime scene he was speeding toward.

October 22. The killer was right on time.

NICOLE TWISTED THE KITCHEN TOWEL in her hands as she stared at her front door. The best night of her life had suddenly turned sour.

Of course she understood that Ryker was a detective. Emergency phone calls and life-or-death situations were part of his job description. The fact that he'd rushed out so quickly wasn't the problem.

His hastily thrown out *I'll call you* wasn't the problem, either. Although it did occur to her that he hadn't asked for her phone number. A small pang of regret stabbed her in the chest. I would be a shame if he didn't call.

But the bigger problem was, he'd lied to her about the call. Or at least he hadn't told her the whole truth. She'd heard him say the date. Seen the look on his face as he listened to the caller. It didn't take a genius, or even a detective, to figure out what that phone call was really about.

Nicole shivered. Ryker thought that the man who'd broken into her home, who'd taken one of her chef knives, who had already killed three women, had struck again.

RYKER SAT ON HIS HAUNCHES and studied the victim's position. She was sprawled across the concrete floor of the patio, the back of her nightgown and the concrete floor around her drenched in blood. Ryker followed the trail of blood with his eyes, back to the patio door. He'd check with CSI about the blood patterns later, but from what he could tell, she'd been stabbed in the back just about the time she'd reached the patio door. She'd made it outside before she collapsed.

Drip patterns down her sides and the blood around her body told him she hadn't died right away. She'd bled out right here where she'd fallen.

He took a quick look around the patio. It was the neighbors on the west side who'd called 911. The apartment to the east had a privacy fence. Bill had already questioned the couple that lived there. Apparently, neither one had heard anything.

He bent down, trying to get a good look at the victim's face. She was older than his previous victims. He wasn't a good judge of age, but he figured she was in her late thirties at best. A frisson of doubt slithered through him. If this was the work of his serial killer, the man had stepped outside the normal actions expected of serial murderers—again.

This victim's age was an anomaly. Ryker rubbed the spot in the middle of his chest where the frisson of doubt had lodged.

What if this killing wasn't connected?

Ryker studied the knife wound just inside her left shoulder blade. He lifted his arm and mimicked the motion that would have been necessary to make that wound. The killer had wielded the knife above his head. He wasn't proficient with a knife as a weapon. A pro would more likely have kept his arm low, and stabbed her in the lower back—the kidneys.

Nope. He was certain his guy had used a weapon of convenience—again. If it *was* his guy.

Ryker sent a quick glance around the small patio. The weapon. Where was it? Every other time, the killer had left the weapon at the scene. Except for last year, when he'd escaped with Nicole's knife.

Ryker studied the body again. It was conceivable that the weapon could be under her, but not likely. Not given the bleeding pattern. If she had fallen while running away from the killer who had just stabbed her, the knife couldn't have ended up beneath her.

He touched the cut nightgown with a gloved finger. He couldn't tell much about the knife wound because of the blood. But the cut in the gown was only about an inch long. It wasn't a very big knife. The blade that made that cut in the nightgown had to be less than an inch wide.

An ominous thought occurred to him. The knife that had been stolen from Nicole wasn't a big knife. He'd looked at her knife case the night of her near attack, but all he could remember was that the empty slot where the missing knife should have been stored wasn't very long. He remembered looking at her knife case and feeling thankful that the man hadn't taken one of the ominously long, thick-bladed ones.

Dr. David Miller, the new medical examiner who'd taken over when Hiram Crouch had retired the previous December, stepped through the door. "Ryker. Got another one?"

Ryker rose from his crouch. "Looks like it. How's business?"

"It's been slow. I reckon it's picking up now."

"I'll leave her with you. I want to look around inside and check with Bill about what the neighbors said."

Dave crouched down beside the victim. "Hey, sweetie," he said. "Let's see what you can tell me."

"I need everything you can give me about the knife he used. We haven't found it yet. I've got a feeling he took it with him."

Dave nodded without looking up.

Ryker headed for the patio door, then turned back. "Dave? How old do you think she is?"

The medical examiner turned her head so he could see her face and neck. "Late thirties or early forties."

Ryker nodded. "That's what I thought." He stepped through the door into the kitchen, carefully avoiding the blood spatter on the tile and the crime scene photographer who was taking photos of every inch of wall and floor.

"Don't suppose you've found a weapon yet," he said to Bill, who was writing something on a small pad.

Bill shook his head, and finished scribbling before he looked up. "Nope. Nothing."

"That's odd."

"Only if the killer is your guy."

Ryker gave a reluctant nod. "Anything missing from the kitchen?"

Bill shook his head, then pointed at a worn brown couch with his pen. "It looks like Ms. Terry was watching TV. May have fallen asleep on the couch. The killer probably saw her through the open window there."

Ryker glanced at the window, then at the door facing, where wood was splintered. "And nobody heard him kick the door in?"

"Apparently not. Although, look at that lock. My nine-year-old nephew could break in here."

Ryker glanced around. The crime scene photographer was standing in the doorway to the patio and a second crime scene investigator was lifting fingerprints from the front door. "Bill," he said, leaning close to Bill's ear, "what if he used the knife he stole from Nicole?"

"Hello, boys," an obnoxiously cheery voice said.

Ryker whirled. It was Lon Hébert, a reporter for the local newspaper, the *St. Tammany Parish Record*. He cursed under his breath.

Bill wasn't so circumspect. "What the hell are you doing here, Hébert? This is a crime scene. Take your ugly, scrawny ass out of here. Tom—" he called to one of the uniformed deputies.

"Aw, Bill. Give me a break. I need a big story. It's been so quiet around here that I was about to run a piece on alligators being run over on the freeway." Hébert laughed. "Delancey, talk to me."

"How do you even know about this?" Bill demanded.

Hébert grinned. "It's called a police scanner, Bill."

"Get out of here," Ryker said, his voice deadly quiet. "And make sure you clear anything—and I mean *anything*—with the sheriff's office before you print it."

Lon held up his hands. "Fine. Fine. I'll call the deputy chief and see if I can get a statement." He turned and left.

Ryker watched him leave. "You think he heard what I said?"

Bill shook his head. "No idea. I didn't see him come in."

"Well, what do you think? I think I need to look at matching Nicole's missing knife with Jean Terry's wound."

Bill shrugged. "You could. But isn't that quite a leap, even for you? Just because we haven't found the weapon yet? You really are trying to connect this to your mysterious serial killer, aren't you?"

"Come on, Bill. Think about it. Yesterday was October 21. He broke in and killed her. No sexual assault." He looked around the room and spotted a purse, upturned on the kitchen counter. "He dumped her purse. Is anything missing?"

"Nope. Not even her cash."

"That's typical. Not even a pretense of a robbery." Ryker's pulse raced with excitement. It was tragic that another young woman was dead, but maybe now he could take this fourth murder to his chief and finally get him to link the cases and treat them as the work of one man—a serial killer.

THREE HOURS AFTER HE'D arrived at the scene of the crime, Ryker was in the St. Tammany Parish Crime Lab pacing back and forth.

"Wearing a hole in my floor is not going to make me go any faster." Dr. Dave Miller was in scrubs, standing over the autopsy table, examining Jean Terry's fatal wound.

Ryker hated the autopsy room. The previous M.E., Dr. Crouch, who was eighty if he was a day, had treated the victims like sides of beef. The fact that Ryker had known a woman who had ended up on Crouch's table hadn't helped.

Dave was the total opposite. Every move he made was kind and respectful. It made a big difference to Ryker, who had never learned to view a dead body as a separate thing from the person she had been.

"What can you tell me about her knife wound?"

Dave was peering through a large lighted magnifying glass. "Not much. I need to cast it, to get a truer representation of the shape and path of the blade. See this *V?*"

Ryker reluctantly moved closer to the table and looked through the magnifier. "That upside-down *V?* Yeah. I couldn't see it earlier, because of all the blood. What would make that kind of wound?"

"Oh, it's a knife all right. Single-edged. That's a common pattern. It's called forking. The blade entered her back here," Dave said, pointing at the right side of the wound. "And exited here." He shifted his finger to the left side.

"What do you mean?"

"She was most likely on her feet. Her attacker was behind her, chasing her." Dave pushed the magnifier away and raised his arm, demonstrating. "He stabbed her with a downward motion. The blade entered between her shoulder blades, angling toward the right. He held on to the knife as she jerked and probably stumbled or fell. In any case, the blade exited at about a thirty-degree angle from where it entered."

"That's forking? I remember the term from Forensics, but I don't think I've ever seen a wound like that."

"How many stabbing deaths have you investigated?"

"Only one—two years ago. The weapon was a fireplace poker."

"Messy."

"No kidding. Especially after Crouch got done with it."

Dave didn't comment. Another point in his favor. Ryker

wanted to bite his tongue. It was never good practice to talk about a colleague, present or former.

"This upside-down *V* is typical of a stabbing," Dave continued. "It's unusual for a victim to remain still while being stabbed."

"What are those marks on the edges of the cuts?"

"The knife's guard. The attacker struck with force. He buried the blade up to the guard. It bruised the skin."

"The guard? Is that like the hilt?"

"Yep. Hilts refer to swords, but it's the same thing. It's always good to have those marks on a wound like this. If I had a weapon to compare it to, that contusion could give us a match." Dave pulled the magnifier down again and peered through it. "Now I need to concentrate."

"Sure. I've got to write up my report. Let me know as soon as you know anything."

"Definitely."

As Ryker pushed open the door, Dave called out to him.

"Oh, Ryker, your victim had breast cancer."

"Yeah?"

Dave nodded. "Double radical mastectomy, and evidence of radiation."

"Is that relevant?"

"Hard to say. I'm curious to see if they got it all, and how much of the lymph nodes they got. I'll order her medical records, and take a biopsy, just in case."

"Thanks, Dave."

Ryker headed to the precinct and wrote up everything he'd seen and done at the crime scene. Then, in a different document, he wrote his impressions of the murder, and how it fit his theory of a serial killer, from the date to his concern that the weapon used could be Nicole's missing knife. He included Dave's information about Jean Terry's cancer, although he had no reason to think it had any bearing on her death.

Twice he was interrupted by phone calls. The first was from one of the deputies who'd run the kid in the other night, telling him that the boy was seventeen, had no priors, not even as a juvenile, but that he'd given them a tip that helped in a drug ring case they were trying to put together.

"Great," Ryker had said. "Glad to help. Do me a favor and get your sergeant to tell my boss, will you?"

The deputy had laughed and said he'd try.

Then, before Ryker could get back to work, his twin brother, Reilly, called.

"Hey, old man." Reilly's nickname for Ryker referred to the fact that Ryker was older by seven minutes.

"Kid. What's up?"

"I heard about the murder. Another notch on your serial killer's belt, eh?"

"Yeah. I'm hoping this one will give me something concrete I can take to Mike."

"Maybe so. Did you see Mom's e-mail?"

"Nope. Been a little busy to follow the Delancey soap opera."

"Well, it did ramble a bit, but the gist was reminding everybody about the anniversary barbecue."

Ryker winced at Reilly's implication. Their mother tended to ramble when she drank, whether talking in person, on the phone or via e-mail.

"I haven't forgotten about the party."

"Well, take a look at her message. She's changing the date because Dad's got to meet with his parole officer on their anniversary."

Ryker cursed under his breath. How many ways could his dad's skewed loyalty interfere with all their lives?

"I'll check it," he growled.

"So, you going to bring a date?"

"What do you think? If I can't even check my mail, when do I find time to date?" Ryker tried to ignore the mental image of Nicole's beautiful naked body that rose in his brain. "What about you?"

"Not only do I have no time, I have no prospects."

"That's sad, kid. Truly sad."

"Yeah, well." Reilly sent a few choice and colorful words across the airwaves.

"Same to you," Ryker said, deliberately changing the subject from their dysfunctional family. "How's SWAT?"

"Pretty slow right now. We're doubling up on exercises and drills."

"Good. See if you can learn how to aim better." It was an old joke between them. Although they were identical twins, Reilly had inherited the sharpshooter gene. It was Ryker who'd had to work at his marksmanship.

"Right. Call me if you want me to take your handgun proficiency test for you."

Ryker winced at the faint bitterness in his twin's voice. Reilly had wanted the detective position that had been given to Ryker.

"Trust me," Ryker said wryly. "You couldn't shoot bad enough for them to believe you were me."

The backhanded compliment earned a reluctant laugh from his brother. Ryker's desk phone rang. "Hey, kid. I gotta go. Work calls."

"Guess I won't see you until the party, then. Bye."

Ryker hung up his cell phone and picked up his desk phone's handset.

It was Dave. "Ryker. I've got something for you."

"I'll be right there." He sped over to the lab and ran to the autopsy room.

"Whoa!" Dave said as Ryker slammed open the door. "There's no fire here."

"Sorry. What've you got?"

"Take a look at this." Dave pointed to a white elongated carving that lay on an exam table.

Ryker's heart thumped when he saw it. It was the casting of the knife wound. Although the casting didn't look like any knife Ryker had ever seen, he knew from the look on Dave's face that he'd come to a conclusion about the knife that had been used to stab Jean Terry.

"Well?" Ryker said, not even trying to keep the excitement out of his voice.

"From the shape of the casting, and the appearance of the wound, I'd say the knife's blade is around five and a half to six inches long. It has a curved return and a tapered bolster. I'd be willing to bet the blade is flexible, based on the shape of the wound."

"Return? Bolster?"

Dave grinned. "Yeah. I suddenly developed a need to know a lot about knives. If you're so sure you've got a serial killer on your hands, I want to make sure I don't miss anything that might help you prove it." He pulled up a diagram on his computer. "Here's a breakdown of the parts of a knife. See there? The return is basically the end of the blade. The bolster is a collar that joins the blade with the handle."

"So what does all that mean? Can you identify the knife?"

"If I had a knife, I could tell you how it compares to the knife that was used. I will say, in the short amount of time I've had to do research, I've concluded that the knife used to kill your victim was a boning knife."

"A boning knife?"

Dave nodded. "Usually used by chefs to debone meat. The blade can be stiff or flexible. This one was flexible."

Ryker's pulse pounded in his head. "This could be it." He clasped Dave's shoulder and shook his hand. "This might be my break. If that wound was made with a chef's knife, it could be the knife that he took from Nicole."

"Nicole?"

"Nicole Beckham. Last year's victim. She's a chef. The killer was scared off by her roommate, but he got away with one of her knives. I don't know which one."

"Bring her knives in. I'll see if they match."

"Dave, I can't tell you how much I appreciate your hard work on this. Will you be around today? Tomorrow?"

"I'll be here all afternoon. Tomorrow's Saturday. My daughter has a soccer game out of town."

Ryker headed back to the precinct, feeling like a weight had been lifted off his shoulders. "Don't get excited," he warned himself, but it was too late.

If Nicole's missing knife could be matched with that wound, he'd have the proof he needed to convince Mike that there was a serial killer on the loose in St. Tammany Parish.

Chapter Four

Ryker didn't sleep a wink all night. He'd carried the four case files of the previous victims home with him, as well as copies of Dave's findings about Jean Terry's stab wound and Bill's notes. He went through all four of the files again, comparing everything he could find to Dave's and Bill's notes as well as his own. By the time the sun came up he had reinforced his belief that the three deaths plus Nicole's near attack were the work of one man.

He looked at his coffee mug in distaste. He'd drunk coffee all night while he'd worked. Now he needed water. Water and a shower.

He took his mug into the kitchen and exchanged it for a cold bottle of water. He gulped half of it as he walked back to his desk.

He sat on the edge of the desk and read over his notes one more time, including the victims' birth dates, which he'd just matched up during the night.

October 25, 2006: Daisy Howard, born in October of 1985 (21), was stabbed with her fireplace poker in her apartment while her fiancé was out of town. Model.

October 22, 2007: Bella Pottinger, whom he'd dated briefly in college, and who was born on November 1 of 1976 (30), was killed by a single slash to her carotid artery. The weapon was a broken wine bottle from her wine cooler. Professor of administrative justice.

October 24, 2008: Jennifer Gomez, born in October of 1985 (23), a bank teller, was strangled with her phone cord.

October 20, 2009: Nicole Beckham, born in October of 1983 (26), barely escaped being stabbed with a knife from her chef knife case when her roommate came home.

October 22, 2010: Jean Terry, born in October of 1973 (37) real estate agent, was stabbed in the back with a chef's boning knife on her patio.

He nodded as he gathered up the files and loaded them back into the box. If he could bring his chief proof that the knife stolen from Nicole's chef knife case was consistent with the knife that had killed Jean Terry, maybe Mike would let Ryker connect the cases.

The trouble was, he couldn't find anything in Nicole's case file about which of her knives had been stolen. The CSI reports described the knife case, the engraving on the other knives and the fact that of the nine knives originally in the case, eight were still present and one slot was empty. But not a single report said anything about the specific knife that was missing. From Dave, Ryker knew that most chef knife kits contained between twelve and sixteen utensils, not all of which were knives.

He looked at his watch. It was after seven o'clock in the morning. He needed to take a shower. Then he'd head over to Nicole's apartment to find out which of her knives the killer had stolen. It had to be the boning knife. It was the only thing that made sense.

He thought about his words to Mike.

It's a shame that another woman has to die to convince you. Damn, he hated to be right about this one.

RYKER KNOCKED FOR A THIRD time on Nicole's door.

"Nicole?" he shouted, rapping harder. His pulse was pounding in his temple, even though he tried to reason with himself. She'd probably gone to the restaurant, or shopping, or even out of town for the weekend. She hadn't mentioned anything about it, but then, they hadn't talked much. They'd been too busy with other things.

He looked over the landing down to the small parking lot attached to the building. He had no idea what kind of car she drove. Nor did he have her cell phone number.

He vaulted down the stairs and loped the three blocks from her building to L'Orage. The restaurant was closed. Shading his eyes, he peered through the glass front doors, then pounded on them. There were lights toward the back, where the kitchen was located.

He debated going around to the back and banging on the kitchen door, but before he made up his mind, he saw movement from the kitchen area.

As the figure grew closer, he saw that it was Nicole. Relief washed over him. No matter how irrational it was, he'd been worried that something had happened to her.

She glared at him as she unlocked the beveled glass doors. "We're closed," she said.

"I need your cell phone number," he blurted.

Her brows knit and she cocked her head. "Okay. Maybe you'd better come inside." She stepped back to let him in, then closed and locked the door.

The front of the restaurant was dark. For the first time, Ryker noticed that the windows were tinted, making the light from the sun appear a dark, watery green color. He'd never been to the restaurant during the daytime.

"What is wrong with you?" Nicole said. "And keep your voice down. The restaurant owner is in the kitchen." Her brow was still knit in a small frown.

Ryker realized that to her, his actions might seem less like those of a detective than a needy boyfriend. He took a deep breath. He had a huge stake in this case he was trying to build. Another woman had died. He *had* to stop the killer before the next anniversary date.

"Okay. I went to your apartment this morning, and you weren't there. I thought the restaurant wasn't open for lunch on Saturdays."

"It's not, but we still have work to do."

"I need to get your cell phone number, in case I need to get in touch with you."

"That's what the emergency is?" she said on a sigh. "I was afraid—"

"What? Oh, that something had happened with the case?" He nodded. "It has, but it's not bad. Okay, it is bad, but I've got information that could be very good."

"Nicole, is everything all right?" The speaker was a large black man in a massive white apron.

"Everything's fine, Job. Thanks."

Job scrutinized Ryker, then nodded. "You call me if you need me."

"Job?" Ryker said, once the man had gone back into the kitchen. "Is that really his name?"

"Just like in the Bible," Nicole said. "Job Washington is the owner of L'Orage. He watches out for me."

"I'm glad. That makes me feel a little better. Now give me your cell phone number and take mine." Ryker quickly recorded Nicole's number and gave her his.

"Tell me what this is all about. That call you got this

morning—another woman was killed, wasn't she? I saw something on the news."

He nodded, and reached out and placed his hand over hers on the table. "She was stabbed."

Nicole met his gaze, then pulled her hand away.

He knew what he was about to say was going to upset her, but he couldn't think of an easier way to do it. Maybe if the information about the stolen knife had been noted somewhere in her case file. Then he wouldn't have to tell her the specifics about Jean Terry's stabbing in order to get the information he needed.

He took a deep breath and met her gaze. "Which of your knives was stolen?"

Nicole heard the suppressed intensity in Ryker's voice. It matched the intensity in his blue eyes. But it was his words that ripped through her insides.

"Wh-which knife?" she stammered. She'd heard him loud and clear. She automatically parroted what he'd said because she needed time to absorb what his question meant. She had the feeling that the answer she gave was going to turn her world upside-down.

He nodded. "I know there are a bunch of different knives in your case. Which one did the intruder take?"

She opened her mouth to ask why, but her lips felt numb. She shook her head.

"Come on, Nic. Which knife?"

She tried to swallow, but her mouth was dry. In that instant, she didn't think she could have spoken if her life depended on it. Maybe it did.

"It was the boning knife, wasn't it? Five- to six-inch flexible blade."

She felt as though he'd hit her in the chest. That was how hard her heart was beating. She closed her eyes for a brief instant, trying to blot out the grisly images that suddenly rose in her mind. "Th-that woman was stabbed with my knife?" she rasped.

Ryker nodded and reached for her hand again. His warm fingers closed over hers. To his credit, he looked as if he'd rather be tortured than answer her.

"That means—"

"It means the man who broke into your apartment and tried to attack you with your own knife has killed four women. You're his only mistake."

RYKER'S WORDS SLAMMED into Nicole's chest like she imagined bullets would feel. *You're. His. Only. Mistake.*

"What do I do now?" she asked, forcing the words through numbed lips.

Ryker let go of her hand. "Do what I told you. Be careful. Take reasonable precautions."

She nodded. She'd do anything he told her to. Because suddenly the danger he kept talking about was ominously real. A man was out there, with *her* knife, killing women.

"But he killed that—other woman. Why would you still think he's after me?"

"I can't afford to think anything else. We don't know if he thinks you can identify him. Your name was in the paper last year after the break-in, so he probably knows who you are, although he may not know where you live now. But I'm not willing to take any chances."

Nicole swallowed hard, and bit her lip. She opened her mouth to thank Ryker for protecting her, but he spoke first.

"I need your knives."

She was shocked. "My knives?" She tried to ask why, but her lips still felt numb.

"I need to take them to the medical examiner. I'm hoping

he can positively identify the murder weapon as a match to your set of knives."

Nicole shuddered at the thought that her missing knife had caused someone's death. "I bought another boning knife," she said.

"You did?" Ryker's eyes sparked. "The same brand? The same knife?"

She nodded.

"That's even better. Dave can match it to the casting he made. I may finally be able to link two cases. Yours and Jean Terry's."

"Jean Terry? She's the—the latest victim?"

"Yeah. She was stabbed in the back."

Nicole wanted to put her hands over her ears. She didn't want to hear any of the specifics. Her active imagination had already given her an image of the poor woman being stabbed. She didn't want a name, and certainly not a face, to go with that grisly image.

She clasped her hands together for a brief moment, trying to force the picture of her knife buried to the hilt in a woman's back out of her brain. Then she stood. "I'll get my case."

He followed her to the kitchen.

She held it out. "When can I get it back?"

"I'll try to get the rest of the knives back to you as soon as I can, but the boning knife will probably go into evidence. You'll have to get along without it." He took the case. "Don't worry. I'll take care of them."

He turned to leave, then turned back. "Keep your cell phone on you at all times. What time do you get off tonight?"

"Eleven. We're working on inventory this morning, but I have a regular shift tonight. So I'll be done around eleven, as usual."

Ryker nodded. "I'll pick you up."

A wave of relief washed over Nicole like a sudden shower, surprising her. She hadn't realized how worried she was. But she tried to protest anyway. What she'd told him last night was true. She was *not* going to act like a victim. "You don't have to—"

His glare paralyzed her throat. She swallowed again and nodded. "Okay," she rasped.

A slight smile lightened his features. "That's better. Remember what I said. Reasonable precautions." He headed toward the door.

Nicole stood and followed him to the door, unable to tear her eyes away from his casual, loose-limbed gait as he walked to his car, folded his long legs into the front seat and drove away. She didn't know whether to be thankful that he was so determined to keep her safe, or terrified that he thought it was necessary.

WITHIN THIRTY MINUTES, Ryker was back in the forensics lab with Dave.

"I was just about to take off," Dave said. "My daughter's soccer game is this afternoon."

"Sorry," Ryker said. "Hopefully this won't take long. I've got Nicole's knives here. She bought a new boning knife, same brand as the one that was stolen." He opened the case and laid it out on a table.

Dave set the casting he'd done from Jean Terry's fatal wound down on a high-definition overhead projector, then laid the boning knife from Nicole's case next to it. He positioned them parallel to each other facing the same direction, and stood there, studying the high-resolution image projected on the screen.

Ryker stuck his hands in his pockets and waited. He tried to look at the objects analytically, like Dave was, but as far as he could tell, the casting was barely recognizable as a knife at all. He couldn't see a lot of resemblance to Nicole's new boning knife.

As hard as he tried to maintain an open mind, he was fast losing his conviction that the knife and the fatal wound were a match.

"Well?" he finally said, unable to wait any longer.

"Hmm," Dave said. He pressed a button on a computer at his elbow, typed briefly, then pressed another button. A printer sang out, its harsh sound splitting the air. Dave took the printout, then crossed the room and pulled a transparency out of a file folder and brought it back to the projector. He removed the knife and the casting and positioned the transparency so that it was projected onto the screen. Then he adjusted the focus.

"What's that?" Ryker felt like a kid who'd been told to be patient. It was all he could do not to fidget like a ten-year-old. He thought the picture was of the *V*-shaped wound, but he was out of his element here, so he couldn't assume anything.

"It's a film of the wound." Dave studied it for a few minutes, then took the knife over to the lighted magnifier and studied it from all angles.

After what seemed to Ryker like an hour, Dave finally turned off the magnifier's light and flipped off the overhead projector.

He folded his arms.

"Dave!" Ryker said, exasperated.

Dave smiled. "I can't say with a hundred percent certainty, but—"

Ryker held his breath.

"But I'm about ninety percent sure that the weapon that killed Jean Terry is a match to this boning knife from Nicole Beckham's chef knife case."

Ryker blew out a breath he hadn't known he was holding. "Ninety percent? That's great! That's enough." He clapped Dave on the shoulder. "Thanks, Dave! When can I have your written report?"

"Monday."

"Monday?" That tempered Ryker's elation a bit. "Two days? But I've got to convince Mike that I have a connection."

Dave cocked an eyebrow at him. "It's Saturday. You won't get to Mike before Monday anyway."

Ryker's phone rang. He glanced at the display. "Speaking of the devil," he muttered.

"I'm out of here," Dave said. "If we don't leave right now, my wife and I will miss the beginning of the game."

Ryker waved at Dave as he answered the phone. "Delancey here."

"Ryker, get to my office. Now!" Mike Davis's voice boomed through the phone.

"What's up?" Ryker asked as he turned toward the door.

"Now!"

"Yes, sir." He snapped the phone closed as he reached his car. He couldn't figure out what had happened. As much as Mike blustered, he never lost his cool.

But just now, he'd sounded anything but cool. Ryker cringed. What crisis could possibly be bad enough to fluster the big deputy chief?

"No, sir," Ryker said to Mike a few minutes later. "I haven't seen it."

Mike shoved the morning newspaper across his desk toward Ryker.

There, in black-and-white, was the front-page article that had Mike worked up.

Parish Sheriff Denies Connection Among Victims Of October Killer.

October Killer. Ryker's chest tightened. Not only had the press gotten wind of his theory of a serial killer, they'd already named the case.

"Now, I haven't talked to the press," Mike growled. "And neither has the sheriff. So where the hell did this reporter get this?"

Ryker's heart sank to his toes. *Lon Hébert.* "Well, yesterday morning at the crime scene—" He paused.

"Delancey!"

"Lon Hébert showed up at the Jean Terry crime scene not ten minutes after I got there. He claimed he heard about the homicide on a police scanner—"

Mike broke in with a long, colorful string of curses, ending with "Son of a bitch! What the hell did you say in front of him?"

"Mike, nothing, I swear. I'd just mentioned something to Bill about the knife wound and Nic's missing knife, when Hébert showed up."

Mike's normally florid face turned beet-red, and he bit right through the toothpick between his teeth. "'*Nic's* missing knife'? Who the hell is Nic?"

"Nicole Beckham. Last year's victim, whose roommate arrived home in time to scare off the killer."

"I don't believe it," Mike snapped. "I should—but I don't. Of all the stupid stunts."

"Hébert said he was going to call you for a statement. He didn't?"

"Hell no, he didn't."

"When I told him to get out I reminded him to check anything he decided to print with the office here. I'll talk to him—"

"No. I'll send Crenshaw. What you're going to do is sit

down and take me through the cases. I've got to meet with the sheriff in one hour at his golf course. His tee time was delayed because of this article." Mike leaned back in his chair. "He's going to rip me a new one, so I'm going to do the same for you. Sit!"

Ryker sat.

"I warned you about talking about your theories. Now look what you've done. You've made it clear to everyone in this office that you believe we've got a serial killer. And now you've involved the press. I could put you on suspension for that."

"I've never—" Ryker stopped. He'd started to say he'd never spoken to anyone outside of the department, but after last night that was no longer true. He'd talked to Nicole about it. "I may have been too vocal, but—"

Mike held up a hand. "Spare me. I know. Women are dying. Okay, I'm here. I'm listening. Convince me that we've got a serial killer."

Ryker leaned forward. "I was in the medical examiner's office when you called. Dave just confirmed that the boning knife that killed Jean Terry is a match to the knife that was taken from Nicole Beckham's apartment last year on October 20."

"I thought you didn't recover a murder weapon from the Terry scene."

"We didn't. But Dave, Dr. Miller, took a casting of the wound, and it matches the new boning knife that Nicole bought to replace the one that was stolen."

"Have you got Miller's report?"

"He'll get it to me Monday. He—we—didn't expect you to be working today."

Mike's florid face darkened. "Neither did I. And I sure didn't figure I'd be trekking out to the golf club to get my ass chewed by the sheriff."

"I'll be glad to go."

"Absolutely not. I'm not putting you within a hundred yards of the sheriff." Mike stood and reached for his coat, then turned and pointed at Ryker. "I'm not happy about this. But I'm also not happy about that woman being killed. You put your cases together. Work them as a serial killer case. But suspension won't be all you're looking at if your theory turns out to be wrong. I can't even tell you what the sheriff will do to you *and* to me. I hope you don't have to wait until another woman dies before you can solve it."

Ryker stood. "Me, too, sir. Me, too. How many men can I have?"

"One. Crenshaw."

"One? But—"

"Don't push me, Delancey. You can use my secretary, Anne-Marie, for paperwork and phone calls. And get me that M.E. report first thing Monday."

Ryker opened his mouth to tell Mike that one person plus a piece of the deputy chief's secretary wasn't enough, but Mike was already out the door, and anyhow, Ryker knew that he was getting off easy, considering it very well could be his fault Hébert had gotten wind of the connection between Jean Terry's case and Nicole's missing knife. He didn't need to press his luck.

His gaze lit on the newspaper headline. He picked up the paper Mike had shoved toward him and quickly skimmed the article. His eyes zeroed in on the last paragraph.

Sources tell us that a knife belonging to a previous victim was the weapon used to kill the latest victim, whose name is being withheld pending notification of next of kin. The chef, Nicole Beckham, whose knife was stolen during a foiled attack on October 20 of last year, could not be reached for comment. The same sources reveal that she is helping with the investigation and has been an invaluable asset.

Damn it! He folded the paper and slapped it against his leg. Lon Hébert might as well have drawn a target on Nicole's back. Any reporter worth their salt knew better than to name a victim without clearing it with the sheriff's office. And then he'd said that she had been invaluable to the investigation. If the killer wasn't already sure that Nicole could recognize him, he would be now.

Ryker called Bill Crenshaw. "Bill, has Mike talked with you?"

"I just passed him in the hall. I just got off the phone with the newspaper office. Can't reach Hébert. Apparently he hightailed it out of town for the weekend as soon as he turned in the story."

"Son of a bitch! Listen, Bill. You didn't tell anybody what I said at the crime scene about the knife, did you?"

There was a pause on the other end of the phone, and then a few choice curse words. "What the hell kind of question is that?"

"I know. Sorry. You think Hébert heard me?"

"He said something about a scanner, but I think he's got a friend inside the sheriff's department."

"Yeah? Who?"

"Well, I'm not accusing anybody, but you've heard the saying. *Telephone, telegraph, tell-a-CSI.*"

"You think it was one of the crime scene investigators who worked the scene?"

"Both Masters and the new guy—Jones—were in the room when you said what you did about the knife."

"You think they heard me?"

"I barely heard you, but it's not impossible. CSIs sure like to think they know it all."

"I'd like to punch Hébert's lights out for putting Nic's

name in the paper. I tell you what, though. That article got me what I've been trying to get all along. Mike agreed to let me combine the cases."

"No way!"

"Didn't Mike tell you he's putting you on the cases with me?"

"Nope. He was grousing about getting his ass chewed by the sheriff."

"Dave matched the wound to Nicole's missing boning knife. I brought her case of knives over for him to compare."

"Hold on a minute. How did he match something to a missing knife?"

"Well, to its replacement. That just happened about two hours ago. Listen, Bill," Ryker added, "Mike's putting you on the cases with me. The October Murders, since the reporter already named it for us. Can you meet with me this evening so I can go over the case files with you?"

"Wish I could, but I'm on my way up to Baton Rouge to a ball game. I'm not on duty again until Monday."

Ryker sighed. "Okay. First thing Monday, then."

"Right. Monday."

Ryker left Mike's office and headed to the evidence room to check out the files until Tuesday. He was disappointed that Bill wouldn't be available until Monday, but he understood. Nobody was as committed to solving this case as he was. He'd already put in hours of off-duty time trying to prove there was a serial killer out there. He couldn't expect anyone else to give up their free time.

But now that he had a partner to work with on the case, he needed to make sure he had every bit of evidence lined up. He understood all his notes and scribbling, but Bill wouldn't. And Ryker needed Bill up to speed as soon as possible.

Maybe a new eye looking at the evidence could pinpoint what he was missing. Because he had to be missing something. There was no perfect crime. One way or another, the killer would trip up. And Ryker intended to be there when he did.

Chapter Five

"Job, you go on home. You've been here all day. And this was supposed to be your Saturday off."

"We had to get the inventory done."

Nicole shrugged out of her chef's coat and hung it on the rack beside the kitchen door. Then she turned back to the long counter to retrieve her knife case—and remembered that she didn't have it. Ryker had it.

Job took off his apron and tossed it into the laundry bin. "It was a good day. We finished the inventory *and* handled a big dinner crowd."

"Yes, it was, but I've got to admit I'm exhausted." She looked at her watch. Ten after eleven. Ryker had told her he'd pick her up. Had he forgotten?

"Are you sure you're okay?"

"I'm fine. I just wish Ryker had told me the paper was going to print that."

"Me, I hate newspapers. They ruin lives and say it's the public's right to know. Vultures."

"I guess I should have expected it, after Ryker took my knives to match with the victim's wound." Nicole shivered. "But I didn't."

"Speaking of that boyfriend of yours, you sure he's coming?"

She sent a glare Job's way. "He's not my boyfriend. He's—he's a detective. He said he'd be here."

"I think he'd like to be your boyfriend."

She felt her face heating up. Did it show? The fact that she and Ryker had— She stopped that thought right there. "Job, don't talk like that. We're not in high school."

"That's for sure," Job retorted.

Nicole's face grew hotter. She turned around and checked the pockets of her chef's coat, although she knew she hadn't left anything in them. But she needed time for her fiery cheeks to cool down.

Job stuck his signature fedora on his bald head. "Come on, Nicki. I'll take you home."

Just then a knock sounded on the front door of the restaurant. Nicole jumped. Why was she so jittery all of a sudden? It was a rhetorical question. She knew why. A woman had been killed, and Ryker was convinced that the murder weapon used was *her* missing knife.

"That's him now." She started for the door.

"I'll get it," Job said. He beat her to the door and scrutinized Ryker through the glass before he opened it.

"Hi, uh—Mr. Washington."

"Job. Call me Job."

"Job. I'm here to pick up Nicole." Ryker's gaze slid past Job and met her gaze. He raised his brows. "Ready?"

Job stepped between Ryker and Nicole. "All this time I thought you were an admirer," he said in an accusatory tone.

Ryker looked surprised. "I'm a big fan. You've got a great chef."

"Humph." Job adjusted his fedora. "Not too smart, letting the newspaper shine the spotlight on her like that."

Ryker nodded. "I agree. If I'd known, I'd have stopped it."

Job eyed him. "Nothing better happen to Nicki, you understand me?"

"Yes, sir."

"Don't worry," Nicole said. "It's all right. Detective Delancey has my best interests at heart."

Job took a step away from the door, so Ryker could come in. "I'm headed home. I'll go out the back and lock up there. You make sure the front is locked and the alarm is turned on."

"I will. Thanks." She set the alarm and locked the front door behind them. As they walked across the street, Ryker looked around.

"Where'd Job go?"

"He parks behind the restaurant."

"Ah. So *he* parks behind the restaurant. *He* drives to work."

"He lives in Bush. That's several miles from here. I live three blocks away. Speaking of which, are you really going to drive me three blocks?"

"Yep."

"It's silly," Nicole muttered as she climbed into his car on the passenger side. She watched him as he got in and cranked the engine, thinking the same thing she'd thought when she'd first met him on the night of her near attack, and again last night.

Detective Ryker Delancey was startlingly good-looking with light brown hair, blue eyes and lashes that stirred a breeze when he blinked. His features were clean and chiseled. His mouth was wide and straight, and looked as if it was made for smiling. It occurred to her that he didn't smile much.

As if he'd heard her, he glanced her way, and his mouth turned up slightly. He reached into the backseat and set her chef's knife case on her lap.

"My knives," she said. It had surprised her how incomplete she'd felt all day without them. Her mother had given them to her when she'd graduated from culinary school.

In ten years, she hadn't been without them, until today. She opened the case and looked inside. The boning knife slot was empty. The empty slot taunted her with danger, just like it had that night. "You kept my boning knife."

He looked over at her as he pulled into the parking lot behind her building. "Why didn't you get it engraved, like the others?" His head nodded slightly toward the case.

"I don't know. My mother—my mother gave the set to me." She closed the case and ran her fingers along the polished teak. Then she realized Ryker was still looking at her. She shrugged.

"I guess I thought I'd eventually get the other knife back. Silly of me."

"You might still, if we catch him."

She shook her head. Her fingers closed around the case's handle. "Please, don't even say that. I don't want it. Not after—" She shuddered. The idea of using that knife—even seeing it—horrified her. It had blood on it now. Human blood. She would never be able to look at it, never be able to touch it, again.

Ryker pulled out into the street and within a few minutes, he turned into the tiny parking lot behind her building. He killed the engine.

"Which car is yours?" he asked before Nicole could grab the door handle to get out.

"It's the silver Ford Fusion over there."

They got out and Ryker surveyed the parking lot. "Way over there?"

Nicole closed the passenger door.

"Bring it over here and park it next to your stairwell."

"I'm not going to do that. I almost never use my car.

It would just sit there, taking up space that someone who drives to work every day could use."

Ryker rounded the front of his BMW, his fists clenched, and got in her face. "Did you think that was a request?" he growled.

Nicole stiffened. He'd morphed from handsome protector to angry commander in a flash. She took a step backward.

Ryker checked himself and unclenched his fists. "Sorry. But you need to understand what's going on here."

She clutched her knife case handle in one hand and her purse strap in the other. "So tell me. What *is* going on here? Because I'm getting confused. Your serial killer only attacks once a year, right? Well, then, he's got his quarry for 2010. Or were you thinking you'd lure him out by making sure he and everybody else in the Greater New Orleans area knew it was my knife he killed that woman with?"

"Are you suggesting I gave that reporter that story?" His brows drew down, turning his handsome face into a threatening mask.

"I don't know what to think," she said shakily, taking a step backward.

Ryker's face transformed immediately. "I'm sorry, Nic. If I'd known that reporter had that information, I'd have stopped him, one way or another."

"But you didn't. And now—"

A pickup truck roared down the street and careered into the parking lot. Ryker's arm snaked around Nicole's waist and pulled her to him and away from the unpredictable path of the vehicle. She heard him mutter "Bastard!" under his breath.

"Let's go upstairs," he said. "I don't like you standing out here in the open."

His hand on the small of her back, he guided her to the

stairs, where he waited for her to go first. The idea of him following her up the stairs, gazing at her backside, which would be at his eye level, made her really self-conscious. She wished she had a jacket, or a long top that covered her butt. Or a better butt, she thought wryly.

At the top of the stairs, she waited with her keys proffered. He took them and unlocked her door, then stood aside while she entered first. Then he glanced around the landing and the streets below before he came inside and closed and locked the door.

And here they were. Just like last night. Only now there was this *thing* between them. Nicole's knees threatened to buckle as the image, the feel, the scent of him hit her. His hands, his body, his mouth, had showed her a whole new dimension to sex. Now she had no idea what to do or say.

If anything, he was acting more like a cop than he had yesterday, when he'd come up to her apartment to convince her of the danger she was in, and ended up making her feel safer than she could ever remember feeling.

She looked at him. He appeared relaxed, and yet ready for anything, like a predator waiting for its prey. His intensity gave her chills. At this moment, she couldn't reconcile the two sides of him. The tender lover was gone and in his place was a warrior chief, ready to do battle.

Ryker took a folded sheet of newsprint out of his jacket pocket and held it up. "I brought this in case you didn't get to read it all."

"Oh, I read it. And heard it read to me over and over again by the kitchen staff and the waiters. If I'd stepped out of the kitchen, I'm sure the diners would have had a lot to say about it, too."

"Damn it," Ryker muttered.

"Maybe it's not that big a deal. My name was in the paper last year."

He glared at her. "Yes, and you quit your job and moved to a different town. Don't you understand what this means?"

She tried to ignore the faintly nauseated feeling below her breastbone that told her she did understand. "I understand what it doesn't mean. I am not moving again."

She walked around the island into the kitchen, a futile effort to put distance between her and what Ryker was saying. It didn't help.

"I got permission to connect the cases."

"Connect?" Her heart thumped in her chest. She knew what that meant, but she didn't want to go there.

"Want some coffee?" she countered, and turned without waiting for an answer. It took a couple of minutes and a bit of concentration to grind the espresso beans and start them to brewing. Then she reached to open the refrigerator to retrieve the milk.

Ryker's hand wrapped around hers. "Stop ignoring me," he growled.

She jumped. "Stop sneaking up on me!" She could feel a flutter in her throat. It was her pulse. "I'm not ignoring you," she finished lamely.

"The hell you're not. You heard what I just said. Your knife links your case with Jean Terry's, and therefore with all the others. And now, because of that reporter, the October Killer knows we're onto him."

Nicole stared at him. "The October Killer?"

He nodded at the newspaper. "Didn't you notice that?"

"Of course I noticed it. You're not seriously going to call him—"

"Hey. The reporter sensationalized the cases by giving him that name," he said wryly. "That's the name we're stuck with." He let go of her hand and stepped back around the island and sat down on a bar stool.

She fixed them each a decaf cappuccino, concentrating on not letting her fingers tremble, and set his in front of him. "But Jean Terry is his victim for this year, right? If he stays true to form—"

"He won't. Listen to me, Nic. He knows we're onto him. And he knows why. It's because of you. You are a threat to him. And now he knows where to find you. If he didn't already."

And there it was. What she hadn't wanted to hear. Or face. She clutched the sides of the cup for warmth and stared down into the pale tan foam. "I guess I've been pretending that none of this has anything to do with me."

Ryker's gaze scrutinized her. "You can't live like that. Ignoring the truth is dangerous—especially right now. Do you have someplace you could go, until we catch this guy? Your mother? Your dad?"

"My mother is dead. And there's no father in the picture."

"I'm sorry. What about a friend?"

She shook her head. "The people at the restaurant are my friends. A couple of girls in Chef Voleur. But there's nobody I could just demand to take me in."

She unwrapped her palms from the cup and then took a sip of coffee. "If you're so worried about my safety, why don't you assign somebody to watch my apartment at night? Doesn't the killer always strike at night?"

"You want to know what kind of manpower my deputy chief gave me to catch this serial killer? One man. *One*. Bill's a good cop, but still." Ryker shook his head and sniffed. "And yeah, the killer has always struck at night—in the past. But now he's got to be feeling cornered. Like we've turned a spotlight onto him. Not only did the newspaper give him a name, they announced that two of the murders were linked by a weapon—your knife."

Ryker tossed back the last of his coffee and set his mug down. When he looked up at her, his eyes were burning with intensity. "I'll stay here."

"What?" Nicole said. "Here? No. I mean—"

"Don't panic," Ryker said quickly, his mouth turning up. "If I had a man to assign to you as a protective detail, he'd already be on the job. But I don't. This is strictly precautionary. I'd do the same thing for any witness. I need to make sure you're safe, because I'm about to mount an aggressive and very intense investigation into these killings. We're going to stir up the waters. This killer will become very uncomfortable. And the closer we get to him, the more danger you're in."

"I don't understand. You're talking about here? In my apartment? But—"

He held up his hands. "Hey, Nic. Don't worry. I'm a cop. You're my victim. That's all. The other—" he nodded toward the bedroom "—I crossed a line. I apologize. It was wrong of me to take advantage of you."

"Take advantage?" Nicole wasn't sure whether to feel indignant or hurt. "As I recall, we were both quite willing."

Ryker's expression grew stony. "In any case, it was a mistake. It won't happen again."

Seeing his expression, Nicole decided she didn't have to choose. She felt both indignant *and* hurt in equal measure. She straightened. "I see. Well, that's a relief. Okay, then, the couch is all yours. If you want sheets and pillows, they're in the closet beside the bathroom." She turned and put her cup in the sink.

Ryker watched as she strode toward her bedroom. "Nic," he called. "I'll need a key."

She whirled and glared at him. For a second, he thought

she was going to object, but she retraced her steps and rummaged in a kitchen drawer. Finally she came up with a lone key on a key ring shaped like a chef's hat. She slapped it onto the kitchen counter.

"There." She spun and walked back through the bedroom door, then paused with her hand on the knob, looking at him.

"Don't leave the toilet seat up." She slammed the door behind her.

He smiled as he lay down on the couch, testing it out. She always had to have the last word. It was something that could easily become very annoying, he was sure. But to his chagrin, he found it cute.

He turned on his side, then returned to his back, stuffing a throw pillow behind his neck. Not too bad.

He heard sounds coming from her room. He sat up and listened. It sounded like slamming drawers. He'd made her mad, or hurt her feelings. He hadn't meant to, but he had meant what he'd said.

It had been a mistake for him to sleep with her. He knew it now, and he'd known it then. Hell, it was the first thing veteran cops warned rookies about. *Don't get involved. Ever. Not with a victim. Not with a witness. And for damn sure not with a suspect.* It was never a good idea. *Never.*

He gave the throw pillow a good solid right hook before he lay down on it again. If it was a bad idea in general, then it was a triple bad idea for him—with her.

Because no matter how many ways he'd tried to spin it all day, it always came back to one thing. Sex with Nicole was the best he'd ever had. Any time. Anywhere. And that was going to make it hard as hell for him to maintain his professional detachment.

But he had to. If he let himself worry about Nicole on a personal level, it could undermine his effectiveness as a law enforcement officer and sabotage his ability to protect her.

Maybe, when all this was over—

No! He pounded the pillow again. No thinking about what might happen later. This was now. He had a killer to catch.

MONDAY MORNING OVER cappuccino, Ryker outlined the rules for Nicole. She would provide him with her schedule. He'd take her to work and pick her up. When he wasn't available, he'd arrange for Bill or Job to drive her. "You don't go anywhere without one of us."

"I can't do this," Nicole protested. "I feel like I'm the prisoner. I have a life—a job. I'm in charge of buying the protein for the restaurant several days a week. I take a yoga class on Saturdays. I—" She stopped short, her breath hiccoughing like a sob.

Ryker stood, stretching out the stiffness in his back from lying on her couch. He buckled on his holster. "Then do what I said in the first place. Get out of town until this is all over."

She lifted her chin. "No. I am not leaving my home."

He studied her. "What is it, Nic? What's the big deal about moving?" He gestured around him. "You've been here less than a year. It's just an apartment."

Her head jerked slightly, as if she were dodging a blow. "I told you I am not moving."

"I don't understand," Ryker countered. "What's wrong with moving? I've moved a bunch of times. It's no big deal."

"No big deal?" She squeezed the mug more tightly. "Where did you spend your childhood?"

"Why?"

"I want to know."

Ryker sent her an odd look, but he answered her question. "Here. Well, over in Chef Voleur. That's where my family's from. I grew up in the same house my father grew up in."

Nicole nodded. "That explains a lot. I spent my childhood going from one broken-down apartment to another, each one smaller and shabbier than the one before. The last place I lived with my mother was a room in a boarding house."

She clenched her jaw. "Then last year, I moved from my beautiful apartment in Chef Voleur to here. Not as nice. Not as large." She shook her head. "I am not going on that downslide again."

"Nic, I'm—I'm sorry."

She didn't say a word. She just finished her coffee and put her mug in the sink. Apparently that particular conversation was over.

He adjusted his shoulder holster and shrugged into his jacket. "Okay, then. Ready to go?"

After he dropped Nicole off at L'Orage, he headed for Mike's office. When he got there, the big man was chewing on a toothpick and studying a report.

Ryker rapped on the door facing.

"Come on in," Mike said without looking up.

"Is that—?"

"Dave's report," Mike growled. He shoved the pages across his desk to Ryker. "Looks like you've proven your connection, Delancey."

Ryker skimmed Dave's report. It was basically what Dave had told him, except that instead of ninety percent certainty, Dave had expanded his certainty that the wound was made by the same brand and type of knife that had been stolen from Nicole's kit to ninety-five percent. Ryker read the notation Dave had made.

The wound was made by a boning knife with a six-inch flexible full tang blade, curved return and tapered bolster. These characteristics are unique to this type of knife, as well as this brand's signature guard (ref. ill. IV), which left a distinctly shaped contusion on the victim's skin.

"He did it," Ryker muttered. He looked up. "He did it! Ninety-five percent certainty that the knife used to kill Jean Terry is the same knife stolen from Nic—Nicole Beckham."

Mike leaned back in his chair and tossed the toothpick he'd macerated into his trash can. "How many open cases are you working right now? *Not* counting your serial killer cases."

Ryker took out his notebook. "I'm due to testify Tuesday morning in a domestic violence case. That should be the end of that one. And I've got to drive to Angola for a parole hearing on Thursday. The only other active case I have is the Terry case."

Mike nodded. "I've switched Crenshaw's open cases to Dagewood and Phillips. They're not happy, but I'll deal with them. They'll manage, unless we're deluged with homicides. I want you to take Crenshaw through every single page of your October Killer's cases. By the way, the evidence room tells me you have the files checked out."

"Yep. I was reviewing them."

"I want a report on my desk tomorrow detailing the similarities between the cases. The sheriff wants to see everything we've got. He's less than thrilled about having to explain a serial killer in St. Tammany Parish, and he's determined not to bring in the Feebs. Want to see his denture marks on my ass?"

Ryker held up his hand laughing. "Thanks, but no. I

don't need that picture in my head." He sobered. "Do you think we'll have to call in the FBI?"

Mike took a toothpick out of his shirt pocket and stuck it between his teeth. "I hope not. I've only got one ass. Get this thing cleaned up yesterday. Got it?"

"Yes, sir." Ryker stood. "Can I have this?" He brandished the M.E.'s report.

Mike nodded. "Yep. Dave sent me two copies. That one's yours."

Ryker found Bill Crenshaw at his desk, working on the computer.

"Bill. How soon can we get together and go over these cases? Mike says he's freed you up."

Bill scowled at him. "Freed me up? Yeah, if you don't count the notes I've got to type up for Dagewood and Phillips to bring them up to speed on my two cases. That alone is going to take me all day."

"Then tonight. Come over to Nic's apartment when you finish."

Bill's brows rose. "Nic's apartment?" He grinned. "You're living at *Nic's* apartment?"

Ryker groaned inwardly. He hadn't meant to say it like that. "She's my only living victim, Bill. I can't put her in protective custody, so I'm staying there—*just* to make sure nothing happens to her." He wrote down the address for Bill. "When can you be there?"

"Not until after six. Later unless you're going to feed me."

"I'll pick up something from L'Orage."

Bill nodded as he went back to typing. "Takeout from the finest restaurant in Mandeville. This October Killer case might turn out to be a cushy assignment after all."

Chapter Six

Ryker unlocked the door and stood back to let Nicole into her apartment that night. Even though she knew he and Bill Crenshaw were working there, the sight still surprised her.

A dark-haired, dark-eyed man in his early thirties who could have been a linebacker for the New Orleans Saints sat on her couch. He was surrounded by sheets of paper and sticky notes. The coffee table was groaning under the weight of five file folders, and several beer cans were lined up on the floor next to takeout boxes from L'Orage.

"Sorry about the mess," Ryker muttered as he locked the door. "This is Detective Bill Crenshaw. He's working with me on the October case."

Bill Crenshaw set an empty beer can down on the floor and made getting-up motions.

"Don't—" Nicole said, holding up a hand. "Please."

"Bill, this is Nicole Beckham."

Bill's dark eyes met Nicole's gaze, then slid all the way to her shoes and back up. He smiled and nodded. "Nice," he said.

Ryker made a growling sound from behind her.

"To meet you," Bill appended. "Nice to meet you. Thanks for letting us use your place."

The glint in his eye told her that he knew, or at least

inferred, that there was a lot more to it than just *using* her place. She let a corner of her mouth turn up, but she raised one brow, hoping he got the message that what she and Ryker were doing at her place was none of his business.

To his credit, Bill looked away, back at the sheets of paper in his hand. Then he looked at her again. "By the way, did you make that spaghetti?"

"The fettuccini alla carbonara with seared asparagus?" Nicole knew she was being pompous, but she'd taken special care with the meal she'd made for Ryker and his fellow detective. It was her signature dish, and she didn't particularly like it dismissed as *spaghetti*.

"Yeah," Bill said. "That. It was great. I never liked asparagus, but that was pretty good."

"Thank you," she said stiffly. "I see you paired it with a fine domestic beer." She turned to Ryker, who was watching her sheepishly, and gave him a small smile to soften her critical words.

"I'll let you two get on with your work." She headed for her bedroom, taking a detour to the kitchen to fetch a bottle of water and a glass of chilled white wine. She was dying for a shower but she didn't want to take it while Ryker and Bill Crenshaw were sitting less than fifty feet away from her bathroom door.

She closed the door to her bedroom and set the water and wine down on her bedside table. She started to undress, stopped and crossed the room to turn the lock on the door. The metallic click reverberated in the air. She winced.

After undressing, she pondered whether to put on jeans or to go ahead and get into her pajamas, although she really didn't want to put on clean pajamas without showering. It had been a long day anyway, and just before closing time one of the waiters had bumped into her and spilled salad dressing on her blouse. So she smelled like balsamic vinegar, a fact that Ryker had politely failed to mention on their short ride from the restaurant to her apartment. She'd seen his nose twitch though.

She sat down on the bed in her underwear and took a long sip of white wine, savoring it as she sighed with exhaustion.

"Damn it," she whispered. She wanted a shower. Now. She looked at her watch. Eleven-thirty. It could be hours before Ryker and his buddy got through with whatever they were doing, and she didn't feel like going to sleep smelling like vinegar.

She set her mouth and stared at the bedroom door. Beyond it, she could hear the low, decidedly masculine murmur of the two men as they talked about the October Killer.

She took another, longer sip of wine, followed it with a deep breath, then stood. She'd made up her mind. This was her home, despite the fact that two large, virile men were sprawled all over her living room just waiting to leer at her.

No. On second thought, she doubted they were thinking about her at all, other than as the lone surviving victim of a killer. But that was their job. Hers was to plan, prepare and cook delicious dishes for hungry diners. She was due back at L'Orage in less than twelve hours, and she couldn't go to sleep smelling like a salad.

Determinedly, she stripped and tossed her clothes into a basket in her closet. Then she grabbed a bathrobe from the hook on the closet door and wrapped it around her, cinching the sash tight. Another sip of wine and another long breath and she was ready.

When she turned the knob and stepped out of her bedroom, Ryker was pacing and Bill was poring over a dog-eared manila folder. Neither one of them acknowledged her.

"—no connection at all," Bill was saying. His tone told her it wasn't the first time he'd said it.

Ryker shrugged. "That's why finding Nic's knife is so important." He ran his palm over his short hair. "Until Jean Terry was killed, I had *nothing* linking the cases except the dates, the victims' birthdays and the very fact that he *wasn't* consistent about weapon or age or race. I talked to the families and friends of the victims, reviewed every receipt, every tax record, every piece of paper I could find, but the victims have nothing in common but their birthdays."

"I'm surprised Mike didn't jump on the dates of the murders and the victims' birthdays."

"I actually thought he would last year. Maybe if the killer had succeeded in killing Nic—" Ryker cut his words short and sent an apologetic glance at Nicole.

Only then did she realize she had paused with her hand on the bathroom door handle to listen to them. She twisted it, hurried inside and closed the door behind her.

Maybe if the killer had succeeded in killing Nic.

She leaned back against the door, feeling woozy. Her hand went to her stomach as Ryker's words bounced through her like a pinball.

Killing Nic. Killing Nic.

Kill.

With nausea roiling up into her throat, she turned on the cold water and splashed her face.

BILL LEFT WHILE NICOLE was in the shower, taking a notebook full of notes with him.

Ryker gathered up the empty takeout containers and beer cans and threw them away, all the while listening to the sound of the shower running.

What a putz he was, carelessly tossing out his theory that Mike would have caved last year had Nicole been killed without noticing that she was standing right there. He'd clamped his jaw as soon as he'd said it, but it was too late. She'd been less than twenty feet away, the color draining from her face. Then before he could backtrack, before he could apologize, she'd rushed into the bathroom and slammed the door.

He sat down on the couch and stacked the case files on the end of the coffee table. One was missing. Nicole's. Bill had taken it with him to review. Ryker picked up the file on top. It was the first victim, Daisy Howard, the case he'd gone back and found after he'd begun to suspect that he had a serial killer. Ryker opened it and sat back, barely glancing at the meager information. After all this time, he had it memorized.

Bill had posed some good questions and suggestions. He'd volunteered to reinterview the families of the victims to see if maybe there was a slender thread of connection that Ryker had missed.

Ryker pinched the bridge of his nose, trying to massage away the headache that was starting, then rubbed his eyes. He heard the pipes squeak as Nicole turned off the shower. Within a few moments, she opened the bathroom door and emerged in a puff of steam. She was wrapped in a pale blue waffled robe and her hair was wet. He stared, thinking that he liked her delicate features and fresh pink skin better without makeup.

"Hi," he said.

She licked her lips and clutched the lapels of her robe tight at her neck. "Hi." She turned toward her bedroom.

"Nic, I'm—"

She paused.

He started again. "I'm sorry about earlier. I forgot we

weren't discussing the cases at the office. Detectives have to be able to analyze crime scenes, corpses and evidence rationally and without mincing words." He spread his hands. "Sometimes we even joke about it. It's not respectful to the victims, but that's the way it is."

Nicole waved a hand and shook her head. "It's all right. I understand. I'm not thinking about cute little flop-eared pet bunnies when I butcher a rabbit."

Ryker frowned, then laughed. "I guess that's the same—sort of."

"Well, I need to change—"

"Right. You're probably exhausted. Thanks for the food. It was great, as usual. You'll have to forgive Bill. He likes to act like a good old country boy. He might have called it spaghetti, but you should have seen him eat it. I suspect you gained a new patron at your restaurant."

She nodded, her gaze flickering from him to the pile of folders on the coffee table, and she looked as if she was going to say something else, or ask something, but apparently she changed her mind.

"Good night," she said, and disappeared into her bedroom, closing the door behind her.

Ryker closed the folder and tossed it onto the coffee table and got up to get some water. He'd drunk a couple of beers with dinner, although he'd have preferred a good chardonnay, and now he was thirsty.

About the time he drained the glass, he heard the bedroom door open.

Nicole came out carrying a wine goblet and a water glass. She was dressed in blue pajamas. They were cotton and rather loose, but that didn't matter. The soft material gave hints of her beautiful, curvaceous body as she moved. Hints that beneath the deceptively modest cotton, she was naked. The modest top and pants were almost sexier on her than her bra and panties. Almost.

He swallowed and set the glass down on the kitchen counter. He had an almost uncontrollable urge to apologize for being there in her apartment.

She took a couple of steps toward him, then paused. "I just wanted to get some water."

"Oh, yeah. Sure." Ryker stepped toward her then pressed against the counter so she could get by him. There was barely room for the two of them standing sideways. He felt the tips of her breasts brushed against the thin cotton of his T-shirt as she slid past.

He went back over to the couch and sat down, repeating over and over silently, *She's a victim. She's a victim. She's not sexy, she's a victim.*

He picked up Daisy Howard's file again, just to have something to do. He heard water running. Then it cut off.

"Are those the case files?"

He looked up. Nicole was standing there, pointing with the hand that held the filled water glass.

"Yep. All except yours. Bill took yours with him to study."

She drank her water, never taking her eyes off the folders. After a few seconds, she started to turn toward her bedroom, and then paused. She looked at him, at the files and back at him.

"Tell me about them."

"About who? You mean the women? No."

Her eyes widened.

"I mean, I don't think it's a good idea. You don't need to know—"

"Yes, I do," she interrupted. "I do need to know." She swallowed. "Maybe I could help."

Ryker couldn't quite suppress a wry chuckle. Everybody was a detective these days. The TV shows perpetuated the myth that anyone—a housewife, a crime writer, a fake psychic—could solve murders. Still, he supposed it couldn't hurt.

At least it couldn't hurt his case. He wasn't so sure about whether it might hurt Nicole to know the details of the murders committed by the man who had almost succeeded in killing her.

"Okay," he said. "Sit down over here." He'd show her the victims' pictures and tell her about the murders, but he wasn't going to let her see everything, certainly not the crime scene photos or the autopsy pictures.

Nicole sat down next to him on the couch and put her glass on the coffee table. Then she clasped her fingers tightly together in her lap. Hearing about the murdered women wasn't going to be easy for her.

He opened Daisy's file. On top of the pages was a five-by-seven color photo of a young black woman with close-cropped hair. "This is the first victim. Her name was Daisy Howard."

She unclasped her hands and picked up the photo. Her hand shook. "She's— She was really beautiful."

"Yeah. She was a model. She lived in Chef Voleur and worked in New Orleans."

"You said she was the first?"

He nodded. "She died in October of 2006. That was before I made detective. I didn't know about her until last year. After your case, I talked to the other detectives about my theory and somebody mentioned Daisy. And sure enough, her case fit the pattern."

"What's that picture?" Nicole set the picture she was holding down and reached for the corner of a photo that peeked out from behind some papers.

Ryker stopped her hand with his. "You don't want to look at that one." It was the crime scene photo of Daisy, lying in her own blood, with the blood-covered fireplace poker beside her.

"Why? Is it—?"

He carefully and deliberately set her hand back in her lap. She intertwined her fingers again.

Ryker fanned the corners of the dog-eared pages with his thumb as he talked. "On the night of October 26, Daisy was home alone. Her fiancé was out of town. The killer apparently broke down the front door and surprised her coming out of the bathroom. He grabbed the fireplace poker and stabbed her in the stomach. Several times." Ryker shook his head. "If her fiancé hadn't been out of town, or if the neighbors had been more responsible, she might have lived. The M.E. estimated time of death as 6:40 a.m."

Nicole's gaze snapped up to his. "A.m.?"

"A neighbor out to pick up his morning paper saw her front door ajar and called 911. We don't know exactly what time the killer broke in, but besides the blood spatter all over the living room, the blood pool beneath her had been spreading for several hours. The center of the pool was still wet when the crime scene analysts arrived."

"But she was dead."

Ryker nodded. "Later, the detectives found a neighbor across the street who said he'd heard something around eleven, but he didn't hear anything else, so he didn't bother to check on it."

"That's so awful!" Nicole shook her head. "You said she fit the pattern. What pattern? Why did you think she was killed by the same man?"

"The similarities. Even though the victims seem to be chosen randomly, they're not. Whoever this guy is, he's got an agenda."

"An agenda? You mean other than just to kill? I thought serial killers couldn't help themselves."

"That's usually true. Plus they generally escalate, and this guy has stuck with once a year. He could be what psychiatrists describe as a mission-directed killer. Most serial killers are obsessive-compulsive or bipolar. As you say, they can't help themselves. It's practically impossible for a serial killer to keep himself reined in. The more he kills, the less effect it has on him, so he escalates. The time between killings becomes shorter and shorter. But this guy—you could set your calendar by him. And he chooses his targets carefully."

"You know a lot about serial killers. Have you had a case like this before?"

Ryker shook his head. "No. I've read a lot in the field of profiling though. And last year I consulted with one of the best profilers in the Department of Justice about the anomalies in this guy's choice of victims."

"How? How did he— Why did he choose me?"

Ryker closed Daisy Howard's file. "He seems to have a way to access birth records, addresses. Each victim was born in October, between October 22 and November 1."

"My birthday is—"

"The twenty-fifth." Ryker glanced at his watch. "Today, at least for twelve more minutes. I'm sorry. I ruined your birthday evening. If I'd been paying attention, I wouldn't have invited Bill over here."

Nicole sent him an odd look. "Don't worry about it. I don't do birthdays."

That surprised Ryker. In his family, birthdays, anniversaries, holidays might as well be holy days. The whole family usually gathered, or as many as possible. Even while his father was in prison, serving the term his mother's dad should have served, the tradition had continued. They'd even taken a birthday cake to the prison one year.

Ryker couldn't imagine not celebrating. "Don't do birthdays? Come on." He smiled at her. "What are you—ninety? You mean Job didn't bake you a cake?"

Nicole rose quickly. "Do you want some coffee?" she asked, already on the way to the kitchen.

His brow wrinkled. What was wrong with her? First the vehement refusal to consider moving. Now she didn't do birthdays. Did the birthday thing have something to do with her childhood, too?

He moved from the couch to a bar stool, leaving the case files behind, and assessed her as she brewed the espresso and steamed the milk. Her shoulders were tight. Her back was stiff, and her chin was slightly lifted. He'd like to get his hands on those shoulders and massage all that tension out until she was relaxed and languid under his touch.

He gave himself a mental shake. *Focus,* he ordered himself. *She's your victim.*

She set a steaming cup in front of him and then tasted her own. "What about the second murder?" she prompted. "How did she die?"

He shook his head. "No. We're not talking about them anymore. You'll have nightmares."

She sniffed and her mouth quirked up wryly at one corner. "You don't?"

He inclined his head. "Perks of the job."

She looked past him to the folders stacked on the coffee table. "The second death was in 2007."

Ryker didn't like it, but having her knowledgeable about the way the killer operated fit with his philosophy of *forewarned is forearmed,* so he acquiesced.

"The second victim was Bella Pottinger." As always, when he said her name, he had to stop himself from flinching. Bella and he had dated briefly when he was a sophomore at LSU and she was a grad student. They'd never been serious, but he'd liked her.

When he'd caught her case, he'd felt a responsibility to her, to find her killer. "She died on October 22. Her birthday was November 1. She was thirty. Mike thought her age and her birthday were enough to keep her from being part of the pattern."

Nicole sipped at her coffee, then licked foam off her upper lip. Unexpectedly, Ryker's body reacted to the sight of her small pink tongue. He'd tasted that tongue, felt it on his lips, his ear, his neck—

He cleared his throat and took a swallow of hot coffee to cauterize that dangerous train of thought.

"What happened to her?" she asked.

"The killer slashed her throat with a broken wine bottle," he threw out gruffly, amazed that talking about Bella's awful death didn't quell his desire for Nicole.

She winced and her eyes closed.

"Sorry. I told you it wasn't a good idea to talk about this tonight."

"Who was next?"

"All right," he said, sighing. He'd convince her that she didn't want to know. "Here goes. On October 24 of 2008, Jennifer Gomez was strangled with her phone cord in her home. On October 20, 2009, Nicole Beckham barely escaped being stabbed with a knife from her chef knife case. Her roommate's arrival scared off the attacker. Then, on October 22 of this year, Jean Terry, who by the way was thirty-seven, was stabbed in the back with a chef's boning knife on her patio. All three have birthdays within two days of each other, although their ages range from twenty-one to thirty-seven." By the time he finished, he felt like a total heel. He sat staring down into his empty cup.

He could feel Nicole's gaze on him. For a few seconds neither of them said anything, then she set her cup on the counter.

"Why was it so hard for you to convince your boss that the deaths are connected?"

He looked up. "It's a lot more complicated than just a few similarities among victims. If you look at the victim profiles, we have three Caucasian, one black and one Hispanic. The weapons, until Terry's case, were weapons of convenience, found in the victim's home and left there. That's not much of a pattern."

"But even so, you thought they were connected."

He nodded. "Another issue is, we actually don't have many murders in St. Tammany Parish."

He turned his cup up to drain the last drops of coffee.

Nicole gestured toward his cup but he shook his head.

"Then you have to consider murder statistics," he went on. "About a third of murders of women each year are linked to domestic violence. In the grand scheme of things, serial killers are rare—maybe one percent of all murders."

Nicole rinsed out the cups and set about cleaning the cappuccino machine. "So I guess the question becomes not why your boss wasn't convinced, but why *you* are."

Ryker shrugged. "The dates, mostly. And the very fact that he isn't organized—that I can't link him by preferred weapon or method of killing. Not even by his choice of victims."

"Except for our birthdays."

"Except that. As far as the evidence goes, he doesn't have a signature. Nor does he seem to take trophies. Jean Terry's murder is the first time he's repeated anything except the birth date."

"The weapon. My knife."

"Right. Hopefully, that will be his fatal mistake."

"So it sounds to me like what you're saying is, he's not really acting like a serial killer."

"That's right. Not if you consider the usual pattern of serial murderers. They generally stay within their own ethnic group. Their victims will usually be connected— age, gender, even body type or hair color will be consistent. And they almost always take trophies."

"So your guy isn't playing by the rules."

"And there's the rub," Ryker said on a yawn. "When is a serial killer not a serial killer?" He stood and stretched. "I'm tired. You must be exhausted."

Nicole finished rinsing the cups and cleaning the cappuccino machine, then dried her hands. She came around the island headed for her bedroom.

Ryker stopped her with a hand on her arm. "Hey, Nic," he whispered, turning her toward him, rubbing the smooth, supple skin of her shoulders with his palms. "I'm sorry about your birthday."

"I told you, I don't—"

He shushed her with his index finger against her lips. Then he leaned down and gave her a gentle kiss. It might have been just a birthday kiss, if they hadn't slept together. If he didn't know those lips, that coffee-and-melon scent. If she hadn't opened her mouth and reminded him of the taste and feel of her little pink tongue.

When he felt his body readying itself for sex, he pulled away. The look on her face almost drew him back in, but he bit his cheek and took another step backward. "Everybody ought to get a birthday kiss," he whispered with a smile.

Her tongue flicked out over her lower lip, followed by her teeth, lightly scraping. Her eyes crinkled a bit at the corners. "I guess I can't argue with that," she replied. "Thanks."

She turned and headed for her bedroom. But instead of closing the door behind her, she turned and stuck her head out. "Ryker?"

"Yeah?" He had his shirt half-unbuttoned.

"How do you know that Daisy was his first?"

"What?"

"If this man is a serial killer, how did you decide that Daisy was his first victim?"

The question hit him like a slap to the face. It shouldn't have, but it did. Nobody at the office had ever questioned him about that. Maybe because they didn't want to encourage his theory, or maybe because they knew him and figured he'd covered every possibility. Which he had.

"I went through the 2004 and 2005 St. Tammany Parish records and didn't find a case that bore any similarities whatsoever."

"What about other parishes?" She leaned against the door facing, pushing a hand through her already tousled hair. "Could the killer have been working in another parish, too? Like Orleans Parish or Tangipahoa?"

His fingers stopped fumbling with his shirt buttons. He looked up and shook his head slowly.

"What if he started somewhere else? Or is killing more often than once a year in other parishes, but just once a year in St. Tammany?"

"Other parishes' records. Why didn't I—? Nic, I could kiss you!" Ryker started toward her but she held up a hand, looking slightly panicked.

"No! I mean—" Her face grew red. "I don't think that would be a good idea." She reached behind her for the doorknob, then sent him a teasing smile. "And besides, you already did. Good night," she said firmly, and disappeared into her bedroom, closing the door behind her.

Ryker stared at the door for several seconds as her words

spiraled through his brain. He felt like banging the heel of his hand against his forehead. What an idiot he was. He'd dug through St. Tammany records for 2004 and 2005, and not just the few murder cases, either. He'd studied each and every case involving a woman. Muggings, assaults, even accidents. But he hadn't checked old cases in surrounding parishes. Maybe because he'd been getting such a hard time from Mike about wasting time on his serial killer theory.

But now—now he had a task force and approval to work the case as a serial case. Granted it was a task force of two and a grudging approval, but that was better than anything he'd had before.

If he were very lucky and could manage to dig up enough new evidence to reassure his deputy chief and the sheriff, he just might be able to catch the killer the media was calling the October Killer.

Chapter Seven

Ryker was gone by the time Nicole got up the next morning. She was relieved and yet at the same time oddly disappointed.

"Stop it," she admonished herself as she made coffee. She was not going to get used to having someone there in her apartment with her. It was too easy to become accustomed to having someone beside her when she went to sleep and woke up. She'd had that little enough in her life. And it distressed her how much she longed for it.

Ryker Delancey had one thing on his mind. Catching his serial killer. If she made the mistake of thinking he was hanging around for any other reason, she was going to be in for a lot of heartbreak when the case was over and he went back to his own apartment and his own privileged life.

She looked across the kitchen island at her couch. He'd made an effort to fold up the sheet. It lay in a lopsided, uneven square on the arm of the couch, waiting for him to return tonight. The pillow he'd used was still where he'd left it, a slight indentation testifying to the fact that he'd lain there.

Nicole had to quell an urge to walk over, pick up the pillow and hold it to her nose. She blinked, and the sensual promise of the pillow faded, and all she could think about were the photos of the dead women. The victims of the same man who'd tried to attack her. Five women, so different and yet not so different at all.

How were they connected in the killer's mind? A model, a professor, a bank teller and a real estate agent. One black, one Hispanic and three white. She took her cup into the bedroom to sip as she dressed.

A knock on her door startled her and she spilled a few drops of coffee. She looked at the time. Not even eight-thirty. Job was coming by to walk her to the restaurant, despite her protests, but he wouldn't be there until ten. She crossed to the door and opened it as far as the chain would allow.

"Yes?" she said.

"Nicole Beckham? I'm Lon Hébert from the *St. Tammany Parish News*."

Nicole's heart thudded in her chest. "Yes?" she said coldly. "You're the reporter that ran that article about me."

He flashed a toothy grin. "That's right. I'd like to talk to you."

"I'm sorry, I—"

"It won't take long. I'd like to get your reaction to the October Killer's latest murder. The victim was stabbed with your knife."

"I don't—I have no comment. Please go away." She pushed the door but the reporter's foot kept her from being able to close it.

"Are you afraid he'll come after you again?" the man persisted. "With your own knife?"

"If you don't get away from my door I'm calling the police." She pushed against the door again.

"Hey, I'm just doing my job. Is it true that Detective Ryker Delancey has placed you under his protection?"

"I'm getting my cell phone," Nicole said desperately, and backed away from the door. She grabbed her phone off the kitchen counter and pressed Ryker's number as she walked back over to the door.

"Ryker?" she said when he answered. "There's a reporter here trying to break down my door."

"I'll be right there," Ryker said.

"Okay, okay. Give me a break," the reporter replied at the same time. "I'm not breaking your door." He backed away and Nicole pushed the door shut and locked it.

"It's okay, Ryker. He backed off."

"Make sure he's gone."

She looked through the peephole. The small, dark-haired man was standing on the landing looking thoughtfully at her door. Then he shrugged and headed down the stairs. "He's headed downstairs. He's gone."

"When's Job coming to pick you up?"

"Around ten."

"Don't even crack the door until you know it's him. Understand?"

"Yes. I'm sorry to bother you."

She heard him sigh. "It's not a bother, Nic. My job is to keep you safe." He paused. "Do you want me to come over?"

She heard the thinly disguised impatience in his voice. He was obviously busy. Plus, she was fine. The fact that the reporter had sought her out bothered her a little, but he was gone, and hopefully he'd gotten the message that if he came back, he'd have to deal with Ryker.

"No, of course not. I'm fine. Ryker?"

"Yeah, hon?"

"He knew that you're staying here. He asked if it was true you had me under your personal protection."

"He said that?" Ryker cursed. "I'm sorry, Nic. This

is probably going to get worse before it's over. Hang in there."

"I told you. I'm fine. I'll talk to you later." Nicole hung up and glanced at the front door, then stepped over to double check all the locks.

As she did so, the reporter's voice echoed in her head. *Are you afraid he'll come after you again, with your own knife?*

"Yes," she whispered to the empty room.

RYKER SPENT THE MORNING in court, testifying in a domestic violence case that had ended with the wife going to the hospital and the husband going to lock-up. Ryker testified that when he'd arrived on the scene he'd witnessed the man shove his wife down their front steps. His testimony sealed the DA's case against the man.

Back at the Chef Voleur office, he met with Mike's secretary, Anne-Marie Lafitte. He briefly reviewed the cases with her, then asked her to go through the five files and make notes of anything she found that the women had in common.

"No matter how insignificant," he'd told her. "The same brand of toothpaste. Same credit-card company. Anything."

Then he searched out Bill, who had just finished bringing Dagewood and Phillips up to speed on his open cases. Charles Phillips shot Ryker a dirty look and muttered something derogatory as he lumbered toward the conference-room door. Ryker and Bill had discussed how such a large man could move so fast when he wanted to.

Ted Dagewood was more vocal. "Delancey, you finally got your little serial killer fantasy past the boss, didn't you? Your mama must be so proud." The acerbic detective was tall and fit, and considered himself a ladies' man. Word was his wife kept him in line though.

Ryker had to bite his tongue to keep from shooting an insult back at him. He managed not to speak until Dagewood sauntered on down the hall.

"Jerk-ass," Bill said.

"What you said, and more. Did you get in touch with Hébert?"

"Nah, every time I called over there, they told me he was out."

"Yeah, out harassing Nic."

"He's been bothering her? What'd he do?"

"He went to her apartment. She called me and told him I was on my way over, so he backed off. He's probably back at his office by now."

"I'll go remind him what he's supposed to be doing," Bill said.

"No. I will. I've got a couple of things I need to say—just him and me."

"You *really* don't want him messing with Nicole, do you?"

"He knows I'm staying over there—to protect her."

"Somebody around here's got a big mouth."

Ryker looked past Bill and saw Dagewood moseying back down the hall toward them. "Look who's back," he muttered.

Bill casually turned around as Ryker braced himself for another smart-ass comment from the cop.

"The boss sent me to find you," Dagewood said sarcastically.

"Yeah?" Ryker responded. "Something about my serial killer fantasy?"

Dagewood smiled, as if pleased that he'd managed to get to Ryker. "Nope. He wanted me to let you know that some crazy old man called, ranting about his daughter being murdered."

"Where?" Ryker was instantly on alert.

"Don't get your boxers in a twist, Delancey. He's been calling for years. Like I said, he's a crazy old dude."

"Why have I never heard of him, and why did Mike say to tell me?"

"Hey. Who am I? Your secretary? Boss asked me to deliver a message and I did." Dagewood pushed past them and walked away.

"I've got to go see Mike. How far along are you on reinterviewing the families?"

"I've talked to two. Nothing new. I'm going to see Jean Terry's parents this afternoon."

"Good. Anne-Marie is reviewing the files and making notes on similarities between victims. Maybe we'll get somewhere. Talk to you later." Ryker headed to Mike's office, where he found the deputy chief on his way out.

"No time, Ryker. Got a meeting with the sheriff."

"I'll walk out with you. Why'd you send Dagewood to tell me about the crazy guy that called?"

"Because I was leaving and I saw him in the hall."

"I mean, why do I need to know about this guy? Dagewood said he's been calling for years about his daughter's death."

Mike nodded as he pushed open the door to the parking lot. "He's called a few times over the years. Seems his daughter was killed in a mugging, and he thinks we should be tearing up the state looking for the killer."

"Who did it?"

"Case was never solved. She was shot in a back alley in the French Quarter. No physical evidence to speak of. It was raining."

"She was shot? Sounds like a mugging gone bad—or a drug deal. Why's the guy calling St. Tammany?"

"Who knows? I've got to go. Anne-Marie has the phone logs. Check with her."

"Thanks, Mike." Ryker started to turn, then checked himself. "Hey, Mike—"

"What?"

"You never said why you're telling me about this guy."

Mike shrugged. "She was young. She died around this time of the year if I remember what the old man said. Maybe she's one of yours." He clicked his remote and the lights on his Buick blinked.

Ryker watched him drive off. Why would Mike think a mugging in New Orleans had anything to do with a serial killer in St. Tammany Parish? He thought about the question Nicole had asked him.

How do you know Daisy was the first? The answer was he didn't. He'd gone through St. Tammany cases with a fine-toothed comb, but he hadn't expanded his review to other parishes.

He blew out a frustrated breath. New Orleans. Orleans Parish. It would take him half a lifetime to sift through the murders, much less all the cases written up as home invasions, domestic violence and however else a murder might be misclassified.

He glanced at his watch as he headed toward Anne-Marie's desk. He might have to wait until tomorrow to ream the reporter.

Today was Nicole's evening off, and he'd promised her he'd be there to pick her up at six o'clock, and would make gumbo for her. He barely had enough time to run by the grocery store. What she didn't know about the evening was that he was going to take her to his house, where he had all the spices and herbs, not to mention the right pot—his grandmother's gumbo pot.

His brain flashed on an image of Nic in his apartment eating gumbo and laughing. In an instant, lust overwhelmed him and his body reacted. Damn it, he had to stop acting like a randy kid.

This would not be an intimate evening of spicy stew and spicy sex. For one thing, he had homework—the telephone logs Anne-Marie had pulled for him.

Maybe that would be enough to dampen his craving for Nic's body. He was supposed to be protecting her, not lusting after her.

BY THE TIME DINNER was over, Ryker had come to regret bringing Nicole to his apartment. For one thing, his kitchen was *way* smaller than hers, and she'd insisted on helping him.

So they'd kept bumping into each other. Each bump had escalated Ryker's lust, until by the time the gumbo was ready, he was sweating and having trouble controlling his breathing.

Now she was sitting on his couch with a glass of wine, and he was washing the dishes.

"What's this?" she asked.

He turned to look. "Telephone logs. I've got to go through them tonight."

"Telephone logs of what?"

"Phone calls from a man wanting to know why we haven't caught his daughter's killer."

"Is she one of the victims?"

He shook his head. "Not one of the five known victims."

"Can I read them?"

Ryker dried his hands and tossed the towel onto the

kitchen counter. "Nope. I haven't had a chance to read through them yet. Are you ready to go?"

"Sure." Was he crazy or did he hear a touch of disappointment in her voice? Maybe she was thinking the same thing he was, that hot spicy gumbo should be followed by hot sweet sex.

Back at her apartment, Nicole took a shower while Ryker settled onto the couch with the stack of computer printouts and two messy dog-eared bound notebooks.

Anne-Marie had apologized for the messy logs. "We only started recording phone calls three years ago," she'd said, "when we were finally allotted funds to buy new equipment. Prior to that, the logs were handwritten. It took me a while to find them all."

He shuffled through them. There were five sets including the one that had been recorded today. Three were computer-generated transcripts. The other two were flagged, handwritten pages in a spiral-bound notebook.

He began reading that day's transcription. At the top of the page was the date and time, and the telephone number and name of the caller, Albert M. Moser, plus his address in Covington, LA.

I'm calling about my daughter. When are you going to find the bastard that killed her?

Sir, I'll try to help you, but first I need your name.

You know my name. Why do I have to start over every time I call? I just want my daughter's murderer caught.

I apologize for your inconvenience, sir. Please tell me your name and I promise I'll try to help you.

Moser. Albert Moser. My baby girl's name was Autumn. You haven't done anything, have you? What do I have to do to get your attention?

Can you give me a date? When was your daughter killed?

See, you don't even know when she died. It was today. October 26. My baby died and nobody even cares. Five years ago today. Do you hear me? Today is her birthday.

Ryker's pulse sped up. *Today*, October 26, was Autumn Moser's birthday. She fit the pattern. "I'll be damned," he whispered.

"What's wrong?"

Ryker looked up to see Nicole wrapped in her blue waffle-knit robe. Her hair was wet and beginning to wave around her face. Her cheeks were pink from the hot shower, and they matched the color of the polish on her toes. Her sexy toes.

He swallowed.

She touched the lapels of her robe, ensuring that it wasn't gaping open. "Is that one of the phone logs?"

"Yeah." He heard the excitement in his voice.

"You've found something," she said, taking a step forward. "Tell me."

"Today is the anniversary of her murder, and it's her birthday."

"Oh, my God! She was killed on her birthday? That's so sad. When was she killed?"

Ryker fanned the transcripts like a card hand. "The earliest log Mike's secretary found is from 2005."

"2005?" she repeated. "Wasn't Daisy's murder in 2006? That means this girl could be the first victim."

He heard his own hopes echoed in Nicole's voice. But the revelation was not all joy. "I can't know that, or even if she's connected at all, until I find her case file."

He stared at the 2005 telephone log. "I went through 2005 case files in St. Tammany. She wasn't in there."

"Do you think anything in the phone logs tell you where she was killed?"

"I hope so. I've got her name now. Hopefully I'll eventually be able to find her case file, unless it's been lost or destroyed."

"I want to look at them."

"I've already told you, I'm not supposed to let non-authorized personnel read them."

"Didn't you tell me you wanted me to be able to protect myself?"

"What I said was that you should exercise reasonable precautions."

"You don't think I can take care of myself?"

"Not against a killer I don't."

She paused, assessing him. Then without another word, she walked over and sat down on the couch beside him.

Close beside him.

Too close beside him.

He breathed in the scent of watermelon and clean warm skin. Her cheeks were still rosy from the hot water and when she stretched out her legs and propped her feet on the coffee table, the robe separated, revealing long lean calves, pretty knees and a hint of a well-shaped thigh.

Ryker sucked in a breath to clear his head, but it didn't help. The air around her was still suffused with the scent of watermelon.

"Here. This is the first transcript." He handed it to her and started reading the second one, from 2008. Within a second he saw that it was practically identical to the first. Different phrasing, but the same message.

You don't even know when she died. It was today. My baby died and nobody cares. It's her birthday.

He handed that one to Nicole and checked the third

computer-printed sheet, this one from 2007. The year Bella had died.

The only real difference in this transcript was the last sentence.

You cops are so blind. Look around you. Girls are dying.

Ryker opened the spiral-bound notebook that was labeled 2006. It was dog-eared and ragged, stuffed with sticky notes and scraps of lined paper. Ryker gave a quick nod of thanks to Mike for sharing Anne-Marie with him. She was good. It would have taken him days to find the entry on his own. He turned to the flagged page.

Finding the entry was one thing. Deciphering it was another thing entirely. It was six lines in the middle of the page, dated October 26, 2006.

Ryker made out the name Daisy Howard, and the name Phillips. He studied the smudged scribbling. Damn Phillips. He'd used a pencil.

9:30. Call fm A. Moser. Daughter dead. Blames us. Didn't try. Raving. Not much sense.

Then two lines that were completely indecipherable, except for the word *nutcase*.

"Great," Ryker said in disgust. "Thanks, Phillips."

"What now?" Nicole leaned over to look at the notebook. Her arm and the side of her breast pressed against his arm. He swallowed.

"I can't read Phillips's writing. Hell of a lot of good that's going to do me."

"Let me see." Instead of taking the notebook from his hand, she leaned even closer.

Ryker didn't move a muscle, afraid if he did she'd back away. But what little information he'd gleaned from the transcripts were fast melting in the heat that was building inside him.

"Nine-thirty. Call from A. Moser. Daughter dead a year now. Blames us. Didn't try. Raving. Not much sense."

"Yeah, I got that much."

Nicole angled her head and shot him a look, then went back to the note. "*L-S-T. Y-R.* Last year." She took the notebook from him and held it at different angles. "Her *B-D-A-Y.* Birthday. And I think this is *M-G-G* or *M-Y-Y.*" She pointed.

Ryker remembered what Mike had said. "It's MGG. Mugging."

"Okay." Nicole placed her forefinger on the page and indicated each word. "Nine-thirty. Call from A. Moser. Daughter dead a year now. Blames us. Didn't try. Raving. Not much sense. Last year. Her birthday. Mugging. *I-M-O*—in my opinion, guy's a nutcase."

Ryker pulled his notebook from his pocket. "Say it again so I can write it down. Next time I look at that mess I won't remember what it said."

She repeated it and he wrote it down word for word. "Great, thanks."

"How about the last one?"

Ryker saw the flag Anne-Marie had stuck on the page for October 26 of 2005, but when he turned to the page, he found a sticky note from her.

Ryker. I couldn't find an entry of a phone call from Moser in this log. I looked thoroughly, but you might want to double-check. Anne-Marie.

Nicole leaned in farther, and Ryker was sure he could feel the outline of her nipple against his biceps. She read the note aloud. "That's the year his daughter was killed. It would make sense that he wouldn't call on that day, doesn't it?"

"It does." Ryker had to move. Either that or he was going to turn and pull Nicole to him and kiss her senseless. That was how crazy her breast pressed against his arm was making him. He sat up and tossed the transcript onto the coffee table, then ran a hand through his hair. "I wish he'd mentioned where she was killed."

"You know it wasn't in St. Tammany."

"I do know that. But that leaves Tangipahoa, Orleans, Jefferson—" He let his head drop back against the couch cushion.

"You're going to talk to Moser, aren't you? He can tell you where she was killed."

"Yeah, if he doesn't fill me full of buckshot first. The man's angry. And despite the fact that Phillips thinks everybody's a nutcase but him, I'd be willing to bet that this time, he wasn't exaggerating."

Chapter Eight

Nicole frowned at Ryker, who was rubbing his eyes tiredly. "You don't really think Moser will shoot you if you go to see him, do you?"

Ryker looked up at her and smiled. "Worried about me?"

"Yes. Of course I am. Why can't you send some policemen to pick him up and bring him in?"

"I need to approach him carefully. I'd rather not upset him any more than I have to. I hope I can gain his trust, make him understand that I'm doing my best to catch this killer."

Nicole touched his arm. His biceps were firm, the skin warm and vibrant under her fingers. She pushed the memory of his lean, strong body molded to hers out of her head. "You're a good man," she said.

He looked at her, the intense blue of his eyes igniting like a flame of pure oxygen. "Just doing my job," he murmured, dipping his head slightly.

She licked her suddenly dry lips and his gaze flickered toward her mouth, lingering there. She stepped closer.

He drew in a sharp breath, then bent his head and brushed her lips with his, so lightly it might not have been his lips at all. It might have been nothing more than his breath.

She waited for him to kiss her again, but he didn't. Instead, he looked down, then lifted his head.

Just doing my job.

She understood. Because she was the same way. Doing a job well required focus. And focus and distraction didn't go together.

"Can you take a break?" she whispered with a small smile.

Two lines appeared between his brows. "Not while your protection is my responsibility."

"You're way too serious. You *are* protecting me 24/7 by just being here."

His jaw flexed and she reached up to soothe the tense muscle with her fingertips. Then she lifted her head and kissed him.

It took him a second or two to respond, but he did, and his response took her breath away. He pulled her to him and pushed the robe off her shoulders, then caressed her body with his large warm hands just as he caressed her mouth, cheeks and neck with his lips.

He guided her into the bedroom and laid her down on the bed while he shed his own clothes. Then he joined her, pressing his length against her. She shivered at the feel of his warm body touching every inch of hers.

"You've got to quit using that watermelon stuff," he whispered, "because even though I know this is a really bad idea, I can't resist it."

Nicole decided not to be offended by his declaration that making love with her was a really bad idea. She chose to interpret his words as concern that getting caught up in lovemaking might compromise her safety.

As they kissed and explored each other's body, Nicole's doubts dissolved in the sweet flood of desire that enveloped her. Her body softened, opened, readied itself to take him in. His fingers and tongue drove her closer and closer to climax.

Finally she sat up and pushed him down onto his back. He looked surprised.

"My turn," she whispered as she straddled him. She felt her face burn in embarrassment at her bold move, but he brushed her warm cheek with his fingertips and smiled at her.

Bending until she could reach his lips, she kissed him deeply, intimately, and pressed her bare breasts against his chest. She could feel his breathing quicken. His hands traced her thighs and slid up to her waist as he ground himself against her, groaning with pleasure. He lifted her to what she felt was a dizzying height, then lowered her onto his hard, pulsing erection.

Her entire body was shivering—shattering—with reaction. His hands slid from her belly around to her hips and bottom, and thighs, and back up until his thumbs joined in caressing her intimately. She arched at his touch.

She tried to keep control, but her body melted into climax too quickly. Ryker thrust upward again and again, until she cried out. Then he guided her as her limbs gave way and she crumpled. He tucked her against his side and rested her head on his shoulder.

His palm slid slowly up and down her arm and he planted a kiss on top of her head.

As she lay there, reality began to creep back into her brain. And slinking in around behind reality were the doubts. She grimaced, trying to push away the doubts and regain the sense of perfect communion and safety that she'd felt while they were making love.

But as had been true all her life, any time she began to believe in safety, began to depend on it, it was snatched away from her like a rug jerked out from under her feet.

Her reality was chaos and fear. The chaos of life on a downward spiral. The fear that each day brought her closer to abandonment.

Even though she fit perfectly against Ryker's body with her head nestled in the hollow of his shoulder, she would never fit into his world. His was a life of family, home, security. She could daydream about those things, but she knew when all this was over, he'd go back to his life, and all she'd be was a victim he'd sworn to protect.

The differences in them created a wall around her heart. She wasn't trying to build it up, but still it grew, brick by brick, row by row. By the time this case was done, it would be impenetrable.

Ryker stirred and Nicole pulled away, thinking he wanted to turn over and go to sleep. But instead, he doubled a pillow under his head and touched her chin with his fingertip, urging her head up.

"Hey," he said.

"Hey." She took a deep breath and yawned.

"You ready to go to sleep? I'll go back to the couch."

"No." She'd answered way too fast. Needy. Desperate. All the things she never wanted to be. "No. I'm not sleepy," she said more casually.

"Good. Can I ask you something?"

"Sure. Anything." That was a lie. There were a lot of things she didn't want him asking.

"Why don't you like birthdays?"

The question felt like an arrow to her chest. *Thud.* She wasn't even sure she knew—not exactly.

"Is it the same reason you're so dead-set against moving?"

Okay. This was getting too close to home. Nicole sat up, fumbling with the edge of the sheet to cover her breasts.

Ryker slid over so she could pull the sheet up to cover

her. Then he patted the bed next to him and held his arm out. For an instant all she wanted to do was run away. She didn't want to answer his questions. Didn't want anyone— certainly not him—delving into the dark places inside her.

But she couldn't resist his invitation to sink back into him. Being held by Ryker Delancey was the safest place she'd ever been.

"Nic? I didn't mean to upset you. You don't have to tell me if you don't want to. I'd just—" He paused for a second, as if he weren't quite sure of himself. "I'd like to know you better."

"My mother wasn't well. Looking back, I think she may have been bipolar, but all I knew when I was little was that my mother wasn't the same as other mothers." Nicole took a shaky breath. Ryker's arm tightened around her shoulders.

"The first place I remember living was a nice bright house with her and my dad. But he died, and we had to move to a small apartment. It wasn't bright at all. I had a hard time understanding why we couldn't stay in our big bright house. I was eight at that time. Mama got a job cleaning offices, but her shift was from ten o'clock at night until six o'clock in the morning."

"Who stayed with you?"

Nicole shivered. "Nobody."

"You were in that apartment by yourself every night?" His embrace grew tighter. "God, Nic."

"In some ways it was a good thing. I learned to be self-sufficient. When I was thirteen I got a job helping out at a local diner. That's where I learned how to cook. The man who owned the diner had been an executive chef, but he'd had a stroke and couldn't use his left side very well. He somehow got me a scholarship to culinary school. I don't know what I'd be doing now if it weren't for him."

Ryker was quiet for a moment. "What about your mother?"

"She died soon after I graduated."

"You said she gave you your knives."

Nicole smiled sadly. "She did. She cashed in an insurance policy to buy them. I was so mad at her for not using the money for herself."

Ryker pulled her close and tucked her head under his chin.

She lay there, listening to his heart beat steadily and strong as she splayed her fingers across his chest and down his lean, sculpted abs. This was what heaven must feel like. Warm. Safe. Intimate.

AFTER TALKING WITH Charles Phillips to see if he remembered anything other than the notes he'd jotted down about Albert Moser's phone call three years ago, which he didn't, Ryker headed over to Mandeville, to the offices of the *St. Tammany Parish Record,* to have a talk with Lon Hébert about boundaries.

Hébert was at his desk, typing on a computer keyboard with two fingers. He glanced up as Ryker approached.

"Detective Delancey," he said, turning back to the computer screen. "I was going to call you for a statement." He hunted and pecked a few more times, then pushed his chair back. "Have a seat. What can I do you for?"

Ryker stayed on his feet. "You can stay away from Nicole Beckham. And you can keep her name out of your rag."

"Hey! Lay off the police brutality. I was just doing my job."

"So your job is to put victims of crimes in danger?"

"What the hell are you talking about?"

Ryker took a step closer to the seated reporter. "I'm talking about printing her name in the paper. Linking her with the Jean Terry case. Revealing the information about her knife. By the way, I need to know who told you that."

"I told you that day. Police scanner."

"I don't buy that. You were there too quick, and the police scanner didn't give you the information about the knife."

"No." Hébert smiled up at Ryker. "It didn't. Doesn't matter, though. I'm not revealing my sources. You need to leave. You're stepping over the line here."

"Yeah?" Ryker's ears were burning, he was so angry. "You think I'm over the line? Bud, you crossed the line days ago. Don't let me catch you anywhere near Nicole Beckham. And if you publish one more thing about the October Killer without checking it with me first, you're going to be real sorry."

Hébert vaulted up out of his chair, sending it rolling backward until it hit the next desk. "You got no right coming in here and telling me what I can and can't do. I'm a journalist. It's my job to let the public know the truth."

"If anything happens to Nicole as a result of what you printed, I'll haul you in as an accessory." Ryker took a step backward. He needed to cool off before he did something stupid yet gratifying, like punching Hébert in the face.

By now several people had come out of offices or stopped what they were doing and were staring at the two men.

Hébert looked around and then took a step toward Ryker, who towered over him by at least five inches. "You get out of here before I call security."

Ryker lifted his chin. "Watch yourself, Hébert," he warned, then turned on his heel and left.

By the time he'd driven from the newspaper office to

Albert Moser's address in Covington, he'd calmed down a little. He didn't look forward to talking with Moser, given the man's anger and pain at the police's failure to find his daughter's murderer. It would be a change from his fiery exchange with Hébert, though. No matter how upset and angry Albert Moser was, he was a victim. His child had been murdered.

Moser's home was a typical 1980s-style suburban ranch house that looked a little worse for wear. The trim on the brick house was way overdue for a paint job. The yard had at one time been landscaped, but overgrown shrubs and a carelessly cut lawn told Ryker that Moser probably lived alone and was probably depressed.

When Ryker pressed the button for the doorbell, he didn't hear anything inside. So he rapped on the door, waited thirty seconds, then rapped again.

Finally, he heard movement from inside. The sound of footsteps approaching and a lock turning. Then the door opened.

Albert Moser was a medium-height man who looked to be in his mid-to-late sixties, although Ryker figured he might be a little younger than that. He wore a plaid shirt that was mis-buttoned and a pair of worn, baggy dress pants. His thinning hair was combed, but he hadn't shaved in several days.

"Mr. Moser? I'm Detective Ryker Delancey." He held up his badge. "May I come in? I have some questions about your daughter."

Moser's dark eyes narrowed. "About Autumn?"

"Your daughter who died," Ryker said gently.

A grimace of pain crossed Moser's face. His eyes narrowed a bit more. "You have news?" he asked hoarsely.

"No, sir. Not yet. But I'm hoping after we talk I'll have

a better understanding of what happened. I hope to be able to give you some answers."

"Really?" Moser eyed Ryker with disbelief. After a couple of seconds, he stepped backward. "You might as well come in."

As Ryker entered the dark foyer, he noticed a framed picture on the wall. "Beautiful woman," he commented, nodding at it.

Moser looked at the picture, then at Ryker. "My wife. My daughter drew that when she was thirteen years old."

"Your younger daughter? Autumn?"

Moser nodded. "Right that way, into the living room."

Ryker stepped down a step into the large sunken room. The only light was the pale glow that filtered in through the curtains. Moser sat down in a recliner and turned on a table lamp. It hardly helped.

After a brief look around, Ryker chose to sit in an easy chair to Moser's right. The position of the chair gave him a straight shot to the front door. He was pretty sure Moser was harmless, but he always liked to be prepared.

"So Autumn was an artist."

"She liked to draw. She was good, too, but she never did anything with it."

Ryker nodded.

"What do you want with me?" Moser demanded, before Ryker could speak again. "If you're here because I called— I have a right, you know. I can call and ask what's being done to find her murderer. You can't stop me from doing everything I can." Moser put his hand on a post-bound book sitting on the table at his right hand. It looked like a scrapbook.

"Yes, you do have that right, Mr. Moser. And my visit is about your daughter. I'd like to find out about her death. It could be linked to several other murders in this area during the past few years."

Moser frowned, traced the binding of the scrapbook, then seemed to realize what he was doing and pulled his hand away. "Other murders? What do you mean?"

"You may have seen something in the paper about the October Killer?"

Moser didn't speak.

"There have been four deaths in the past five years, all during the last full week in October, all women whose birthdays were during that week."

"Like my Autumn. Her birthday was yesterday." His voice cracked.

"I know, and I'm sorry for your loss. I'd like to find out everything I can about her death. It's possible she was the first victim of this killer."

Albert Moser's face drained of color and his eyes widened. "What did you say?"

Ryker knew he'd heard him. He'd spoken to enough grieving family members and enough evasive suspects to understand that the question was automatic, an unconscious attempt to gain a bit of time to process the information he'd just heard. Moser's reaction seemed to indicate that he'd never considered that his daughter's murder might be linked to the other, more recent murders in St. Tammany Parish.

"Where did the shooting take place?"

Moser blinked rapidly. "Where?"

Ryker leaned forward and propped his elbows on his knees, trying to display open and friendly body language. The older man was clearly stunned by Ryker's mention of the October Killer.

"I apologize if these questions are upsetting, Mr. Moser,

but I need this information. It could help us find your daughter's killer."

"Right," Moser said. "That's all I've wanted all this time." He took a shaky breath. "It was her birthday. She'd decided to go to the French Quarter. Autumn was a head-strong girl. She never learned responsibility like my older girl, Christmas, did. Christy's a doctor now."

Ryker didn't comment. He didn't want to interrupt the flow of the man's memories. He jotted a quick note to find out where Christmas Moser lived.

"Autumn had gotten in with some bad people. She was doing drugs, I don't know what kind. I figure that's why she was down in the French Quarter that night. It was her birthday, you know."

Ryker nodded, then made a production of slipping his notebook out of his pocket and opening it. There was no reason to point out to Moser that he kept repeating himself. He was heartbroken about his daughter, and frustrated that the police hadn't found her killer. Making an effort to show the man that he was paying attention was the least Ryker could do for him. "Yesterday. October 26, right?"

Moser shook his head. "A father shouldn't outlive his child. It's a sad, sad thing, Detective. It can make you crazy. Make you think things, do things, you never thought—" He pulled a handkerchief out of his pocket and blew his nose. "I tried to tell the policemen back then that I knew who'd killed her, but they didn't care."

That surprised Ryker. "You know who killed your daughter?"

"She was running around with a married man. He wouldn't leave her alone. She swore to me she'd quit him, but he kept calling her. Begging her to see him. Threatening her. About a week before she died, she let on that she was afraid he'd kill her if she didn't go back to him."

"You told the police this? The New Orleans police?"

"I sure did."

Ryker watched Moser. He couldn't decide if the man was the nutcase Phillips had claimed he was, or if he was right about the married man. "What happened? Did NOPD arrest him? Question him?"

Moser folded his handkerchief and wiped his eyes. "Nope. I never knew his name. She never would tell me. Said it'd get him in trouble and he'd lose his job."

"So she thought you would know him?"

Moser looked at him in surprise. "Know him? You think that's why she wouldn't tell me? Because I know him? Hell, I don't know all that many people."

"Maybe it was someone well-known. A celebrity or a politician. Someone in the public eye."

"Humph. I doubt that. If it was somebody rich, I'd have known. Autumn would have gotten him to buy her stuff, and I never saw any stuff."

"Maybe he bought her the drugs," Ryker suggested.

Moser sent him a calculated glance. "Maybe so."

"One last question, Mr. Moser. Why call the St. Tammany Sheriff's Office about your daughter's killer? Why not call the NOPD?"

"I called them, too. But I'm pretty sure the man who killed her lives around here."

Ryker knew he could get information about Autumn Moser from her case file, but there was something about her father that made him want to keep asking him questions. Ryker had a gut feeling that Moser knew something that could help him, if he could just dig it out.

"Where did your daughter live?"

"She'd moved back in with me. She'd lost her job and had to give up her apartment."

"And you're sure you never saw or met the man you believe killed her?"

Moser stood and pocketed his handkerchief. His hands were shaking. He obviously was ready for Ryker to leave.

Ryker stood, too. "Only a couple more questions, Mr. Moser. The more I know, the closer I can get to finding the person who murdered your daughter, and these other young women."

"My girl's not part of this October Killer thing. That man killed her."

"I assume the police went through her things?"

Moser nodded as he headed toward the front door. Ryker glanced around one last time. The house was typical. The large living room. Kitchen and dining room off to one side. A hall on the other side leading to the bedrooms. Through the door to the kitchen he could see slips of paper and pencil drawings on the refrigerator door.

"I wonder if I could see her room? It might help me find the man who killed her."

"No. I mean, there's nothing there. What the police didn't take, I threw away. I couldn't stand it, having her things around. I took everything to the dump." Moser opened the door. "I'd like you to leave now. I don't want to talk about this anymore."

Ryker stepped past him, then turned and handed him a card. "Here's my phone numbers, office and cell. If you think of anything that might help me, please call. And believe me, Mr. Moser. I'm committed to finding the man who killed your daughter."

Moser stared at the card for a second, then took it.

Ryker started down the sidewalk.

"Detective," Moser called out. "What happened to the

girl they talked about in the newspaper? The chef—the one who survived?"

"She's fine. Doing well," Ryker said noncommittally.

"That article said she's helping with the investigation. Is that true? Or is it one of those things the paper prints because it sounds good?"

Ryker's anger at Hébert for exposing Nicole in the newspaper flared. "That's not something I can talk about," he parried.

Moser frowned. "But it was in the paper."

"I'm afraid that's all I can say. Call me anytime, Mr. Moser."

As Ryker drove off, Moser was still standing on his stoop, fingering the business card.

Chapter Nine

Albert Moser closed and locked his front door with trembling hands, then sat down in his recliner. He set the detective's business card on the end table next to his scrapbook, but his unsteady hand knocked it onto the floor.

For a moment, he just stared down at it as his thoughts raced dizzily.

Finally, someone had paid attention to his desperate calls. His work had paid off. Detective Ryker Delancey was looking into his daughter's death.

But there was a problem with that. Detective Delancey was certain that his daughter's death was connected with the October Killer murders. That would send him in an entirely different direction. Albert's direction. And he couldn't have that happen.

He stood and paced. He'd gotten the police's attention. But not in the way he'd planned. Where had his plan gone wrong? He'd figured having a second young woman die the last week in October, one year after Autumn died, the police would be reminded of his daughter's case and dig deeper.

But when he'd dug into his insurance records to find young women near Autumn's age, and with birthdays near hers, there had only been one woman who lived in New Orleans. Her home was in the Garden District, in a gated community. Albert knew he'd never be able to get to her. So he'd had to go with women who lived in older houses, in apartments, in neighborhoods where he could get to them. And because he'd always lived and worked in St. Tammany Parish, that was where he'd written most of his insurance policies, and that was where most of them lived.

So he'd killed a young model who lived in Mandeville but worked in New Orleans. He'd chosen her because she was exactly the same age as his daughter. Same birthday, same year. Then he waited. Nobody called. Nobody came to talk to him. If the police even remembered his daughter's murder, they didn't do anything about it. He'd called the St. Tammany Parish and the New Orleans police and complained, pointing out the similarities between the cases. Begging them to find his daughter's murderer before someone else died. But nobody listened.

Then the next year had rolled around. Albert had tried to ignore the calendar, but the urge to do something had been too strong. So he'd killed the second young woman.

Now he was in too deep. At some point, maybe last year when he'd failed to kill Nicole Beckham, his focus had changed. It was no longer a desperate attempt to send the police back to the first October murder. Albert put his palms on either side of his head and squeezed.

It had become vengeance. He had lost his beautiful Autumn, so he'd taken other beautiful young lives.

He bent over and picked up Detective Ryker Delancey's card off the floor. Delancey had said that Nicole Beckham was helping with the investigation, but he'd refused to tell Albert just how she was helping.

He thought about her in her dark bedroom, sitting up in bed so that the light from her window caught the gold highlights in her hair and the fear in her eyes. He'd stood there in her doorway, clutching the knife he'd found in a case on her kitchen counter, ready to dive at her and sink its blade deep into her belly.

But the sound of a key rattling in the front door had startled him. With one last glance at her wide eyes staring directly into his, he'd kicked open the kitchen door and escaped.

He rubbed a hand over his thinning hair. At the time, the newspapers had indicated that neither Nicole nor her roommate had seen anything. But Albert knew from the articles about his daughter's death and from television that the police never released all the information they had. They always held something back.

He opened the scrapbook that sat beside his chair. He had all the newspaper clippings from all the killings. He turned to the articles about Nicole Beckham. He knew them all by heart.

What could they have held back about her attack? Albert was dreadfully afraid the answer was that she had seen his face.

He'd watched her during the past year, wondering if she would recognize him. He'd even eaten at her restaurant a few times. Once she'd emerged from the kitchen to greet a couple who'd asked to meet the chef. She'd smiled and glanced around the room, but she hadn't reacted. Had she not recognized him? Or had she not noticed him?

He turned to the newspaper clipping from two days ago, that told about Nicole Beckham's knife being used in the killing of Jean Terry. He read the article again, looking for any clue that Nicole could identify her attacker.

Then he looked at the detective's card once more. Delancey was the man he'd seen with Nicole. He'd thought the man was a cop, and now he was sure. That certainty led to another. There was only one reason a police detective would be sticking that close to a victim. Nicole Beckham wasn't just Detective Delancey's only living victim.

She was his only witness.

Albert couldn't afford to have her identify him. Not now. Not when the police were finally looking into his daughter's death.

"ABSOLUTELY NOT, JOB!" Nicole said as she sat up in bed and pushed her hair out of her face with the hand not holding the phone. "We've never served frozen fish and we're not going to start now."

Job sighed. "I've called my mother to stay with the kids while I take Merina to the doctor. As soon as we're done, I'll head over to Henri's."

"By then all the decent fish will be gone. Plus, you need to be with your wife. Thursday is my day to buy fish anyway. You know Henri watches out for me like his own daughter. I'll be fine."

"You should call your boyfriend, let him know you're going."

"He's not my boyfriend," she said automatically, wishing Job would figure out that his joke wasn't funny. "He's going up to Angola to testify at a parole hearing today."

"What about his partner?"

"Bill's going to the Quarter to talk to the police and get the Moser girl's case file. I could be halfway to the river by now if we weren't still on the phone. Don't worry. I'll see if I can find some black drum fish."

"I've got to go. Merina is really hurting."

"You tell her I'm thinking about her. I've never had a kidney stone, but I hear they're awful."

Nicole hung up and got out of bed. Six o'clock. She was already late if she wanted the best-looking fish. She tossed on a pair of jeans and a T-shirt and ran a brush through her hair. She'd get the fish, take it to the restaurant and come back and shower and dress. Even with Job out, she didn't have to be cooking until ten. She'd have plenty of time.

NICOLE CHECKED THE REARVIEW mirror. The car behind her was way too close. She took her foot off the gas. "Okay. I'm slowing down. Pass me already."

But he didn't. He stayed on her tail. She turned off the distracting radio and tightened her hands on the steering wheel. The slap-slap of the windshield wipers was annoying enough. She didn't like this road in sunny weather. She hated it in the rain.

Henri LaRue owned three fishing boats on the Tchefuncte River near Madisonville. He and his four sons fished every day and supplied fresh fish to several restaurants on the north shore of Lake Pontchartrain. She or Job made a point of driving to Henri's several times a week to pick out the best fish for L'Orage's famous *Poisson du Jour.* The regulars looked forward to the variety of fish L'Orage featured at different times of the year.

The road that led from the highway down to Henri's was narrow and old. It wound along the serpentine banks of the river. Nobody but folks going to and from the market used it, and Nicole usually recognized most of the cars. But not this one.

She glanced in the mirror again. The car had fallen back a few feet. Thank goodness, because the rain was coming down faster now, soaking the blacktop and running off onto the marshy shoulder. That shoulder bothered Nicole. With the once-white lines faded into near invisibility and the crumbling shoulder, it was hard enough to drive the narrow road on a clear morning. Each time Nicole met a car passing in the opposite direction, her heart jumped into her throat and stayed there until she was safely past.

The car following her had crept up close again. She couldn't see the driver's face. He had the visor flipped down for some reason.

Through the rainy haze she spotted familiar bright orange shrimp boat nets sticking up over the trees to her right. It was the *Cara Mia,* a fishing boat owned by Thierry Martin. That meant she was only about four miles from the highway. Better, there was a relatively straight stretch of road ahead.

"Okay, you're in a hurry. I get it. Come on." She wished the driver would turn on his headlights. The heavy clouds and pummeling rain made it hard to see.

Frustrated, she lowered her window and gestured for the car to go around her. Thank goodness he sped up. Nicole held her breath and kept her speed steady, waiting for him to go around. But he didn't.

"It's okay," she shouted. "I know this road. You can pass!" She waved again, soaking her arm and the sleeve of her T-shirt. She raised the window and threw both hands in the air in a quick gesture of extreme frustration.

"What is the matter with you?" She gripped the wheel again, tighter. "Okay, if you won't pass me, I'll just stay out of your way."

She sped up, going as fast as she dared. She blew out a breath, trying to calm her racing heart. She hated driving in the rain. "There. Have all the road you want."

But when she looked in the rearview mirror, he was back on her tail. "What—?" Her breath caught. Her irritation faded and a growing sense of uneasiness took its place.

What if passing her wasn't what he was trying to do?

She sped up a little more and felt her pulse thrumming in her throat. The rain seemed to have let up a little, but she still had to concentrate to avoid dropping a tire off the edge of the marshy shoulder.

Something bumped. The cooler in the backseat that held the fish shifted. What was that? Had she hit a turtle? An alligator? She glanced in the rearview mirror just in time to see the car behind her slow down. Before she could react, it sped up again. *A lot.*

She braced herself. He was speeding toward her.

The bump shoved the car forward and flung her head back, bouncing it hard against the headrest. Whoever was in that car was doing this on purpose. She squeezed the steering wheel so hard her fingers cramped. A check in the mirror told her he was about to ram her again. She hit the gas.

The car fell behind. Nicole took a shaky breath, the first in quite a few seconds. She hadn't realized she'd been holding it. She checked her speedometer and winced. She was driving way too fast for the road and conditions.

But she knew the highway had to be just ahead. A mile at the most.

Movement in her mirror caught her eye. He was coming at her again. She floored it, her heart pounding, her hands screaming with cramping pain.

She took a winding turn and her right rear wheel slid off the road into the mud. She had to fight to keep the car from fishtailing. She couldn't keep up this speed. She'd crash.

Sweat prickled along her forehead and the nape of her neck. She glanced at her purse on the seat beside her. Her cell phone was right there, in the front pocket. She wanted to let go of the wheel and grab the phone and dial 911, but she couldn't. She was deathly afraid of driving off the road again.

The dark car filled her mirror, he was that close. *Objects in the rearview mirror are closer than they appear.*

She chuckled hysterically. That was impossible. That car couldn't get any closer.

Then simultaneously she felt the impact, heard the crunch of metal on metal and felt her head slam backward into the headrest.

Her hands slipped off the wheel and it spun toward the right.

No! God! Please!

She struggled to straighten the vehicle. The back wheel spun. The car wobbled and wove, and another crashing blow hit her from behind.

Then as the metallic shriek faded, the world began spinning. The rain made swirly patterns on the glass and the windshield wipers counted the seconds in slap-slaps as things inside the car bumped and slid.

Her head felt as if it was spinning around on her neck in the opposite direction from the world.

Then it all stopped. With a thud and a loud wet plop. Okay, not everything stopped. The world continued to spin, but somehow, Nicole knew that it wasn't really the world now—it was her head. She closed her eyes to try to set herself, or the world, or whatever was wrong upright again. When she opened them she saw her hands glued to the wheel. The knuckles were white. The tendons strained like fishing line pulling a really big catfish, and the veins stood out like faint blue rivers.

She blinked and dared to look beyond the wheel, beyond her hands to the outside of the car. She was looking up. At the edge of the road she'd recently been on. Black mud spattered the windshield and the side windows. Amazingly, the rain had stopped.

How was she going to get all that mud off her windshield if the rain had stopped? That thought made her realize that the wipers had stopped, too. In fact, the car was no longer running. She couldn't hear anything except an occasional low groan. At first she thought it was a person. Had she hit someone? Had the driver of the other car run off the road too?

But after a couple of seconds she realized the groan coincided with small backward movements of the car.

She was sliding downhill. That wasn't good.

Nicole listened to her oddly calm thoughts and wondered why she wasn't panicking. Was she dreaming? Or had the slamming of her head against the headrest knocked her out? Given her a concussion? She was pretty sure that calm was not the appropriate emotion for her predicament.

From somewhere she heard the roar of a car's engine and the slamming of a door. Then a muffled yell rang out. Her first reaction was relief. Someone was here to rescue her. But with excruciating slowness, she realized that wasn't the most likely conclusion.

The figure that had risen up and was now looming above her was far more likely to be the driver of the car that had forced her off the road. He was coming to finish her off.

She needed her purse. Her cell phone. To her surprise, it was right there, next to her hand. It had slid over onto the console. She fumbled in the front pocket and pulled out her phone.

To her utter surprise, her hand wasn't even trembling. She dialed Ryker's number.

"Ryker, I need help," she said when he answered.

In front of her, the figure moved. He came closer to the edge of the road. Then he pulled something out of the pocket of his rain poncho and pointed it toward her.

"Nic? What's wrong? What's happened? Nic!"

"Oh, it's a gun," she muttered. At that instant a metallic thud and a zing split the air. She tried to duck down below the dashboard but her safety belt hindered her.

"A gun? Nic! Where are you?"

Her shoulder and chest hurt where the belt pressed into her. Fumbling blindly, she finally got the belt unhooked. "I'm on Henri LaRue Road, off Highway 22."

It amazed her how calm she felt and sounded, even though two more shots pinged into the front of her car. "I'm in the mud and he's shooting at me."

"Good God, Nic! Who's shooting at you? Hang on, I'm calling 911."

He was gone for a second. Then she heard his beloved voice again. "You did say Henri LaRue Road, didn't you?"

"Yes." She wanted to look and see if the man was coming down into the mud after her, but she figured it wouldn't be a good idea to stick her head up. A fourth shot and the odd thud of something hitting the safety glass of the windshield convinced her she was right.

"Nic, are you hurt?" Ryker was back. "They're coming. Right now. What's going on? Did I hear gunshots?"

"Of course. I told you. Can you please hurry? I'm scared."

"You should hear the sirens in a second. Stay down, Nic. I'm on my way."

Nicole heard a note in Ryker's voice she hadn't heard before. He sounded scared. Not possible. Ryker Delancey wasn't scared of anything.

Vaguely, distantly, she heard a familiar wail. Sirens. He'd been right. They were coming. Thank goodness.

"Ryker? I hear them," she said, but he'd hung up.

A string of curses filled the air, out of tune and out of sync with increasingly loud sirens. Then more gunshots peppered the car. Nicole cringed and shifted so she could cover her head with her arms. She felt a peck on her cheek. When she touched the place, her fingers came away smeared with blood. She didn't touch it again. She wasn't sure she wanted to know how bad it was.

One last gunshot ricocheted off metal, then a car engine fired up, revved and roared away, almost drowned out by the sirens, which were getting really loud. Then she saw the reflection of blue and red flashing lights.

The police.

They were here. Nicole lifted her head to look out the windshield but when she did, the seat fell out from under her. She thumped back down on her butt.

The car was moving—downhill. Then she felt it tilt sideways. Her breath caught on a sob.

"Ryker!" she screamed, but she knew that the sound coming out of her mouth was no more than a whisper.

"Ma'am? Hello? Ma'am, are you all right?"

"I think so," she called. "Are you going to shoot me?"

"What? Ma'am? I'm a fireman. I'm here to rescue you. Can you hear me? Don't move, just speak."

She took a deep breath and tried to call more loudly. "I think I'm okay."

"Ma'am, can you tell me who you are?" The voice was a little closer. Nicole carefully raised her head, doing her best not to move enough to disturb the car. She saw a man in a fireman's uniform with a harness around his torso. He was trying to walk down into the mud hole, but he kept slipping. Two men up on the road were holding on to the harness.

"Be careful," she called.

The fireman grinned. "Don't worry about me, ma'am. What's your name?"

"Nicole Beckham."

"Good, Nicole. You just sit right there and we'll have you back up on the road in no time. What happened to your cheek there?"

"I think a bullet hit me."

"It's not bleeding much. Probably a ricochet. Did you feel anything else hit you? Are you bleeding anywhere else?"

"No."

"Are you sure? Not hurting anywhere? Legs? Feet? Can you wiggle your toes?"

She tried. "Yes. I can." For some reason, she wanted to cry. His questions were painting a lurid picture for her of all the things that could have happened, and she was suddenly terrified. "Can I get out now?"

"Let's wait a minute, okay, Nicole? Can I call you Nicole?"

"You already did."

"That's right, I did." He chuckled. "Okay, Nicole, when I get to the front of your car, my buddies up there are going to throw me a chain. I'll hook it to the frame. When I do, the car might slide a little bit. But that hook's going to keep it from going any farther. How does that sound?"

His words were reassuring, but she noticed that his smile didn't reach his eyes. "Okay. I guess the ditch is deeper than I thought it was."

"Maybe a little. Now, I need you to sit tight." The fireman turned his head. "Ready for the chain!" he shouted.

A huge chain was lowered to him. He grabbed it and bent down, under the front of the car.

She heard the scrape of metal against metal and felt a bump, then the sickening feeling of the car seat dropping out from under her again. She cried out.

The fireman's head rose above the front bumper. Then the rest of him, most of which was covered in black mud. "Nicole?" he called out. "You still with me?"

"I'm here." She barely heard her own voice over her pounding heart.

"Good. I'm coming to get you out."

He nodded to the men above him and they lowered him some more, until he was beside the driver's door.

"Can you undo your seat belt?"

She nodded and did so.

"Okay. I'm going to try to open the door. There's a lot of mud over here, but if we can get the door open, you'll be out of here in no time. If we have to go through the passenger door, it might take a little longer."

"I didn't just run off the road into a ditch, did I? This is deeper than that."

"Don't worry, Nicole. I promised Ryker I'd get you out of here in one piece, and that's what I'm going to do. You just do everything I say and we'll be having café au lait together in no time."

"Ryker? You know Ryker?"

"I sure do. Since he was a snot-nosed kid." The fireman grinned again and Nicole realized he looked a little familiar. "We're cousins. My name's Shel Rossi."

"Shel? For Shelton?"

"Nope. I wish." He chuckled as he pulled a tangle of yellow straps from his backpack. "This is a harness. I need you to get this part right here around your chest under your arms. Then wiggle this long strap between your legs."

Nicole managed to get the straps under her arms, but she couldn't lift herself out of the seat enough to maneuver the webbed strap down her back and between her legs.

"I tell you what," Shel said. "I'm going to get this door open first, then if you'll allow me, I can help you get the crotch strap around and fastened."

"I don't care what you do, Shel, as long as you get me out of here."

Chapter Ten

Shel reached for the door handle. It took some struggling, and several times Nicole thought the car was going to go sliding backward, but finally he got the door open.

"Now if you'll forgive me," he said. He pushed the strap of the harness down between her back and the seat, until he'd stuffed it under her butt. "Okay, can you brace your legs and lift your butt?"

She did and he reached between her legs and grabbed the strap. Before she knew it he had it fastened to the chest strap.

"Okay. You're all secured and ready to go. Don't tell Ryker how much fun we had." He winked at her.

She laughed.

Then he grew serious. "I'm ready to lift you out. I want you to concentrate on not getting your legs or arms tangled in the steering wheel or the seat belt. I've got your harness attached to mine, so you're not going anywhere without me. And the only place I'm headed is back up to the road. Okay?"

Nicole swallowed. "Okay."

By the time Shel was done, Nicole felt as if her arms had been jerked out of their sockets and her legs had been tied in knots, not to mention the bruises she was sure she had from the punishing straps. But Shel's strong arms held on to her as he half walked, half slid up the muddy slope, helped along by the firemen pulling on his harness.

Finally, more than one pair of strong arms hauled her and Shel up to solid ground. Shel unhooked her harness from his and turned her over to a waiting EMT.

"Thank you, Shel."

"Don't mention it. Tell Ryker to bring you around to meet the family one of these days." The mud-covered fireman touched the brim of his hat and headed toward the fire truck.

After the EMT had determined that the scratch on her cheek and some bruises from the seat belt and the harness were her only injuries, he helped her get as much mud off her as possible, then gave her a pair of scrubs and left her to change inside the ambulance.

By the time she emerged, Ryker was loping across the road toward her. She'd barely climbed down from the back of the ambulance when he grabbed her and pulled her fiercely to him.

She slid her arms around his waist and reveled in his tight, strong embrace. "Ryker! Oh, Ryker. I'm so sorry!"

"Nic! Are you all right?" His chest was heaving and his heart was beating double-time. Beating for her.

"I'm fine now. I—"

Suddenly, he let go of her and took a step backward. He glanced around, his cheeks flushed. He cleared his throat as the emergency medical technician approached. "How is she?" he asked.

"She's fine. Just a scrape on her cheek, and she'll have some bruises from the rescue harness, but otherwise, she's a-okay."

"Thanks," Ryker said gruffly. As the EMT headed away, he turned back to Nicole, a frown marring his even features. But before he could say anything, Shel Rossi came up. He'd shed the harness and the backpack and jacket, but he still had on the firemen's pants with red suspenders holding them up. The white T-shirt he wore revealed a very nice, buff torso. He clapped Ryker on the back.

"Shel." Ryker turned and held out his hand. "Thanks."

"No prob, cousin. That's a really nice—witness you've got there."

Nicole smiled at Shel's teasing tone but Ryker wasn't amused. "What's the story on the car?"

"Hard to tell. The rain's washed away any evidence we might have found on the road—tire tracks and such. The front of the vehicle is peppered with gunshots. They're looking for bullets or casings. But again—" Shel glanced skyward. "The rain."

"Yeah. Who's the detective?"

"Baron Treehorn, from Madisonville. He's over there."

Ryker nodded. "I know him. We've talked a few times."

"I've got to go talk to my chief." Shel turned to Nicole. "I sure am glad you're okay, Nicole."

"Thank you again, Shel. You kept me from dying of fright."

"My pleasure." Shel paused, eyeing Ryker. "She was incredibly brave, Ryker. Watch that Delancey temper."

Shel wasn't even out of earshot when Ryker turned on her.

"What the hell were you doing? I told you that you were not to go anywhere without me or Job or Bill. That meant *anywhere!*"

He was furious, and a little scary. Nicole swallowed hard, then stood up straight and lifted her chin. "I don't know if you noticed, but I've had about all the excitement I can handle for one day, so I'd appreciate it if you'd wait until tomorrow to scream at me like a banshee. Like Shel said, watch your Delancey temper." She felt like crying, but she channeled every bit of fear and panic and terror into matching Ryker's anger. It worked fairly well.

Ryker's face reflected surprise for an instant before it resumed its former furious scowl. "You almost got killed. Do you know that?" He took her arm and pulled her over to the edge of the road.

"Look down there," he ordered her. "That mud down there is deep, and it's worse than quicksand. A couple more minutes and neither you nor your car would have ever been seen again. I'll ask you one more time, what the *hell* were you doing out here?"

Nicole barely heard his last words. She was staring down at her car, which was slowly being winched up out of the ditch. The winch's motor shrieked, the chain creaked and a low, wet sucking sound provided a bass undertone. Her car was almost wheel-well deep in black mud.

"Worse than quicksand?" she repeated. Gone was her righteous anger. Gone was her pride at Shel's declaration of how brave she'd been. The tears that hadn't quite made it to the surface before emerged, and the terror that she'd managed to keep locked away while Shel Rossi was saving her life erupted like a volcano. Suddenly she was shaking all over.

She wrapped her arms tightly around herself, but as hard as she squeezed, trying to hold herself together, she still felt as if she was falling apart. A sob escaped her tight throat. Then another one. Then tears overflowed.

Ryker started to say something, then stopped and clamped his jaw. After a couple of seconds, he took a deep breath.

"Come on," he said gently. "I'm going to put you in my

car. You're obviously freezing. I'll see if anybody has any coffee."

"Shel s-said we'd h-have café au lait," she wailed, knowing she sounded like a child but unable to stop the tears or the shivers.

Ryker guided her to his car and settled her in the passenger seat. Then he got in, started the engine and turned on the heat. "You stay right here until I get back. Understand?"

Although his words were commanding, his voice was still gentle. She nodded.

"I will," she said through chattering teeth. "Where— where are you going?"

"Just over there, to talk with the detective and see if anybody's got a thermos of coffee. I'll be back soon."

"Okay." Nicole rubbed her arms and hunched her shoulders. The warm air from the car's heater penetrated the chill on her skin, making her shiver even more.

But her skin would warm up.

It was the cold knot of terror lodged beneath her breastbone that she was afraid would never thaw. Terror due to a man in a black hoodie who wasn't going to stop until she was dead.

The heater's blast finally began to seep through her clothes and skin. She took a shaky breath and sighed. Several yards away, Ryker was talking to his cousin Shel. Shel was obviously describing how he'd gotten the strap around her and pulled her to safety.

Then the two of them walked over to her car, where a young man wearing a CSI jacket was taking photographs. Shel spoke to the photographer, who pointed to several places on the fender as he answered. Ryker followed the two men's words carefully. After a few seconds, he grimaced and brushed a hand over the top of his head, leaving his hair spiked.

The gesture she'd seen before made Nicole's heart squeeze in love and gratitude. If anyone could thaw the icy block of fear inside her, Ryker could. She was safe now. Ryker was here.

NICOLE WASN'T SAFE ANYWHERE. The realization nearly paralyzed Ryker. He'd never admit it to a living soul, but the sound of Nic's voice on the phone saying those awful words had frightened him more than anything he could remember, including the time his twin brother, Reilly, had nearly drowned trying to race Ryker in their grandma's pool when they were six.

I need help. Her words had sliced through his heart like one of her super-sharp knives. The fear and hope and bravery in her voice had cut even deeper than that.

Then she'd said something about a gun. A gun. He'd been halfway to Baton Rouge, headed toward Angola, when she'd called. He'd turned right around and sped here, his lights flashing. He'd made a quick call to Angola to let them know that an emergency had come up and he couldn't make the hearing. He'd already faxed them his written statement.

Then he'd spent the rest of the time trying to call her back, but she hadn't answered. He'd prayed that the reason she wasn't answering was because the police were there and she was fine, and not because she'd been shot or taken hostage.

He stalked over to the detective in charge. "Baron, what's the story here?"

"Ryker," the tall gaunt detective greeted him. "I haven't had a chance to talk to the victim, but—"

"Nicole. Her name is Nicole Beckham."

Detective Baron Treehorn nodded. "Ms. Beckham. From what my crime scene folks tell me it looks like she was forced off the road. See the back of her car there?" He pointed with his pencil.

Ryker had already taken a quick look at the car, but he stepped around to the rear. Some of the mud had been scraped away, and he could see the dents in the fender.

Treehorn stood beside him. "It appears the vehicle struck her from the rear twice, maybe three times. It'll be easier to tell once we've washed it. I'm hoping we can get some paint transfer to help us ID the vehicle. Then there are the bullet holes." He walked around to the front of the car and Ryker followed.

"Eleven."

Ryker had already counted them. And when he had, he'd almost lost his footing, that was how bad his knees had trembled. Seven in the frame and four in the windshield, at—he measured the distance from the road down the bank to Nicole's car with his eyes—twenty-five feet. Thirty at most. "Damn." It looked like a long way down there, but it wasn't. Not for a bullet.

"Yeah. We've recovered a couple of casings. 9 mm. With any luck we'll match it to a gun that's already in the system. If we're real lucky we'll get a fingerprint off one of them. I doubt we'll be that lucky though, what with the rain and mud."

"Where do you want to talk to Nicole? Not out here."

"No," Treehorn agreed. "We'll go to Beau's, up the road. They've got pretty good coffee and a private room. How does that sound?"

"Good. Thanks. I'll drive her in my car if that's okay with you."

"Fine by me. See you there."

Ryker got in the car and put it in gear.

"I guess they didn't have any coffee?" Nicole asked tentatively.

"We're going to a restaurant up the road," he said as he carefully turned around. "They'll have coffee. Detective Treehorn has some questions. It won't take long."

She continued to rub her arms and her shoulders were still drawn up and in, as if she were trying to make herself as small as possible.

It hurt him to see her like that. So small and vulnerable. Almost breakable. "I shouldn't have yelled at you so loud."

A short laugh escaped her throat. "So loud?"

"Okay, I'm sorry I yelled." He took a breath. "But damn it, Nic. You could have been killed." His throat tried to close up on the word. He swallowed as he turned into the parking lot of the restaurant.

It was a catfish house. The dashboard clock read nine o'clock, not prime business hours for a catfish place. Then he noticed a worn sign over the door. Breakfast.

He parked the car.

"Job's wife had a kidney stone."

"What?" He wasn't sure he'd heard right. "Job's wife? What are you talking about?"

"Job had to take her to the emergency room. So he couldn't go to the market."

Ryker's heart wrenched. "The guy shot eleven bullets at you, Nic. Eleven!"

Her eyes closed and she nodded. "I know. I heard them."

Ryker's heart squeezed so tightly in his chest that he nearly gasped. *She heard them.* Crouching there, not knowing if the next bullet would be the one that hit her. Not knowing if anyone could save her. "Damn it!"

She cringed.

"Ah, Nic. Don't." He pushed a strand of hair back from her face and brushed the backs of his fingers against her cheek. "I thought—" What? He'd thought what? That he'd die if she were hurt? That he'd gotten her killed? That in that instant when he'd heard her small, brave voice asking for his help, he'd fallen in love with her?

No! What kind of thinking was that? She was a victim of a crime. His job was to protect her. That was it. That had to be it. He pulled his fingers away.

"I'm sorry, okay?" she said. "I never thought it would be dangerous in the daytime. All this is so hard on Job. I don't want him to lose his restaurant because I can't go anywhere without a babysitter."

"Have you asked Job what he wants, because I'm pretty sure I know what he'd say. He'd say nothing's more important that keeping you safe."

"I know," she said brokenly. "He'd close the restaurant down if he thought that would help me."

"That may be what he has to do."

"He will not. I won't let him—oh, no! I forgot about the fish."

"The fish?" Ryker shook his head in confusion. "What fish?"

"The black drum. In the cooler in my car. I was going to smoke it with alder wood for tonight's *Poisson du Jour.*"

"Really? Fish? When are you going to start worrying about yourself?" A harsh chuckle erupted from Ryker's throat. "Fish," he repeated in disgust.

"But Job needs it for the menu tonight."

"Job and the restaurant need to take a backseat, Nic. You're the one everyone's worried about. Job can get along without you for a few days."

She clasped her hands together until her knuckles were white. "No, he can't. The sous chef quit two weeks ago. He can't handle everything by himself."

Ryker saw Treehorn gesturing to him. They needed to

get inside and get Nicole's statement. "We'll talk about this later." He got out of the car and walked around to open her door.

"I'm not going to let you bully Job into closing the restaurant," she declared as she got out.

"Let's go." He needed to get this interview over with so he could take her back to his apartment and lock the door. He'd like to handcuff her to the bedpost to be sure she couldn't get away, but that might be considered unlawful restraint.

BY THE TIME TREEHORN was satisfied that he'd squeezed every drop of information he could out of Nicole, and Ryker had driven back to his rented house in Chef Voleur, it was after six.

Nicole was exhausted. She'd held herself together all day with the last dregs of her energy and will. Now she felt depleted, wrung out. All she wanted to do was get into the shower and stand underneath the hot pouring water and cry.

But Ryker argued that she needed to eat something. His insistence that he knew best for her was the last straw. She snapped at him and stomped off to the bathroom.

It wasn't until she was ready to turn off the hot water and get out of the shower that she realized she didn't have any clothes except the scrub shirt and pants the EMT had given her. When she stepped out into the steam-filled bathroom, she saw a sweatshirt hanging on the door hook. It hadn't been there before.

Ryker had come in while she was in the shower. Which meant he'd heard her sobbing. Her face burned. She'd already shown him what a cowardly wimp she was. Now he knew she was not only a wimp, she was a crybaby.

She pulled the sweatshirt over her head. It hung nearly

to her knees and the sleeves flopped five inches over her hands. She pushed them up. The fleece shirt was wearable, and long enough that she wouldn't embarrass herself. Because she didn't have any clean underwear either. She quickly rinsed out the panties and squeezed them in a towel. Then she hung them on a towel rack. Hopefully they'd be dry by morning.

Rooting around under the sink, she came up with a hairdryer. She quickly dried and finger-combed her hair. Then she wiped steam off the mirror. Not too bad, although her nose and cheeks were shiny without makeup. Nothing she could do about that though.

She stepped out of the bathroom and shivered.

"Cold?"

Ryker's voice came from his tiny kitchen, where he was making his Morning-After Eggs. Their familiar savory smell made her stomach growl. She closed her eyes and took in the dark smell of coffee and the crisp scent of toast.

When she opened her eyes, Ryker was watching her with an unreadable expression on his face. She ran her palms down the front of the sweatshirt.

"There are socks in the top drawer of my dresser if you want to get a pair."

She glanced toward his bedroom. "I can't go into your drawers," she said.

He sent her an exasperated look. "Suit yourself."

Her toes curled on the chilly hardwood floor, convincing her that warm socks were more important than saving herself from the slight embarrassment of seeing his underwear drawer. She grabbed a pair of white-and-gray athletic socks and pulled them on. The heels rode up way past her ankles, but they were warm.

When she came back into the front room, Ryker had two

plates of eggs and two mugs of coffee on the table and was retrieving the toast from the toaster.

Nicole sat down, spooned sugar into her coffee and took a long swallow. "Oh, that's good," she said.

He sat down next to her and held out a plate of toast. She took a piece. "It's not cappuccino," he said.

"It's good," she said around a mouthful of eggs. She polished off the food in no time.

Ryker ate more slowly, watching her the whole time.

By the time Nicole had finished her eggs and two pieces of toast and had a second cup of coffee, she was feeling much better. Her head was clearer and her thoughts were less scattered.

As she swallowed the last drops of coffee, she thought about the time. "Oh, no! What time is it?" She looked toward the windows. "Is it after dark? I can get to the restaurant in time to help with the late diners and close up."

She vaulted up, the wooden chair legs squeaking across the hardwood floor. "Come on. We need to go by my apartment first so I can change clothes."

"No."

"What? Seriously, Ryker. I've got to get to work."

He glared at her.

"You can't just keep me here."

"I'm sure going to try. Sit down."

Nicole barely heard him. She glanced around the living room. "Where's my purse? I need to call Job and let him know I'm on my way."

"Nic! Sit down!"

She heard that. She dropped back into the chair, biting her lip. "You're a bully," she muttered.

"Maybe so," he snapped. "But I wouldn't have to bully you if you'd listen to me. I talked to Job this morning, while Treehorn was interviewing you. My grandmother's chef had a son who's also a chef. The son retired a couple of years ago. I got my aunt Claire to call him. He's agreed to fill in." Ryker gave her a smile that looked a little smug. "So you don't have to worry about Job and the restaurant."

Nicole stared at him, trying to process his words. She'd heard him, but the things he'd said seemed almost like a foreign language.

His grandmother's chef's son would fill in for her. What kind of family had a personal chef? Much less have such influence that they could command someone to drop everything and rush to their aid.

The Delanceys, obviously. Con Delancey had run Louisiana politics for years, and his wife, Lilibelle, had been wealthy in her own right. It was a wonder Ryker hadn't recruited an army of Delancey family members or employees to bodyguard her.

In her mind's eye, Nicole watched as another few rows of bricks were laid on the growing wall between Ryker and her. She had no one, not friends, not even family, that she could call to her aid with no notice.

She had nothing to offer him. She was so far out of his league that she wasn't even in the same zip code as his league. Whatever she'd thought about in her deepest fantasies, whatever Cinderella story she'd subconsciously written in her head, she had to delete it and fast.

There were no Delanceys in her future. And there were certainly no poor, scared Beckhams in his.

"Nic?" Ryker's voice penetrated her racing thoughts and she realized it wasn't the first time he'd called her name. "What's the matter? Are you sure you're okay?"

She licked her lips and consciously tried to relax her aching jaw enough to give him a smile. "You've thought of everything, haven't you?" She waved a hand. "Hire a chef, bully a victim. Anything to find your killer. It looks like you're going to get what you wanted in the first place. You've got more money than King Midas. Why don't you just hire a mover, find me a place in another state and plunk me down there, out of your way?"

"Nic—"

She held up a hand and shook her head. "No. Stop wasting your energy fighting with me about every little thing. I give up. You're the boss. I'll do whatever you say."

"I'm not—"

"And then when all this is over, I'll go away. I'll move—again—and start over again." Her mouth curled in a wry smile. "It's what I'm good at. But right now I am kind of tired. Let me wash these dishes before I fall asleep face-down in the eggs."

Ryker deftly scooped her plate up before she could get her hands on it. He sent her a brief smile. "What eggs?" he teased. "You ate every last crumb. I should have made more."

"That was perfect." Perfect, just like everything he did. He was the perfect cop. The perfect egg-cooker. The perfect lover. And he'd never be hers.

"Come on, I'll put you to bed. The sheets are fairly clean," he said apologetically. "You should be comfortable. I'm sleeping on the couch."

He gestured for her to precede him into the bedroom. Then he walked around her and turned down the carelessly draped comforter. He took a swipe at the sheets to smooth them.

"I'll be right out there on the couch."

"Are you sure Job will be okay?" she asked. "Maybe I should call him. I want to check on Merina."

"You can call him if you want, but he's at the restaurant and everything is fine. He's been showing Richard Tesch around the kitchen and getting ready for tonight. His wife passed the kidney stone and is back at home."

He turned to go again. As he reached for the light switch, she thought of something else.

She was quiet for a moment, then, "Ryker? He must have been out there all night. He knew you were gone. He saw me get in my car. Do you think he was watching me all this time?"

He shook his head. "I don't know. Maybe since that article in the paper. He was definitely waiting to get you alone. Which reminds me, you'll be working days for a while. You'll act as sous chef for Richard, and I'll pick you up around six. No more early mornings or late nights."

"He thinks I can identify him."

Ryker didn't answer.

"Could we get that reporter to say that I can't?"

"No," he said quickly, then grimaced. "That wouldn't be a good idea. I don't want you mentioned in the newspaper again. Do you need anything?"

You. "No."

"Get a good night's sleep." Ryker turned out the light and pulled the door closed until it was open just a crack.

"Ryker?"

He pushed the door open. "Yeah? You know you can't go to sleep if you're talking."

"I'm sorry. I didn't mean to get into trouble. I wish I was brave—"

"You are brave, Nic." His voice was quiet. "Do you know how many people would have panicked if they'd driven off the road into a ditch? Not to mention if they had to work with a fire and rescue specialist to free themselves. Shel was very impressed with you." He paused. "So am I."

Ryker impressed? She stared at his silhouette, backlit by the light from the living room.

"Now go to sleep!"

"Yes, sir." As if ordering her would work. She'd been *that* close to dying. She doubted whether she'd ever be able to sleep again.

Chapter Eleven

Ryker was going over Treehorn's report and transcript of his interview of Nicole, which the detective had e-mailed him, when he saw a movement in the corner of his eye. He looked up. It was Nicole. She stood in the doorway of his bedroom dressed in his sweatshirt and socks, looking like a waif.

"Hey. What's wrong?"

She spread her hands. "I don't know. I can't go to sleep. Every time I doze, I see that man standing above me, pointing a gun at me."

"Come here." Ryker held out his hand.

"I'm okay, I just—can't get that image out of my head."

"Come on. Treehorn e-mailed me the transcript of your interview, and the final sketch the forensic artist did of the man who ran you off the road."

"Sure. That'll help me sleep."

Ryker chuckled. "At least it'll give you something to do."

She sat down beside him, pulling the hem of the sweatshirt as far down over her legs as it would go.

Ryker watched her hands. She was covering up her nakedness under the sweatshirt. He'd been in the bathroom.

He'd seen her delicate panties hanging on the towel rack, dripping water.

He felt himself stir at the thought of her smooth, beautiful body covered only by his sweatshirt. Stir and grow hard. He sucked in a deep breath and tried to distract himself by concentrating on Treehorn's interview questions and her answers. When that didn't work he tried picturing her car sliding deeper down the muddy shoulder toward the ditch as a dangerous killer shot at her.

It helped, a little.

"Is that my interview?" she asked.

He nodded, adjusting the laptop to hide his arousal. "You told Treehorn you didn't recognize the man?"

"I could barely see his face. He had on a dark hooded sweatshirt."

"Here's the artist's rendering of your description. You did a good job." He clicked to open the file.

"No, I didn't. I couldn't give very many details at all. Mostly what I saw was that gun."

"Take a look." Ryker clicked and the face she'd described filled the screen.

She laughed nervously. "He looks like that sketch of the Unabomber."

"Not really. Here's the other sketch he did from your description. The full-length sketch."

When the computer-generated image of the man who'd tried to kill her rose on the screen, Nicole gasped. "Oh! He looked just like that."

The stocky man in dark baggy pants and a black hooded sweatshirt stood looking down and pointing a large handgun directly at the screen.

"That's him. I know you can't tell much. But that's exactly what he looked like before he pulled the trigger."

"You did a good job. We actually can tell a lot. We

can see his build, his relative height. The fact that he's Caucasian."

"The glasses aren't quite right. The frames were bigger. Really big. The kind that older people wear. Like he hasn't bought new glasses in a long time."

Ryker knew what she meant. A lot of men, including Detective Charles Phillips, wore those big old-fashioned glasses. He pulled up the interview again. He read her description. According to her, the man was medium height and rather stocky in build. She'd told Treehorn he seemed to be older, in his sixties.

"You're sure he's in his sixties?" Ryker pointed at the screen.

"Pretty sure." She leaned closer to look at the computer, and her arm pressed against his.

"How did you decide that?"

She shrugged. "Well, the glasses. And the way he stood. The way he moved, I guess. He seemed a little bit bent over. Oh, and his hands looked old."

"That's interesting. If he's that age, he's got to be pretty strong. I mean, he had surprise on his side when he attacked his victims, but the way he killed them took force. The usual profile would suggest a younger man, a loner and underachiever in an undemanding job."

"So he's still not fitting the serial killer pattern. I guess I can see why your boss was so reluctant to let you link the cases. It's a good thing he trusts you."

"Yeah, well." Ryker laughed shortly. "He doesn't so much. He still half believes I got stuck on the serial killer idea because of Bella."

"Bella?"

Ryker bit his tongue, but it was too late. Damn it, that had slipped out. He hadn't wanted Nicole to know that he'd known one of the victims.

"Bella, the second victim? You knew her?"

He had to tell her now. "We dated a couple of times, back in school. I was a sophomore at LSU and she was a grad student."

As he said the words, he felt her stiffen. By the time he'd finished, she was sitting up straight and he could feel the tension radiating from her.

"I'm so sorry about your girlfriend," she said. "I can see why you pursued this serial killer idea so relentlessly."

Ryker heard the pain in her voice. She'd obviously thought he was pursuing this case so relentlessly because of *her*. As the thought crossed his mind, he realized he'd become interested in the cases because he'd known Bella, but it was for Nicole's sake that he was pursuing the killer so relentlessly.

She'd never believe that. Never trust it—or him. It would have made a lot more sense to have come clean with her about Bella in the beginning. Certainly before they'd slept together. "Nic, she wasn't my girlfriend. It was a few dates. Nothing serious, trust me."

"I understand," she said.

He held up his arm, hoping she'd sink into his side.

She didn't.

"Listen to me. Of course I took an interest in the case because I knew one of the victims. And of course I'm sorry she was killed, but the couple of casual dates we had were eight years ago. I hadn't seen or heard from her since then."

She nodded automatically. Damn it, she didn't believe a word he said. He wanted to confess to her that while he was sad about Bella's death, the very idea that Nicole might have been hurt had ripped a hole in his heart that would never heal until he could hold on to her forevermore, keeping her safe at his side.

The unsettling direction his thoughts had taken sent his heart skittering into high gear. At that moment Nicole pushed away and rose. "I'd better get back to bed," she said. "I'm so tired I'm not sure I'm making sense."

"Sure, hon. I know you need your sleep. I'll see you in the morning."

Ryker watched her as she padded back into the bedroom. He listened until he heard a soft sigh and knew she was in bed and settled.

Only then did he allow himself to replay his thoughts. *Forever? Safe at his side?* He wasn't even thirty. His longest relationship had been a few months. He didn't even want to add up how long it had been since he'd had sex, prior to sleeping with Nicole.

So where had the concept of *forever* come from? Marriage, family, kids. Those were things his parents did. Things that existed in the haze of a far-off future.

But they were things that had been creeping into his head ever since he'd met Nic.

He had to stop them, because they couldn't happen. Not now. Not yet. He was letting his hormones—or something—get in the way of the clear head and logic he needed to catch the October Killer.

Maybe it was a good thing Nicole had misunderstood his reason for pursuing this case so relentlessly. The last thing he wanted to do was hurt her. He wanted to pull her into the protective circle of his arms, not push her away.

Not watch her trust in him fade.

He only hoped a spark of trust would remain inside her long enough for him to coax it back into a flame.

After the October Killer was caught.

THE NEXT MORNING Ryker had the Autumn Moser case file in his hands. He sat at his desk, going through the specifics.

Autumn was killed at 11:00 p.m. on October 26, 2005, her twenty-first birthday, in an alley off Basin Street, near the St. Louis Cemetery.

A bad neighborhood even in the daytime. What was she doing down there that time of night? He thumbed through the crime scene photos, the CSI and autopsy reports, until he got to the detective's typed report.

He skimmed it quickly.

Cause of death was three gunshot wounds to the chest.

Purse was spilled and her cell phone was missing.

The scrapes on palms and knees, and mud spatter on her calves suggest she'd fallen while running. However, the entry wound places her face-to-face with her killer at near point-blank range.

Ryker rubbed his temple. If it was a mugging, why would the mugger chase her? For that matter, why would she run, if he were holding a gun on her? And why had the mugger shot her?

On the other hand, if it wasn't a mugger, if it was his serial killer, had he taken her cell phone as a trophy? If so, why hadn't he taken trophies from the other victims?

He flipped the page to read the detective's conclusions. Sure enough, his opinion was that Autumn Moser's death was a homicide at the hands of a mugger.

To be thorough, he flipped through every single page in the file. Toward the back, he found a statement from Christmas Leigh Moser, the victim's sister, stating that she'd been talking to her sister, Autumn, on the phone, wishing her happy birthday, when her sister had screamed. Christmas Moser had heard what she described as gunshots through the phone line before it went dead.

The information on the police report included Christmas

Moser's address and phone number. Ryker called the phone number.

"Dr. Moser," a low, husky voice answered.

"Christmas Leigh Moser?" he asked.

"Yes. Who is this?"

"I'm Detective Ryker Delancey, St. Tammany Parish Sheriff's Department, Ms.—Dr. Moser."

"Yes?"

Her voice went up in pitch.

"I apologize, Dr. Moser. I'm calling in regards to your sister's death in 2005. Do you have time to talk for a few minutes?"

"Can you hold a moment?" He heard her giving orders to someone, maybe a nurse, to change a dressing and increase the flow of an IV, and a couple of other things he couldn't understand.

"Now. Detective Delancey, is it? I can give you about three minutes. I'm making rounds on the pediatric ward here."

"I apologize for calling you out of the blue about this, but I'm looking into your sister's death. I have a statement by you in the New Orleans Police Department case file on Autumn Moser that states that you spoke with her on the phone around 11:00 p.m. on the night of her death."

"That's right."

"You had called her to wish her happy birthday?"

There was a pause, and when Dr. Moser spoke again, her voice was more husky than before. "Yes. I did."

"Can you tell me why you called so late?"

"I'd had an emergency with one of my patients, and had just gotten home."

Ryker tapped a pencil tip on the pad on his desk. Dr. Christmas Leigh Moser wasn't going to provide him any information that he didn't ask for. "You reached her on her cell phone. Did she say where she was?"

"No. Didn't you say you had my statement in front of you?"

"Yes, I do, but I want to get your perspective about the phone call."

"She didn't say where she was, but I could hear vehicles and music."

Ryker jotted that down. "You said you heard her scream."

"Yes." Dr. Moser's voice was becoming brittle. "It sounded like she was running, then she stopped and was breathing hard. I asked her if something was wrong. She said 'Christy!' And then screamed. Then she said something like 'you bum,' or 'you scum' or something." Dr. Moser paused and took a deep breath.

Ryker waited.

"I heard gunshots. Then the phone went dead."

"Do you know how many gunshots?"

Another pause. "Three? Four? I can't be sure. Why are you looking into her case now, after all this time?"

"There have been other murders that may have similarities to your sister's. I want to look at it again in light of these new developments."

"I see. Have you talked to my father? Albert Moser?"

"Yes."

"Then you've seen how he has been affected by my sister's death. I'm pleased to know that you're looking into the case, Detective. I hope you're able to do something. My sister's death has ruined my father's health. I have to go now."

"Thanks for talking to me, Doctor. If I need anything more, may I call you?"

"Please call my secretary and set up a teleconference

time. I can devote more attention to your questions if I'm not rushed."

Ryker took down the secretary's number, thanked the doctor and hung up. Christmas Moser's statement didn't mention anything about what Autumn had said just prior to being shot. Ryker quickly scribbled some notes about the conversation, and put a big star by the words *bum* and *scum*. He needed to ask Dr. Moser more about that. He dialed her secretary's number and made an appointment for a half-hour telephone interview on Monday.

Then he dialed NOPD Detective Dixon Lloyd. "Hey, Dix, it's Ryker."

"Ryker. What's going on up there in Delancey-land?" Dixon's joking name for Chef Voleur was an appropriate epithet, since many of Ryker's large immediate and extended family had grown up and now lived in the town.

"Same old. You know, hanging out at the plantation house in our white linen suits, sipping mint juleps and twirling our gold-tipped canes."

Dixon laughed. "Yeah. That's what I thought."

"What can you tell me about a detective down there— Fred Samhurst?"

"Fred? He's okay. A couple of years away from retirement and about forty pounds away from his running weight."

Ryker jotted notes as he spoke. "Five years ago he caught a case on Basin Street, wrote it up as a mugging. I've got the girl's father saying she was killed by an ex-lover."

"Five years ago? Why's the father popping up now?"

"The daughter was killed on October 26 of 2005. He calls every year around this time. Think Samhurst might have missed something?"

Dixon paused for a beat. "Hard to say. You know how it is."

Ryker did. Dixon didn't want to talk about a fellow detective.

"What makes you think the father's right?" Dixon asked.

"According to Samhurst's notes, the girl was running away from whoever shot her. Apparently fell at least once and scraped her knees and palms. Then she was shot in the chest—three times."

"I remember that case. I think the father has called here a time or two, demanding justice for his daughter. Sad." Dixon paused for a second. "All I can tell you is Fred had a mild heart attack a couple of years ago. He started eating healthier. Lost thirty pounds at least."

"Can you switch me over to Dispatch? I want to see if I can catch up with Samhurst today and talk with him about the case."

"Sure thing."

Ryker thanked Dixon and waited for Dispatch to answer. He made arrangements to speak with Detective Samhurst, and then hung up. Dixon's seemingly offhand comment gave Ryker some insight into the case. Samhurst was still forty pounds overweight after he'd lost thirty. He jotted a note.

Detective Fred Samhurst was approx. 70 lbs. overweight and out of shape at the time of Autumn Moser's murder. Had he taken the easy way out and called it a mugging?

Ryker wanted to get Dave's take on the forensics of the case. He walked the file over to Anne-Marie's desk and asked her to send it to the M.E.'s office with a request to get back to Ryker ASAP with his opinion.

"How's it going with reviewing the victims' case files?" he asked her.

"I've been working on it every chance I get. I'm almost

done. There are a couple of things that might help you, but I can't say for sure until I finish with the last two files."

"You want to give me a hint?"

Anne-Marie smiled. "It's really not much. But I think I'll be able to finish today. So what about this afternoon or tomorrow? I'd like to give it to you all at once. Get your gut reaction. See what you think about it."

"Sounds good. It'll probably have to be tomorrow though. I'm on my way to New Orleans this afternoon to talk to the detective who caught Autumn Moser's case."

"That's fine. First thing tomorrow morning."

"Have you seen Bill?"

"He's in the break room."

Ryker found him there.

"Hey," Bill said. "I was just about to come see you. Jean Terry? Her medical records show that she was in—" he dug his notebook out of his pocket "—in stage four cancer." He met Ryker's gaze. "Dave confirmed that. Stage four—that's bad."

Something in the other detective's voice made Ryker take notice. "So what have you got?"

"Those papers on her dining table? They were insurance forms. She was changing beneficiaries on her policies. Signing them over to her niece. I can't quite figure out what's important about that, but I've got a feeling."

"A famous Bill Crenshaw feeling?" Bill was highly intuitive. Often his "feelings" turned out to be vital pieces of the puzzle. "What kind of policies?"

"The usual, I guess. One was from when she was born. It's got a lot of cash value built up." Bill shrugged. "Like I said, it's not much. By the way, her parents didn't know her cancer had come back."

"Give that info to Anne-Marie," Ryker said. "Maybe it's

something she can connect to another victim. She's almost done going through the files."

"Sure thing."

"And, Bill. We need to dig through 2004 records. I'm afraid we may not have found victim zero yet."

"St. Tammany records? That could take a while."

Ryker nodded. "I know. I'm on my way down to New Orleans to talk to Fred Samhurst, the detective who caught Autumn Moser's case. I'll pick up the 2004 cold case files. They've got a clerk sorting them for me. One way or another we've got to verify where this guy started."

Ryker didn't get much information from Fred Samhurst. He was defensive and claimed not to remember much about the case. When Ryker asked him how he decided that three-point blank shots to the chest didn't throw up a red flag, he'd merely shrugged and shaken his head.

By the time Ryker got back with his trunk stuffed with cold cases from the Eighth District Police Department on Royal Street in the French Quarter, it was after 6:00 p.m. He made it through one box by eleven, when he had to pick up Nicole.

She went straight to bed, claiming exhaustion. But he could tell she was uncomfortable around him, now that she knew that he'd dated one of the victims.

He couldn't blame her. He wasn't sure what was going on between them, either. And he sure as hell didn't understand what was going on inside him. He couldn't stop thinking about her, worrying about her.

Even though he'd watched out for her for a year, he'd only actually known her a few days. Still, he had no doubt in his mind that he would never forget her. Or get over her.

And that scared him almost as much as the October Killer did.

"SON OF A BITCH!" Ryker growled the next morning when he looked at the front page of the *St. Tammany Parish Record*. Right there, below the fold, was the sketch of the October Killer.

"Ryker?" Nicole's sleepy voice came from the bedroom. "What's wrong?"

"Nothing. Go back to sleep." He skimmed the article, which quoted the sheriff as saying, "This sketch was given to police by an unnamed witness who has been helping us with our investigation, after a recent encounter with the man depicted in the sketch. We want all residents of St. Tammany Parish to be aware that a dangerous killer is at large. Anyone who recognizes this man, please notify your local sheriff's office department immediately."

Fury ignited in Ryker's gut as a sense of dread settled on his chest. The things Hébert had written, about how invaluable Nicole's information was to the police, paled in comparison to this.

The sheriff was dangling Nicole as bait.

Burning with rage, Ryker dialed Mike Davis. The deputy chief answered on the first ring. "Don't start with me, Ryker. I'm not in the mood."

"What the hell does the sheriff think he's doing? Do you have any idea what's going to happen now?"

"I said don't start with me. Of course I know what's going to happen. We're going to be getting hundreds of tips from people who are sure they've seen this guy. Not to mention the phone calls from folks who hear something at night or are convinced the meter reader is about to break into their house and murder them. I've already talked to the sheriff about bringing in temporary staff to man the phones."

"The phones don't require trained personnel. Look, Mike. I know you didn't have a choice. Obviously the press release came directly from the sheriff's office. But I can't leave Nicole out there dangling like a worm on a hook. I need protection for her. The sheriff just painted a bull's eye right on her back."

Mike sighed. "I know. I'm already on it. I can give you a uniformed deputy—days only."

Ryker's chest tightened in relief. "That's fine. I'll be with her at night. Have the deputy call me and we'll work out times and places." Finally he had some real protection for Nicole. Protection and security. Surely Nicole couldn't get into trouble with a deputy watching her.

"It'll take me a while. I'll have him get in touch with you as soon as I can work out the logistics."

"Thanks, Mike."

"Yeah, don't thank me yet. I need Crenshaw back. Phillips is out with the flu."

Ryker grimaced. "Flu? Damn it." He understood. Mike couldn't afford to have his small cache of detectives diluted. Especially now, with the whole of St. Tammany Parish in an uproar about a serial killer at large. "I'll get Bill to bring me everything he's got so far."

"Ryker? That's not all."

"Not all? Damn, Mike. I don't have anything else you can take from me."

"Anne-Marie can't work with you. I need her full-time, supervising the telephones."

"She's supposed to have some information for me. I'll get with her this morning."

"Find that killer, Delancey."

"Trust me, Mike. I will." Ryker hung up and stared down at the newspaper's front page for a few seconds. Then he grabbed it, balled it up and flung it across the room.

He went to the bedroom door and rapped on the door facing. "Nic?"

He saw her start, then sit up. "What?"

"Get up. I need to take you to the restaurant. Job's always there by seven, right?"

She threw back the covers and got up, pushing her hair back from her face. "Unless he's going to market. Why?"

"What's he doing today—Saturday?"

"Saturday? He'll be there. We buy everything for the weekend on Friday."

"Good. I'm taking you over there. Sometime this morning, a uniformed deputy will report to you. You won't go anywhere except with him. He'll drive you to work and home and anywhere else you have to go. You will listen to him and do whatever he says. Understand?"

"No," she said, yawning. "What's wrong?"

"The sheriff put your sketch in the paper."

Nicole stared at him, her eyes wide. "Oh, my God, why?" she croaked.

"To show his constituents that he's on the ball on this serial killer case. But ostensibly to warn residents of the parish that there's a killer on the loose."

"What's going to happen now?"

Ryker sighed. "We're going to get hundreds of phone calls from people who are sure they've seen him."

"But that sketch was so vague."

"Yeah. That's the problem." Ryker sighed. "Call Job and make sure he's there, and I'll run you by your house to get some clothes, then to the restaurant."

"What'll you be doing today?"

"What else? Finding a killer."

Chapter Twelve

Ryker drove Nicole to the restaurant and took Job aside. "Have you got a weapon?" he asked him.

"I sure do," Job answered, eyeing Ryker suspiciously. "A 9 mm. I bought it after Katrina. Got me a carry permit, too." He reached inside the apron and pulled out the gun from his belt. "See?"

Ryker was surprised. "You carry that all the time?"

"Ever since I found out Nicki was in danger, I keep it on me all the time."

"I assume you know how to use it?"

Job's eyes narrowed. "I wasn't always a restaurant owner, Detective. Any other questions you got for me?"

Ryker shook his head. "I guess you saw the paper this morning."

"I did. Man, I've got to say, I sure wish I hadn't called her about Merina's kidney stone. If I had it to do over, I wouldn't. I tried to talk her into not going down to Henri's. But you know Nicki."

Ryker almost smiled. "I do know her."

"You want me to watch out for her? That's no problem, son. I've been watching out for her ever since she first walked in that door and asked me for a job. She's like a member of the family."

Ryker nodded. "I'm glad to hear that. It makes me feel better to know you care about her that much."

"One of these days I'm going to turn that question around on you."

"Turn it around?"

Job nodded and his black eyes snapped. "Ask you if you care about her. What your intentions are."

Ryker swallowed. *Don't ask me yet,* he thought. Not until the danger is over. He had to concentrate on keeping Nic alive. He had to lead with his head, not his heart.

"Job, as a law enforcement officer, I can't ask you to risk your life for hers. And I can't compel you to carry or use your weapon. In fact, I can't even condone it."

"You listen to me, son. Nicki'll be safe here with me, because anybody tries to get to her, they'll have to get past me. You think I'm going to make that easy for them?"

Looking at the big man, Ryker knew he meant exactly what he said. "I think getting past you to get to Nicole will be next to impossible." He held out his hand. Job took it.

"I can't tell you how much I appreciate it. I've got a deputy on his way over. He'll be guarding her, too. With both of you, I'm positive she'll be safer here than at my house. This killer attacks his victims when he's sure they're alone. And he's never used a gun. But after yesterday, we know he's got one."

"You go on and do your business. Catch him. We'll keep Nicki safe."

ON THE WAY TO THE OFFICE Ryker got a call from Deputy Harold Ingram, who told him Mike had assigned him to guard Nicole. Ryker gave him the address of the restaurant and his house, then he issued him orders not to let Nicole out of his sight.

"I mean that literally, Ingram."

"Yes, sir. I'm headed over there now. Don't worry, I'm on it. Will you be taking over or will I expect another officer?"

"I'll be there to pick her up. By six, unless something happens. I'll give you a call."

"Six sounds good."

"Thanks."

Ryker opened the door to the sheriff's office and found that it had turned into a madhouse. Phones were ringing off the hook. Several people Ryker had never seen before were answering them. Men in telephone company uniforms were running wires into the big conference room, where six phones sat on the table.

Ryker worked his way through the crowd to his desk. As he did, he spotted Anne-Marie holding a couple of manila folders and talking to a small group of women. She gestured toward the conference room, looked at her watch and apparently dismissed them with instructions about when to return. Then she headed toward his desk.

"Good morning," she said, sinking down into a side chair.

"Yeah? You think so?" he countered, smiling at her.

"No. Just trying to be polite."

"How many telephone people do you have to supervise?"

"Ten, so far." She waved her hand. "And they're setting up six more lines in the conference room. As you can see, it's a madhouse." She smiled wryly. "Do you think the sheriff had any idea what he was doing when he released that sketch?"

Ryker sighed. "That's a really good question. Looks like he was on the ball getting temps in here to answer the phones."

"You're right about that."

"Listen, Anne-Marie, I know you're hip-deep in alligators, so whatever you can give me on your research into the October Killer's case files will be appreciated."

Anne-Marie's dark brown eyes lit up. "Okay. See what you think about this." She set the two folders on the edge of his desk and opened one.

"We've got five victims, right? Daisy Howard, twenty-one, Bella Pottinger, thirty, Jennifer Gomez, twenty-three, Nicole Beckham, twenty-six, and Jean Terry, thirty-seven."

"Right." Ryker's brain flipped through the crime scene photos of the four dead women as she spoke, and he thought about how different they all were.

"I looked at everything they could possibly have in common, but nothing jelled. Not with all five of them."

"You didn't find anything?"

Anne-Marie held up a finger. "Until—"

He sat up expectantly, trying to tell himself not to get his hopes up, but excited by the slight note of triumph he heard in Anne-Marie's voice.

"Until I started looking at their parents. It took some digging, but I finally found something. Records of insurance policies, all from one particular company."

Despite his warning to himself, his heart leaped. "From one company?"

"Yes. The Mark Life Insurance Company. It's based out of Michigan."

Ryker frowned. "And the victims' parents are somehow connected by this company? All of them? Why, because they bought insurance policies?"

"Because they bought insurance policies on their children, specifically their daughters—" Anne-Marie paused. "At birth."

"Insurance policies." Ryker remembered Bill's mention

of Jean Terry's insurance policy, which she was signing over to her sister. "They're connected by insurance policies. What does that mean?" he muttered. "Was someone killing them for their insurance?"

"I have no idea. Mr. Howard told me that the insurance paid twenty-five thousand dollars upon his daughter Daisy's death. Which sounds like some kind of whole-life policy. But it's the only thing I could find that even remotely connects the victims."

Insurance. All five victims. Bought at birth. Birthdays in October.

"Ryker?" Anne-Marie said.

He blinked. "I'm trying to figure out how having that insurance policy could have led to their death. Do you have any idea who sold the parents the policies?"

A telephone company employee walked over and spoke to Anne-Marie. "Ma'am, the phones are ready. Are you ready to test them?"

She sighed and stood. "Yes. I need to get the temps set up. They'll be back in—" she checked her watch "—five minutes." She spoke to Ryker. "I'll leave you the folders. Hopefully you can make some sense out of them. Oh, and to answer your question, just one. Mrs. Gomez told me that her husband wrote the policy on their daughter, Jennifer. The other parents I could reach promised me they'll dig out the policies and see what they can find."

"Jennifer Gomez's father is an insurance agent?"

"Until he died a few years ago."

"And they collected twenty-five thousand dollars on their daughter, too? Have you contacted the insurance company?"

She nodded. "Several times. But they haven't returned my calls. Their number is in one of the folders if you want to try again."

Ryker reached for the folders. "Thanks, Anne-Marie. Maybe I can get a lead out of this."

"One last thing. Mrs. Gomez faxed me the policy on Jennifer. It's in that second folder. I don't know if it will help or not."

"Thanks, Anne-Marie. You did a great job. This is a lot more information than I had before."

She smiled and waved as she headed to the large conference room to set up more telephones in there for tips.

Ryker picked up his phone and called Bill. He needed to get all the information Bill had about Jean Terry's life insurance policy.

Bill had said he had a feeling that the insurance would be important so Ryker wanted to get his take on this information. Maybe together, they could figure out what the connection was between the insurance policies and the October Killer's victims.

RYKER HAD JUST FINISHED talking with Bill and was debating the chances of catching anyone in the offices at Mark Life Insurance Company on Saturday when his phone rang. The screen displayed an unidentified number.

"This is Detective Delancey," he said.

"Detective? This is Albert Moser."

"Mr. Moser. What can I do for you?"

"I've found something in my daughter's things that might help you find the bastard that killed her." Moser's voice was unsteady, as if he were excited or upset. He was probably both.

"I thought the NOPD cleaned out all your daughter's things."

"That's just it. They did. But after you asked me, I decided to look again. What I found isn't much. It's a scrapbook. She'd hidden it behind the headboard of her bed.

It's got notes about him and a couple of things that might belong to him. A key ring. A napkin. Some pictures. But the biggest thing is there's a sketch. You know I told you Autumn loved to draw. This is a sketch of a man. It could be him—the scumbag who killed her."

Ryker frowned. If the police had searched Autumn Moser's bedroom, they'd surely moved her furniture. How had they missed something as big as a scrapbook? A thought hit him. When he was in Moser's house there had been a scrapbook sitting next to him on a side table. What if Moser had manufactured evidence, hoping it would lead to his daughter's killer?

"That does sound promising," he said carefully. "Can you bring it to the office? Or I can have somebody come over and pick it up."

"I was hoping you'd come, Detective. You can see where she hid it. The New Orleans police shouldn't have missed it. But like I've been telling everybody, they weren't the least bit interested in finding the man who killed my daughter."

"I can send a deputy. He'll take photographs and get everything to me right away."

There was a pause, and then Moser's voice took on an angry, out-of-control quality. "You're just like the rest of them, aren't you? Look at all those other women. How can the sheriff's office be working so hard to find their killer, and nobody is trying to help me?"

"Mr. Moser," Ryker said, trying to keep the irritation out of his voice. "You need to relax. I can promise you we're working on your daughter's case, too. We believe the same man who killed her killed these other women."

"Well, you're wrong! This scrapbook could have evidence about that man. You'll know I'm right when you see it." Moser took a deep breath. "Please. I need to put it in your hands, Detective. You're the only person who's ever treated me with respect. The only one who's listened to me. You've got to help me now. It's the last thing I can do for my daughter, and I can't do it without your help."

Damn, the man knew how to lay on the guilt. It was as if he knew how bad Ryker felt that he hadn't been able to stop the killer before now. Ryker checked his watch. He'd planned to run over to the restaurant anyway, to make sure Ingram had gotten there and to see for himself that Nicole was all right. After he drove up to Covington to see the scrapbook Moser had, he could head south to Mandeville and check on Nicole.

"Okay, Mr. Moser. I'll be there in about half an hour. How does that sound?"

"Thank you, Detective. I truly believe this is going to make everything right."

Ryker hung up and stood. Then a thought made him reach for the folders Anne-Marie had given him. While he was at Moser's he could ask him about insurance policies. Maybe he and his wife had taken out a policy on their daughters when they were born. It would be one more link in the chain that proved these deaths were the fault of one man—the October Killer.

He headed for his car, not relishing the eight-plus-mile drive to Covington from the sheriff's office in Chef Voleur. It would put him thirteen miles from the L'Orage Restaurant, and that meant probably an hour before he could get there to check on Nicole—more if Moser was chatty.

Still, this was a small thing to do for the grieving father. Besides, who knew? Moser might be right. The scrapbook could be legitimate. If Autumn Moser had drawn a likeness of the man she was seeing, the man her father was certain had killed her, then Ryker would be that much closer to catching the killer.

ALBERT MOSER HUNG UP his phone and smiled. He sat in his daughter's Ford Focus, which he'd picked up that morning from the parking garage where it had been ever since her death, and which was parked across the street from the Chef Voleur Sheriff's Office.

He waited until he saw Delancey's white BMW pull out of the sheriff's office parking lot and turned north, toward Covington.

"That takes care of you, Detective," he muttered. "For now." He'd known by the tone of the detective's voice that he was skeptical about the scrapbook.

Thinking about it now, Albert realized he hadn't needed to put the scrapbook together and make it look as if it had been taped behind Autumn's headboard. Just telling Detective Delancey that he had a box of things the NOPD had returned to him would have sufficed.

Too late now. The scrapbook was there, sitting on the table beside Albert's chair. It was there because Albert had put it there the night before.

If Delancey decided to break into his house while he wasn't there, he'd find it, just like Albert told him he would.

Albert turned the Focus southward, toward Dupre Street in Mandeville, where L'Orage Restaurant was located. He was glad he'd kept Autumn's car serviced and stored in the parking garage all this time. Autumn's tags and stickers were years out of date, but if he drove carefully and stuck to back streets, that was no problem. He hadn't come this far to let carelessness spoil his plans.

His fists tightened on the steering wheel. What a stupid girl Nicole Beckham was, giving a description of him to the police, and letting them stick it on the front page of the newspaper. The sketch had bothered him. It hadn't really looked like him, but it still made him feel conspicuous. As if everyone he passed was checking him out thinking, *Is that the October Killer?*

But in any case, this was the second time Nicole had seen him. He couldn't chance her identifying him. He had to move quickly, while Detective Delancey was on his wild-goose chase.

It would take the detective at least thirty minutes to drive to Albert's house. Another few minutes to realize that Albert wasn't going to answer his door. A few more minutes if he decided to break in to ensure that Albert was all right, but Albert knew he couldn't count on that. Nor could he count on the time it would take Delancey to get back to the restaurant. Once the detective realized he'd been duped, he'd call and send every patrol car available to the restaurant.

He'd watched Delancey all night, determined not to let him out of his sight for one second until he could put his plan into motion. Early this morning Delancey had taken Nicole to the restaurant, then headed for the sheriff's office, which was exactly what Albert had counted on.

Twenty minutes. That was all he needed. Once he was done, the last person who could identify him as the killer would be gone. He'd drive to the restaurant, go inside and take care of her and whoever else was there, switch cars again and be on his way home in less than fifteen minutes.

He had a prescription refill waiting at his pharmacy in Covington. He'd pick it up. That would give him an alibi and explain why he hadn't been at home when Delancey got there. He'd remembered the prescription at the last minute.

He glanced at his scrapbook sitting on the passenger seat. "I'm sorry, Autumn. I tried to get justice for you. If something happens—at least you'll know I tried." He sighed. "And so will your sister. Even if she can't forgive me, maybe at least she'll understand when she reads the note I left for her."

At that instant, Albert's cell phone rang. He nearly jumped out of his skin, and almost sideswiped a car in the other lane. Pulling the phone from his pocket, he looked at the display.

Christy.

No. He couldn't talk to her. Not right now. He tried to keep his eyes on the road, but the damn phone kept ringing.

Finally, it stopped. Albert breathed a sigh of relief and went to set it down in the console.

It rang again. Christy wasn't going to stop calling until he answered. She knew he never went anywhere without his cell phone. She'd made him promise he wouldn't. If he didn't answer, she'd call the deputy who patrolled his neighborhood to check on him.

Albert pressed the answer key. "Christy," he said breathlessly.

"Dad? What's wrong? You sound out of breath."

"No, I—"

"You've got to get more exercise. I worry about you sitting in that house all day every day."

"Christy," he interrupted. "What do you want?"

"I'm back from the seminar in Germany. I was just checking to see how you're doing. I was thinking, if you don't feel like coming up here for Christmas, maybe I can get a couple of days off and come down there. We could at least go out for Christmas dinner. I got you something in Germany."

"That sounds good." He paused, thinking desperately. "I can't talk now. I've got corn bread in the oven. It's burning. Let me call you back."

"I'm glad you're cooking corn bread. But, Dad, are you sure you're okay? You sound funny."

"I'm fine, Christy-girl. I'm fine. Bye." Albert dropped the phone into the console and grabbed the steering wheel with both hands. They were white-knuckled, with blue veins crisscrossing the rough, wrinkled skin. He made a right turn, hardly slowing down at all. He had to hurry to get to L'Orage in time. He had to kill Nicole Beckham. Maybe, once she was dead, Delancey would focus on his daughter's death.

If he could just get one detective to listen to him, they'd be able to track down the man who killed Autumn. He'd tell them to talk to her friends to see if they'd met the man, something the NOPD had failed to do. They'd look seriously at the sketch she'd drawn. Albert knew the man in that sketch was Autumn's killer. He just knew it.

NICOLE LIFTED THE LID off the pot and sniffed at the chicken stock she was reducing. The aroma made her mouth water. She was acting as sous chef for Richard Tesch, since she wasn't going to be here for the dinner service. Deputy Ingram had told her Ryker would be picking her up around six.

Still, it felt great to be cooking anything, even chicken stock. She liked the kitchen on Saturday mornings. It was her favorite time. Since they weren't open for lunch on Saturdays, she and Job were the only ones there in the mornings. Richard and the rest of the staff weren't due in until two o'clock.

She drew in a deep breath. The kitchen was quiet and warm, and smelled delicious. Like home, or at least like Nicole had always imagined home would smell.

Job was humming an old hymn and kneading a huge ball of bread dough in preparation for baking his signature homemade French bread. A second bowl of dough was sitting on the top of the stove, rising. The aroma of yeast and flour mixed with the rich smell of the chicken stock to fill the kitchen.

Nicole dipped the hot stock into a smaller pot, separating it from the chicken bones and skin.

"Let me get that, Nicki," Job said, washing and drying his hands. He put on oven mitts then picked up the heavy pot and lid and drained out the last of the broth. "I'll take these out to the Dumpster. Stock smells real good today."

"It does, doesn't it?" She smiled at him. "Why don't you tell Deputy Ingram to come in and have some lunch? The tea has steeped enough. I'm going to sweeten it and put it in the refrigerator, then I'll make us all a chicken sandwich."

The deputy was making his half-hour rounds, checking all sides of the restaurant and the surrounding buildings. Nicole liked him. He was polite and quiet and appeared to be very good at his job.

Job pushed open the heavy door that led from the kitchen out into the alley where the garbage Dumpster was. Nicole set the smaller stockpot back on the gas and turned it to high. It took a couple of hours on high heat to reduce the stock to the consistency she liked.

She grabbed the ten-pound bag of sugar and turned back toward the island, where a large jug of tea sat.

Outside, she heard Job's muffled voice, and the deputy's answer.

Then she heard several pops.

She jumped and dropped the bag of sugar. White crystals slid with a whishing sound across the dark red tile. She watched in a strange panicked daze as they bounced and sparkled.

Then came another pop, different in pitch.

Oh, no! She knew that sound! *Gunshots.* Someone was shooting.

"Job!" she cried. She stared at the back door, willing him to pull it open and walk in, followed by Ingram. Maybe she was just jumpy. Maybe the pops had been a car with bad sparkplugs or bad valves or something.

She took another step.

More pops sounded, deeper, louder, closer to the door. Then a harsh cry.

Dear God! That was Job's voice. They *were* gunshots and he was hurt.

"Job!" she screamed.

Again, her first instinct was to run to the kitchen door and fling it open to check on Job and Ingram. But something—Ryker's warnings about precautions, as well as her own instinct for self-preservation—kept her rooted in place.

If the killer was out there, if he'd shot Job and the deputy, what could she do, except get herself killed?

I need to help Job, she objected.

Ryker's words reverberated in her head. *Exercise reasonable precautions.*

But that was to keep her from getting hurt. He hadn't told her what to do if someone else were hurt on her account.

All at once a different sound reverberated outside the door.

Footsteps, crunching on pavement.

Let it be Job, she prayed. *Please, let him be okay!*

But what if it wasn't?

As she watched, the door swung open, but nobody appeared. She looked around. The pantry was right beside the exterior door. No escape that way.

The swinging doors that led out into the dining room were on the other side of the room, around the big granite-topped island. She'd never make it. And there was nothing behind her but the industrial-size refrigerator.

She measured the distance to the dining room with her eyes. Maybe she *could* make it if she could skirt the big island that stood between her and the swinging doors fast enough. But that was a long way, and she'd be exposed if whoever was out there shooting came inside.

At that very instant a dark figure stepped through the door into the kitchen. Having nowhere else to go, she ducked behind the big stainless-steel stove, putting its bulk between her and the man.

It was him. The man who'd tried to kill her on the River Road. He had on those ridiculously big, thick glasses and that black hooded sweatshirt. But this time the hood didn't shadow his face. This time his head was bare.

His hair was gray and thin on top, she observed aimlessly as he lifted his arm and pointed the gun at her and pulled the trigger. She felt a little swish of air close to her cheek as she ducked. She cried out at the same time as the report rang out—much louder than a pop.

A second shot rang out, then the man cursed. She heard his shoe soles crunching in the sugar. He was headed straight for her. And there was only about thirty feet from the door to the stove.

Nicole crouched down and doubled her fists, praying that a bullet wouldn't hit her.

THE FARTHER RYKER DROVE, the more worried he got. He really needed to know that Ingram was there and that everything was all right. He dialed the number Ingram had called him on. No answer.

Damn it, he should have verified with Ingram that the number was his cell number. He looked at his watch.

"Screw it," he muttered, swinging left into a driveway and turning around. "Moser can wait. Nic can't."

He couldn't justify driving all the way out to Covington until he'd verified that Nic was okay. As he sped toward L'Orage he tried the office receptionist, but of course the line went straight to voice mail. All those tips and panicked calls about the serial killer.

"We are experiencing an increased number of calls at the current—"

He cut the connection, then tried Dispatch. Same thing. So he dialed Mike's cell number. Mike answered on the second ring. "What?"

"Mike. What's Ingram's cell number?"

"Ryker, what the hell?"

"I can't get through, and he's not answering, if the number I have is his cell."

Mike told him to hang on for a second. He came back with the number.

"Damn it, that is his cell number. Something's wrong. Mike, send backup to L'Orage Restaurant, 101 Dupree Street, in Mandeville. Now!"

"You got it."

Ryker stuck his cell phone in his jacket pocket and turned his blue lights on. He gripped the wheel with both hands and hit the gas.

He made it to the restaurant in eleven minutes. A light blue Ford Focus was parked carelessly near the entrance to the alley that ran behind the restaurant. He pulled in right behind the little car and threw his BMW into Park without bothering to cut the engine. Then he jumped out and drew his weapon.

The first thing he saw when he rounded the rear of the Focus was Ingram, crumpled on the ground. Fear stole his breath. The killer was here. He needed an ambulance. He pulled out his cell phone as he scanned the alley, letting his gun's barrel follow his gaze. Closer to the kitchen door, he saw a mass of white, moving slowly.

God, no. Not Job!

Mike's gruff voice came on the line.

"Mike," Ryker snapped. "Two men down. One an officer. Send a bus with the backup. Hurry!"

He pocketed his cell phone and knelt and touched Ingram's neck. The deputy didn't move, but his skin felt warm. He was alive—maybe.

"Backup's coming. Hang in there," Ryker whispered as he headed toward Job. He couldn't afford to wait to see if Ingram responded. He had to get to Job.

And Nicole!

Job lay on his side, his right hand flung out. The 9 mm semi-automatic lay a few inches away from his fingers. A huge red blossom of blood stained the front of his apron, but even though he was wounded, Job was inching slowly toward the door. He was trying to get to his gun.

"Job!" Ryker called softly, stooping to check on him. A gunshot from inside the kitchen stopped him.

Nicole!

Job grunted and pushed himself an inch farther.

"Job," he said, his breath whooshing out. "It's okay. Backup's coming. Hold on, man."

"Nicki," Job whispered.

"I know. I'm going in after her." Ryker stepped over to the door and set his shoulder against it, ready to push it open.

"Let her be okay," he whispered.

Chapter Thirteen

Nicole cringed as a bullet ricocheted off the stainless-steel edge of the oven's door. She had no time left. The killer was almost on top of her.

Fear arrowed through her, sharpening her sense of hearing and smell to super-powers. The sound of the killer's shoes crunching on the sugar seemed deafening. Her nostrils burned and her stomach turned at the overwhelming stench of hot chicken stock mixed with the faint odor of gas coming from the burning eye.

Just then a shadow appeared on the tile floor beside her. The shadow of an arm holding a gun. This was it. She was going to die, crouching in the corner like a coward.

No. She would *not* die like this. Not without a fight. Ryker had told her she was brave. He'd said he was impressed.

He'd be so disappointed in her if she didn't try to defend herself. But—hadn't he also said there was no way she could protect herself against a killer?

She was sure he was right. But she had to try. She took a deep breath, trying to draw in courage. The pungent scent of chicken broth sharpened her senses. An idea slammed into her brain in the fraction of a second it took for the killer to take another step and aim down at her.

Without having any hope that her sudden brainstorm

would work, she rose, screaming, "No!" and shoved at the hot stockpot with her bare hands.

The pot tumbled, splashing scalding-hot chicken stock everywhere. The man screeched. The gun went off. Nicole winced at the sound and used all her energy to dive past him toward the island. She felt a jarring impact and a sharp burning sensation in her side.

A bullet? Had she been shot? As her body spasmed with pain, she fell short of the island and her head slammed against something hard. Stars burst before her eyes.

The last thing she heard was a beloved familiar voice yell out, "Freeze, you son of a bitch!"

THE MESS ON THE KITCHEN floor was treacherous, but although Ryker slipped, he regained his footing immediately, unlike the killer, who was prostrate, rolling in hot liquid with steam rising from his clothes.

Ryker grabbed a handful of the man's sweatshirt, which was soaked with what smelled like chicken soup, and pushed the barrel of his gun into the back of the his neck. He put his weight on one knee right in the middle of the man's back.

"Shut up!" he yelled. "On second thought, don't. I'd love to shoot you right here for resisting arrest."

"I'm burning up! She burned me!" the man screamed.

Ryker buried the nose of the gun in the man's flesh.

"Okay, okay! Don't shoot!"

"Give me your hands," Ryker ordered him. The man tried, but he couldn't move with Ryker's knee pressed into his back.

"Nic?" Ryker called out, but she didn't respond. His heart was racing so fast already that he didn't think it could go any faster, but the ominous silence sent it into overdrive. He felt as if he couldn't breathe.

At that instant, he heard sirens. *Backup.*

Hurry, damn it! I've got to check on Nicole.

Footsteps crunched on pavement and the door slammed open. "Delancey?"

It was Ted Dagewood. The voice grated on Ryker's ears, but he was happy to hear it.

"Ryker!" It was Bill, running in around behind Dagewood. Bill tapped him on the shoulder. "I got him."

Ryker rose and stepped back. Bill dragged the man to his feet and shoved him facedown on the kitchen counter. Dagewood pulled out handcuffs, grousing. "Damn, this place stinks to holy hell."

Ryker heard more footsteps. A quick glance through the open door told him the EMTs had arrived. He saw one bending over Job.

As Bill and Dagewood marched the killer out the door, Ryker scanned the kitchen.

"Nic!" he shouted. "Where are you?" Then he saw her. She was lying just around the end corner of the island. Her pale, still face terrified him.

He bent over to touch her neck, to check and see if she was alive. But his hand hesitated just above her skin.

What if she wasn't? What would he do? His fingers began to shake.

Then her eyelid twitched.

Ryker's heart turned completely upside down in his chest and spasmed in relief. It hurt. God, did it hurt. But he relished the pain. *She was alive.* He touched her, felt her warm skin against his fingertips, and his vision grew hazy.

"Ryker?" she whispered without opening her eyes. "Is that you?"

He bent his head and touched his lips to her temple. "Yeah, hon," he rasped. He had to clear his throat. "It's me."

She squinted and moaned. "My head hurts. And my hands. And my—my side."

"Stay still. The EMTs are here."

"No, wait. Where's Job?" she whispered. "And Deputy Ingram?"

"Excuse me, sir," a voice said from behind Ryker. "I need to get to her."

Nicole's hand reached out for him. Ryker took it. "Don't worry. I'm not going anywhere," he whispered to her. Then he stood and let the EMT do his job.

He still couldn't see worth crap. He rubbed at his eyes and was surprised when his knuckles came away damp.

He glanced around at the kitchen. The floor was covered with sugar and chicken broth. The smell was overwhelming at best. Sickening at worst. What the hell had happened here? And why had Job and Ingram been outside, leaving Nicole alone in the kitchen? He shook his head. It would take a while before everything was sorted out.

His gaze spotted something on the floor, pushed up next to the foot of the island. He bent down and retrieved a pair of glasses, thick lenses with heavy frames. Just like Nicole had described.

The killer's. Here was one thing he could find out right now. The identity of the October Killer.

"Nic, I'll be right back," he promised, then turned and headed outside, where Bill and Dagewood were putting the suspect into the back of a squad car. Ryker strode over to the vehicle.

Dagewood turned toward him. "Your girl all right?" he asked.

Ryker nodded, a little surprised at the concern in the man's voice. Not like the Dagewood he knew. "I hope so." He gestured toward the car. "Who is he?"

The detective shook his head. "No idea. He's not talking.

The EMTs say we've got to take him to the hospital. He's got burns from that chicken broth. His hands and face are already popping out with blisters."

Bill had just closed the car door when Ryker stepped over to it. He pulled the door open again and leaned down to look inside.

The man's face was distorted by the blisters of second-degree burns, but Ryker still recognized him, even without his glasses.

"Albert Moser," he breathed, his throat closing in shock.

Albert Moser's pale blue eyes stared at Ryker seemingly without recognition. His raw, blistered face was blank.

"Moser, what the hell? Did you kill all those girls? Don't tell me you killed your own daughter?"

Moser just kept staring at him for a moment, then looked away. Ryker tossed the glasses into the far seat. He spoke to the deputy at the wheel. "Those are his glasses."

He straightened and closed the car door, then rapped on the roof to indicate to the driver that he could go.

Bill eyed him. "You okay?"

Ryker didn't feel okay. The shock of seeing Moser sitting there had drained the last of his energy. "I'm not sure. Do you know who that is?"

Bill shook his head.

"That's the father of the girl who was murdered in New Orleans. Albert Moser."

"The one who kept calling? Begging us to find his daughter's killer? That doesn't make sense."

"No, it doesn't."

"So what the hell does that mean?" Bill asked. "Is he the October Killer?"

"Hell if I know. I'm as confused as you are. More. I talked to the man. Sat in his living room. Told him I'd do everything I could to bring his daughter's killer to justice."

Bill met Ryker's gaze. He looked as stunned as Ryker felt. "He shot Ingram and the restaurant owner? He tried to kill Nicole? Why?"

Ryker couldn't do anything but shake his head. "Your guess is as good as mine. As soon as he's done at the hospital, let's get him in and talk to him. Oh, and can you get a warrant to search his house? He called me earlier to tell me he had a scrapbook that belonged to his daughter. Now I can see that it was probably a lie, to lure me as far away from Nicole as he could, but we need to search everything. House, car, everything."

"Detective Dagewood?" A uniformed deputy walked up. "That blue Ford Focus over there? It's got expired tags. I mean years expired. I ran them and they belonged to an Autumn Lynn Moser."

Ryker stepped over. "That's Albert Moser in the police car that's pulling out. The Focus must have been his daughter's car."

Dagewood nodded. "Get it towed to the pound," he ordered the deputy, then turned to Bill. "Include that vehicle in the warrant, would you?"

"Detective?" the deputy continued. "There's something in the front seat. A big book of some kind. Like an album."

"Leave it alone until we get the warrant," Dagewood told him. "Just get it towed. And don't let anything happen to that book."

Bill clapped Ryker on the shoulder. "You okay?"

Ryker shrugged. "It's going to take a while to sort all this out. What's the word on Ingram and Job?"

"They're both headed to the hospital. I think Job's okay. The bullet was a through-and-through. His right shoulder.

Ingram—I don't know. That coward sneaked up on him and shot him in the back."

"Damn. Where are they taking them? To St. Tammany?"

Bill nodded. "St. Tammany Regional Medical Center. Why don't you go check on Nicole? I'll take care of things here. We can talk once you know she's okay."

Ryker opened his mouth to protest. It was his case. He should be taking charge of everything. But at that moment, he heard the kitchen door open and saw an EMT walking Nicole out. Nicole had white gauze covering both hands and a small strip bandage on her forehead.

Ryker met them halfway up the alley. "How is she?" he asked the EMT.

"Doing fine. Her hands are burned, just first degree, but they'll be painful for a few days. And she'll have a nasty bruise on her head and her side where we think the stockpot hit her, but she's fine. She's going to need some help for a day or two, though."

Ryker looked at Nicole, whose face was still pale. "No problem. I'll take care of her."

"Where's Job?" Nicole asked. "Nobody will tell me anything." Her eyes brimmed over with tears. "I heard the gunshots. He's been shot, hasn't he?"

"Hey, Nic. Listen to me." Ryker put his hands gently on her shoulders. "Job's gone to the hospital, along with Deputy Ingram. Job was shot in the shoulder, but he's doing okay. Ingram isn't in as good a shape as Job, but the doctors are taking good care of him." He looked at the EMT. "Are you taking her to the hospital?"

When the EMT shook his head, Ryker continued. "What do I need to do about her hands?"

The young man shook his head. "We iced them for a few minutes. Just keep them clean and bandaged. I've given her a tranquilizer, and the physician on call will call a prescription for a painkiller in to her pharmacy. Do you know where it is?"

"Nic? Your drugstore?"

She shook her head. "I don't—"

Ryker took out a business card and scribbled the phone number of a pharmacy near his house. He handed it to the EMT. "Have them call it in there."

"I can take a shower, can't I?" Nicole asked the EMT.

"You could, but it's not going to feel good on those hands." He looked at her, then at Ryker, then back at her. "You could—ask someone to help you clean up."

"I told you, I'll take care of her."

Nicole's face turned pink.

"Come on, Nic, let's go. I'm taking you home and putting you to bed."

"I want to go see Job—and Deputy Ingram."

Ryker shook the EMT's hand and thanked him, then he led Nicole past the ambulance and the blue Focus to his car. He opened the passenger door and helped her inside, then reached around and fastened her seat belt for her.

"Ryker? Was that him? The October Killer? Who is he?" Her voice faded.

"I'll tell you all about it later, okay?"

"Okay," she said drowsily.

He kissed her on the forehead, near the bandage. Her skin was warm. She looked up at him as he pulled away. Her eyes were dilated, and the lids were heavy. The tranquilizer had kicked in. He closed the passenger door and got in on the driver's side and started the engine.

"Ryker?"

"Close your eyes, Nic. Rest."

"Are we going to…?" Her voice faded.

"We're going home, hon. I'm taking you home."

RYKER GOT NICOLE to his house and bathed and into bed, then he ran out to the drugstore on the next block to pick up her prescription. When he got back and brought the tablets and a glass of water into the bedroom, she was asleep.

For a few moments he stood there, staring down at her. He'd had a hell of a time getting all the chicken broth and sugar off her. He'd made her sit on the toilet seat so he could undress her and wash the sticky, smelly goop off. She'd protested, but it hadn't taken her long to agree that she couldn't do it herself and she wouldn't sleep a wink covered with the sticky mess.

So she'd sat still while he removed her blouse and carefully washed her face, neck arms and torso with a soft terry washcloth and warm water.

She'd endured his ministrations. That was the best spin he could put on it. She'd closed her eyes when he'd started bathing her chest and back and belly. When he'd told her to stand so he could take off her pants and wash her legs and feet, she'd obeyed, acting like a doomed prisoner.

Touching her, ministering to her, had him hard and groaning to himself in no time, but her sad, exhausted demeanor quickly turned his lust into concern.

Could she just be drowsy from the tranquilizer? He'd like to believe that, but he was pretty sure there was more to it than that.

He'd finally gotten her reasonably clean and helped her put on one of his undershirts. Then he'd led her from the bathroom into the bedroom and helped her into bed.

Now as he watched her, all the horror of finding her in that kitchen at the mercy of the October Killer came back to him in spades. "I am so sorry, Nic. I didn't take care of you."

She murmured something, then sighed quietly and her breathing evened out. She was sound asleep.

As he bent down to kiss her forehead, he heard the un-mistakable ring of his cell phone out in the living room. He slipped out the door and pulled it shut, then answered the phone.

It was Bill. "How's Nicole?"

"She's asleep. What have you got?"

"Between the EMTs and the crime scene analysts, we've got a pretty good picture of what happened. Moser must have either been at the restaurant already when he called you, or he was watching the sheriff's office to be sure you headed toward Covington. From the way he parked the Focus, it was pretty obvious he'd planned to go in the kitchen door. But I think seeing Ingram surprised him. Ingram had his back to the street, checking the alley when Moser shot him."

"Damn," Ryker said. "In the back."

"Yeah." Bill went on. "Job told us he'd come out to get Ingram to go inside and have a sandwich. When he heard the shot, he drew his gun but Moser managed to shoot him in the shoulder before he could get a shot off."

"And he left both of them to die in that alley in their own blood." Ryker pushed his fingers through his hair. "I don't know, Bill. I guess he fooled me completely. I can't picture him as a cold-blooded killer."

"You never know what people are capable of," Bill agreed.

"So he went straight inside to find Nicole?"

"Yep. Nicole had ducked behind the stove to hide."

Ryker allowed himself a grim smile. "Good for her. Where did all that sugar come from?"

"From what she told the EMT, she'd been about to sweeten a jug of tea, and dropped the bag when she heard the shots. She hid behind the stove, which was big enough to shield her until Moser got close. Then she shoved the pot at him. Burned the crap out of him. The EMT said the pot must have bounced off Moser and hit her in the side as she dived for cover."

Ryker's eyes pricked with emotion. She'd saved herself. She'd done what she'd told him she could do ever since he'd first spoken to her. She'd taken care of herself.

He cleared his throat. "Are they going to release Moser from the hospital?"

"Yeah. I think we'll be able to get him in for questioning within the next hour. You going to be able to make it? I can handle it if—"

"I'll make it. See you there."

Ryker hung up and rubbed his eyes. He went back into the bedroom to check on Nicole. She was still asleep. He touched a strand of her hair, pushing it away from her face.

"You didn't need me after all, did you?" he whispered. "I guess keeping a hot pot of chicken broth on the stove could qualify as *reasonable precautions.*" He bent over and pressed a kiss to her cheek. "I love you, Nic. I know you don't trust me. I know you think we're too different. But I swear—" He stopped, his heart in his throat.

She'd moved.

Holding his breath, he watched her stir, heard her murmur something, then wince, as if she was in pain.

He thought she'd said his name.

"It's okay, Nic. You're home. You're safe."

She made a little noise in her throat, then settled down and her breathing evened out.

He hadn't meant to wake her. Surely she hadn't heard him. His heart in his throat, he started to back out of the room, and then thought about clean clothes. If he was going to interrogate Moser, he needed to shower and change.

He headed into the bathroom and splashed cold water on

his face. He looked at himself in the mirror for a second. He needed a shave and his eyes were red—because he kept rubbing them. Not because he'd been close to crying.

He took a quick shower and shaved. After he dressed, back in the living room, he grabbed his cell phone and dialed his brother.

"I heard about the shooting, old man. Are you all right? What happened?"

"I'm fine. Nicole's got burns on her hands. Just first degree, but they're going to be painful. She's asleep now, here at my house. I've got a thousand things to do and I don't want to leave her alone. Would you—?"

"Your timing sucks." Reilly sighed. "Okay, let me call and tell Jen that I can't do dinner tonight."

"I thought you said you didn't date."

"I don't. It's for damn sure that Jen won't go out with me again after I stand her up."

"Reilly—"

"No worries, Ryker. I'm on my way."

AN HOUR LATER, Ryker was sitting across from Albert Moser in an interrogation room at the sheriff's office in Chef Voleur. Under his folded hands was a scrapbook. The first half of it contained pictures of a young happy family—husband, wife and two daughters. The pages were filled with pictures of the girls at every age, from infancy to adulthood. Both of them were beautiful.

The second half of the book contained enough evidence to put Albert Moser in prison for the rest of his life.

"If you don't talk to me, Albert, I'm going to have to assume that you not only killed these lovely young women, but you killed your daughter, too."

Moser looked at Ryker with undisguised agony in his eyes. Ryker was certain he hadn't killed his own daughter.

But nothing else had worked to get Moser talking. So he'd resorted to baiting him with the accusation that he'd killed Autumn.

"Listen to me, Albert. I can't begin to understand the pain you must be going through. I lost my older sister several years ago, but as bad as that was, I'm sure it's not much compared to losing a child. I've seen what's in this scrapbook. You had two beautiful daughters, and someone took one of them away from you."

Moser was looking at his hands. He didn't react to Ryker's words.

"All the women you went after were babies you'd written life insurance policies for, weren't they? That's how you found them. How you chose them. You knew when they were born because you had their insurance policies." Ryker took a deep breath. He was pulling out all the stops.

"It's all right here in your scrapbook. The policies. The newspaper clippings about the murders. Why'd you do it, Albert? To cover up your murder of your daughter? You wrote a policy on her, too, didn't you? Twenty-five thousand dollars. That's a lot of money. And it's not like Autumn was a good girl. Not like your older daughter, Christmas. Autumn didn't deserve that money, did she? You knew she'd only use it to buy drugs—"

Suddenly, Albert Moser sprang up out of his chair and lunged at Ryker. He didn't get very far, because his hands were cuffed, and Ryker easily sidestepped him.

"You're wrong! You bastard, you're wrong!" Moser collapsed on the scarred wooden table, sobbing.

Two uniformed deputies appeared at the door, but Ryker waved them away with a shake of his head. He glanced at the two-way mirror and held up his hand, palm out, hoping Mike and whoever else was watching would get his message. He just needed a little more time.

Albert Moser was about to break.

Ryker went around the table and helped Moser back into his chair. Then he sat down again. "Tell me how I'm wrong, Albert. All I have to go by is this scrapbook. I see the insurance policies, the newspaper clippings. What I don't see is anything that shows me that your daughter is any different than the girls you killed."

"I loved my Autumn. I'd have done anything for her," Moser said brokenly. "She was my baby. But after her mother died, she got a little wild. She got mixed up with some lowlife—some married man. *That's* who killed her. If I could have got my hands on him, I'd have beat him to death. I'd have made him suffer before he died."

"But you killed Daisy Howard and Jennifer Gomez and Bella Pottinger and Jean Terry instead. What did they do— that they deserved to die? You know, each one of them was somebody's baby, too."

Moser shook his head back and forth, back and forth. "I know. It hurt me—so bad. But I had to get the police's attention. Police don't care anything about girls who get killed walking around in dangerous alleys late at night. They figure those girls get what they deserve." He stopped shaking his head and looked at Ryker. "That's what the detective told me. He said my daughter, my girl, shouldn't have been out there. Said I should have taken better care of her."

Ryker grimaced. Samhurst shouldn't have said that. "He was wrong. I know. You tried your best to take care of your daughters, didn't you, after your wife died. So why did you kill those other girls? Was it to get the police's attention?"

"Sure. I figured if women kept dying on the same day every year, the police would take notice. They'd look back at other cases, and they'd find Autumn's case and reopen it. Then they'd find the man who murdered her."

Ryker had expected something like what Moser was telling him, but he was still stunned. Moser had thought that he could get his daughter's case reopened by repeating the murder. He'd killed a woman each October, on or near his daughter's birthday—the day she'd died.

Ryker rubbed a place in the center of his forehead that was hurting, then studied Moser. How had the man made the leap from getting his daughter's case reopened to killing women with similar birthdays?

"But, Albert, Autumn was killed in New Orleans. Wouldn't it have made more sense to focus there?"

Moser shook his head. "I would have, if I'd had data on young women there. I only sold a couple of policies in New Orleans. Most of my clients, especially for the babies, were in St. Tammany Parish. But Autumn lived here, right here in Covington. The St. Tammany sheriff should have avenged her death."

"Albert. I want you to calm down. I'll be back in a minute. I'm going to get you some water." Ryker exited the room and nodded at one of the deputies. "Stay in there until I get back."

He opened the door to the viewing room and stepped inside. Mike and Bill Crenshaw and Dagewood were there.

"What do you think?" he asked them.

"He's crazy as a loon," Dagewood said immediately. "If he killed his own daughter—"

"You really think he did? I don't," Ryker responded. "Bill?"

Bill Crenshaw shook his head. "Hard to say. I'm inclined to think he's not crazy, but what he did was sure a crazy stunt. Hard to imagine why he'd think killing women in

St. Tammany would make the NOPD sit up and take notice about just another mugging."

"Ryker, book him. Let the lawyers sort it out," Mike said around the toothpick he was chewing. "You're holding the damning evidence right there in your hand. He's obviously the October Killer."

Ryker ran his fingers through his hair, leaving it spiked. He looked at Mike and Bill and Dagewood in turn. "I don't like it. We're going to put him away for the rest of his life, and he still doesn't know who killed his daughter. I feel like somehow we're letting him down."

"Letting down a murderer? Damn, Delancey, you're more of a wuss than I thought you were." Dagewood's voice carried an unmistakable note of disdain.

Ryker glanced at Bill and Mike. They were more polite, but from the expressions on their faces, they thought the same thing.

Ryker sighed. He had a lot to do before he could go home, including the difficult task of calling Albert Moser's other daughter and telling her what her father had done.

Chapter Fourteen

Nicole woke up thinking about home. She lay there for a few seconds, trying to figure out why she was thinking about something she'd really never had.

We're going home.

You're home.

Who in her dreams would be saying things like that?

Ryker? Was it his voice she'd imagined telling her that everything was okay? That they were going home?

She moved to push herself upright in bed, and her palms and fingers burned. "Ow," she muttered and looked at them. They were covered in snow-white gauze. She stared at them blankly.

The bedroom door, which was cracked, pushed open. "Hey, Nicole. You all right?" a vaguely familiar voice said.

Ryker? "My hands hurt. What hap—?" She gasped. "Oh, I remember. Job! How's Job? And that Deputy Ingram? Did you check on them for me?" She squinted at the silhouette in the doorway as he spread his hands. "Sorry to disappoint you, but I'm not Ryker," he said gently. "I'm Reilly."

She stared at the familiar chiseled features that were vaguely outlined in the pale light that came from behind him. "Not—?" She gaped at him. "You're who? I don't understand—"

"I'm Ryker's twin brother, Reilly."

"Tw-twin? You're twins?"

"Yeah. Identical. Sorry about the scare. Ryker didn't think you'd wake up. Can I get you something?"

"Identical? Twins?" Nicole was certain she was still dreaming. "Ryker told me he had brothers, but he didn't mention a twin."

Nicole saw Ryker's twin brother's silhouetted jaw tense and his body stiffen. She looked more closely.

"I could turn on the light if you like."

She nodded. He reached for the switch and the room was flooded with light. She found herself staring at a human being that was as much like the man she knew as anything on earth could be. An identical twin. Of course there were some differences. Reilly's hair was longer. And he wasn't quite as heavy as Ryker.

"This is too weird," she whispered.

Reilly laughed. "We get that a lot. Do you need something? Some water?"

She shook her head. "Where did Ryker go?"

"He had to interrogate Moser."

"Moser? The man whose daughter was killed? Why?"

Ryker's twin brother moved a little farther into the room. "He's the one who attacked you, Nicole. And he had a scrapbook filled with newspaper clippings of the other deaths. I'm not sure, but I imagine they're going to book him for murder."

"Murder? That can't be right. His own daughter was killed. That doesn't make sense."

"Nope. It doesn't. But he shot your friend Job and Detective Ingram, and tried to kill you. Don't worry. Ryker'll get the truth out of him."

Nicole shuddered. "When's Ryker getting back?"

"I don't know. He might stay all night if he's close to breaking Moser."

She winced at Reilly's words. *Breaking Moser*. It sounded so cruel.

"Hey, you need to get back in bed. Ryker told me to give you a painkiller if you woke up. You were asleep when he got back from the pharmacy with them. He said they were on the bedside table here." Reilly walked over to the table and picked up the plastic vial. "One every six hours as needed."

He started to open the vial.

"No," Nicole said sharply. "I don't want a pain pill. It'll make me groggy."

"That's what it's supposed to do. You're supposed to be sleeping as much as possible, so your hands can heal."

She looked at her hands again. "The chicken stock," she whispered, wincing. "It was really hot." The pot had burned her hands. They hurt.

"I heard how you overpowered Moser with hot chicken soup." Reilly grinned.

Nicole didn't feel much like laughing.

"Now how about taking your medicine?"

"No." She shook her head. "I'm fine. The EMTs gave me a tranquilizer. That's already made me sleepy."

Reilly paused and gave Nicole the once-over. "Okay, if you're sure. I'll bet your hands are hurting, though."

"Nothing I can't handle."

Reilly nodded, as if he'd expected no less from her. He sat down in a chair near the bed. "So what are your plans? I mean now that the threat is over."

Nicole's heart squeezed. She hadn't even asked herself that question.

What was she going to do? First of all, try to figure out how to live without Ryker Delancey.

Ryker didn't know it, but she felt as if she'd known him for a year. Ever since he'd started coming to the restaurant several nights a week. It had irritated her at first. Seeing him there in the restaurant night after night kept the memory of the killer's foiled attack uppermost in her mind. But it hadn't taken her long to realize that she'd never felt so safe in her life.

What would it feel like to have all his protective, responsible qualities, plus his love, forever? So wonderful it didn't bear thinking about.

She realized what she had to do. It would break her heart, but not as badly as waiting for Ryker to tell her.

"Hey," Reilly said. "Are you all right? You look like you're about to cry. I think you should take one of those pills."

Nicole shook her head. "My plans? I need to go home—" Her throat closed on the word *home*. She cleared her throat. "Back to my apartment. Will you take me?"

Reilly stood and held out both hands, palm up. "No. No way. I'm not incurring the Wrath of Ryker. He told me to stay here with you, and that's what I'm going to do."

She frowned at him. "You always do everything your twin brother tells you to?"

A spark lit Reilly's eyes that reminded her so much of Ryker her heart squeezed painfully in her chest. "Not always."

"If you won't take me I'll call a cab."

Reilly arched a brow at her. "You gonna go like that?"

Her cheeks blazed. "No." She had to think for a second. The tranquilizer had done a pretty good job. "No. He's got a sweatshirt I can wear. It'll look like a mini-dress. A weird one, but it'll cover me."

"Listen, Nicole. I'm just the babysitter here. Why don't

you lie down for a little longer and we'll talk about this when you're feeling better?"

There was nothing Nicole wanted to do more than go back to sleep. She wanted to recapture the dream in which Ryker had promised her that they were going home. But that wasn't going to happen. She and he had had the *home* discussion. They were too different.

Her life had been one continuous downward spiral until she'd stopped it by taking control of her destiny. She would never have the kind of home and family Ryker had, but she could make a home for herself. It would be small and inexpensive, but it would be hers. And as long as she could take care of herself, nobody would be able to take it away from her.

"No," she said firmly. "I'm going *home*." She threw back the covers and stood up in the flimsy undershirt Ryker had given her to sleep in.

Reilly took one look at her and his cheeks flamed. "Okay, I'm—I've, I'll just wait in the living room. When you're ready I'll take you to your apartment."

He left the room muttering, "Ryker's going to kill me."

Nicole smiled a sad little smile as she looked around the bedroom for Ryker's sweatshirt. Spotting it draped across the top of a dresser, she quickly donned it and looked for her shoes. Stepping into the bathroom, she checked her hair. It was a mess, but there was nothing she could do about it with her hands bandaged.

Looking from the mirror to her hands, she made up her mind. The EMT had said the burns on her hands were first degree. Which meant they'd be red and they'd hurt, but they were not going to blister and they weren't going to scar. She could use them, carefully. She peeled off the gauze and looked at her palms and fingers. Red—definitely. Rather bright.

She stuck her tongue to the pad of her thumb. *Burned.* Gingerly, she picked up Ryker's comb and pushed it carefully through her hair, gritting her teeth at the burning of her fingers. Good enough.

Then she stepped out into the living room.

"I'm ready."

Reilly turned around and stared at her as if she were an assassin. "I can't change your mind?"

She just stood there.

"Not even if I tell you Ryker will skin me alive?"

"Sorry."

"What about if I tell you what a complete idiot he is? My stubborn, clueless brother is head over heels for you. Seriously. He's always dated around. I'm not sure he's ever had a real serious relationship. But this past year—" Reilly shook his head. "All I can say is, he's never acted like this before—ever."

"Like what?" Nicole hadn't meant to ask, but the words had come out before she could stop them. She didn't want to let Reilly get her hopes up.

"Like a man in love. Obsessed. This past year he's taken it as his personal mission to keep you safe. I know for a fact he hasn't been out on a date in at least a year. Maybe longer. Every time I talked to him, he was at your restaurant, going to it or coming back from it." Reilly gave her a searching look. "My opinion? If you're not here when he gets home, he'll be devastated."

"Devastated? Ryker?" Nicole laughed and shook her head. That did it. He'd gone too far. Embellished too much. So she knew he was lying.

Ryker Delancey didn't love her. To him, she was a means to an end. Because of her, he'd caught his killer.

His job was done. And therefore, so was hers.

IT WAS AFTER MIDNIGHT when Ryker got home. He was ready to hit the sack, but he wanted to check on Nicole first. Part of him hoped she'd taken a pain pill and gone to sleep, but part of him wanted to gather her in his arms and tell her—what?

He had no idea what he would say. All he knew was when he'd entered the kitchen and hadn't seen her, he'd been terrified that the October Killer had shot her. In that moment, he'd known that life without her wouldn't be worth living.

"Hey, kid," he greeted his twin, who was stretched out on his couch. "How's Nicole?"

Reilly sat up yawning. "She's fine."

Ryker headed across the room. "She's asleep, I hope."

"I guess," Reilly said.

Ryker turned at the tone in his voice. Reilly had gotten up from the couch and was reaching for his leather jacket.

"What do you mean you guess?" He pushed the bedroom door open and saw the empty bed. He glanced toward the bathroom, but the door was open and the lights were out.

He whirled. "Where the hell is Nic?"

"I took her to her apartment," Reilly said evenly as he pulled his car keys out of his jacket pocket.

"You what?" Ryker roared at his twin brother. "What the hell's the matter with you? She's in no shape to take care of herself. I can't trust you to do a damn thing."

Reilly frowned, but he stood his ground. "She wanted to go back to her apartment. You didn't tell me I was guarding a prisoner. I thought I was here to keep an eye on a victim of a crime." He shrugged. "She asked me to take her, and I did."

Ryker advanced, fists doubled at his sides. "You let her

bully you, didn't you? I should have known. A rent-a-cop could have done a better job." Ryker pushed his fingers through his hair. "Get out of my way. I'm going after her."

Reilly didn't move from in front of the door. "You'd better listen to me, old man. I'm only going to tell you this once. You're an idiot. I'm warning you, you'd better be careful with her. She's not a trophy, something you can just take because you want it, like captain of the football team or a detective position with the sheriff's office. She's a living, breathing and, by the way, beautiful human being, with a mind of her own." Reilly opened the door, then turned back. "And if you had a lick of sense, you'd realize—"

"What?" Ryker stepped closer and got in his brother's face. He clenched his fists at his side. "I'd realize what?"

"That you're about to let your stubborn need to control everything and everybody lose you the best thing that ever happened to you." Reilly headed down the steps and out to his car, leaving Ryker standing there.

Ryker stepped outside and started to slam the door. He'd go get Nicole and bring her back here. She'd be better off here.

Wouldn't she? Damn Reilly, he thought as his brother started his Camaro and pulled away from the curb.

Why had she left? He'd told her he'd take care of her. He'd guarded her and protected her. What more could she want?

For some reason the word *forever* whispered through his mind.

NICOLE WENT BACK to the restaurant three days later. Her hands still hurt but they were much better, and she was going crazy in her apartment.

She was surprised to find Job there. His right arm was

in a sling, but it didn't slow him down a bit. Richard was planning the menu and Job was explaining to a kitchen staff person how to properly knead bread dough.

When Job saw her he grinned and hugged her with one arm. She hugged him back and told him how sorry she was that she'd gotten him mixed up in her problem.

Job just shook his head and hugged her tightly again. "I'm just glad you're back. You sure you can make it the whole evening? How're your hands?" he asked.

"They're sore, but I'll be fine. I'll leave early if I have too much trouble."

Job's thick brows drew down. "I don't want you to be hurting, but if you think you could stay at least until eight o'clock, I'd be most appreciative."

Nicole nodded, although she thought his request on her first day back was odd. Usually Job bent over backward to keep her from working too much. "Think you can make the tea?"

"Absolutely," she replied.

THAT EVENING, one of the waiters came into the kitchen with a panicked look on his face.

"Nicole, there's a man out there demanding to see the chef."

Nicole glanced at Richard. "Someone wanting to compliment you, Richard."

Richard just smiled at her blandly.

"No, no, ma'am," the young waiter said. "He wants to see whoever made the desserts. He's furious."

Job chuckled and Richard sniffed. "Sure am glad you made the desserts tonight, Nicole."

"I was careful," she said. "Granted I made all cold desserts so I wouldn't have to get near the stove with these hands, but I know they were good. I tasted them."

"I can't go back out there," the waiter whined. "Not unless—"

"It's okay, Tim. I'm going." Nicole carefully dried her hands on her dish towel and straightened her shoulders. When she pushed through the swinging door into the dining room, she saw about a dozen patrons. Some were digging into their entrees, some were lingering over coffee. Others still held menus.

Then she saw him.

Ryker was sitting at his regular table with a tiramisu in front of him.

There is nothing wrong with that tiramisu, she thought. *This is just a ruse to get me to talk to him.* She arched an eyebrow and strolled over to his table in her most regal manor. "Is there a problem, sir?"

He looked up at her and she could swear she saw a flicker of fear in his blue eyes. He started to say something, but instead he swallowed.

"Ryker? Is something wrong?" Something other than the dessert. His hesitation was beginning to scare her. Was he here to give her some bad news? Was Moser not the October Killer?

At that thought, Nicole's knees went weak and she had to grab the back of a chair to steady herself.

Ryker cleared his throat and spoke. "Chef, there's something in my tiramisu," he said.

"Something—?" She looked at the dish in panic. What in the world? A strand of hair? A fly? Her cheeks heated.

Behind her, she heard smothered chuckles. She glanced toward the kitchen and saw Job and Richard standing there with pained looks on their faces. What was going on?

"Well?" Ryker snapped.

"I—I'm sorry. I'll take it back." When she reached for the dessert dish, Ryker caught her hand in his.

"No. Not yet," he said loudly. "First I want you and the entire restaurant to see what's in it." With his other hand, he pointed at the edge of the whipped cream.

Nicole stared at him. There was something definitely fishy going on. His cheeks were pink and his eyes still held a flicker of wariness.

He still held on to her hand, so she obediently bent down and squinted at where he had pointed on the creamy dessert. She couldn't see anything. She started to raise her head and there it was. A spark of light. A *bright* spark of light.

"Do you see this?" Ryker asked as he fished the sparkly object out of the whipped cream and held it before her eyes.

It was round and gold and covered with snow-white cream. Nicole couldn't speak.

"Is it yours?"

She shook her head dumbly, staring at it, her brain refusing to form a coherent thought.

"Are you sure?" Ryker's voice rose. What was he trying to do?

By this time the other diners had stopped and turned toward them, and out of the corner of her eye, Nicole saw that the rest of the kitchen staff and Ryker's brother Reilly had joined Job and Richard in the doorway.

"What are you doing?" she whispered to Ryker.

He swallowed. "I'm trying to ask you to marry me." He picked up her left hand and slid the whipped-cream-covered ring onto her third finger.

"So?" he asked, sliding out of his seat and onto one knee. "Will you marry me, or will you leave me kneeling here in the middle of all these people with whipped cream on my hands?"

Nicole sank to the floor in a crouch. "Ryker, how can we—I mean, we hardly know each other."

"What do you mean?" he asked with a smile. "I've had dinner with you nearly every night for a year." Then he took a deep breath and his face turned serious. "I know I haven't been very nice to you, but I was trying to keep you alive. I need you, Nic. My family is huge, and in a lot of ways wonderful and a lot of ways awful. But it's time for me to have my own family. Will you be my family? Will you build a home with me? A place we can always be safe together?"

Nicole could barely breathe. "Are you sure?" she asked. "We're so—different."

Ryker shook his head. "No, we're not. We both want the same thing. Love. Happiness. Security. Now, I'll give you one more chance to have the last word. Will you marry me and let me give you a home?"

Nicole's heart soared as she smiled and kissed his lips. "You've already given me a home. My home is in your heart."

* * * * *

THE PAEDIATRICIAN'S PERSONAL PROTECTOR

BY
MALLORY KANE

DID YOU PURCHASE THIS BOOK WITHOUT A COVER?
If you did, you should be aware it is **stolen property** as it was reported
unsold and destroyed by a retailer. Neither the author nor the publisher
has received any payment for this book.

All the characters in this book have no existence outside the imagination of
the author, and have no relation whatsoever to anyone bearing the same name
or names. They are not even distantly inspired by any individual known or
unknown to the author, and all the incidents are pure invention.

All Rights Reserved including the right of reproduction in whole or in
part in any form. This edition is published by arrangement with Harlequin
Enterprises II B.V./S.à.r.l. The text of this publication or any part thereof may
not be reproduced or transmitted in any form or by any means, electronic or
mechanical, including photocopying, recording, storage in an information
retrieval system, or otherwise, without the written permission of the publisher.

This book is sold subject to the condition that it shall not, by way of trade or
otherwise, be lent, resold, hired out or otherwise circulated without the prior
consent of the publisher in any form of binding or cover other than that in
which it is published and without a similar condition including this condition
being imposed on the subsequent purchaser.

® and ™ are trademarks owned and used by the trademark owner and/or its
licensee. Trademarks marked with ® are registered with the United Kingdom
Patent Office and/or the Office for Harmonisation in the Internal Market and
in other countries.

First published in Great Britain 2011
by Mills & Boon, an imprint of Harlequin (UK) Limited,
Eton House, 18-24 Paradise Road, Richmond, Surrey TW9 1SR

© Rickey R. Mallory 2010

ISBN: 978 0 263 88560 6

46-1111

Harlequin (UK) policy is to use papers that are natural, renewable and
recyclable products and made from wood grown in sustainable forests. The
logging and manufacturing processes conform to the legal environmental
regulations of the country of origin.

Printed and bound in Spain
by Blackprint CPI, Barcelona

To Daddy, my hero and my biggest fan.
I know you and Mama are dancing.

Chapter One

Reilly Delancey was late. He hurried up the steps of the St. Tammany Parish courthouse, through the metal detectors and into the large central hall, fingering the knot of his tie and wishing he hadn't tied it so tightly.

He spoke to a couple of fellow officers who were waiting to testify in other cases. They had the same resigned expression on their faces that he was sure was on his.

A quick glance at the courtroom schedule told him that the McGilicutty case, in which he was testifying as the lead hostage negotiator, was in Courtroom Three. He rushed to the door, only to be stopped by the assistant district attorney who'd prepped him.

"Judge Simmons just got here," Hale Dunham told him. "It'll be at least twenty minutes before we need you."

"Simmons is hearing the case? It'll be thirty. I'll get a cup of coffee."

"Be back in fifteen," Hale warned.

"Eighteen," he countered and headed toward the small kiosk on the far side of the hall. If Simmons had just entered the courtroom, it would be ten minutes before he finished straightening his robes and arranging his gavel and pens. Then another twenty before the preliminaries were over. Simmons questioned everything.

He ordered and paid for his coffee and dumped sugar into

it, then stood sipping it as he glanced around at the hubbub in the courthouse.

Two detectives walked by. Dagewood and Phillips. He didn't remember their first names. They worked with his twin brother, Detective Ryker Delancey. Phillips was loud and overweight, but basically he seemed like a good guy. Dagewood, on the other hand, was arrogant and rude.

As if to prove Reilly's opinion, Dagewood stopped in front of him. "Well," he said. "If it's not the Delancey that *didn't* make detective."

Reilly bit his tongue. Somehow, Dagewood had figured out how badly Reilly had coveted the position Ryker had gotten, and he mentioned it every chance he got.

"Dagewood," Reilly responded noncommittally, taking his own shot. The big detective liked the uniformed officers to address him by his title, so Reilly never did.

"So what's up today?" Dagewood continued. "Defending a traffic ticket?"

Phillips chuckled at the old joke.

Reilly sipped his coffee and didn't answer.

"Come on, Ted," Phillips said. "I didn't get any breakfast. By the time we get back to the office, all the doughnuts'll be gone."

"Hang on," Dagewood said. "I haven't tried the coffee here. If it's good enough for Delancey…"

Phillips laughed again and the two stood in line.

Reilly ignored them as his gaze slid over the crowd. He half expected to see Ryker. His brother was here for the sentencing hearing of the man who'd killed four women in St. Tammany Parish over the past five years.

Reilly and Ryker didn't normally see each other a lot these days. They ran in different circles since Ryker was a detective and Reilly was SWAT. But Reilly had babysat his brother's injured star witness a few weeks ago while Ryker was booking

Find, try & love more books like this!

Visit millsandboon.co.uk

EXCLUSIVE 15% OFF ALL ORDERS!

SEE OVERLEAF
FOR DETAILS

MILLS & BOON®

You can find all Mills & Boon titles at our website

millsandboon.co.uk

For a limited time only, we are offering you an **EXCLUSIVE 15% OFF** when you order online. Simply enter the code **15NOV11** at the checkout. But hurry, this offer ends on 30th November 2011.

PLUS, by ordering online you will receive all these extra benefits:

- Purchase new titles **1 MONTH AHEAD OF THE SHOPS.** Available in paperback and as eBooks!

- Order books from our huge backlist at a discounted price

- **Try before you buy** with Browse the Book

- Be the first to hear about exclusive offers in our eNewsletter

- Join the M&B community and discuss your favourite books with other readers

Terms and Conditions:
- Offer expires on 30th November 2011
- This offer cannot be used in conjunction with any other offer.
- Code can only be redeemed online at www.millsandboon.co.uk
- Exclusions apply
- Discount excludes delivery charge.

NOV11

the killer. She wasn't just his star witness either. Since two weeks ago, she was his fiancée.

Ryker engaged. Reilly shook his head. Hard to believe. Before his older brother—older by seven minutes—had met Nicole Beckham, he'd never even dated anyone seriously.

As his thoughts wandered and his coffee cooled, his gaze settled on what just might be the most striking woman he'd ever seen. She was tall and slender, with midnight-black hair that fell to her shoulders and a confident walk that had more eyes than his following her.

As soon as he realized that most of the males in the central hall were watching her, it became obvious that she wasn't paying attention to any of them. She was headed straight for him.

Or more likely, for the coffee kiosk.

Whatever she had her eyes on, Reilly would bet a month's pay that she'd get it. She was the confident, super-cool type who got whatever she wanted. He swallowed a chuckle as he watched her mow down the men in her path with a glare. Her high heels clicked with purpose on the marble floor.

He couldn't tell where she was looking behind the narrow, black-rimmed glasses she wore, but he managed to resist the urge to glance behind him. He kept his gaze on her face. He was dying to know if her eyes were as black as her hair and her glasses frames. He got his answer when she stopped directly in front of him.

They weren't black. They were green. And flashing with irritation. At him.

At him?

"Detective Delancey," she said, propping a hand on her hip.

Reilly shook his head and muttered his automatic response. "No, I'm not—"

"Don't start with me again, Detective. You must be so

proud. My father is barely recovered from the heart attack he suffered in *your* jail less than two weeks ago. But he was determined to stand before the judge and plead guilty. How could you be so quick to catch him, but no one can find my sister's killer? Why don't you spend some time on that!" She paused to take a breath.

Reilly jumped at the opportunity. "I'm not Detective Delancey," he said quickly. "People make that mistake all the time. I'm—"

She jerked off her glasses and took aim with those laser-sharp eyes. "What do you mean you're not—" She stopped, frowning at him.

Reilly assessed her more closely as, behind him, Phillips chuckled. Then Dagewood spoke up loudly. "Need any help there, *Officer* Delancey?"

Without the glasses shielding her eyes, he could see something behind their cool expression. Something that was far from cool and far from confident. The lids were rimmed with red and faintly puffy. Her generous mouth was pressed into a severe line, and the skin along her jawline appeared stretched tight. He could see pale blue veins under the delicate skin of her neck. The black-haired beauty was wound tight as a spring about to break.

He replayed her words in his mind, fitting the pieces together.

Detective Delancey—

My father…pleaded guilty—

She was the daughter of Ryker's serial killer. That surprised him. He wracked his brain, but couldn't come up with the man's name.

"No. You're not Detective Delancey," she said, shaking her head.

He shrugged, intrigued that she'd arrived at that conclusion so quickly. Usually it was the other way around. He'd had people actually argue with him about which twin he was, and so had Ryker. Which was funny, because he didn't think he and his brother were alike at all. Both of them had always been lean, but Ryker had put on a little weight in the past year. And Reilly was a lot less OCD about haircuts and clothes and life in general.

"Sorry," he said to the woman. "It happens a lot. Especially if I'm dressed up." He ran his finger under his collar again. "Which is as seldom as possible. I hate suits."

The tension around her mouth softened a bit.

"I'm Officer Reilly Delancey. SWAT." He held out his hand.

From behind him he heard, "The Delancey that didn't make detective," followed by Phillips's annoying laugh. One day he was going to punch Dagewood.

She ignored or didn't notice his hand as she sent a swift, withering glance toward the two detectives. "Where is Detective Delancey?" she asked, looking at her watch. "He disappeared as soon as the judge dismissed us. I thought maybe he'd be out here."

"My guess is, if he's not scheduled for another court appearance, he's gone to check on his fiancée," Reilly replied.

The woman in front of him stiffened even more.

"To check on his fiancée? Of course. That's exactly what I'd do after I put a sick old man in prison. Or maybe I'd go to Disney World."

Reilly's hackles rose at her sarcasm, although he could hardly blame her for being upset. After all, she'd just witnessed her father plead guilty to what—four counts of murder? Still, he leaped to his brother's defense, choosing his next words carefully.

"My brother's fiancée was injured on the day your father was arrested," he said carefully. "She had a doctor's appointment this morning."

Her sharp glance and the grimace of pain that passed fleetingly across her face told him she understood what he hadn't said. Ryker's fiancée's injury had been at her father's hand.

"I'm sorry about your father—and your sister," he offered.

Her mouth tightened. "Why?" she asked. "You don't know me. Or my family."

"I know a little about your father's case. How the death of your sister—"

"How can I find Detective Delancey?" she interrupted, two bright spots of color appearing in her pale cheeks.

Despite her words, what he heard was *that's none of your business*. And it wasn't. He'd crossed a line. He immediately backtracked.

"He's probably already left the courthouse. If you want, I can make sure he gets in touch with you."

She glanced at her watch, then back at Reilly. Suddenly she appeared unsure, and that surprised him. She didn't seem like the type to ever be unsure of anything. She might be wrong, as she was in thinking he was Ryker, but she would always be sure.

"Hand me your phone," he said.

She put her glasses back on and gave him a narrow look. For a moment he wasn't sure she was going to comply. But finally her hand snaked inside her purse and she handed him a smart phone. He quickly programmed his number and name into it, then pressed Call. His cell phone began to ring. He dug it out of his pocket, answered it, then hung up her phone and handed it back to her.

"What's your name?" he asked without looking up.

"Dr. Moser," she said without hesitation.

He raised his gaze to hers.

"Christy—Moser." She stared for an instant at the display

on her smart phone, then stuck it into the pocket of her jacket.

Reilly finished entering her name into his phone. "Okay. I'll get my brother to call you."

"How soon? I need to find out what happens next. How long my father has before he—" She stopped and cleared her throat. "I have to go," she said. She fingered the watch on her left wrist and looked at it for the third time. Or was it the fourth?

"Yeah, me too," he said, checking the time on his phone's display before he pocketed it. His seventeen minutes were up. He had to get to Courtroom Three.

Christy Moser turned and walked away. Reilly watched her excellent backside sway in the black fitted skirt. It was amazing how high-heeled shoes affected a woman's walk. In a good way.

Dr. Moser. He'd have to ask Ryker what kind of doctor the serial killer's daughter was.

CHRISTMAS LEIGH MOSER stood at the front door of the house where she and her sister Autumn had grown up in Covington, Louisiana. Yellow crime-scene tape crisscrossed the doorframe, garish against the dingy white paint.

She stared at it, aghast. Why was her dad's house a crime scene? Nothing Detective Delancey had told her had indicated that her father had done anything here. Horror churned in her stomach, mingled with shame.

She hadn't been in the house since her sister's death. She should have made more of an effort to get back here to see her dad. But two years of residency plus a fellowship in pediatrics at one of the foremost children's hospitals in the northeast made it difficult to get home to sleep, much less take a trip thirteen hundred miles away.

She'd called him every week—well, nearly every week.

How had she not known something was dreadfully wrong with him? How had she not realized he'd gone off the deep end?

A twinge under her breastbone gave her the answer to that. She *had* known something was wrong. Known it and ignored it. She'd chalked up his monotone answers and disinterest to mild situational depression, and had encouraged him to get out more, see his friends, get back to playing golf. She'd told him he should talk to someone and suggested that he ask the pastor of his church about a grief-counseling class or a therapist.

She thought about the one time she had visited her dad in the past five years. She'd attended a seminar in New Orleans. She'd met her dad at a restaurant for a hurried dinner before kissing him on the cheek and rushing back to her hotel room to prepare for a talk she was giving the next day.

Now here she was. Too late. Her family home had become the home of a killer.

She shuddered, swallowing hard. Shock and revulsion and fear had dogged her steps ever since she'd received the phone call telling her that her father had been arrested. The call had come less than twelve hours after she'd talked to her dad. When she put the times together, she realized that within an hour of their conversation, he'd shot two people, a policeman and a restaurant owner, and had tried to kill a third.

He'd done it with the misguided notion that he could force the police to reopen Autumn's case.

Guilt washed over Christy like a blast of hot summer wind, stealing her breath and leaving her back and neck prickling with sudden sweat. The certainty that this was her fault sat like a dead weight on her chest. She'd gone off and left him to deal with Autumn, knowing her younger sister was in trouble with drugs.

If she'd stayed in Louisiana, would her little sister still be alive? Would her father be an active, vibrant man in his early sixties, rather than a deranged murderer?

Rationally, she recognized that her decision probably wouldn't have changed what happened, but rationality and guilt were like matter and antimatter. They couldn't occupy the same space. And the guilt was stronger.

Christy realized she'd become exactly what she'd sworn she'd never be, a workaholic career woman with no time for family, like her mother. Deborah Moser had been a tenured professor at Loyola until the day she'd been in the wrong place at the wrong time.

Christy glanced around the neighborhood where she and Autumn had played as children. None of the neighbors were outside, and there were no cars on the street. She'd once known many of the people who lived here. Where were they now? Resentment burned deep within her. Why hadn't they known something was wrong with her dad?

Why hadn't she?

She looked down at the key in her hand. Suddenly, she needed to go inside and look at her father's things. See her sister's room. Wallow in some more guilt.

She slipped the key into the lock and turned it. The door opened easily, silently.

Christy ducked under the crime-scene tape. She pushed the door wide. The first thing that struck her was how dark the inside of the house was. The second, that it had been that way ever since their mother had been killed when Christy was sixteen and Autumn was twelve.

Leaving the front door open for light, she stepped over to her father's recliner and turned on the lamp on the side table. The glow was feeble. After a couple of seconds, her eyes adapted to the dark and she could see a little bit.

Smudged gray dust outlined a large square on the side table.

She wiped a fingertip across it. Fingerprint dust. It had to be. The peculiar color distinguished it from household dust.

Looking at the table, Christy knew immediately what had lain there. Dad's scrapbook. More pain gnawed at her heart. Ever since she could remember, he'd kept it. How many times had she sat in his lap as he'd pasted pictures of her and baby Autumn in the leather-bound book and carefully, in neat, precise printing, labeled each one with their name, the date and a sweet or funny comment?

But that image quickly morphed into the memory of Detective Ryker Delancey showing her the pages in the back of that beloved book, behind the family pictures. Pages containing baby photos of girls she didn't know, with comments written beside them in a shaky hand she hardly recognized as her father's.

Those were her father's victims, and Detective Ryker Delancey had made her look at them, made her read her father's careful notes about where they lived, when their birthdays were and when he planned to kill them. Then the detective had demanded to know if she'd seen them before.

Of course she'd never seen them. Angrily she swiped her hand across the table's surface, obliterating the dust outline of the book. Did the detective know he'd destroyed every last good memory from her childhood? Did he care?

She dusted her hands together. She should leave. She knew she wasn't supposed to cross crime-scene tape. But this was her home, or it had been. Didn't she have a right?

She glanced desperately around the dimly lit room, hoping to find something—anything—that would give her an explanation for why her father had done what he had. Something rational that she could take to the police and say, "Here, look. This is what he was doing. Now it makes sense, doesn't it?"

But she knew there was nothing to find. No rational explanation, no sane reason.

She blinked and realized her gaze had settled on a framed picture Autumn had drawn of their mother. It hung on the wall above the television. Christy's eyes filled with tears. Their mother had been beautiful and smart. Autumn had looked just like her. She stepped over and touched the glass. More dust. She sneezed.

Guilt and embarrassment tightened her chest, making it difficult to breathe. Anyone coming into this sad house would immediately see how badly she'd neglected her father.

She reached into her purse for a tissue.

"Freeze!" a harsh voice barked.

Shocked, she turned. The unmistakable silhouette of a uniformed police officer darkened the doorway.

"Wait!" she called out, her hand still inside her purse. "I'm—"

"I said freeze!"

She froze.

The harsh beam of a flashlight swept her, blinding her as it passed over her face. Finally, the beam stopped on her hands.

"Hold it!" he barked when she started to pull her hand out of her purse. "Don't move that hand."

"Oh, no. It's okay. I was just—"

"Stop! Now I want you to lift your hand out of your purse, thumb up."

Christy frowned, but tried to comply. She raised her hand until her thumb was visible over the edge of the purse's clasp.

"Okay," the officer said, his gun still pointed at her, his eyes bright in the dimness of the doorway. "Now—slowly, lift your hand all the way out, and if I see *anything* in it, I'll shoot."

Numb with fear, she did what he said, spreading her shaky fingers to demonstrate that they were empty.

The officer's stance relaxed a bit. "Drop your purse. Do it!"

She dropped it.

"How'd you get in here?"

"Please," she said. "I'm—"

"How?"

"My key. It's in my purse."

The officer shone the beam of the flashlight in her face again. "Are you alone?" he asked.

"Yes. Of course."

"Step outside," he continued, backing across the threshold. "Keep your hands where I can see them."

She complied, following him until she was on the porch and he had backed down the steps to the sidewalk. She saw the police car parked behind her rental car.

"Who are you?" he snapped, once he got a look at her in the afternoon sunlight.

"Chr-Christmas Leigh Moser. Albert Moser is my father."

"Your father?" He rubbed a hand across the bald top of his head.

She understood the slight note of bewilderment in his voice. Until twelve days ago she'd thought the same thing. Serial killers didn't have daughters, families, lives.

"Don't you know you're not supposed to cross crime-scene tape?"

Christy shrugged carefully. "I'm sorry," she said innocently. "I've never been involved in a crime before."

The officer touched the microphone on his shoulder. "Sneed here. I'm at the Moser scene. Cancel backup. It's the perp's daughter." He aimed a stern gaze at her. "You need to leave, ma'am. If you go to the sheriff's office over on

Columbia Street and fill out the proper paperwork, you can get access to the scene once the crime lab has released it."

Horror enveloped her like a dark cloud. "The *perp?* The *crime lab?*" Her stomach turned over again and acrid saliva filled her mouth. She swallowed hard.

"Why is my father's house a crime scene?" she demanded, her voice hollow to her own ears. "He didn't do anything here." She shuddered as the scrapbook's pages rose before her inner vision and the court bailiff's bland voice listing the women her father had killed played over in her mind. "Did he?"

He sniffed. "The suspect's residence has been declared part of the crime scene, as have his vehicles."

"I see," she said, feeling numb. "Thank you."

The policeman gestured toward her car. "Now get on out of here," he said as he holstered his gun.

She had no choice but to obey him. She walked past him down the sidewalk. As she did, the microphone attached to his shoulder crackled. The only words she could make out were *Moser* and *hospital.*

"What?" she exclaimed, turning back toward him. Her heart thudded painfully. Her father? Hospital? Oh, no!

The policeman spoke into his mic. "I've got the daughter here. I'll let her know."

"Ms. Moser," he said. "That was the dispatcher. Your father has suffered a heart attack. He's being taken to St. Tammany Parish Medical Center."

"Oh, no!" Christy breathed. "Not again!" She started toward her car.

"Ma'am?" the officer called after her. "I can get you there faster in the squad car."

Christy stopped in her tracks. "Thank you," she said.

As she got into the police car and the officer cranked it and sped away, blue lights flashing, she prayed, "Please don't let my father die before I get there. I need to tell him how sorry I am."

THREE HOURS LATER, after her father had been moved from the emergency room to the cardiac care unit, Christy left the hospital. The nurse in charge had told her that she wouldn't be able to see him again until morning. She argued that she was a physician and demanded to see the doctor in charge. But when the cardiac specialist found out she was a pediatrician, he'd smiled apologetically and told her the same thing. It was a hospital policy. Intensive-care visiting hours must be observed—by everyone.

So she'd called a taxi to take her back to her dad's house to pick up her rental car. Then, exhausted, she headed to the Oak Grove Inn, a bed-and-breakfast she'd booked in Chef Voleur, stopping along the way to pick up a bottle of wine.

After her flight the night before, she'd barely had time to unload her bags and fall into bed. Then this morning she'd been up at dawn, unable to sleep with her father's nine o'clock sentencing hearing looming. Now more than twelve hours later, her dad was in the hospital, and all she wanted to do was go back there and sit with him. But she couldn't. The last thing the nurse had told her was to rest. "It's the best thing you can do for your father now. It won't help him if you're exhausted."

Irritatingly, it was the same thing she told worn-out parents of her young patients. It was bitter medicine to swallow, but she knew the nurse was right.

She took a deep breath and squeezed her burning eyes shut. She vowed to take the nurse's advice.

As she approached the inn, which was on a quiet street in a residential section of Chef Voleur, she thought about the difference between the north shore of the Pontchartrain and Boston. As much as the north shore had grown over the last twenty years, the cities still retained a lot of small-town character.

She pulled into the small parking lot. A loud roar announced a big pickup pulling in beside her. Living in Boston for six years, she'd forgotten how many pickups were on the roads in Louisiana. She couldn't remember ever seeing one in Boston proper.

She got out, grabbed her purse and the bag holding the wine and headed for her cottage, sending a vague smile toward the darkened windows of the pickup. As she walked past the main house toward the third of four tiny cottages lined up behind it, a motion-sensing light came on. But her cottage was dark. Someone—the maid?—had turned off the light she'd deliberately left on this morning.

Behind her, heavy footsteps crunched on the tiny seashells that were mixed with gravel to form the path to the cottages. The driver of the pickup, probably.

Her big-city instincts kicked in and she clutched her purse tightly against her ribs as she quickly inserted the key into the door and turned it.

The crunching footsteps came closer.

It's just the person in Cottage Four, she told herself as she opened the door to slip inside.

A crushing blow hit her on the back and sent her sprawling onto the floor.

Chapter Two

When the blow slammed Christy to the floor, the bag containing the bottle of wine flew out of her hands and landed with a thud in front of her.

Still driven by the momentum of the blow and the weight against her, she pitched forward, hands out to break her fall. She hit the hardwood floor hard and felt a distinct, painful snap in her right wrist.

Pain and panic immobilized her for an instant as a heavy body landed on top of her. He straddled her, pinning her down.

Her heart pounded violently and her limbs quivered. The man grabbed a fistful of her hair and slammed her face down onto the hardwood floor. He put his mouth near her ear. She could smell stale cigarettes on his breath.

She tried to suck in enough air to scream, but his weight pressing her chest into the hardwood floor was too heavy. She tried anyway. All that came from her lips was a feeble squeak.

"Shut your mouth," his gravely voice whispered.

Christy's hands were pinned underneath her, and her right wrist pulsed with a sickening pain. Using her left hand, she tried to move, to roll, anything to get him off her. Nothing worked and every tiny movement intensified the piercing agony in her broken wrist. It was making her nauseous.

Whatever the man intended to do to her, she couldn't stop him. He was too strong and she was too weak.

"Please—" she rasped. "What do you want—?"

His hand pushed her cheek harder into the floor. "Go back where you came from," he growled. "Or you're as dead as your sister."

Terror sliced through her like a razor blade. *Her sister's killer.* He'd followed her. Just as the thoughts whirled through her brain, he grabbed her hair again and banged her head against the floor—twice. The blows stunned her.

At some point, she was aware that his crushing weight was gone. Dazed, her head spinning and her wrist throbbing, she managed to roll over onto her side.

Where was he? Dear God—she couldn't see anything in the dark. Was he really gone? Or was he hiding in the shadows, preparing to kill her?

Instinctively she reached for the tiny can of Mace she carried in her pocket, but when she moved her hand, the pain nearly took her breath away.

She rolled onto her back and tried to reach it with her left hand. It was awkward—almost impossible. Tears welled in her eyes and slid down her cheeks. Tears of frustration, of pain, of paralyzing fear.

Finally, she got her fingers on the object in her pocket, but it wasn't the Mace. It was her smart phone.

Desperately she grabbed it, trying to press the buttons for 911. But her fingers were shaking too badly. The device slipped from her fumbling fingers and clattered across the hardwood floor.

No!

"Help!" she whispered, her lungs deflated by sobbing. She rolled onto her stomach and reached out with her left hand, feeling along the floor. Where was it?

"Where are you?"

She gasped, at first thinking it was her attacker's voice. But no. This voice was tinny, mechanical. Was it her phone? She squinted.

There. She saw the light from the display. Thank God. But it was halfway across the room.

Forcing a deep breath into her spasming lungs, she tried to pull herself up enough to crawl toward it, but her right wrist was useless. Worse than useless. If it didn't stop throbbing, she was going to throw up. The pain was making her sick.

Giving up on trying to move, she cried, "Help me!"

God, what was the name of this place? Her brain was so fuzzy, and she hurt so bad. "Three—! she cried breathlessly. "Cottage Three," Christy sobbed. "Please hurry!"

REILLY DROVE LIKE A bat out of hell toward the Oak Grove Inn. What if he was wrong? What if he'd misunderstood Christy Moser's sobbing words? The only *cottages* he knew about were on Oak Street in Chef Voleur, about two miles from his Covington high-rise condo.

He should have asked her where she was staying when he'd gotten her phone number. Now it was too late. Something had happened to the beautiful black-haired serial killer's daughter, and she'd called him—because his number was the latest number in her phone.

"Christy? Christy can you hear me?" he yelled into his phone. "Hang on. It's Reilly Delancey. I'll be right there." He kept talking to her because the line was still open. He had no idea whether she could hear him or not. Holding his breath, he listened. Was that a sob? Or harsh, panicked breathing?

"Christy. Talk to me. Where is Cottage Three? Is it Oak Grove Inn?"

"Oak—?"

Fear arrowed through him at her weak, rasping voice. "Christy? I'm coming. Hang in there."

He careered around the corner onto Oak Street and into the driveway of the B&B. His brain registered three vehicles in the parking lot. A silver Avalon with rental plates, a light blue pickup with Louisiana plates and a Prius with a Mississippi vanity tag that said LVG CPL. He pulled into the parking lot beside the pickup and vaulted out of his car.

Cottage Three. As he sprinted toward the row of small cottages lined up on the grounds of the Oak Grove Bed-and-Breakfast he grabbed his weapon and flashlight from his belt.

"Hey!" he shouted. "Guerrant! Guerrant, you in there?" The owner, Guerrant Bardin, lived in the back of the main house. "Call the police!"

"What the hell?" he heard just as a motion-sensing light flared.

"Call 911!" Reilly shouted. "Get the police over here. A woman's been attacked."

More lights came on. He saw Bardin standing on his back porch in boxer shorts and a T-shirt, with his phone at his ear.

The door to Cottage Three was standing open. Reilly slowed down and approached carefully, holding his gun and his flashlight ready.

He rounded the door facing and the flashlight's beam hit a female body sprawled on the hardwood floor.

Christy! Horror turned his blood to ice. Then she moved and gasped, and relief flooded him. Automatically, he swept the room with the flashlight's beam and called out to no one in particular, "Clear."

Then he crouched beside the black-haired beauty and brushed her silky hair out of her face. "Christy?" he said softly. "Hey, Christy, talk to me."

"No—" she moaned, trying to push him away.

"It's okay. I'm Reilly Delancey—" He took a breath. "The police," he clarified.

At that instant, crunching footsteps approached. Reilly whirled, aiming flashlight and gun at the doorway. "Hold it right there," he barked.

"What's going on?" a voice growled. He heard the unmistakable sound of a shotgun shell being chambered.

"Guerrant? It's Reilly Delancey. Did you call the police?"

"Hell yeah, I did." Bardin stepped into the doorway and reached around to flip on the lights. He'd pulled on blue jeans over his boxers. "Oh, crap. What happened?"

"I think she was attacked. Don't touch anything. Wait out there for the police."

"Is she alive?"

As Bardin spoke, Christy moved her right arm and cried out in obvious pain.

With the lights on, Reilly saw that her slim skirt was ripped, her stockings were torn and one foot was bare. Beyond her, toward the bathroom, her purse had slid across the floor and spilled. A bottle of wine in a paper bag had rolled into a corner. Her phone lay just out of her reach.

"Guerrant, guard the door. If you see anything, holler. I need to clear the area." Reilly slipped out the door of the cottage and canvassed the area. He didn't see anyone. He checked the seashell-and-gravel path that connected the cottages. It ended at the fence that surrounded the inn's grounds. The fence was green chicken wire, designed to disappear amid the landscaping. It would be absurdly easy for someone to climb it and vault over. He shone the flashlight into the thicket on the other side of the fence. Nothing.

He circled around the cottages, just to be sure there was nobody lurking, then walked up to the door where Guerrant was standing guard.

"Didn't see anybody here," Guerrant reported.

When Reilly entered, Christy was struggling to sit up. She looked up at him. There was a scrape on her cheek. She blinked. "Reilly Delancey," she said hoarsely. "Not the detective."

"Are you okay? Are you hurt?"

She squeezed her eyes shut. "The scaphoid bone in my wrist is fractured, although it's not displaced. Please help me up."

Scaphoid bone? Reilly had no idea what she'd just told him, but he had heard the words *wrist* and *fractured*. "No. You stay right there. Don't move. I'm calling—"

Christy pushed herself up using her left hand and pressed her right hand protectively against her ribs.

"—the EMTs," Reilly finished with a sigh. Super-confident. Super-cool, even after being attacked. Even with a broken wrist. Did that come from being a physician? Or from what must have been a very difficult childhood? Either way, he was glad she was alive.

Giving up on the notion that she might listen to him, he crouched beside her, ready to steady her if she felt faint or got sick. She looked a little green around the gills.

"Help me up," she ordered. When she tried to move, her mouth tightened and the tension along her jawline increased.

He had his phone out. "No. You'll wait for the ambulance—" he started.

Using just her left arm, she struggled to get her feet under her. With a sigh, he slid his hands under her arms and helped her to her feet. "Do you ever listen?"

"I—know my own body," she replied, putting a notion in Reilly's head that he quickly banished.

She teetered between one high heel and one bare foot. Earlier at the courthouse, he'd observed that she was just about as tall as his nearly six feet. But now, as she put her weight on her bare foot, she seemed small. Her shoulders under his hand felt bony—feminine—sexy.

She still appeared dazed, and if the situation weren't so dire, she might have looked comically awkward with one shoe on and one shoe off. He gently pushed her down into the chair, a little surprised when she didn't protest.

He watched her carefully. She held her wrist cradled against her, protecting it. A large red area on her forehead was swelling and turning purple. Her lips were white at the corners. The scrape on her left cheek blossomed with tiny beads of blood, like early morning dew on a red flower.

She caught him checking out the scrape. "It's nothing more than an abrasion." She tentatively pressed it with a finger. "I'll probably have a mild contusion," she said, then added, "a bruise." She frowned. "And a larger one on my forehead."

"Your wrist—" Reilly started.

"I told you, it's not displaced. It won't need setting. I'll wrap it and get a wrist guard. There's no need for medical treatment."

"That's not your call," Reilly informed her as he dialed one-handed. "What happened?"

She shook her head as if trying to clear it and touched the bruise on her forehead. "I was hit from behind. Knocked to the floor. I thought—" She stopped.

Reilly ordered an ambulance then hung up. "You thought what?"

She shook her head again. "Nothing. The man said, 'Go back where you came from or you're as dead as your sister.'"

The words shocked Reilly. "He said that? Those exact words? Are you sure?"

"Yes."

Although she looked like a frightened, hurt young woman, her reply was confident and smooth.

"What else did he say?"

"Nothing. He got off me and left."

"Did you get a good look at him?"

She shook her head. "I tried to turn over and get up but my wrist—" Her voice gave out.

"You're positive it was a man?" Reilly asked.

She looked at him frowning. "Of course."

"Why 'of course'?"

But before she could answer, the crunch of heavy boots on seashells and gravel announced the arrival of the police. Two uniformed officers appeared at the door to the cottage, their weapons drawn.

Reilly indicated the badge at his belt. "Deputy Reilly Delancey, SWAT. Dr. Moser here was attacked." He didn't know the officers, but both of them glanced his way when he told them his name. He'd long since stopped being surprised by that.

In and around Chef Voleur the name Delancey always drew a reaction. Depending on the situation and the people, the reactions were vastly different. Reilly figured the two officers knew or had heard of Ryker.

One of the officers stepped over to Christy and the other faced him.

"Delancey? Deputy Buford Watts. How'd you get here?"

"Dr. Moser is involved with a case of my brother's, Detective Ryker Delancey. I had given her my phone number in case she couldn't reach him."

The officer's gaze sharpened. "Moser. Not—the October Killer?"

"There's no reason to get into that," Reilly responded, knowing as soon as the words left his mouth that he was wrong. Given what her attacker had said, there was definitely a reason to get into that.

"No? Do you know who attacked her?"

"Not yet."

"Her father killed half-a-dozen women," Watts said, his gaze studying her.

Four, Reilly corrected silently, sending an apologetic look toward Christy. The deputy was being deliberately insensitive.

"What if it was a victim's family member?" Watts continued. "Have you gotten specifics?"

"Just got here myself," Reilly answered. "I'd like to be in on your interview though."

The officer didn't have any objection. Within a few minutes, Christy, who was still refusing medical treatment, Reilly and the two officers were seated at the dining room table in the main house of Oak Grove Inn.

"Now, Ms. Moser," the first officer started.

"It's *Doctor* Moser," Reilly inserted, just as Bardin's wife bustled in, wrapped in a voluminous fleece robe.

"For goodness sakes! What are you doing to this poor girl?"

Reilly tensed at Ella Bardin's use of the word *girl.* He glanced at Christy sidelong, trying to send her a signal not to insult Ella, but she wasn't paying any attention to Ella's choice of words or to him. She was staring into space and frowning.

"Get out of the way, all of you," Ella continued.

"Ella—" said the older officer.

"Buford Watts, you just hold your horses." Ella turned to Christy. "I've put some water on to boil, and I'll get you a cup of tea in just a minute, unless you'd rather have coffee?"

Christy realized that Ella was talking to her. She looked

up and her stiff demeanor softened just a little, barely enough to notice. "Oh, thank you. Tea is fine."

"And here." Ella Bardin stepped over to a recliner and pulled an afghan off the back of it. "Cover up with this. The very idea—" this aimed at the three men "—of leaving her sitting there in that torn skirt. What kind of gentlemen are you?"

Watts answered, "The kind who're trying to find out who attacked her, Miss Ella." His words were measured.

The younger officer grinned at Ella. "I sure could use something warm to drink, Miss Ella."

Ella looked at him. "I'm sure you could," she retorted as she started back toward the kitchen.

Watts turned his attention back to Christy. "Dr. Moser, could you tell me your full name please?"

She straightened. "Christmas Leigh Moser. That's L-E-I-G-H."

Watts's eyebrows raised, then lowered.

Reilly's did too. *Christmas.* He thought about what Christy had said about her sister, and remembered Ryker mentioning Moser's other daughter. Her name was odd too. Summer? No, Autumn.

He assessed Dr. Christmas Leigh Moser. Somehow, the name, which could easily have seemed silly, fit her. He wasn't sure why he thought that.

Buford Watts wrote something on his pad, then addressed Christy again. "Good. Now if you would, tell me exactly what happened."

"Certainly," she said coolly. "As you obviously already know, my father is Albert Moser." She waited for confirmation from the officers. They nodded.

"I flew in from Boston late last night." She paused. "I had to find physicians to take my patients before I could leave," she explained. "I went to his arraignment this morning. Then this afternoon I received a call that he had suffered an MI—a heart attack, so I went to the hospital." She stopped to take a fortifying breath. "He's in the cardiac care unit. I left there around six o'clock, stopped at a liquor store to pick up a bottle of wine, then drove here, to the inn. I parked in the lot out there."

"That's your car? The rental?" Deputy Watts asked.

She nodded. "Just as I parked the car, a light-colored pickup pulled in next to me. I walked to my cottage—Cottage Three," she amended. "I unlocked the door, but before I could enter, something hit me from behind. The blow knocked me to the floor. I landed on my wrist and fractured the scaphoid bone."

Both officers' gazes went to her right hand, which she held against her torso. At that moment, Reilly saw the flash of red lights through Ella Bardin's lace curtains and heard the crunch of tires on shells and gravel. "There's the ambulance," he said, earning him an angry glance from Christy.

"I told you—" she started, but he sent her a look that his brother Ryker had dubbed "The Silencer." It worked. She pressed her lips together and merely glared at him.

The EMTs made quick work of her broken wrist. For the most part, she'd been right. There was little that could be done about the bone that was broken. The EMTs iced it for a few minutes, then applied a pink cast that covered her palm and half of her thumb, and extended about four inches up her forearm.

"You need to ice your forehead too," he said, scrutinizing the bruised skin. "It'll help keep the swelling down, and maybe prevent a black eye."

"I know," she responded archly.

The EMT glanced over at Reilly, then applied a small bandage to her cheek. The bandage was also pink, with ladybugs on it.

Reilly was pretty sure Christy had no idea what was on the bandage. The wink one of the EMTs gave him on the way out confirmed it. Their way of getting her back for lecturing them about the futility of putting a cast on a scaphoid fracture.

Once the EMTs were gone, the officers resumed the questioning.

"You were saying that someone knocked you to the floor," Buford Watts prompted her.

She adjusted the ice pack. "Yes. I'd just unlocked and opened the door when I was hit from behind. The man landed on top of me. I tried to roll over, or buck or kick, but he was too heavy."

Reilly noticed a faint shiver tense her muscles. He doubted the officers saw it. They seemed mesmerized by her striking appearance, or maybe her calm recitation of what had happened.

Watts asked the question Reilly had asked her before. "You know it was a man? Did you get a good look at him?"

"No." A sharp syllable. "I was on my stomach and he was on top of me. But it was a man. No question." She met each officer's gaze, but didn't look at Reilly. Then she took a deep breath. "I know because he was straddling me."

Reilly's breath stuck in his throat. "Did he—?" he croaked, earning a stiff glance from the officer in charge. This wasn't Reilly's case. Not technically. For their purposes, he was merely a witness—the first person the victim had called.

Christy Moser looked directly at him for the first time since they'd come into the house. As before, when he'd looked into her eyes at the coffee kiosk, he thought he saw something underneath their cool darkness.

She gave a slight negative shake of her head. "I wasn't raped," she said quickly. "But it was obvious that he was male."

The younger officer's face turned pink. "Yes, ma'am,"

he said, then cleared his throat. "Did he—did he take anything?"

She shook her head. "Nothing. Apparently his only purpose in attacking me was to give me a message."

"A message?" the officer echoed.

Christy opened her mouth but before she could speak, Ella Bardin was back with a steaming mug of fragrant tea. "Here you go, dear. I'm sorry it took so long, but I wanted to wait until the EMTs were gone."

The two officers eyed the hot drink with covetousness in their gazes, but if Ella Bardin noticed, she gave no sign of it. Christy thanked her and held the cup in her left hand.

"You said the attacker left you a *message?*"

"That's right. He pushed my face against the hardwood floor and said, 'Go back where you came from or you're as dead as your sister.'"

Reilly watched the two officers. Both of them sat up straight in their seats.

"Your sister?" Watts said.

At the same time the younger officer echoed, "Get out of town?"

Christy Moser held up the hand with the cast. Her fingernails were perfectly manicured, except for the right index one, which was raggedly broken. "Let me explain," she said, much more calmly than the officers' outbursts. She took a quick breath and continued.

"My sister was murdered five years ago, on Bienville Street in the French Quarter. Her death was ruled a mugging, but my father was certain that she was murdered by a married man with whom she was having an affair. The night she died was her birthday and she'd gone down to the Quarter to celebrate."

The word *celebrate* took on an ironic tone. Reilly wondered just how much Christy knew about her sister and the man she'd been seeing.

"I've been in Boston for the past six years, doing a residency and then a fellowship in pediatrics at Children's Hospital. I had—" She paused and a fleeting shadow crossed her face. "I wasn't aware of everything that was going on. However, I believe that my attack this evening proves that my father was right. My sister's death wasn't just a mugging. And apparently whoever killed her feels threatened by my presence here."

Reilly noticed that the two officers seemed bewildered. He sympathized with them. He'd barely kept up with her rapid-fire explanation and conclusion, and he had the advantage of knowing something about the case from Ryker.

The lead officer looked at Reilly then back at Christy. "I think we need to get an official statement from you— downtown. And I'm going to call CSI to look for trace from the man who allegedly assaulted you."

"Allegedly?" Her voice was frosty.

"Legal terminology," Reilly commented in an effort to soften the officer's words. He was afraid if Christy stiffened any more, she'd break.

Turning to Watts, he said, "Can the statement wait until tomorrow? Dr. Moser is exhausted."

Watts sent him a glaring look, but nodded. "Sure. We can take the official statement tomorrow. But Ms.—Dr. Moser, you might want to give some thought to what you want in the official record. If you're prepared to make a written sworn statement to everything you've just told us, then you are accusing the man who assaulted you and threatened your life of killing your sister. If we're able to find any trace evidence and match it to someone, your statement accuses that person of murder."

Christy waited a few seconds, watching the officer closely,

but he didn't say anything else. She nodded. "That's exactly right, Officer. I am definitely accusing the man who attacked me of murdering my sister."

Chapter Three

After the police finished questioning Christy, they cordoned off and locked Cottage Three, holding it as a crime scene until the CSI team could process it the next day.

Ella Bardin insisted that Christy sleep in the front bedroom of the main house of the Oak Grove Inn, the Lakeview Room. It didn't look out over any lake Reilly had ever seen, but there were photos of famous lakes all over the room, including Lake Pontchartrain. After Ella made sure the room was in perfect condition, she excused herself, saying she had an early morning. Tomorrow was French toast day and she had to get up at five o'clock.

Reilly deposited the few items the officers had allowed Christy to grab from her cottage onto the antique dresser and turned to say good-night to her.

She was standing in the middle of the room, watching him carefully. She definitely looked the worse for wear. She'd twisted her glossy black hair into some kind of knot, but it was coming undone. Her torn skirt would have been indecent if not for the black lace slip. Her stockings were in shreds, and she'd long since discarded the single shoe and her jacket.

Her expression reflected her experience. It was at once angry, bewildered, frustrated and scared. Reilly felt an odd urge to cross the room and pull her into his arms. But Dr.

Christmas Moser wouldn't appreciate him peeking beneath her tough exterior. In fact, he knew what she'd say if he tried to offer comfort.

That does not accomplish anything, Officer. Surely you realize that.

"I heard your father had a heart attack," he said. "He's in the cardiac unit?"

She nodded.

"I'm sorry. You don't need any more stress right now."

"What's on your mind, Officer Delancey?"

The question surprised him. He'd already noticed her keen observation of the officers as they checked out her and her story. His grandmother's saying, "doesn't miss a trick," certainly applied to her.

"I'm not sure what you mean," he parried.

"I doubt that."

He inclined his head in agreement. If she was up to answering questions he had plenty to ask. "All right. How long did you say you'd been in Boston?"

"Six years." She reached up with her right hand to push a strand of hair out of her eyes and winced when the cast got in her way.

"Six years. And did you say you hadn't been home?"

"No. That's not what I said," she answered firmly, although Reilly thought he saw a flicker in her eyes that indicated that she wasn't telling the whole truth. As a sniper and sometimes leader of the hostage negotiation team for the St. Tammany Parish SWAT team, he'd made it a practice to study kinesiology—facial expressions, body language, all indicators of stress.

"I believe I said I hadn't known how badly my father was taking Autumn's death. Of course I've been home in the past six years."

"How many times?"

Christy lifted her chin. "Is all this on the record, Officer?"

He shook his head.

"Then I'd rather wait and give my statement once only, at the police station."

"No problem," he said. "I'll pick you up at eight o'clock, out front."

Her eyes went wide. "What?"

He smiled and nodded toward her right hand. "You can't very well drive with that cast on."

"Certainly I can," she shot back, but her right fingers twitched.

"Yeah? Touch each of your fingers to your thumb."

She set her mouth and lifted her hand. But the cast was too restrictive. She couldn't make her fingers and thumb touch. "I told the EMTs not to immobilize my thumb," she complained.

"Eight o'clock," he repeated. He thought he heard a feminine growl. "And in the meantime, you call me if you need me."

"There's no reason for you to appoint yourself my chauffeur. I'll take a taxi."

Reilly lay his hand on the cast where it covered her knuckles. "There is a reason. You asked me to help you."

She looked at his hand, then up at him. One day, he promised himself, he was going to explore that vulnerability she kept locked behind her snapping green eyes.

"I thought you were your brother at the time."

"Still," Reilly said with a grin. "You did ask. And you called me when you were attacked. I figure that makes it my responsibility to keep you safe. I have no intention of letting that guy get within a hundred yards of you. Consider me your knight in shining armor, until I'm sure you're no longer in danger."

"I don't need a knight—"

"Don't start with me, damsel," he said teasingly, touching her lips with his forefinger. "Whether you think you need me or not, you've got me."

CHRISTY WAS FUMING by the time Reilly Delancey left. She prided herself on being able to handle any situation. As a pediatrician specializing in trauma, her working life was all about emergencies.

Involving kids. Not herself. She glared at the cast on her wrist. How careless of her to break her wrist. Still, it shouldn't hinder her too much. As if to mock her, a throbbing ache began beneath the cast.

Reilly Delancey was a bully. Somehow, and she wasn't sure how, he'd gotten her to agree to ride with him. She sniffed. It was ridiculous. She could drive. A simple wrist cast wouldn't be that big a problem.

She wriggled the fingers of her right hand. A shooting pain made her gasp. Well, she amended, she could drive if she had to.

She was disgusted with herself. She should have been more careful. She'd seen dozens of children with wrist fractures because they instinctively reached out to break their fall. Tucking arms into the body and rolling was much safer. *If* one had time to react.

To be fair, she'd had no time. But now she had to live with a pink cast for several weeks.

She held up her hand and grimaced. *Pink.* Her colleagues in Boston would give her hell about that. Almost any color would have been better than pink. But the EMT had sworn the only colors of paste he had were pink or fluorescent green.

Now that she thought about it, wasn't the color added after

the paste was mixed? And wasn't the default color of the paste white? At the time she hadn't felt like protesting. So she had a pink cast and there was nothing she could do about it tonight.

She glanced at her watch. After ten o'clock. Reilly Delancey had told her he'd pick her up at eight in the morning. She needed to get some sleep.

Stepping into the bathroom, she reached up with her left hand to loosen her hair as she looked in the mirror. And stopped cold.

The EMT had applied a pink strip bandage with ladybugs on it. *Ladybugs.* She frowned at her image. Reilly Delancey was behind this. She was sure of it. He was nothing but trouble, and she didn't need any more trouble than she already had.

She quickly undressed, dropping the skirt and the shredded stockings into the trash can in the bathroom. Digging into her suitcase, she unearthed her pink satin pajamas.

Staring at them, her face flamed, even though she was alone. Damn those EMTs and Reilly Delancey. How had he known—?

She stopped that thought right there. He couldn't have known that she loved wearing pretty, feminine lingerie under her utilitarian work clothes. Although—his blue eyes *were* awfully sharp, and it looked as if he never missed a trick.

After a painful few minutes spent getting the pajamas on, she turned back the covers awkwardly and climbed into bed. But when she tried to relax and clear her mind, she couldn't stop her thoughts from racing.

—where you came from or you're as dead as your sister.

—Mr. Moser, do you understand that by pleading guilty, you are giving up your right to a trial?

—I did it. I killed those girls.

Your father has had a heart attack—

Christy turned over and squeezed her eyes shut. But closed eyes couldn't block the mental image of the emergency room technician loading all the heart monitors and IVs onto her father's gurney and wheeling him onto the elevator to take him up to the cardiac care unit.

Christy hadn't been able to take her eyes off her dad. Against the white sheets he looked small, frail, vulnerable. He looked nothing like the man who'd reared her and her sister.

Her eyes stung and hot tears squeezed out between her closed lids. Sniffling and telling herself that tears never solved a problem, she turned over again and tried to find a comfortable position for her wrist.

But despite her resolve, the tears kept on coming. They slid over the bridge of her nose and down her cheek to the pillow. When had her family fallen apart? When had her dad changed from a big, strong parent, raising two daughters on his own, into a deranged killer?

WHEN REILLY GOT TO THE Oak Grove Inn the next morning, Christy was waiting in the foyer.

"Morning," he said with a smile, which faded as he took in her injuries. "Wow, they weren't kidding about that bruise. Did you put ice on your forehead?"

"Of course. Otherwise I *would* have a black eye. You're late."

Reilly nodded. "Miss Ella caught me as I was leaving last night. She told me to wait until eight-thirty so you could eat breakfast. French toast day today, right?" He reached out and wiped a speck of powdered sugar off her chin. "Hard to eat with a cast on, isn't it? Think how tough it would be to drive."

Christy swiped at her chin with two fingers. "Are you ready to go?"

"Yep." He opened the front door and stepped aside to let her precede him out the door. This morning she had on brown pants and a cream-colored top with long sleeves that stretched over the cast on her wrist and a short brown sweater. He didn't see any buttons anywhere. She'd picked an outfit that was easy to don.

"You look nice," he commented as he followed her to his car.

"Thank you," she said stiffly. She reached for the passenger-door handle with her left hand, but he stretched around her and opened the door. When he did, her hair brushed his cheek. A bolt of lightning-hot lust shot straight to his groin.

Damn. His reaction surprised him. So much that he'd almost gasped. He immediately straightened, putting the door between him and her, but not before his nose caught a subtle floral scent that was very familiar to him. Christy Moser smelled like the gardenias that grew in his grandmother Lilibelle's garden.

As Christy climbed into the car, Reilly swallowed. When had he gone from merely admiring her figure and feeling protective of her to lusting after her? Of course, as soon as he asked the question he knew the answer. About two seconds after he'd first spotted her walking across the courthouse lobby.

In fact, he'd woken up in a very uncomfortable state this morning, with the dregs of a sexy dream involving the two of them and dozens of ladybugs floating in his head.

He tried to make small talk on the way to the sheriff's office. He pointed out the Christmas decorations that lined the streets of Covington and made comments about Christmas in the South, where shorts and sandals were more appropriate attire than parkas and boots.

Christy seemed distracted, staring out the window at nothing. Probably thinking about her attack the night before and the statement she was going to have to make in a few minutes.

As he pulled into the parking lot at the sheriff's office, she turned to him. "I never heard from Detective Delancey. I need to talk to him."

Reilly winced. He'd forgotten to call Ryker. "I'll let him know. I'm going to see him this morning." He wanted to ask Ryker about Autumn Moser's case. Whether, after Albert Moser's confession and the connection between the murders he committed and his daughter's death, the case was going to be reopened.

If it was—

"You told me you'd let him know yesterday."

"Yes, I did," he said rather testily. "But the day got busy, for you as well as me." He cut the engine and got out of the car. He knew that Christy had more than one reason to be upset and irritable. And he couldn't deny how beautiful and sexy she was, but he was getting a little tired of her officious attitude.

He walked around the car and opened the passenger door for her.

"Thank you," she muttered as she got out. He followed her into the building and directed her down the hall to the interview rooms.

Buford Watts was standing near the break room, drinking a cup of coffee. When he saw them, he set the coffee mug down on the top of a bookcase and stepped up to Christy.

"Morning, Ms. Moser."

Reilly started to correct him, then bit his tongue. If Christy wanted to remind the man that she was a doctor, she could do it herself.

"Good morning," she responded evenly.

"I've got a room set up for us. It's right through there." Buford pointed the way to Interview Room Two. The door was open. Christy entered and Reilly followed, but Buford stopped him at the door.

"Don't you have something to do this morning, Delancey?"

Reilly shook his head. "This week the SWAT team is practicing and recertifying weapons skills. I finished yesterday." He gave Buford a bright smile. "You said I could sit in on the interview."

"The interview last night. Nobody said anything about this morning," Buford said.

"Well, do you have a problem with me sitting in?"

The deputy muttered something under his breath and went into the room. Reilly entered behind him. Buford indicated a chair for Christy to sit in, then sat directly across from her, with the tape recorder in the middle of the table.

Reilly moved a chair to a neutral spot at the end of the table, neither on Christy's side nor Buford's.

Buford turned on the tape recorder and went through the required preliminary information—date, name, location and so on. He quickly and casually ran through the questions he'd asked Christy the night before.

Then he leaned forward and picked up a folder that was lying near his right hand. "Ms. Moser—Dr. Moser that is—our crime scene investigator team went over to the Oak Grove Inn this morning and checked out Cottage Three. They didn't find any trace evidence specific to your case."

Christy stiffened. "What do you mean? Are you saying I made up the attack?"

"Now, now, Miss. I'm not doubting you were attacked. That was obvious. But as good a housekeeper as Miss Ella is, there was a lot of hair and dust and stuff on the floor of that cottage. CSI told me they didn't find anything that could be definitely linked to last night."

Christy tried to fold her hands in front of her but the cast interfered. The fingers and thumb of her left hand played with the edge of the cast. Her gaze flickered to Reilly and away.

"What about the pickup that followed me into the parking lot?"

"Well," Buford reached into his pocket for a small notepad. "That belongs to a Chester Ragsdale. He lives over in Covington. Him and his wife had a spat over the weekend, so he's been staying there in Cottage One the past few days. He said he's gonna try to go home today." Buford took a breath. "My partner talked to him and to the couple from Mississippi who were in Cottage Two. None of them saw or heard anything."

Reilly saw and felt Christy's frustration.

"So you're telling me there's nothing you can do to find the man who attacked me?"

"I'd like you to think back on last night. I know you're awfully upset about your daddy. I don't suppose anyone can blame you for that. And I'm sorry to hear that he's in the hospital. But I do have to ask these questions. When the person knocked you down, tell me again what he said."

She eyed him narrowly. "He said, 'Go back where you came from or you're as dead as your sister.'"

Buford tapped his pencil on the desktop and watched it. "And you're sure about that?"

"Yes." The word was coated in frost.

"Why do you think somebody would go to all that trouble to warn you to get out of town?"

"Officer Watts," Christy said in measured tones. "Five years ago, my sister was shot while I was on the phone with her. I heard her scream. I heard the—shots." She took a breath and sent a quick glance toward Reilly. "The only times I've been back in Chef Voleur since her funeral were once for a seminar three years ago, and then two weeks ago. I flew down here to check on my father after I was notified about his first MI, while he was in jail."

"MI?"

"Myocardial infarction—heart attack."

Watts nodded.

Christy brushed her hair back, a typical sign of discomfort or deceit. Reilly didn't think she was being deceitful.

"I flew back to Boston the same day." She stopped and looked at Watts.

He looked at the eraser tip on his pencil, then back up at her. He raised his eyebrows. "You flew in when your father was put in the hospital. What about when he was arrested?"

She shook her head. "I was busy—on call. I couldn't leave my patients."

The detective nodded and wrote something on his notepad.

"Don't you see?" she asked. "The man who attacked me is the man who killed my sister—" Christy's voice gave out. She swallowed and spread her hands. "He knew I'd be here for the sentencing."

Her words hung in the air. She looked at Buford, then at Reilly, then back at Buford. Her eyes were bright with unshed tears. "Isn't it obvious? The man who killed my sister knows she was on the phone with me. He obviously is worried that I heard something and can identify him."

Reilly didn't say a word. Buford sat still, his eyes on Christy, as if he were weighing her words. Then he sat up straight. "All right. I think that's all for now, Ms. Moser." He reached for the tape recorder.

"What?" Christy stared at him. "That's *all?* Are you saying you don't believe me?"

Buford punched the off button on the recorder, ejected the tape and stuck it into his shirt pocket. Then he pushed his chair back. Its legs screeched along the floor. He stood with a grunt.

"Why, no, ma'am. I'm not saying that at all. I *am* at a loss to explain how this man who you think killed your sister found you, watched you and followed you, when you'd only been in town for around twenty-four hours."

Christy didn't stand. "You're at a *loss?* I don't see how it could be any clearer, Officer. My father's arrest and arraignment were in all the papers. If my father is right about my sister's death, and I believe he is, then the man who killed her is the married man she was seeing." She stopped long enough to take a breath.

"He knew she had a sister. Even if he didn't know who she was talking to on the phone, her phone is missing. Isn't it logical to infer that he took her phone and saw my number? Naturally, he would expect me to show up at the courthouse. It would be simple for him to spot me there and follow me. Wouldn't it?" She addressed that question to Reilly before turning her icy gaze back to Buford Watts.

"I have to agree, Buford," Reilly said. "It's a theory."

Buford nodded his head. "It coulda happened that way. I just can't make a case for it."

Reilly thought of something. "What about her clothes?" he asked.

Buford had picked up his pencil and was studying the end of it. He frowned at Reilly.

"Her clothes. The skirt, jacket and blouse. Did CSI test her clothes?" Reilly asked him.

The older officer picked up the manila folder and paged through the sheets. "I don't reckon they did."

"Nobody thought about testing her clothes?"

Buford sent Reilly a narrow gaze. "You were there, and being so all-fired helpful. Why didn't you think of it? Hell, you coulda hired somebody to do it for you."

Reilly didn't bother answering him. The resentment had been bound to surface sooner or later. He and Ryker both caught a lot of flak because of their infamous, wealthy grand-parents. It was no secret that the Delancey grandkids weren't hurting for money, or that a lot of that money had been made in Louisiana politics, off the backs of citizens.

"I put the skirt and stockings in the trash," Christy inter-jected. "In the bathroom."

"Buford, call them now. Before Ella Bardin puts out the trash. Get the skirt and stockings. Her blouse and jacket too."

Buford nodded irritably and left the room.

Reilly looked at Christy and gave her a rueful shrug.

She sniffed. "Why do you think I left Louisiana?" she said archly.

"It's not the place," he said. "It's the people. There are good people and bad people everywhere."

When she winced, he realized that his words had hit too close to home.

IT WAS AFTER ONE O'CLOCK before Deputy Watts was done with questioning Christy and forcing her to read her tran-scribed statements. She'd slowly and meticulously made changes to the transcription using her left hand.

To his credit, the deputy had ordered in po' boy sand-wiches and iced tea for lunch. To his discredit, the po' boys weren't seafood. They were piled high with ham and cheese and mustard—loads of mustard. Christy had picked at hers, tearing off bits of the delicious French bread and washing it down with sweet tea.

Reilly stayed with her the whole time. She didn't want him to know how much that meant to her. She didn't want anyone to know that. It bothered her that in two days Reilly Delancey had become the one constant in her suddenly out-of-control life.

She'd heard of the Delanceys. Everyone who'd grown up in Louisiana had. Because of their infamous grandfather, they were all stinking rich. Didn't have to work a day if they didn't want to. So why had Reilly and his brother become cops? She assessed Reilly. He looked sincere and genuinely delighted with his sandwich. But she didn't know him. She couldn't take the risk of depending on him.

She'd never allowed herself to depend on anyone—never looked to a man for validation—except her father. She wasn't happy that Reilly Delancey had appointed himself her protector. Even if she had no idea how she'd have gotten through last night and this morning without him.

"Are you sure you don't want something else to eat?" he asked for the third time as he drove her to the hospital to see her father.

"I'm positive," she responded shortly. Her stomach was growling, but she was about to see her father for the first time since he'd been admitted to the cardiac care unit. Even if she could have eaten, she was pretty sure she wouldn't have been able to hold it down.

Reilly placed his hand at the small of her back as they walked through the halls to the doors of the CCU.

"Thanks for bringing me here," she said dismissively. "What time will you pick me up?"

Reilly looked at his watch, then at a sign beside the door. It listed visiting hours as twenty minutes every hour between 7:00 a.m. and 7:00 p.m.

"I've got a few things to do. What if I pick you up at four-thirty? Then you can have three visits with him."

She nodded. "That'll be good. The nurse told me yesterday

that if it wasn't too busy this afternoon, I could stay a little longer." She took a shaky breath and sighed.

"Christy? You're sure you're okay? I can get back here earlier if you need me to."

She shook her head. "No. I need to be with my dad as much as I can, before—"

Reilly gave her a searching look before nodding. "I'll see you at four-thirty then." He turned and headed back toward the front of the building.

She knew what Reilly was thinking, as clearly as if he'd spoken aloud. How could she sit there at her father's bedside, knowing he'd killed four young women? How could she still view him as her dad, as the man who'd reared her and taught her the values she now embraced?

"I don't know," she whispered as she pressed the automatic door opener and showed the nurse her visitor's badge. She braced herself for the woman's reaction when she said, "I'm here to see Albert Moser. I'm his daughter."

Chapter Four

While Christy visited with her father, Reilly searched out Ryker in his office.

"Hey, old man," he greeted his older-by-seven-minutes brother. "How's Nicole?"

His brother's normally solemn face lit up at the mention of his fiancée. "She's fine. The burns on her hands are almost healed."

"Thank God they were only first-degree."

"Thank God I got there before Moser shot her," Ryker said hoarsely.

Reilly had never seen him so passionate about anything or anyone. Things had always come easy for his brother. Ryker had excelled at everything. And beaten Reilly. In high school, Ryker was quarterback, leaving Reilly to settle for wide receiver. Ryker had graduated top of his class. Reilly was second.

Both had joined the St. Tammany Parish Sheriff's Department, but Ryker had gotten the coveted detective position. Reilly, who was the better shot, had been chosen for SWAT.

And now, Ryker was getting married and once again Reilly was one step behind. *One step,* hell—he corrected himself. He wasn't even dating anyone.

"Speaking of Moser," he responded. "I've got a few questions about his daughter's case."

Ryker sent him an arch look. "Moser's daughter that was murdered? That's an NOPD case. It was shelved as a mugging five years ago."

Reilly sat down in the chair across from Ryker's desk. "Albert Moser's older daughter sought me out at the courthouse yesterday. Thought I was you. She gave me an earful before I could get a word in to tell her she had the wrong twin."

"Oh, yeah, *Doctor* Moser. The Ice Queen."

Reilly smiled and shook his head. "Ice Queen? Yeah, not so much. She was attacked last night at her cottage at the Oak Grove Inn."

Ryker sat and pushed folders out of his way. He leaned back. "I heard about the attack. I've just started looking into Autumn's case again to get a better read on Christy's situation. She okay?"

"Broken wrist and contusions."

"How're you involved? Other than your obvious preference for tall gorgeous brunettes. Tell me she doesn't have green eyes."

Reilly pointedly ignored him. "Yesterday, I told her I'd have you get in touch with her, and I gave her my cell number."

"Your cell number. Why didn't you give her mine?" Ryker's blue eyes sparked with mischief.

Reilly didn't bother to answer. "When she was attacked, she managed to grab her phone and quick-dial my number."

"So you were first on scene?"

"Yeah. I called for backup, but by the time I got there the guy was gone." Reilly took a breath. "You won't believe what he said to her."

Ryker waited.

"He told her, 'Get out of town or you're as dead as your sister.'"

"He said that?"

Reilly nodded. "So what did you find out about the case? Is NOPD going to look at it again?"

"Doubt it. I called Dixon Lloyd at the Eighth, down on Royal Street in the Quarter, and got the name of the detective who caught Autumn Moser's case. His name was—" Ryker grabbed a small notepad that lay on the corner of his desk and paged through it for a few seconds. "Fred Samhurst."

Reilly grabbed a piece of paper from Ryker's trash can and made a note. "Samhurst. What'd he have to say?"

"Where are you going with this, kid?"

"Christy could have been killed last night. Her life was threatened. And if the man who attacked her didn't kill her sister, he knows who did."

"Well, Moser never gave up the notion that his daughter was killed by someone she knew. He thought it was a married man. He said his daughter told him the man was obsessive about keeping the affair quiet. Said his reputation and his career would be in jeopardy. Who's handling Christy's case?"

"Wait a minute," Reilly said. "Go back to the married man. His reputation and career would be in jeopardy?"

Ryker shrugged. "That's what he told me. I thought maybe it was someone Moser knew, and that's why she wouldn't tell him. But Moser insisted he didn't know anybody who would be fired if he was caught having an affair."

"But she thought Moser would recognize him?"

"I thought about that. Maybe he wouldn't have *known* the man. Not personally. Maybe the guy was a celebrity or a politician. Someone in the public eye." Ryker leaned back in his chair. "Moser nixed the celebrity idea. Said if the man were rich, Autumn would have made him buy her stuff. He was right about that. There was no sign in her belongings that someone was spending money on her."

"So maybe what he bought her was drugs," Reilly said.

Ryker's brows drew down into a frown. "Why all the questions? What are you up to, kid?"

"I want to help Christy. I want to find the bastard who attacked her and see what he knows. What I don't understand is why no one listened to her father. Why wasn't Autumn Moser's case reopened a long time ago?"

"I can't answer that. I can tell you that the detective who caught the case probably missed something."

Reilly laughed without humor. "Yeah? You think so?"

"Do you want to hear what I know? I've got plenty to do. I could just let you dig it up yourself."

"Don't go all big-brother master detective on me, Ryker." Reilly hated it when Ryker took that supercilious attitude.

"Fine. Dixon didn't want to rag on a fellow detective, but he did tell me that a couple of years ago Samhurst had a mild heart attack. Said he lost a lot of weight—maybe thirty pounds or so—which left him about forty pounds overweight."

"Are you kidding me? He was that overweight and out of shape? No telling what he missed. How in hell is he still on active duty?"

Ryker shrugged. "Everybody's shorthanded."

"What else did Dixon tell you?"

"Nothing. I talked to Samhurst, but he didn't have much to say. He got real defensive and claimed he didn't remember much. I asked him why three point-blank shots to the chest didn't throw up a red flag, but he didn't have an answer."

"Three shots to the chest? That's how she died? Holy—" Reilly felt a sick weight in his chest. "No wonder Christy wants someone to reopen the case. Did you know she was on the phone with her sister when she was shot?"

"Yep. She gave me the gist of the conversation, and I got copies of her sister's case file from NOPD."

"Yeah? What about the sister's phone? Christy said it turned up missing."

"That's right. It was never recovered. Frankly, I think Samhurst blew it, big time. He never should have written it up as a mugging."

"That does seem outrageous. A mugger unloading point-blank into a young girl when any night of the week the Quarter is crawling with drunk guys with full wallets. And what would a mugger want with a phone that could be traced to him?"

Ryker nodded in agreement. "What I don't get, is if the doctor's so all-fired intent on catching her sister's killer now, where was she back then?"

"In Boston, doing her residency or something."

Ryker shook his head. "Think about it. If she'd come home and stirred all this up with NOPD, maybe somebody would have looked at Samhurst's conclusions more closely. It could have saved four young women's lives."

That sick weight in Reilly's chest got a lot heavier. "Yeah. I have a feeling Christy hasn't missed that point."

Ryker nodded grimly. "Okay. I can give you a copy of my files and report. But, kid, I don't know what you think you're going to do—"

Reilly stood. "I'll tell you what I'm going to do. I'm going to find out what happened to Autumn Moser."

Ryker stared up at him. "How exactly? Are you going to go barging into the Eighth Precinct of the NOPD and demand justice?"

"You just get me your reports. And everything you've got on the sister's case."

"Reilly—"

"I may not be a detective, but I'm a law-enforcement

officer. And if I can't do anything through official channels, I'll do it unofficially."

Ryker stood too. "This isn't like you, kid. Tell me you're not trying to get into Christy Moser's—"

"Hey!" Reilly snapped. "Of course not. Come on, Ryker. You saw her. She looks tough as nails on the outside, but she's about to fall apart."

"Well, I definitely saw the tough-as-nails part. And, by the way, the gorgeous part. But falling apart? Nah, she seemed perfectly together to me."

"Well, she's not. Think about it. She's lost her mother and her sister and may lose her father, and now her life is being threatened. She needs someone on her side."

"Okay, Christy Moser's life sucks right now. Why are you getting involved? If she needs protecting, give her the number of Dawson's security agency. She can pay for a bodyguard." Reilly glared at his brother, but before he could open his mouth, Ryker blew out a breath between his teeth. "Don't tell me you've appointed yourself her knight in shining armor?"

Reilly didn't like Ryker's sarcastic tone. "Well," he drawled, "it's not like I'll be the first Delancey twin to do that."

Ryker's lips thinned. "Be careful, Reilly. Don't lose your job over this woman."

"Trust me, old man. If it comes down to my job or her life, it will be an easy choice. I don't intend to let Christy Moser out of my sight until I'm sure she's no longer in danger."

REILLY LEFT RYKER'S office with the Autumn Moser file and headed over to the office of the SWAT commander. He needed to let him know what he was going to be doing, and he didn't want to try to explain over the phone.

Errol "Ace" Acer had been on the St. Tammany Parish SWAT team since its inception in 1980. He'd been SWAT

commander for three years. Reilly was one of fourteen officers who, in essence, had two bosses. Mike Davis, the chief
deputy of the Chef Voleur office of the St. Tammany Parish
Sheriff's Office, and SWAT commander, Acer.

He wanted to get Ace's approval before going through the
chief deputy for his request for leave. He drove over to the
SWAT leader's office.

"Ace, got a minute?"

Acer looked up, his rugged, lined face grave. When he
saw Reilly, a corner of his somber mouth turned up. "Sure,
Delancey. Sit."

"Thanks." Reilly didn't want to spend a lot of time chewing
the fat with the veteran SWAT officer, although he usually
enjoyed it. He needed to get the okay from him and put in
his request to Mike Davis before he had to get back to pick
up Christy.

Ace stacked the papers he'd been perusing and set them
aside with a sigh.

"Problem?"

Ace shrugged one shoulder. "Nothing new. The parents
of that kid that shot his buddy over at Ramey Middle School
are suing the department."

"Damn," Reilly commiserated. "That was as clean a talk-
down as we've ever done."

Ace nodded. "Right. You did a terrific job."

Reilly shook his head. "Everybody did. We were lucky
that time."

"Damn straight."

The bottom line of any SWAT team conversation after
an incident, whether it was a talk-down or a takedown, was
always the same.

We were lucky that time.

Damn straight.

Reilly had never been in a situation that had turned out

"unlucky," which meant that a police officer had been killed. There had only been one incident like that—eleven years ago. One was enough.

"But you're not here to keep me company. What's up?" Ace leaned back in his chair and intertwined his fingers behind his head.

"I want to take leave, and I wanted to ask you first."

"Leave?" Ace's white eyebrows shot up. "Since when? And why are you asking me? Administratively, you're under Mike."

Reilly had never taken any time off, not in the entire four years he'd been on the force. "It's kind of a personal issue," he said. "You're familiar with the October Killer case?"

Ace nodded.

"Moser's daughter is here for the arraignment, and she was attacked last night."

The SWAT commander didn't comment, nor did his expression change. He just waited.

"The attacker told her if she didn't get out of town, she'd be 'as dead as her sister.'" Reilly sat forward. "I want to see if I can help her get her sister's case reopened."

Ace closed his eyes for a moment. "You know that's going to be touchy, since your brother's the primary on her father's case." Typically, he didn't waste words or time. He got straight to the point.

"Yes, sir. Actually, I'm not asking to be excused from SWAT duty. I'll still be on call 24/7. I just wanted to let you know and see if you approved of me taking time from regular duties before I put in my request to Deputy Chief Davis."

Ace sat up. "Sounds good to me. Go for it."

Reilly stood, a little surprised. He'd half expected Ace to react the same way his brother had. But if Ace thought Reilly was being foolish to run off chasing an ice-cold case, he kept his opinion to himself. "Thank you, sir. I'll make sure that Dispatch knows I'm still on call."

Reilly drove back to Chef Voleur and caught Deputy Chief Mike Davis just as he was leaving his office.

"Chief, have you got a minute?"

"On my way to see the sheriff. What is it?"

"I want to take some leave. About a week. Maybe two."

"Leave? Before Christmas?" Mike blinked. "Can Ace spare you from the SWAT team?"

"I talked to him earlier. If you approve, I'll take time from my regular duties but I'll still be available for SWAT duty."

Mike stopped at the door to the parking lot. "What's this about, Reilly?"

Reilly took a deep breath. "Well, sir, I was the first one on the scene at the Oak Grove Inn last night, where a woman was attacked by an unknown assailant."

Mike's eyes narrowed. "Yeah?"

"The woman who was attacked is Albert Moser's daughter. Her attacker told her to get out of town or she'd end up as dead as her sister."

"Moser? The October Killer? Delancey, what the hell are you up to?"

"Sir, she appealed to me to help her find her sister's killer. I want to do that."

"That's an NOPD Detective Division issue, since the girl was killed down in the French Quarter." Mike pushed open the glass door. "Besides, it's a cold case."

"I'm not asking you to approve what I want to do. I'm just asking for time off."

"You're skating on thin ice here, Delancey. I can't defend you if anyone complains."

"Yes, sir. I understand that. Can I get the leave?"

Mike scowled. "I'll have to verify it with Jean-Marie. She's working on the leave schedule for the holidays now. But if you'll agree to work over Christmas, I can probably swing a week right now."

"Thank you, sir."

"Why in hell are you getting mixed up with the October Killer's daughter?"

Reilly didn't see any need to go into detail about *why* he became involved, so he just repeated the facts. "Yesterday, Christy Moser asked me to help her find her sister's killer. Last night she was attacked by someone who threatened her life." He set his jaw and looked at Mike Davis steadily.

"I intend to make sure that the person who got close enough to Christy Moser to threaten her doesn't get that close to her again."

CHRISTY SAT IN THE backseat of the taxi with her head against the seat and her eyes closed, trying to will herself to stop crying. It had been awful the day before, seeing her dad dressed in the ugly orange prison jumpsuit with his hands cuffed in front of him. But as bad as that had been, it didn't hold a candle to seeing him lying in the cardiac care unit, with wires and tubes running everywhere.

Her father was only sixty-two, yet he looked a decade older, if not more. He'd already seemed to age since his first heart attack, which occurred soon after he was arrested. But now, lying so still in that bed, in a mesh of wires and tubes, he looked ancient, shrunken, his complexion nearly as gray as his hair.

His nurse told her they'd sedated him to keep him calm. He reacted when he heard her voice, but he didn't respond. All he did was moan or mutter unintelligibly.

Christy held her breath to keep from sobbing. The man in the cardiac care unit wasn't the man who'd reared Autumn and her, who'd been so strong when their mother had died, who'd celebrated all their achievements and all their special moments with photographs and pages in the big family album he'd kept all their lives.

"Ma'am?"

Christy heard the voice and realized it wasn't the first time she'd heard it. She opened her eyes. It was the taxi driver. The car was stopped.

She squinted through the window. She was here. Her dad's house.

"Oh, thank you," she said as she got out. "Please wait for me."

"Hey, lady. Fares are stacking up. I can't afford to wait. You call the dispatcher when you're ready to go. You owe me thirty-two dollars."

She handed him two twenties. As he pulled away, she reached into her purse and retrieved her key. Thank goodness the officer who'd caught her here the other day hadn't taken it away from her.

She walked up to the door, where new crime-scene tape had replaced the old, and unlocked it. She ducked beneath the tape and entered the house.

The first thing she did was go to the kitchen to look for light bulbs. She was shocked at what she saw. Her dad had never been an excellent housekeeper. He usually ate takeout off paper plates and left them sitting on the kitchen table for days at a time. Often as not, when he made a pan of cornbread, he'd leave the skillet sitting on the stove.

But today, to Christy's shock, everything was spotless. The kitchen table had been wiped and polished. The stove was clean, the sink was empty and there was no old food or grease smell. Even the coffeepot had been cleaned.

A profound sadness shrouded Christy. Her dad had known. He'd known he wouldn't be coming back here. She could imagine him that morning. He'd cleaned up as best he could, because he'd expected to die that day. The day that he lied to her and told her he was making a pan of cornbread for his lunch.

Christy moaned and dropped into a kitchen chair, giving in to a few minutes of helpless sobbing. When she was all cried out, at least for the moment, she got a glass from the cupboard and filled it with tap water and drank. Then she wiped the glass clean and put it back where it belonged. She didn't want to mess up the kitchen her father had cleaned so meticulously. Or telegraph to the police that she'd been there.

Wiping her eyes and pulling in a deep, sustaining breath, she retrieved a box of light bulbs from under the sink, then headed back through the living room and into her sister's bedroom.

She tried the overhead light and the lamp, expecting the bulbs to be burned out, but they weren't. Maybe the police had added new bulbs while they were searching the house. Or maybe her dad had never turned on the lights in Autumn's room since her death.

Christy set the box on Autumn's bedside table, noticing that the police had spread gray fingerprint dust here too. She surveyed the room. The bed had been pulled out from the wall, the drawers of Autumn's dresser were standing open and clothes were piled and scattered, as if careless police hands had rifled through all of them.

Tears welled in her eyes again, but she dashed them away with a swipe of her fingers. She didn't have time to wallow in grief and guilt. She had to get back to the hospital before four-thirty. The rest of her day would go a whole lot easier if Reilly didn't catch her showing up in a taxi, when she was supposed to be there waiting for him.

She looked at Autumn's closet, wondering how thoroughly the police had searched it. Not thoroughly enough, she prayed as she set her purse on the bed and braced herself for the task of searching through her sister's things.

First, she surveyed the racks of clothes and the shelf above the clothing rod. Autumn's taste had always been eclectic, running from black and silver Goth outfits to wild tropical prints and skinny jeans. On the shelf were motorcycle boots sitting alongside sexy, strappy sandals. Her sister's taste in clothes hadn't changed much since Christy had left home when Autumn was sixteen.

She eyed a pile of clothes in the bottom of the closet and wondered if they were Autumn's discards or if they'd been dropped there by the police when they searched. It didn't matter. Not anymore.

Christy pushed the clothes aside and moved a couple of pairs of shoes and a single sock away from the interior wall near the left side of the door. Then she bent down and reached out to slip her thumbnail behind the baseboard.

"Ow," she muttered, pulling her cast-wrapped hand back. Her broken wrist did not want to bend in that direction.

At that moment she heard a car door slam. She froze, not daring to breathe. After a few seconds she heard what sounded like a front door closing, probably across the street. She blew her breath out carefully as she glanced at her watch. She only had about twenty minutes before she needed to get back.

She should have called the taxi back as soon as the grumpy driver left. She had no idea how long it would take to get a taxi out this way. But now that she thought about it, a taxi sitting in front of the house would cause questions. She certainly didn't want the neighbors calling the police to report a suspicious vehicle.

Quickly, she slid farther into the closet on her knees, maneuvering so she could use her left hand to pry the baseboard loose. Christy had never hidden things from her parents. Well, almost never.

But from the moment Autumn could walk, she'd been a pack rat, saving little treasures and secreting them away. She'd been six when she'd discovered the loose baseboard in her closet and the hollow space behind it. She'd shown it to Christy and made her promise never to tell their parents.

Christy never had.

The baseboard fit tightly against the wall. No one would suspect it was loose. Christy slipped her fingernails between the baseboard and the wall and pulled gently. The board gave.

Her heart jumped. *Don't get too excited,* she warned herself. Autumn at six, twelve or even sixteen, hadn't been the same person as Autumn at twenty-one. It could have been years since she'd hidden anything in her secret place. The chance that there might be something there that would give Christy a clue to who had killed her sister was minuscule.

Christy pried the baseboard away from the wall, noting that the adhesive was a piece of chewing gum. *Chewing gum.* She giggled and her heart twisted.

She had to maneuver more before she could slide her hand into the empty space. She cringed, hoping no spiders had taken up residence in her sister's hiding place.

Her fingers immediately encountered a wad of rolled paper. She pulled it out and gasped. Twenty-dollar bills. A lot of them, rolled up and secured with a pink Cinderella ribbon. The sight of the dirty money wrapped with the innocent ribbon was heartbreaking.

"Oh, Tum-tum," she whispered, using the nickname she'd given her sister when Autumn was a baby. "What were you doing?"

Reaching in again, she found a cardboard box. It was barely small enough to fit through the opening, and it took some fancy maneuvering with her left hand to get it out. It was taped up with duct tape. Setting it beside the roll of twenties, she explored the space one more time. In the farthest corner she could reach, she felt some coins and a length of what felt like more ribbon. She pulled them out. The dusty ribbon matched the ribbon used to tie up the bills.

She looked at the coins. Two were Louisiana quarters. But the third disk wasn't a coin at all. It was a button. A brass button, with a few navy-blue fibers attached to it with matching thread.

Christy secured the piece of board back against the wall and crawled out of the closet. When she did, she spotted a cell phone charger plugged into the wall. She grabbed it. Autumn's phone—the phone she'd used to call Christy the night she'd died—had never been found. Christy quickly searched the room, knowing she wouldn't find it. The police had already turned the house upside down. She wondered why they hadn't taken the cord. She looked at it, then put it in her purse, not really knowing why.

She got to her feet and grabbed a tissue out of a box on Autumn's bedside table. She didn't know if it would do any good, since she'd already handled the coins and the button, but she wrapped them in the tissue and stowed it, the box and the roll of twenties in her purse. As much as she was dying to see what was in the box, she knew she needed to get out of there and back to the hospital.

She headed back to the kitchen, set her purse down on the counter, washed her hands and dried them with a paper towel. Then she inspected her clothes. Her pants were covered with cobwebs and dust. Muttering a mild curse, she looked in the junk drawer. A roll of masking tape. Just what she needed. She took a strip of tape in both hands and slid the sticky side along the material of her brown pants, lifting away the dust and cobwebs. As soon as her clothes were halfway presentable, she'd call another taxi.

With any luck, Reilly would never know she hadn't been at the hospital the whole time.

Chapter Five

At four-thirty on the dot, Reilly parked in front of St. Tammany Parrish Medical Center and went inside to pick up Christy. She was nowhere to be found. The waiting room receptionist told him she'd called a taxi.

"Damn it," he muttered, heading back to his car. He should never have left her alone. He should have given her a half hour to sit with her dad and then made her go with him. But after her assault, her dad's heart attack and the grilling Buford Watts had given her this morning, he'd figured she was too upset and exhausted to run off on her own. In fact, she'd almost leaned on him as he'd walked with her to the cardiac care unit earlier. *Almost*.

He'd thought maybe she'd decided that it wasn't so bad having him beside her. Well, she'd shown him. She'd given him the slip the first chance she'd gotten.

Clever, Doc. But not for long.

Hopefully, she'd decided to go back to her room and rest. He headed to the Oak Grove Inn to make sure she was okay. He'd get Ella to check on her, and if she was asleep, he wouldn't bother her. Tomorrow was soon enough to fuss at her for not waiting for him. But a niggling voice in the back of his mind told him Christy Moser was not the type to spend an afternoon in bed.

When he vaulted up the steps of the white clapboard main

house at the bed-and-breakfast, Ella met him at the door, broom in hand.

"Afternoon, Reilly. Watch out."

Reilly stepped back barely in time to miss being coated with the dirt and dust she swept across the threshold.

Once Ella was done, she looked up, past Reilly. "Where's Christy?"

"She's not here?" Reilly asked, not really surprised.

"No." Ella's sharp bird eyes scrutinized Reilly. "D'you lose her?"

He clamped his jaw. "No, I did not lose her." He just didn't know where she was.

Ella gripped her broom like a weapon. "Well, shoo. Get back out there and find her. She doesn't need to be running around on her own. She's hurt and heartsick."

"Yes, ma'am," Reilly said as he backed down the steps, dusting off his pants. Okay, that was a waste of time. Think like her. As he got into his car and cranked the engine, it hit him.

Her dad's house. He muttered a string of curses. Of course. He'd bet six months' pay that she'd taken a taxi to her childhood home. It was still cordoned off as a crime scene, but a few strips of yellow tape wouldn't slow Dr. Christy Moser down a bit.

As he backed out of the B&B parking lot, he speed-dialed Ryker's number to get Albert Moser's address.

When he pulled up to the house, a taxi pulled up behind him. Reilly walked over to the vehicle and handed the guy a couple of twenties.

"Thanks," he said. "You can go on."

The driver shrugged and took off.

Reilly walked up the steps and ducked under the crime scene tape. As he stepped into the living room, Christy hurried out of the kitchen, hiking her purse strap over her shoulder. When she saw him, she stopped and stiffened. "Oh," she said.

"*Oh?*" Reilly crossed his arms and leaned against the foyer wall. "That's what you've got to say? Just *oh?*"

"I—have a taxi coming."

"Not anymore."

She glanced past him at the door then back. "What are you doing here?" Amazingly, she managed to insert a note of righteous indignation into her voice, but the little quaver at the end of the sentence took the starch out of her effort.

"Looking for my damsel in distress." Reilly had to bite his cheek to keep from smiling. She was a tough one all right—on the outside. "The question is what are *you* doing here?"

Her left hand tightened on her purse strap. "I just—I just wanted to see my dad's house. He—" She paused. "He needs his reading glasses."

She was lying. She might as well have been wearing a sign. *I'm a really bad liar.*

"Yeah? He's feeling well enough to read?" he asked mildly.

"Uh, no. Not yet. But I want to make sure he has them when he does feel better." She nodded toward the table next to the big recliner. "They should be—right there, but—" She shrugged. "They're not."

"Maybe the nurses put them with the rest of his things when they admitted him."

"No—" She stopped again, narrowing her eyes at him. "Maybe. I just wanted to help."

There was that note in her voice again. Tough, but underlain with a vulnerability, a note of doubt, as if she wasn't quite sure what exactly she was trying to say. And again, the little quaver at the end. Reilly studied her. Was she on the verge of crying?

He had a feeling she would not appreciate him seeing her

cry. She already resented him for being there to help her when she needed help, whether she would admit it or not.

He longed to take that quaver out of her voice, longed to offer her a shoulder. But she wouldn't accept it or appreciate it. So all he did was step a little closer, close enough that she couldn't ignore him. Close enough to be there if she chose to reach out.

An odd sound came from her. Was it a smothered sob? She was looking down, so he bent his head slightly to meet her gaze.

"It's okay," he said softly. "It's okay to want to see your home. It must not have been easy, coming in here."

Her head shook slowly from side to side, but she still stared at a place on the hardwood floor, not meeting his gaze.

"I'd have brought you," he murmured. "You didn't have to come alone."

"I didn't know he was in such bad shape," she moaned. "I didn't know. I'd have come home. If I'd known he was so sick—I'd have—" Her words got swallowed up by a sob.

Reilly didn't want to make the wrong move, but he couldn't suppress the urge to do something to comfort her. He took a step closer and put a gentle hand on her shoulder.

When he did, she turned toward him. He slid his arm around her and exerted just the slightest pressure. It was enough. She came into his embrace and pressed her face into the hollow of his shoulder. Her breaths were hot against his skin, even through his shirt, and they came in little puffs. She was crying.

It wasn't easy—her crying. It was stifled, bottled-up, piti-ful, like a kid trying to hold its breath and cry at the same time. It was obvious Dr. Christy Moser never cried.

"Christy, it's not your fault. What your father did. It's not your fault." He rubbed her back, aware that his resolve to be just a shoulder she could cry on was dissolving fast. Despite his good intentions, he couldn't ignore how sexy her bony, feminine shoulders were. He lowered his gaze to the graceful curve of her neck and the little bump at the top of her spinal column. Even that was sexy as hell.

He swallowed and closed his eyes. "Not your fault," he whispered again and again as he basked in the feel of her slender, supple body pressed against his, and savored the damp warmth of her breath against his skin.

Then, after what could have been a couple of seconds or a dozen minutes, Christy stiffened and pulled away. She turned her back on him and swiped at her eyes with her fingers.

"Excuse me," she said in a muffled voice and headed for the kitchen.

Reilly moved to the kitchen doorway, just to make sure she was all right. And, he had to admit, to be sure she didn't sneak out the back door. She turned on the water tap and splashed her face several times, then pulled a paper towel from a stand to pat her skin dry.

When she turned around, her cheeks were shiny and pink, and her eyes, though rimmed with red, were bright. "Please accept my apology," she said evenly. "This has been a difficult couple of days."

Reilly started to tell her that *difficult* was a mild word for all she'd been through, but he saved his breath. She already knew that.

"Let's go," he said. "You'll want to take a shower and freshen up before dinner."

"I'm not really hungry. I'll probably just ask Ella for a sandwich or—"

"*I'm* taking you out to dinner. You could use a little relief from all the stress and pain of the past few days."

"No, I shouldn't. I ought to go back to the hospital—"

"Hey," he interrupted, placing his fingers lightly against her lips. "You don't get a vote. You're going to dinner with me and that's final. Oh, and I hope you have something casual, because you wouldn't want to ruin your fancy designer pants on the rough wooden seats."

"I don't feel like going out."

He put his hand in the small of her back and ushered her out the front door of her father's house. When he turned to lock the door, her purse bumped heavily against his arm.

"Damn," he said. "What've you got in there? A .38?" As soon as he said the words, a rush of apprehension washed over him. "Tell me you don't have a gun."

"I don't have a gun," she responded.

"How do women walk around with that much stuff hanging off their arms?"

"We're stronger than you think," she said, her mood lightening marginally, although he didn't miss the way her arm tightened around her bag.

Reilly got her settled in the passenger seat of his car and got in on the driver's side and started the engine.

"By the way, Doc," he said offhandedly. "Don't run off without me again. Remember, there's somebody out there that wants you dead."

SEVERAL HOURS LATER, Christy sighed and crumpled the paper towel before tossing it atop the growing pile on the scarred wooden table. "I'm stuffed. I'd forgotten how good boiled crawfish are."

Across from her Reilly grinned, causing sparks to fly from the brightest blue eyes she'd ever seen. She couldn't stop her own mouth from turning up in response.

"That's what you get for running off to Boston," he said, and turned up his mug of beer.

She smiled and shrugged, not letting herself slide back into self-recrimination for leaving her father and sister behind. Reilly had been right. She needed a respite from the stress and grief and guilt. Shrugging again, she commented, "Clams are good too, you know."

He grimaced in mock distaste. "Ugh. Bottom feeders."

"Oh, as opposed to mudbugs?" The nickname for crawfish had come from the crustacean's habit of burrowing into the thick mud of the bayou.

"Mmm," was Reilly's only comment as he popped the head off another crawfish and expertly peeled it and popped the savory bit into his mouth. "Have some more."

"No. I'm really stuffed." She sat back and sipped at her beer, making a face. Beer wasn't her favorite, but Reilly promised her it was perfect with crawfish. It wasn't.

He pulled the bowl of warm lemon-scented water toward them and dipped his fingers, then wiped them off with a clean paper towel.

She did the same. "This is nice."

"Beau's is a really high-class catfish shack."

Christy's mood darkened immediately. "Didn't I see a sign for Henri LaRue Road on the way here?" She'd tried to ignore it at the time, but his mention of the name of the restaurant reminded her.

Reilly's face went solemn. He nodded. "I'm sorry. Maybe I should have taken you someplace else."

"Don't try to snow me, Officer. Henri LaRue Road is where my father tried to kill Nicole Beckham. Did you think I would miss that fact? You chose this place on purpose."

"I didn't, but—" He angled his head without finishing his sentence.

He didn't need to. What he didn't say rang loud and clear. "But there aren't many places around here that don't have something to do with my father's crimes."

"Christy, I—"

She held up a hand. "Just don't. I can deal with it. I have to, until I can get through here and get back to Boston." She turned her palm up in a helpless gesture. "Mandeville, Chef Voleur, Covington, even way out here past Madisonville. My dad really got around, didn't he?"

Reilly looked down at the crumpled paper towel in his hands, then back up at her. "Why did you go to your dad's house?"

Christy felt heat rising from her neck. She took another drink of beer, hoping to quench the fire before it turned her cheeks red. "I told you. I was looking for his reading glasses."

"No, you weren't."

It was irritating how well he could read her. Of course the reading glasses excuse was pretty lame. She could have said a lot of things that would have sounded more plausible. Insurance information. Checkbook. Even underwear.

She couldn't look at Reilly. Damn him and his blue eyes.

"Okay. I felt like I needed an excuse. I just needed to see the house."

He was silent for a moment. "Did it help?"

Christy gave a short laugh. "I don't know. I grew up there. It was just my dad and my sister and me after my mother died. We were—" Her voice gave out. She cleared her throat and tried again. "We were a family. I wanted to see if the house felt the same."

All of that was true, and she could see in Reilly's softening gaze that he believed her—maybe even somehow understood. But it was hard to hold his clear blue gaze, because she was still lying.

Sure, she'd wanted to see the house. But what she wasn't telling him was that she'd wanted to see what was in Autumn's secret hiding place before someone else did. Who knew what was going to happen to the house, now that her father would be spending the rest of his life in jail—*if* he got out of the hospital alive.

If there was any clue to who killed her sister, it would be found in the items she'd pulled from Autumn's closet. Even now, anticipation and fear burned through her. The box was right there beside her, in her purse. She set her jaw and willed herself not to look toward it.

"You ready to go?" Reilly asked.

Christy nodded as she dampened one more towel in the lemon water and cleaned her fingers before picking up her heavy purse.

Reilly guided her through the restaurant and out to his car. Once they were on their way, he said, "How are you dealing with the cast on your wrist?"

Christy looked at it. The edges near her fingers were already becoming grubby. "It's a pain, to tell you the truth. And look how dirty it's getting already."

"What about your wrist. Does it hurt a lot?"

She shook her head. "Not too much. Only if I twist it." She glanced over at Reilly. "I can't thank you enough for the bright pink cast though. It goes with everything."

Reilly laughed. "Wasn't me. I think the EMTs were a little irritated at you bossing them around."

"I'm a physician. I knew what I was talking about."

"And they knew what they were doing. You did get a black eye."

Christy opened her mouth to retort again, then paused, gingerly touching the bruise on her forehead. "Okay. Maybe I deserved a pink cast."

The rest of the drive back to the B&B was pleasant. Reilly talked about mundane things. How the Saints were doing this year, who was slated to appear at Tipitina's on New Year's Eve. His good-natured banter put her at ease and made her feel like an ordinary person out for a nice evening. It was the first time she'd felt normal since she'd arrived back in Louisiana.

She glanced at Reilly sidelong. Again, as when they were eating the po' boy sandwiches, he seemed at ease and comfortable. An ordinary guy on an ordinary date.

It was hard to picture him as a wealthy heir to an infamous fortune.

She needed to believe he was as honorable and caring as he seemed.

When he pulled into the parking lot at the B&B and shut off the engine, she turned to him.

"Reilly, you understand why I had to see the house, don't you?"

He met her gaze. "Sure. It was natural. Illegal, but natural." He sent her a smile.

"No," she said, placing her fingers on his forearm. "I mean you *really* knew. You understood. I could tell." She paused. "Or at least I thought I could." She pulled her hand away. "Okay, sorry. Never mind. I didn't—"

"No, you're right," Reilly said. "When Ryker and I were six, my dad told us that my grandfather was murdered in my grandmother's house. We'd been there before, but after he told us, I couldn't wait to go see it. It was the same place, the same dark halls and countless rooms where we played and ran, but it was different too. I'll never forget how it felt. It was as if—" He stopped and sent her a sheepish glance.

Christy swallowed. "As if evil had taken over? As if it were haunted by the ghosts of the dead?"

Reilly didn't say anything, but he reached out and took her hand. He squeezed it gently. "I'm sorry, Christy. Nobody can possibly know what you're going through, but I'd like to help in any way I can."

His eyes were soft and intense at the same time—a mesmerizing combination. At that moment, she felt as if he could see straight through to her soul.

"Why?" she whispered.

For a long moment he didn't answer. His gaze slid from hers and drifted down to her lips and back up. Was he going to kiss her? A tiny thrill erupted under her breastbone.

Did she want him to?

He met her gaze again. "I don't know," he muttered, sounding genuinely bewildered. He blinked, then straightened. "Because that's what knights in shining armor do, I guess." His eyes twinkled as he got out of the car and came around to open the passenger door.

He walked her to the door of the B&B. "So what's on your schedule for tomorrow?" he asked.

Christy thought about the box, the twenties and the button in her purse. "Nothing. I'm probably going to sleep in and go see Dad in the afternoon. I can catch a taxi."

To her surprise, Reilly nodded. "If you can, that would be great. I've got a few things I need to catch up on."

"Reilly, you don't have to keep spending your time—"

He touched her lips with his forefinger, a gesture that she was coming to expect whenever she protested. Coming to expect—and look forward to.

"I know I don't have to. But I'm committed now. You asked me to find your sister's killer. I intend to do that."

"I thought you were your brother when I said that."

He took a step closer and leveled that intense gaze on her. "But you don't now."

Her mouth went dry. He was so close she could feel the warmth of his breath on her cheek. "No. I don't now."

He leaned forward and brushed his lips across the curve of her jaw, then turned and headed down the steps back to his car.

Shocked, Christy stood there and stared at his back until he got to his car. He turned around and nodded at her with a grin, then got behind the wheel. He cranked the engine, but the car didn't move until she had gone inside the B&B and closed the door.

"No," she whispered to herself. "You're definitely not your brother."

CHRISTY CLOSED THE DOOR to her room and quickly changed into her pajamas and a robe. Then she sat down on her bed and pulled Autumn's treasures out of her purse.

For a long time, she did nothing but sit and stare at them. The box. The twenties. The tissue-wrapped button.

She looked at the box. It was small and square, the kind of box a bracelet or compact might come in, with a textured white surface barely visible under the wrinkled, crooked strips of duct tape. The loose corners of the tape were coated with dust and cobwebs.

Christy got a pair of fingernail scissors from her makeup kit and carefully cut the tape all the way around the edge of the box lid, then with a fearful intake of breath, she opened it.

A folded, crumpled sheet of lined paper, perforated at the top as if it were torn from a small spiral notepad, was the first thing she saw. She lifted it out with the point of the scissors, wishing she had a pair of surgical gloves. If she showed the contents of the box to Reilly—and she wasn't sure she ever would—she didn't want to destroy any evidence.

Under the piece of paper was a small, white plastic bag filled with white powder.

"Oh, my God, no!" she breathed. "Damn it, Tum-tum. Why would you—" She stopped. There was no answer to that question. Her baby sister was dead.

Christy knew what she was looking at. Illegal drugs. What kind, she had no idea, but she'd seen enough television to know what little bags filled with white powder meant. She didn't want to take the chance of puncturing the plastic bag, so she set the scissors down and picked it up by its edge with her fingernails.

On the underside of the bag was a mark. It was smudged, but it looked like a curved *M* or *W* or *3*, depending on which way she turned the bag. And below it was a number, also smudged. Christy didn't even try to decipher it.

The bottom of the little box was dusted with granules of white powder—and there was something else. A tiny plastic rectangle.

Christy started to reach for the scissors, but something about the shape of the little white-plastic rectangle caused her to proceed with caution. With the tip of a nail, she lifted the rectangle. She grabbed its corner and took it out of the box. It was a tiny computerized card, like the SIM cards in cell phones.

Cell phone.

The police had never found Autumn's cell phone. They'd assumed the mugger took it. They'd questioned her and her dad about Autumn's friends, but neither one of them had been able to name a single one. The best Christy had been able to do was to give them the name of Autumn's best friend from high school, but at the time of Autumn's death, Laurie Kestler had been at college in Florida.

Did this SIM card belong to Autumn? It was the kind of thing she'd always kept in her secret hiding place. Her diary, sheets of notepaper on which she'd scribbled the name of her latest crush, cigarettes. If the tiny device held all the numbers Autumn had saved to her phone, it might hold the critical clue to who had killed her.

Suddenly, Christy's fingers were shaking so badly she dropped the card. It bounced from the bed onto the floor, right next to her bare foot. She picked it up. One careless move and she could lose it. As she stared at it lying on her palm, she realized what she needed to do.

She quickly retrieved her cell phone, turned it off and took the back off it. There, peeking out from a slot designed especially for it, was the SIM card for her phone. She started to pry it out with a fingernail, but stopped.

The card in her phone looked larger than the one she held in her hand. It probably wouldn't work. Still, she wanted to try it. As each minute passed, she became more convinced that locked inside that tiny card's even tinier computer chip was the answer to what had happened to her sister.

No. What if she broke the card, or got it stuck in her phone? She had to wait until she could get to a phone store. But in the meantime, what was she going to do with the card? Put it back in the box? She didn't want to do that. She didn't know if the white powder would hurt the card, but she didn't want to take a chance.

She glanced around the room. The décor in the room was a jumbled, eclectic mix of Victorian and American country. One of the Victorian touches was an antique writing desk, complete with feather pen and paper intended to look like parchment. Christy tore a strip of paper and wrapped the SIM card in it, then tucked the little package into the corner of her wallet.

Back at the bed, she stared at the rest of the box's contents. The bag of powder shone as if it were sprinkled with glitter. She rubbed her face tiredly. What was she going to do with it? A part of her wished she had left well enough alone.

Why had she thought it was a good idea to go sneaking into her sister's room and uncovering her secrets? Yes, she'd probably discovered information that could lead to Autumn's killer, but in doing so, she'd come into possession of an illegal substance.

"Damn it, Autumn. How far are you going to go to ruin my life?"

Chapter Six

As soon as Christy muttered the words, she knew they were unfair and self-pitying. Autumn had ruined her own life. She didn't have the power, not even after death, to ruin Christy's.

It was Christy's own fault that she'd gone snooping in her sister's closet. She could have done the right thing and told Reilly or Deputy Watts about Autumn's hiding place. If she had, she'd have nothing to worry about now. She wouldn't be in possession of meth, or heroin, or whatever that white powder was.

She turned her attention to the piece of folded lined paper that she'd taken out of the box, wondering if she should compound her felony by unfolding it and reading what was on it.

She looked toward her cell phone. What she should do is call Reilly and tell him what she'd found. Her face burned at the thought of how he'd react.

Sighing, she turned back to the sheet of paper. She was in too deep already. What could be worse than finding drugs? No. It was never a good idea to think in terms of *what could be worse*.

There were countless things that could be worse. The note could contain the phone number of Autumn's drug connection. Her dealer. A vision swirled through Christy's head—her calling the number, arranging to meet the person and being shot just like Autumn had been, to protect the killer's identity.

Shaking her head at the absurdity of her imagination, Christy decided to unfold the paper. It had been folded twice, so it was a chore to get it unfolded without leaving finger-prints all over it, even when she used the letter opener from the writing desk. But finally it was spread open on the bed.

Christy stared at the words printed there, her brain in a fog as she tried to make sense of them. It certainly wasn't a drug connection. At least, she didn't think it was.

In penciled block letters, the note read, "Hey. Meet me at the shack. I'm 10-10 at 12. Got some stuff for you. B."

Christy didn't know what 10-10 meant. But *shack* and *stuff* sounded ominous. It *could* be a drug connection. Or a love note. Or both. Christy shivered. Her younger sister had been involved in an entire world that was alien to Christy. She had no idea how Autumn had gotten started using drugs in the first place. Christy had been out of high school before Autumn entered. She'd been in medical school by the time Autumn had graduated, so busy with school and labs and rounding with the doctors at the medical center that she hadn't had time for Autumn.

Guilt washed over her again and again she tried to shake it off. She hadn't had a mother or a big sister to guide her in high school, and she'd done fine.

But Autumn had never been as mature as Christy. Or as careful. Had her sister been taken advantage of? Gotten in over her head and found herself addicted before she realized what had happened? Or had she dived in headfirst, the way she'd always taken on any new project or hobby?

Had Autumn made the conscious decision to send her life down the path that had ended with her murder?

Christy rubbed her face again, pressing on her eyelids to

stop their stinging. No matter how it had happened, Autumn's choices had led her to her death, her father to murder and Christy to this point. She had no idea what she was going to do about the note or the drugs, but she knew one thing for sure.

She couldn't leave Louisiana until she found out what had happened to her sister. She hadn't been there for Autumn when it counted, before her death. But now she had a chance to find the person who had murdered her sister. She had Autumn's SIM card. With any luck, the list of saved phone numbers on that card would contain a clue to "B's" identity.

Christy was convinced that this "B," whoever he or she was, knew something about Autumn's death. And Christy was going to find "B" if it was the last thing she ever did.

REILLY SPENT THE BETTER PART of the night in his apartment overlooking Lake Pontchartrain in Chef Voleur, studying the file Ryker had given him on Autumn Moser. She was killed at eleven o'clock at night on October 26, 2005, her twenty-first birthday, in an alley off Basin Street in the French Quarter, near the St. Louis Cemetery.

Reilly shook his head. That area near the St. Louis Cemetery had always been a rough one. The cemetery was the oldest in New Orleans, and its ancient guests were constantly disturbed by drug deals, muggings and killings.

Had Autumn Moser been down there to score, or had she just been in the wrong place at the wrong time? Reilly fanned the pages, looking for Ryker's signed report. He found it in the back.

Ryker had quoted Albert Moser saying that his daughter had a substance-abuse problem. So Autumn could have been down there to buy drugs. He thumbed through the pages until he came to the crime scene photos. The CSI photographer had caught Autumn Moser's face in several shots. Her expression was serene.

Reilly shook his head. She must have lain there unconscious for a while before she died. Her face muscles had had time to relax from the distortion of fear and pain. Her hair was too black and stringy and the overdone dark eye makeup she wore was streaked, but something about the eyes and mouth was very much like Christy.

He kept thumbing through pages, past the CSI statements and the autopsy report, until he got to lead detective Fred Samhurst's typed report.

Cause of death was three gunshot wounds to the chest.
Purse was spilled and her cell phone was missing.

The scrapes on palms and knees and mud spatter on her calves suggest she fell while running. However, the entry wounds place her face-to-face with her killer at near point-blank range.

He flipped back to Ryker's report. There he saw the same questions that had immediately jumped into his own mind. If the mugger were holding her at gunpoint, why had she run? And why had the mugger chased her, caught her and then shot her?

He returned to Samhurst's statement. Detective Samhurst had concluded that Autumn Moser's death was a homicide at the hands of a mugger.

Christy had said she was on the phone with Autumn when she was shot. He flipped a page and found a typed transcription of a phone call Ryker had made to Christy in Boston.

Reilly read through the transcript.

Det. Delancey: I'm Detective Ryker Delancey, St. Tammany Parish Sheriff's Department, Ms.—Dr. Moser. I apologize. I'm calling in regards to your sister's death in 2005. Do you have time to talk for a few minutes?

Dr. Moser: Can you hold a moment?…Now, Detective Delancey is it? I can give you about three minutes. I'm making rounds on the pediatric ward here.

Det. Delancey: I apologize for calling you out of the blue, but I'm looking into your sister's death. I have a statement by you in the NOPD case file on Autumn Moser that states that you spoke with her at 11:00 p.m. on the night of her death.

Dr. Moser: That's right. On the phone.

Det. Delancey: You had called her to wish her happy birthday?

Dr. Moser: Yes. I did.

Det. Delancey: Can you tell me why you called so late?

Dr. Moser: I'd had an emergency with one of my patients and had just gotten home.

Det. Delancey: You reached her on her cell phone. Did she say where she was or who she was with?

Dr. Moser: No. Didn't you say you had my statement in front of you?

Det. Delancey: Yes, I do, but I want to get your perspective about the phone call.

Dr. Moser: She didn't say where she was, but I could hear vehicles and music.

Det. Delancey: You said you heard her scream.

Dr. Moser: Yes. It sounded like she was running, then she stopped and was breathing hard. I asked her if something was wrong. She said, "Christy!" And then she screamed. Then she said something like, "You bum" or "You scum" or something. I heard gunshots. Then the phone went dead.

Det. Delancey: Do you know how many gunshots?

Dr. Moser: Three? Four? I can't be sure. Why are you looking into her case now, after all this time?

Det. Delancey: There have been other murders that may have similarities to your sister's. I want to relook at it in light of these new developments.

Dr. Moser: I see. Have you talked to my father? Albert Moser?

Det. Delancey: Yes.

Dr. Moser: Then you've seen how he has been affected by my sister's death. I'm pleased to know that you're looking into the case, Detective. I hope you're able to do something. My sister's death has ruined my father's health. I have to go now.

Det. Delancey: Thanks for talking to me, Doctor.

The rest of the transcription was contact information, so Reilly went back to Ryker's report. After the phone call to Christy, he had called a friend of his, NOPD detective Dixon Lloyd, and asked him about the lead detective on the Autumn Moser case.

Lloyd had told Ryker that since the murder, Samhurst had suffered a mild heart attack and lost thirty pounds, which had left him forty pounds overweight.

Even though Ryker had told him about Samhurst's weight, Reilly still stared at the numbers. Samhurst had been seventy pounds overweight when he'd caught Autumn Moser's murder case.

As clearly as if they were on the report in front of him, Reilly could see the words Ryker had not written down. *Did Samhurst take the easy way out and write up Autumn Moser's murder as a mugging?*

If he had, he'd contributed to the deaths of four young women and the destruction of two lives, Albert Moser's and his one surviving daughter, Christy's.

CHRISTY WAS JUMPY AND nervous at breakfast the next morning. Ella had cooked a full country breakfast, just as she did every morning, so the table was groaning under the weight of scrambled eggs, sausage and bacon, biscuits, toast, sweet rolls, juice and coffee. Christy pushed scrambled eggs around the plate, holding her fork awkwardly in her left hand as she pretended to listen to Ella's nonstop prattle. The couple from Mississippi happily shoveled food into their mouths. Guerrant, Ella's husband, drank coffee and stared longingly at the newspaper, which was folded neatly on the corner of the large buffet.

As soon as she could, Christy excused herself and rushed back to her room, afraid to leave the incriminating evidence unguarded for even a few minutes. She closed and locked the door behind her and sat down on the bed, her heart racing.

Not only had she become entangled in her sister's illegal activities, she was involving innocent people. Because Christy had brought Autumn's box here, Ella and Guerrant Bardin were technically in possession of illegal drugs on their property.

She unlocked her suitcase and pulled the box out. She set it on the Victorian writing table and stared at it. The fingers of her left hand worried the fraying edge of the cast on her wrist as she considered what she should do.

She should call Reilly. Right now. She shouldn't hold onto the drugs or the note any longer. Every minute she delayed, she was that much deeper into breaking the law. She was a physician in possession of illegal drugs. She could lose her license. Not to mention that she was endangering the Bardins' livelihood.

She picked up her phone, then hesitated. Reilly was busy. He'd told her he had something he needed to do today. And he hadn't told her to call him if she needed him, the way he had the night she was attacked.

She didn't want to call him in the middle of a meeting, or if he were involved in police business. He'd contact her as soon as he could. She knew that.

For whatever reason, Reilly had appointed himself her personal guardian. He wouldn't waste any time getting back to her.

When he did, she'd tell him everything. Or almost everything, anyhow.

She slid her phone back into her purse. While she waited to hear from Reilly, she was going to take her rental car and go find a cell phone store. She wanted to see the numbers on that SIM card, numbers Autumn had thought were important enough to keep in her secret hiding place.

Christy locked the box inside her suitcase and draped a scarf casually over it. If anyone disturbed her suitcase, she'd know by the position of her scarf. Then she quickly dressed and, after locking the door to her room, headed out to her rental car. It wasn't as easy to drive as she'd hoped it would be, but at least she was able to handle the steering wheel and the automatic shift without too much pain or trouble, even with the cast on her right hand.

At the first cellular store she found, she showed the SIM card and the charger cord to the clerk, who told her the phone that took that cord used a larger SIM card.

So the phone Autumn had been using that fatal night was not the same phone the hidden SIM card had come from. The clerk sold Christy a phone that used the same card and all its accessories, including a fully charged battery that Christy talked him into giving her. She could not wait for the battery to charge overnight.

She sat in her car and went through the saved numbers on the card. There were the usual contact numbers for the cellular service plan, Triple A Wrecker Service, a doctor's office, a pharmacy and a pizza delivery service. The only names that meant anything to her were their dad's, of course, Christy's own cell phone number and a number for Laurie Kestler, Autumn's best friend from high school.

Christy breathed a little sigh of relief that Autumn still had Laurie Kestler's number. At least she could talk to one person who had known Autumn. That is, she could try. After all, the numbers listed on the card were at least five years old.

She hoped and prayed Laurie could tell her who the other names were. Or at least some of them. From what she remembered of Laurie, she doubted the girl would know anyone called *Slick* or *Jazzy* or *Glo*. But maybe she'd be able to identify *Jeff, Tina, Frankie* or *D.B.*

D.B. Could that be the "B" who'd written the note Autumn had hidden in her box? Christy's pulse raced as she looked at the number. It was a local area code. She could just call—see who answered.

Her thumb hovered over the call button, but she hesitated. If someone did answer, what would she say? *Hi there. I think you know something about my sister's murder?*

After staring at D.B.'s number for a moment, she moved her thumb away from the call button and pressed the Down arrow until she got to Laurie.

She dialed it.

"Hello?" a soft voice answered.

"Laurie? This is Christy Moser, Autumn's sister."

There was a slight hesitation. Christy was probably the last person Laurie had ever expected to hear from.

"Um, yeah? Hi?"

"I'm sorry to bother you, but I found your number in Autumn's things and I wanted to ask you a few questions. Do you have time to talk for a minute?"

"I guess," she said hesitantly. "I just put the baby down for a nap."

"The baby?" That surprised Christy. She'd been picturing

Laurie as still twenty-one, like Autumn. "How lovely. Congratulations. Boy or girl?"

"She's a girl. Aynsley. She's three months old." Laurie paused. "Um, my mom told me about your father. I—"

"That's all right, Laurie. I need to find out if you know any of these names." She read the list of names from Autumn's SIM card.

"I—don't think so," Laurie said.

"I know it's been five years, but please think. Are you sure none of the names sound familiar?"

"I didn't know most of the people Autumn hung out with there at the end. We didn't talk much after she got into all the drugs. I'm—I'm sorry."

"Don't worry about it. I know what Autumn was doing. I know she was into drugs. So you can't figure out who Glo is? Spelled G-L-O? Or the initials D.B.?"

"There was a guy named Danny that graduated with us. He had a crush on Autumn, but I don't think his last name started with a B."

"Do you remember anything else about him?"

"No. He played soccer, I think."

"What about a boyfriend? Did you know who Laurie was seeing?"

"I really don't want to—"

"Laurie, listen to me. You're not going to hurt my feelings and you're not betraying Autumn's confidence. You'll be helping us find her killer."

"Okay, but please. I don't want to get into trouble. I should have told the police this back then, but I was in Florida, and they never talked to me."

Christy felt her pulse fluttering in her throat. Maybe Laurie did know something that would lead to Autumn's killer.

"It's okay, Laurie. I *swear* you won't get into trouble." As she finished speaking, Christy heard a baby crying.

"Oh, no, the baby's awake." Christy heard movement through the phone. Laurie must be heading for the baby's room.

"Laurie, just two minutes, please. Tell me what you know."

The girl sighed. "Autumn bragged to me that her boyfriend could get her stuff—you know."

Christy did know. *Stuff* equaled *drugs*.

"Did she tell you anything about him?"

"He was married, and she used to say that he had to protect his reputation and his job. It was like she was proud that he had to keep her a secret."

The baby's crying got louder. Laurie was in the baby's room now.

"I really have to go," Laurie said, then whispered cooing baby words.

"All right. Thanks, Laurie." Christy sighed as she hung up. Not much help. Of course, she hadn't expected much. From what she remembered about Laurie, she could have predicted that Autumn's high school friend wouldn't know Autumn's newer—probably drug-using—friends.

But the bit about the mystery boyfriend was interesting. He had to protect his reputation and his job. What could that mean? Was he a politician? A well-known business-man? The possibilities were endless, unless Autumn was just bragging.

As for Autumn's friends, she had more of a lead than before. Maybe if she could find a yearbook from Autumn's senior year, she could figure out who Danny was. Or even Glo or Jeff.

A phone ringing startled her. For an instant she thought it was the new phone—maybe Laurie calling back. But then she realized it was hers. She looked at the display.

Reilly.

She pressed her lips together as she answered.

"Where are you?" he demanded before she even had a chance to say *hello*. "And please tell me you're not driving your rental car."

"Hi to you too," she threw back at him.

"Christy—"

"I decided to try driving, and what do you know? I can drive just fine." She flexed her right fingers and a pain shot along the back of her hand. She winced.

"I thought you said you were going to take a taxi to see your dad."

"As I just said—"

"So are you at the hospital now?"

"No. I haven't made it over there yet."

"You haven't made it over there. Back to my original question," he growled. "Where are you?"

"On my way back to the inn." She swallowed, pressed her lips together again, then continued. "Can you meet me there? I need to show you something."

There was a pause on the other end. "Tell me you didn't go back to your dad's house."

"I didn't go back to my dad's house today," she said carefully.

She heard Reilly sigh. "Thank goodness. I'll see you at the inn."

Christy hung up and started the car. But her gaze strayed back to the new cell phone. It would be so easy just to call one of those numbers. Yes, whoever she called would be a stranger, but she could tell them that she was looking for a friend of her sister's.

What could it hurt? She picked up the phone and ticked through the stored numbers until she got to D.B. Her thumb hesitated over the call button, but finally, with a deep, fortifying breath, she pressed it.

The phone rang so long she figured it would go to voice mail. When she finally heard a click, she waited, holding her breath, to hear what the message said.

But what she heard wasn't a prerecorded message. After an infinitesimal pause, a voice said, "Who is this?" The question was a cross between a growl and a whisper, definitely male. Was he trying to disguise his voice? If so, that meant whoever was on the other end of the phone thought the caller might recognize him. Laurie's words echoed in her head.

He had to protect his reputation and his job.

She forced air into her lungs. "Is this D.B.?"

The voice lowered in pitch. "Who is this?" he repeated menacingly.

"I'm Christy Moser. I found this number in my sister's phone." Not strictly true, but simpler than trying to explain about the SIM card.

She heard a sharp intake of breath, then the phone went dead. She called back, but that time the phone went straight to a digitized female voice reciting a generic message.

"We're sorry, but the owner of this number has not yet set up a voice mailbox. Please call again."

What if the number was one of those pay-as-you-go phones? If the man who had answered was D.B., would he throw the phone away?

Apprehension grew in Christy's chest. Had she just made a fatal mistake?

Had she just talked to Autumn's killer?

Chapter Seven

After spending the night going over Ryker's file on Autumn Moser, Reilly had planned on sleeping late. If he was up by nine o'clock, he'd have plenty of time to get to an official dress-uniform press conference at the mayor's office.

But at a quarter to six, a call had come in for the SWAT team to respond to a situation at a convenience store. A kid had gone in to rob the store, and had ended up holding the clerk and a female customer at gunpoint. It had taken three hours to talk the kid out.

As Ace had commented afterward, they'd been lucky that time.

Reilly barely made it to the mayor's press conference on time. He'd had no chance to change clothes prior to heading down to the police station on Royal Street to pick up the original Autumn Moser case file. Even though he'd called ahead, he'd had to wait over an hour while the file clerk found it, enduring good-natured ribbing about walking around in his dress blues.

By the time he'd made it back to the inn and discovered that Christy and her rental car were gone, it was nearly four.

He was forced to listen to Ella talk about her nephew, who'd been in trouble with the law but who was a good kid, while he waited for Christy. He nodded and smiled and made the appropriate responses at the appropriate times, all the while swearing he was going to make Christy pay for that twenty-five minutes he'd never see again.

Finally he heard a car pull into the parking lot. Through the glass panes of the front door he saw Christy. She managed to look perfectly at ease as she strode up the walk, although he did notice that the knuckles of her left hand were white where she gripped the strap of her shoulder bag.

Excusing himself from Ella with a comment about official business, he stepped out onto the porch and closed the front door behind him.

"Glad you could make it," he said.

She looked up, then did a double take. "Wow! You're in uniform," she said.

"Yeah. It's been a busy day."

Something about how he looked or what he said bothered her. Her hand tightened even more on the straps of her shoulder bag, and she was staring somewhere in the vicinity of his uniform pocket.

"Apparently it has been for you too. Where have you been?"

She sent him an irritated glance. "I have something I need to tell you—to show you."

Reilly heard the undertone of apprehension, maybe even fear, in her voice. "Okay," he said, glancing back at the front door. He could see a distorted silhouette through the beveled glass. Ella. "Let's go some place where we can talk."

"It's—I need to get something out of my room."

Reilly nodded and opened the front door. "Hurry," he said for Ella's benefit. "We're already late for that appointment."

Christy shot him a questioning glance. He stared at her, willing her to understand that he didn't want to get embroiled in another gab-fest with Ella.

Her gaze flickered and she nodded. "I know," she responded. "I'll hurry." She unlocked her door, slipped inside and closed it firmly.

Reilly glanced over at Ella, who had her mouth open, about to speak.

"Official police business," he said. "Urgent. No time to talk."

Ella's black eyes sparkled and her cheeks turned pink. "Oh, what's it about?" she breathed.

"That's classified," he snapped officiously.

Ella pursed her lips, but her eyes still sparkled. She turned and practically ran toward the back of the house. Going to tell Guerrant that she'd been involved in *official police business*. Reilly blew out a breath. Anything to stop her talking.

When Christy emerged, locking her door behind her, she had that death grip on her purse and her face was pale.

He didn't ask any questions. They got into his car and drove to his condo.

As they got on the glass elevators and he pressed the button for the eighth floor, Christy looked a little taken aback. "What is this?" she asked.

"My apartment. I figured we could talk here without anyone disturbing us."

She nodded, but sent him a narrow glance. A suspicious glance.

Not exactly the response he normally got on the rare occasions he brought a date home with him. The address alone generally had them squirming with lust and greed. And that turned him off. Therefore, he'd be hard-pressed to remember the last time he'd invited a woman up here.

He'd bought the condo because it was easy, not because it was impressive or because he enjoyed flaunting the money he'd inherited from his grandparents. But women generally insisted on being impressed. The condo had turned into an excellent tool for measuring women's reactions. The more impressed they were the less interested he was.

So Christy's reaction intrigued him. He unlocked his door and entered first. He wanted to gauge her reaction when she saw where and how he lived.

Christy stepped into the living room, her gaze immediately going to the glass wall that overlooked Lake Pontchartrain. The sun was setting, and red and gold light sparkled on the lake's restless waters and turned the buildings into silhouettes. He knew it was a breathtaking sight.

She stared at it for a few seconds, then slowly turned her gaze to the rest of the room.

After he'd moved in, Reilly had asked his cousin if she'd pick out some furniture for him. Cara Lynn had done a good job. She'd bought leather and wood—pieces with clean lines and sturdy construction. Like the apartment, the furniture was designed for ease and comfort.

"Nice apartment," she said. "Comfortable."

"Thanks," Reilly said, surprised again. Not only was she not drooling over the address or the view, she seemed to get why he liked it. He scrutinized her as she stepped farther into the room.

"Do you cook?" she asked, checking out the chef's-grade gas stove, the vented grill, the zero-degree refrigerator-freezer and all the kitchen accessories.

"No," he laughed. "I wield a mean can opener though. And I'm particularly proficient at calling for pizza."

She smiled. "That's a waste of a great kitchen."

"Yeah, it came with the place. What can I say?"

She seemed fairly at ease, but he didn't miss the fact that she hadn't loosened her hold on her purse one bit.

He moved to stand beside her. Just as he opened his mouth to ask her what she had to show him, his cell phone rang.

"Excuse me," he said to her, then looked at his phone. It was Commander Acer.

"Delancey," he said.

Ace asked him if he'd finished his report before he left.

"Yes, sir. I apologize, sir. I left it in the printer."

"No problem. I'll get it. 10-4."

"Yes, sir. 10-4." When he hung up and turned, Christy was staring at him, all color gone from her face.

"What's the matter?" he asked.

She didn't answer for a couple of seconds. "I—I'm sorry. I'm just really tired." She looked past him, out at the lake, then back. "Did you say 10-4?"

"Yeah." He smiled. "Just like in the cop shows. Why?"

"What does it mean?"

"It's police code. It basically means *message received and understood.*"

"Oh, right. I think I've heard that on TV, haven't I?"

She wouldn't look at him. He couldn't figure out what had just happened, but while he was on the phone with Ace, Christy's body language had gone from displaying relative calm to spine-cracking tension. What had changed? He watched her carefully as he went on.

"The cop shows love to use them. You'll hear 10-4 a lot. And 10-20 for location. You've heard them ask, 'What's your twenty?'"

"Oh, right." She paused then met his gaze. "Haven't I heard of 10-10 too?"

"Yeah. 10-10 stands for off duty. Nobody really uses them much anymore. A few of the older guys. But there are dozens of codes. Too many to remember."

"I see," she said in a brittle voice. Her shoulders drew up and she dropped her gaze. "Would you mind if I used your bathroom?"

Reilly pointed. "Right back there. There's a half bath at

the end of the hall." As she disappeared he went over the last few moments in his mind.

Something had upset her—suddenly and badly. Was it his short conversation with Ace? They hadn't spoken a dozen words.

She'd asked him about the ten codes, but was that just a diversion, to try and keep him from guessing what was really bothering her?

CHRISTY HADN'T ALLOWED herself to think about anything except walking calmly and confidently until she got inside the guest bathroom and closed the door.

As soon as the latch clicked into place, Christy let out her breath in a whoosh and sat down on the closed toilet lid. Her legs were quivering so badly she wasn't sure she could have stayed on her feet. And she felt nauseated.

So 10-10 meant off duty. As soon as Reilly had said 10-4 on the phone she'd realized she'd heard numbers like that before, on police shows on television. Police shows. *Police.*

Dear God, the man Autumn had been seeing was a police officer. Christy's mouth went dry and her stomach did a double backflip.

Yesterday when she'd found the drugs in Autumn's hiding place, she'd admonished herself for thinking that nothing could be worse than finding drugs. And this was why. There was always something that could be worse.

Of all the people Autumn could have been seeing, a cop was the absolute worst. Everything she'd heard about the mystery man began to make sense. Laurie saying that Autumn told her he had to protect his reputation and his job. Her father declaring that Autumn's boyfriend was afraid of jeopardizing his job.

Christy realized she was panting. Hyperventilating. She put her hands over her mouth. "Oh, dear God," she whispered.

A cop. That explained the brass button too. It was just like the ones she'd noticed on Reilly's dress uniform.

She had no idea what she was going to do. She'd thought she was in trouble when she found the little bag of drugs. But now, she had evidence that Autumn's boyfriend, the man who may have been supplying her with drugs, the man who may have killed her, was a law-enforcement officer.

She had to tell Reilly.

No. She couldn't tell Reilly. He probably knew the man. Besides, she had sense enough to know that a note and a button wouldn't stand up against a department full of cops. She knew about the "blue line." This wouldn't be the first time her family had been on the wrong side of the line that separated civilians from police.

Quickly, aware that she'd been in the bathroom for several minutes, Christy pulled the box out of her purse and opened it. She picked up the note with her fingernails and stuck it down into her wallet, then closed the box.

She'd show Reilly the drugs and the roll of twenties. If she were very lucky, maybe there were fingerprints all over them, implicating whoever had given them to Autumn. If not, well, she'd just have to come up with more proof.

She rinsed her fingers and splashed a little water on her face before going back out to face Reilly.

He was waiting for her, looking concerned. His intense blue eyes searched hers. "Christy, what's wrong?" he asked.

"Wrong?" She looked at him questioningly.

He arched a brow and his expression clearly said, *Give me a break.* Then he touched her left hand.

She looked down and saw that she had that death grip on her purse again. She consciously flexed her fingers and took a deep breath.

"I wasn't telling the truth about why I went back to Dad's house," she said.

He took her hand and squeezed it. "Relax. I know you weren't. Tell me why you really went back there."

"I needed to check something. To find something." She pushed her hair back with her right hand, and a few hairs caught in the pink cast. "Ow," she muttered, jerking her hand away.

"Here," he said, guiding her over to the leather sofa. "Sit down and try to relax. I'll get you something to drink. What do you want?"

She shrugged. "What do you have?"

"Just about anything. That's a big refrigerator."

"Cranberry juice?"

"Yep." He fetched her a bottle of cranberry juice and himself some water. As she took the bottle, he glanced at his watch. "Are you hungry?"

She shook her head automatically. It was obvious she needed to get whatever was bothering her off her chest as soon as she could. He'd call for pizza later, or scramble some eggs. That much he could do.

"Okay, so you went to your dad's looking for something?"

She looked miserable, sitting there on his tan leather sofa with her purse in her lap. She held on to it with both hands, as if afraid he was going to grab it away from her.

"Autumn was never a very trusting person," she said. "She hid things—her favorite treasures, her secret notes. You know, like a kid will."

He waited, knowing she had to start like this. He'd talked to desperate people, grief-stricken people, angry and hurt and terrified people, in his experience on the SWAT team. They rarely told their stories in a straightforward manner. They all were tormented by their experiences, their memories, and they had to let it out somehow. In his time working on the SWAT team, taking his turn as lead negotiator, he'd become a very good listener.

"She was so young when our mother died. Only twelve. It hit her hard. I was older. More mature."

By four years, Reilly thought. Not so much older.

"Autumn had a secret hiding place in her closet, behind a loose baseboard. I was sure the police hadn't found it. I was right." Christy stared at her hands for a long time without speaking.

"So you went there to see if Autumn had left anything in her secret hiding place?" he asked, his voice prodding gently.

"I found a roll of twenties—a big roll," she said, glancing up at him briefly before continuing. "And a box."

There it was. The answer to why she was so protective of her purse. That's what had her so spooked. She needed to tell him about what she'd found. She needed to show it to him, but she was terrified.

"Do you have the box and the roll of bills with you?" he asked.

She nodded.

"Can I see them?"

It took her a few seconds to force her fingers to let go of her purse, but she finally pulled out the roll of twenties and set it on the large glass coffee table. Then she dug into her purse again and came up with a small rectangular box. It was crudely taped up with duct tape.

Reilly waited until she'd set the box on the coffee table. Then he spoke. "Can I look at the box?"

She raised her green eyes to his and he thought of a rabbit watching a hawk diving toward it. His heart twisted. He couldn't imagine what was in the box that had her so spooked.

No, that wasn't true. He *could* imagine what was in it. All too easily. From what he'd read about Autumn, the girl had been deep into drugs. So he was pretty certain, based on how Christy was acting, that he knew exactly what was inside the box. He just hoped he was wrong.

She nodded, and her tongue flicked out to moisten her lips. Her throat moved as she swallowed.

He picked up the box and pulled on the lid. A couple of pieces of duct tape tried to stick, but he peeled them back. He looked inside.

Damn it. A bag of white powder. Exactly what he'd expected. Exactly what he'd hoped he wouldn't find.

"I'm sorry," Christy whispered.

Reilly set the box and lid down. He was furious. Furious and afraid—for Christy. "When did you find this?" he asked evenly.

She swallowed. "I told you, yesterday."

"You had it in your purse when I got to your dad's house."

Her gaze faltered and she nodded.

"It was in your purse when we went to dinner last night?"

"No," she muttered. "It was in my room."

"So you found this at—what—three in the afternoon? We were together all evening, and you didn't think it was worth mentioning?" He could hear the ice-cold fury in his voice, and he didn't miss the growing fear in Christy's body language.

Her fingers were bluish-white from clutching her purse. Her shoulders were tight and stiff and he could detect a fine trembling throughout her entire body.

"Christy, do you know what this is?"

She started to speak, faltered then cleared her throat. "Of course I do." Her voice was brittle.

"Why in hell—" He stopped. It didn't matter why she

hadn't called the police or told him earlier. He had to deal with it now.

"We've got to turn this in."

She nodded.

He put the top back on the box. Then he went to the kitchen and grabbed a plastic grocery bag and put the box and the roll of twenties into it.

Christy hadn't moved.

Reilly sucked in a deep breath. He didn't want to ask the next question, because he wasn't sure he wanted to see how bad a liar Dr. Christy Moser was. Nor did he want the knowledge her lie would give him. But he had to ask. "So, is this everything?"

She glanced up at him questioningly.

"Did you find anything else?"

She opened her mouth but nothing came out.

"What else did you find, Christy?"

She swallowed. "Some ribbon. A few coins."

"Is that all?"

"Reilly, I—"

"Is. That. All."

She looked down at her hands and nodded.

"What about the bag. Did you touch it?"

"Just with my fingernails."

"The inside of the box?"

Her shoulders slumped. "Probably."

"Okay. You found this stuff yesterday and brought it back to your room at the inn, but you didn't open it until this afternoon, and you called me as soon as you saw what was in it."

"No, I—?"

He stopped her with a raised hand. "Listen to me. You did not open the box until this afternoon and you called me right away. You only touched the contents enough to see what they were."

"Are you sure—?"

"Trust me, Christy, you don't want to explain why you kept it for more than twenty-four hours before you told anyone about it."

"Okay." She stood.

"And Christy, I need to be sure, before I take this to the police, that there's not something else I should be giving them."

She shook her head—too quickly, too hard.

He bit his tongue to keep from pressing her. There had been something else in that hiding place. He'd bet his condo on it. But he had to get the drugs and money to the sheriff's office—now. So he was happy to accept her answer at face value, although deep in his heart he knew she was lying.

THEY SPENT THREE HOURS at the sheriff's office while the deputy on duty processed the evidence and took their statements.

The first thing the deputy did when he saw the bag was take a pair of tweezers from his desk drawer and pick it up to examine it. "Did anyone touch this?" he asked.

Reilly nodded at Christy.

"I touched it with my fingernails, but that's all."

While she was talking, the deputy turned the bag over to look at the bottom. "I'll be damned," he breathed.

"What?" Reilly leaned forward.

"That's an evidence marker." The deputy pointed at the smudged letter on the bottom of the plastic bag. "If I'm not mistaken, it's Amber Madden's mark. She's one of the crime scene analysts."

Reilly squinted at the mark and uttered an expletive.

Christy's heart leaped in a combination of fear and

excitement. "What does that mean?" she asked, although she was pretty sure she knew.

Reilly and the deputy locked gazes for an instant. The deputy cleared his throat. "Well, it looks like this bag was logged into evidence. That number identifies the case file."

A pang of fear stabbed Christy deep in her chest. Whoever Autumn was involved with had given her drugs stolen from police evidence. It had to be someone in the sheriff's department.

That information drove home the seriousness of what she was doing. She was withholding evidence. Evidence that could lead to the man who killed her sister.

Reilly scrutinized the mark and the number. "Do we have any reports of missing evidence? This had to have been at least five years ago. The girl who hid this box was killed in 2005."

"This number underneath will identify the case," the deputy said. "We'll know soon enough. To answer your question, there are always a few instances of missing evidence."

"But drugs," Reilly insisted. "Wouldn't that have been investigated?"

Reilly and the deputy exchanged a glance, and then the deputy's gaze flickered toward her.

She looked down at her lap. The deputy was already regretting talking about missing evidence in front of her. Reilly obviously agreed because he sat back in his chair and looked at his watch.

"Anything else, Deputy?" he asked.

The deputy rolled his chair back from the desk. "We'll need to get your fingerprints, Dr. Moser."

He explained to her that they were needed to exclude her from any suspect fingerprints they found on the bag. He got her to give him a crude drawing of the exact location of Autumn's secret hiding place, and interrogated her about other possible hiding places in the house. He explained to her that since the house and lot were still classified as a crime scene, they wouldn't need any additional paperwork to search them again. She signed a statement indicating that she understood.

Finally they were free to go. The money and the box with its contents stayed at the precinct, and the deputy promised to let Reilly know what came of the search of Albert Moser's house.

Reilly and Christy made the drive back to the Oak Grove Inn in silence. He walked her to the door. "I'll call you in the morning," he said. "Can I trust you not to go running off in your car?"

Her eyes sparked with irritation as she nodded. "Yes," she said stiffly, turning the glass knob on the door.

He took a step backward.

She turned back toward him. "Reilly, I'm sorry—" She stopped, her eyes sparkling with unshed tears.

He had an odd urge to pull her into his arms and tell her everything was okay, but the urge wasn't quite as strong as the anger that still burned in his chest. Anger that she hadn't confided in him about finding the box. Anger that she had put herself in jeopardy by holding on to illegal drugs. Anger that she didn't trust him enough to tell him what else she'd found.

And yet, he couldn't stop himself from touching her cheek. "Good night," he said evenly. "I'll watch until I see your lights come on. Try to get some sleep."

After she went inside and closed the front door behind her, he headed back to his car. But he didn't crank the engine until she turned on the lights in the front guest room.

As he put the car in Reverse, the unmistakable crack of a gunshot split the night, followed by the sound of breaking glass and a short, piercing scream.

Chapter Eight

Before the scream had died down, Reilly had his phone in his hand. "Dispatch, Officer Delancey here. Need backup at Oak Grove Inn, Covington. Shots fired."

Then he grabbed his weapon and his high-powered flashlight from his glove compartment and jumped out of the car. He sprinted toward the side of the house from which the rounds had come. He held the flashlight in his left hand and used his left wrist to support the weapon held in his right. He reached the wall and flattened his back against it. He sidled toward the corner.

He heard the front door open. He glanced back. It was Guerrant.

"Get back inside and take cover," he stage-whispered.

He hoped to hell Christy was okay.

Once he reached the corner of the house, he took a deep breath and darted his head out, then back immediately. He didn't see anything that looked human. So more slowly, he rounded the corner, leading with his weapon balanced atop the flashlight.

Once he stepped out of the shelter of the house, motion-activated floodlights flared, illuminating the side yard. He scanned the area, looking for anything odd. Anything that moved.

He examined the ground below the window where thick,

springy grass grew. There would be no way to get a shoe print.

Beyond the fence was the vacant lot he'd gotten a glimpse of the other night, when Christy was attacked. It was a tangle of overgrown hedges, vines and bramble bushes. Sweeping the area with his flashlight beam, he noted that several yards past the fence, the bushes turned into trees.

Whoever had fired the shot could easily have escaped through there. But not without some scratches. He filed that information away to give to the responding officers.

For an instant, Reilly thought about trying to give chase, but it had been at least twenty seconds since the shot was fired. The shooter was probably far gone by now.

He aimed the flashlight toward the back of the house, then toward the parking lot, but nothing seemed out of place. He switched off the light and pocketed it, but kept his weapon ready as he headed back around the front of the house.

When he turned toward the front door, he saw Guerrant standing on the porch with his shotgun. Would Guerrant hesitate to use the weapon if he were threatened? Given his calm expression and the ease with which he held the gun, Reilly was pretty sure the owner of the inn would have no trouble unloading both barrels if the situation warranted it.

"Backup's coming," he told Guerrant as he ran up the steps. "Tell them the shooter went through the vacant lot."

Guerrant nodded. "I already talked to the folks in the cottages."

Reilly ran inside. Christy's door was open. Ella's voice, an octave higher than normal, came from inside.

"Christy!" he shouted as he ran into the room.

Christy was sitting on the edge of the bed, white as a sheet. When she saw Reilly, she started to rise, but Ella, who was fluttering around her like a mother hen, pushed her back down.

"Don't get up, dear. You'll faint." Ella looked over her shoulder at Reilly. "Oh, my goodness," she cried. "What in the world is going on out there?"

Reilly barely acknowledged Ella. He was worried about Christy. "Are you okay? You're not hurt are you?" he asked her.

She stared at him, eyes wide. Her lips were pinched and white at the corners, and her hands were clenched together in her lap.

Reilly started toward her, but was stopped by Ella, who wailed, "Those windows were the original glass."

She gestured wildly at the broken glass, then turned back to Christy. "Oh, my God, you could have been killed."

"Ella," Reilly snapped. "Go make some coffee."

"Oh, my God," the woman said again. "We're going to be up all night." She hurried out of the room. "I'd better make some coffee," she said, as though she hadn't heard him.

As soon as Ella was gone, Christy stood and came to Reilly.

He put his arms around her and hugged her, then pushed her to arm's length with gentle hands on her shoulders.

Tears glistened in her wide, frightened eyes, and one slipped down her cheek.

He stopped it with a finger. She looked unhurt, but her pallor worried him. "Are you sure you're okay?"

She nodded. "I'm not injured. However, I do seem to be having a mild—panic attack." Her breath came in little puffs and she pressed her left hand against her breastbone. "It's so silly how the reaction doesn't set in until after the danger is over."

Her effort to diagnose herself logically, coupled with the indignant note in her voice made him feel much better. He'd hated seeing her terrified and unsure of herself. He knew she hated being that way.

He smiled wryly. "Yeah," he said. "Silly. I'm glad you're not hurt. Tell me what happened. Were you standing at the window?"

"No. I was right there—" she gestured "—in front of the dresser, taking off my watch and jewelry."

Reilly measured the distance between the dresser and the window with his eyes. At least four feet. He walked over to the window. The house was on a traditional foundation, a couple of feet off the ground, so the shooter had to have his back against the fence to aim at Christy where she'd stood in front of the dresser.

"Why in hell would anybody put lacy curtains and nothing else on a bedroom window? There ought to be shades or blinds on these windows." He inspected the broken pane, then turned and walked to the other side of the room and swept the wall with his gaze. Sure enough, about two feet above his head, a bullet was embedded in the wallpaper.

"I guess blinds aren't authentic."

"What?" he asked distractedly as he turned back to look at the window. The trajectory would have put the bullet about a foot behind Christy.

"Blinds," Christy said. "Maybe shades were used back in Victorian times, but blinds probably weren't."

He looked at her, frowning, then realized she was answering his rhetorical question about the curtains.

"Oh, right," he said. A little color was coming back into her cheeks as she calmed down. So he decided not to tell her how narrowly the bullet had missed her.

He turned his attention back to the window. Had the gunman been shooting to kill? Or had the shot been a warning? A second warning to Christy to go back to Boston and forget about trying to find out who had killed her sister.

"It almost hit me, didn't it?" Christy asked, her voice small. "I thought I felt something swish by me." She shivered.

Reilly realized she'd been watching him carefully. She hadn't missed his mental calculations of the bullet's trajectory.

"I don't think he was trying to kill you," he said, hoping he sounded reassuring.

"Why not? He told me he would. Assuming it was the same man who attacked me. If you're just trying to make me feel better, don't."

"Okay," he said. "I didn't check while I was outside, but with those ridiculous curtains and the lights on in here, I'm pretty sure he could see you clearly. If he's any kind of decent shot, he could have killed you if he'd wanted to."

He regretted his honesty when the returning color faded from Christy's cheeks.

"Let's go to the dining room. I called for backup. They'll be here any minute."

As soon as the words were out of his mouth, he heard the sirens coming rapidly toward them. "There they are."

He led her through the front parlor and into the dining room. They sat at same massive table where they'd sat a few nights ago, after she'd been attacked.

Ella came in with a pot of coffee just as Deputy Buford Watts and Guerrant came inside.

Buford didn't look the least bit surprised to see Reilly. "Delancey," he said resignedly. "First on the scene again?"

Reilly didn't bother to answer him. "Did you put out a BOLO for an armed man on foot running from this area?"

"Sure did. We'll see if anything comes of it." Buford turned to Christy. "Ms. Moser. Oh, I'm sorry. *Doctor* Moser. Have you thought about when you might want to be heading back to—" Buford looked at his notepad "—Boston?"

"Buford—" Reilly said warningly.

The deputy shrugged without taking his eyes off Christy.

"I'm not saying—I'm just saying. If I were attacked twice in one week, I might think about heading home."

CHRISTY WAS EXHAUSTED and shivering with fatigue by the time Deputy Watts got through questioning her and Reilly. His men had crawled all over her room, taking pictures, measuring the height of the broken windowpane and the height of the bullet hole in the wall and digging the slug out to preserve as evidence.

She watched dully as the deputy and his men left.

"Christy?"

It was Ella Bardin. "Christy, I really hate to say anything, but—"

"Please, Ella." Christy held up her hand. "You don't have to. I'll go to a hotel. I'm so sorry that I've put you and your husband in danger. And I'll certainly pay for the damage to the room."

"No, no," Ella protested. "I just might have to make up a tall tale, like maybe Jefferson Davis stayed here and somebody took a shot at him." She laughed.

Christy forced a smile. "Maybe that would work," she said. "Thank you so much for the coffee. Can I help you clean up?"

"Absolutely not. You just go ahead and get your stuff together."

Christy sighed. She'd hoped Ella would protest. That she'd insist that Christy could wait until morning to leave, but no such luck. Still, she certainly couldn't blame the woman. An assault and a shooting in the same week was never good for business or for peace of mind.

Reilly came in just as Christy pushed herself to her feet. "Get your stuff together?" He'd echoed Ella's words.

She nodded. "I'm going to get a hotel. I can't subject Ella and Guerrant to more violence."

"Well, you're not going to a hotel. You're coming with me."

Christy saw Ella pause on her way to the kitchen with the coffeepot. She turned around, obviously eavesdropping.

"Could we discuss this in my room?" Christy asked stiffly.

Reilly glanced toward Ella. "Okay, sure," he said, then leaned in close to her ear. "Although there's nothing to discuss."

She turned on her heel and headed through the door into her room. She waited for Reilly to enter, then closed the door behind him.

"I can't go to your apartment," she said. "I'll get a hotel room."

"The hell you will. There's somebody out there after you. If he can get to you here, he can get to you in a hotel. No. You're coming to my apartment."

"And why can't he get to me at your apartment?"

"Besides the fact that there's a security guard on duty 24/7? And it's on the eighth floor? Because *I'll* be there."

"A security guard?" she echoed. He lived in a secure apartment building? "No." She shook her head. "I can't."

"I don't see why not. Get packed."

"Because—" She stopped. She couldn't tell him why she didn't want to stay with him. She wasn't sure she could explain it to herself. She'd like to think it was because he was too overprotective, too bossy.

But that wasn't it. Or maybe it wasn't so much his protectiveness as her reaction to it. She'd always been independent. She liked living alone, making her own decisions, being in charge of her own life.

But as much as she tried to tell herself that Reilly's concern, his larger-than-life presence and his insistence on protecting her were annoying and unnecessary, she couldn't deny how good it felt to have someone concerned about her safety. She could get used to having a knight in shining armor around. And that was going to make it really hard to go back to her solitary, independent life. A life without Reilly Delancey in it.

"Christy? Are you sure you're all right?"

"What?" She realized she'd been staring at him. "Yes, of course. I can go to a hotel," she said unconvincingly, doing her best to look anywhere except at him.

"Get your stuff together." He didn't even bother arguing. "I'm going to check with Buford before he leaves, make sure he's got CSI collecting trace from inside and out."

Christy quickly packed her suitcase, checked around the room to make sure she hadn't forgotten anything and pulled her bag into the living room. She set the key in a dish on the coffee table and sat down to scribble a note on a sheet of Ella's Victorian writing paper.

Reilly came back inside. "Ready?" he asked as he grabbed her suitcase.

She picked up the key and slid the note beneath it. "Yes," she said.

"What's that?" he asked.

"Just a note to Ella to let her know how sorry I am for putting her in danger."

As they headed out to his car, she said, "I'll drive my rental car."

"No," Reilly responded flatly.

"I can't leave it sitting here in Ella's parking lot."

"It's been sitting here this long. It can stay for a few more days."

"But won't it make the...make him think I'm still here?"

Reilly looked at her thoughtfully. "Right. It could put Ella and Guerrant in more danger. I'll call the rental company and tell them to come pick it up. I'll pay any additional fees involved."

"That's ridiculous and unnecessary. I can drive." She dug in her purse for the keys.

"Yeah. That's the problem." With a movement so quick he had no time to react, Reilly grabbed the car keys from her hand. "You can drive, but you're not going to. I have no intention of letting you out of my sight. Now get in the car."

Christy's ears burned, she was so angry. "You're bossy and rude. This is tantamount to kidnapping."

Reilly's eyebrows shot up and he grinned. "Tantamount?"

Christy blew out her breath in a huff. "Bully," she muttered as she got into the car and slammed the passenger door.

CHRISTY HAD BEEN SURPRISED to say the least the first time he'd seen Reilly's condo. The view of Lake Pontchartrain alone had to be worth at least six figures. She'd guessed he'd paid at least a quarter million for it. In Boston, it would have been worth four times that. Although she doubted there were any condos this large in Boston.

Now as he led her down the hall to the guest suite, which was opposite the master suite, she revised her estimate of the condo's cost upward. The place had to be twenty-five hundred square feet, and the guest bath included a spa tub, a separate shower and one entire wall made of glass bricks.

Her amazement must have shown on her face, because he shrugged. "It came with the place," he said, repeating what he'd said the day before about the professional kitchen.

She just shook her head.

Giving her a narrow look, Reilly backed toward the door. "I'll let you—freshen up. If you need anything—"

Christy looked around. "I'm pretty sure there's nothing I could possibly think of that's not already here," she said.

Reilly nodded. "I don't suppose it would make a difference if I told you my cousin Cara Lynn furnished and decorated for me? I asked her to get whatever she thought I needed. Apparently she thought it would be funny to outfit the guest suite like some kind of luxury spa hotel or something."

She met his gaze, then glanced around the suite. There was a basket filled with bottles of water on a library table, alongside an exquisite silk arrangement in a bowl that probably cost more than the refrigerator in her apartment. A plasma TV was mounted above the marble fireplace opposite the bed.

The marble of the hearth extended to the right to form the entrance into the bath and dressing area, where Christy could see sparkling mirrors and shiny chrome fixtures.

"Apparently," she said. When her gaze met his again, he looked sheepish.

"Okay, then," he said. "If you need anything, pick up the phone. It'll buzz in my room and in the living room."

Christy uttered a short laugh. "Okay," she said.

Reilly's gaze faltered as he backed out the door and closed it behind him.

Christy frowned. Suddenly, he'd seemed ill at ease. Was it something she'd said? Maybe she'd embarrassed him about the opulence of the guest suite.

He'd said his cousin had decorated and furnished his apartment. She must have thought he'd have lots of guests. Had his cousin been thinking of female guests? But if so, why would she have thought the females would be staying in the guest suite, rather than in the master suite with Reilly?

Christy stepped past the marble fireplace and entered the bath. Her glimpse of chrome and mirrors and marble had been the tip of the iceberg. The bath was as large as her bedroom in Boston. The shower enclosure was clear glass. The spa tub was gigantic, with an unopened basket of bath accessories sitting on the wide tile ledge around it. The toilet was behind a half wall, and beside it was a bidet.

A bidet.

Christy chuckled softly. She'd love to meet his cousin. She was sure she'd like her. The first thing she'd do would be to thank her for giving Christy the first laugh she'd had in a long time. Then she'd thank her for the spa tub.

Her smile faded. All this opulence didn't fit with the Reilly Delancey she knew. Of course, all she knew was what he'd allowed her to see.

She sighed. She wasn't going to solve the dilemma of who Reilly was tonight.

She eyed the spa tub longingly. Maybe she could relax in the tub for a while. Maybe hot water and some fragrant bath salts would wash away the fear and tension and grime of the evening.

She quickly set her suitcase on the antique luggage rack in the dressing area and dug out fresh underwear and pajamas and her favorite gardenia-scented bath salts, then went into the bathroom and closed the door. A brand-new, snow-white bathrobe hung behind the door.

"Wow, all the amenities for Reilly's *guests*," she murmured. As she reached to turn on the hot water in the tub, she heard an unfamiliar chiming sound. She stopped. Was it a clock? A phone?

Phone. Her heart pounded. It was Autumn's phone.

Christy hurried over to her purse and upended it onto the bed. Where was that phone? It rang again. *There.*

She grabbed it with shaky hands. Who could be calling this number? Laurie? D.B.? Autumn's killer?

Finally, Christy got the phone turned around in her hand and was able to see the display. It was Laurie. She answered.

"Is this Christy?"

"Yes. Yes it is. Laurie?"

"I'm sorry to be calling so late—"

"It's not a problem. What is it, Laurie? Did you remember something?"

"Maybe. Did you say one of the names in her phone was Glo? G-L-O?"

"That's right."

"I think that might be a girl who went to high school with us. Her name was Gloria Soames. I didn't know her very well. She was really into Goth. You know, black clothes, black fingernails and lipstick. All that stuff. She dropped out before senior year."

Christy searched through the spilled contents of her purse, looking for a pen. She glanced at the bedside table. Of course there was a fancy, Victorian desk set complete with pen and notepaper. She grabbed the pen, holding it gingerly in her right hand—the one with the cast.

"Gloria Soames. Can you spell that?"

"I think it's S-O-A-M-E-S."

Christy wrote quickly. "What else do you know about her? Parents? Brothers and sisters? Where she lived?"

"She had a brother. He was older than us. His name was Jason or Jackson or something like that. Christy…" Laurie's voice faded. She knew something else. Something she didn't want to tell.

"Laurie? What is it?"

"You need to know. Glo was into drugs. Bad drugs—you know, needles and all that. And—" Laurie paused and Christy could hear her shaky breathing.

"And what?" Christy held her breath, afraid of what Laurie was about to tell her, but certain she knew what it was.

"Everybody talked about Glo. They all said she'd do anything to get money. Anything, you know?"

"I know," Christy said, rubbing her temples.

"I know that's not much, but—"

"Laurie, do you have a yearbook?"